The PIANIST AND MIN JADE

A NOVEL

C.C Avram

C. C. AVRAM

where words connect

خداوند

ر. د. بهابه

The
PIANIST
AND
MIN JADE

A NOVEL

The Pianist and Min Jade

ISBN: 978-1-946274-97-7 Paperback
ISBN: 978-1-946274-98-4 e-Book
Library of Congress Control Number: 2022948267

First Edition: Wordeee
Cover design: Okomota
Book Layout: Amit Dey

Published in the United States 2023 by Wordeee, Beacon New York

Website: www.wordeee.com
Twitter: wordeeeupdates
Facebook: facebook.com/wordeee/
e-mail: contact@wordeee.com

Printed in the USA

CHAPTER ONE

UNIVERSITY OF MICHIGAN
ANN ARBOR, CAMPUS
MIN JADE
PERSPECTIVE

THERE WAS NO MISTAKING THE steps approaching. More erratic this morning, for sure. Winful wondered what footwear was responsible for the riotous noise on the tiled floor of Dennison Hall and often made a game of guessing before his mad professor came into view, the spurred boots, the metallic heeled pumps, or the sneakers with cleats, lights, and bells. He was guessing the metallic heeled pumps when the mop of curls bounced into his office, flopped down in a chair, and tucked her feet up under her. He was right. The shoes were the tamest part of the outfit, which consisted of a huge sunflower shirt, a patched maxi denim skirt and a floral scarf.

"I guessed right this morning," Winful puffed up, observing the ever-quirky Min Jade, his quarterback in all things cerebral. She was one of the University's rising stars, though nothing about her hinted she was a brainiac; no stern tresses pulled tightly at the nape, no manly tweed suits, or rimless spectacles. Min Jade's otherworldly, ambidextrous brain was something to be reckoned with. In his thirty years at the University of Michigan, only once had he met a genius of her caliber, either as student or faculty. Yet, Min Jade seemed the most ordinary person in the world. Her fierce brainpower, retention, and visual interpretations, her equal versatility in music and the arts, and her ability to see special relationships in unique and fresh ways often mesmerized him. He always looked forward to their morning visits, if for nothing else than to see what she was wearing. This morning something was amiss. There was a childlike innocence about her but most of all, her usual, unbridled enthusiasm and chattiness when nervous, seemed dampened under an aura of melancholy. It was rare that he'd catch a glimpse of it, but when he did, he knew something was wrong. Was it the right time to bring up the conference?

"My, my, you're such a great physics man with such an acute ability for sound dissonance," she deadpanned, checking out her footwear. "How are you this morning, Professor?"

"Middling to fine. What about you?" Winful, who knew his star like a book, had observed she'd been off kilter for the last few weeks.

"I could be better. I'd love some of your calming tea."

"Humm. So, what's going on in your headspace these days?" Winful ambled over to the tea tray in his makeshift kitchen, the window ledge where he kept his precious orchids. Min Jade had three speeds, nervous chatter when she was uncomfortable, laser-focused or teetering. She was teetering.

"It's that obvious, huh?"

"You haven't been yourself for a while now. What's going on?"

"Insomnia. I've resorted to playing show tunes at one a.m.," Min Jade confessed, swiping a mop of her natural curls off her forehead. Min Jade associated music with calm, mostly show tunes and played them any time of the day or night when she felt out of sorts. Last night, it was *Luck, Be a Lady Tonight, Summertime,* and *People.* Although no prodigy like her mother, Min Jade was musically gifted. She had a good voice, perfect pitch, and could hold her own on the piano. It was no coincidence that her mother had named her after her favorite Korean pianist, Min Kim Ye-Kwon. Who on earth would name their American-born child Min Jade, anyway? Min Jade often wished she'd simply been called Kim, which would've stopped the barrage of questions about her Asian name. But no! Jessica Jade would never subscribe to things plain and straightforward. Kim was too ordinary a name for her special girl.

"How long has this been going on?" Winful asked.

"Almost three weeks." Indeed, her insomnia was beginning to feel like an albatross. Like the time her mother had to check her into the hospital to "get some rest." Plagued by constant asthma attacks, Min Jade was used to hospitals and had spent a good part of her childhood going in and out of them, but that time had been different. She'd been admitted to a psychiatric ward.

It was clearly no time to bring up the conference—or was it? "I have a great idea for you," Winful said. "It'll be a distraction. Don't say no," he hurried on when he saw her face scrunched up to object. "Just think about it. Everyone in the department is most impressed with your citations on Google Scholar and Web of Science. Your index is over 100! That's Nobel Prize-worthy. The Dean wants to create a conference around your work."

"*No. No,* Dr. Winful. Not right now. I'm too busy. Really. Plus, as you can see, I'm not in the greatest shape."

"Hear me out. You've been working non-stop. I'd like to arrange for you to take a sabbatical before the conference.

Take six months off. That'll give you a well-deserved rest and us enough time to plan a great event. What do you think? I'm sure Eric will agree even though you didn't officially apply," he handed her a cup of his calming tea.

"A sabbatical? I never thought of that. I sure could use some time away from my lab."

"Where would you want to go if you decided to do it?"

"Austria. Innsbruck," Min Jade surprised herself with the speed of her reply.

"They've produced three Laureates."

"Yes. I know. It seems like a great program."

"Better than great. You could be inspired."

"Meaning, 'pay attention'?" She smiled at her mentor, her dimples deepening.

"Yes, that's what it means since they seem to know how to produce Laureates. You could be a contender, you know?"

"Professor Winful, you are such an optimist. I know how badly you want the University to get a prize, but aren't you overly hopeful here? Indices are one thing, but…."

"Oh, never mind with the reality check. What will you teach if you decide to go?"

"Do I have to teach?"

"Well, you'll want to keep your toes in the pond, so to speak. Maybe just one class. You can manage that, right?"

"I suppose I could teach anything. Nonlinear optics. Harmonic frequencies. Pair creation. Wouldn't it be great if we could figure out how to boost Hercules' power? They may have ideas."

"Advancing Hercules. Now, that would be awesome. We need to get there first and teach those Brits a thing or two," he winked.

Min Jade rolled her eyes.

"What?" Winful rebuffed. For a woman who loved being first, Min Jade was remarkably non-competitive, except with herself. He wished he could make her more so, but she had zero interest. He'd never been able to get her to appreciate the theory of the zero-sum game. For one to win, another must lose. "Think too, Min Jade, of the fact that as a black woman…."

"Professor," she rarely engaged in race conversations, "don't you find particle theory a more interesting subject? I'll have a chat with Victor Yanovsky over in engineering later. He's more up on the competition, you know, and I'll tell you what I find out," Min Jade slurped her tea.

Yanovsky, her sounding board, was a Russian-trained physicist who directed the Guinness award-winning HERCULES laser. Like Min Jade, his research focused on ultra-high-intensity interactions, particle acceleration, and high-intensity X-ray generation. They often collaborated on their research and held each other in high esteem.

"You're thinking it's a good idea then?"

"Not particularly. I'm just answering your question, but the idea of a new perspective could be interesting."

"Think hard!" Winful proffered, picking up his spray bottle and wandering over to his window garden. 'If you do decide to go, though, I'm not sure who'll be left to challenge and stimulate my mind or, for that matter, pay attention to me." Winful pivoted his portly, yet stately, body away from his beloved orchids to look at her. His brown eyes glinted. Running a hand through his thinning gray hair, he leaned into a conspiratorial pose. "Who will teach your classes if you go?"

"Sigmund Fletcher would be my first choice."

He nodded his head. "Yes. Yes. Sigmund's a good choice, but it's doubtful he'd visit me daily." Winful's finger slid along the spines of his alphabetically shelved books. If anyone could get the University a Nobel in Physics, Min Jade would be it. "Ah," he pulled a book from his impressive shelf. "Take this, just in case. I was there last year. Not much could have changed," he handed Min Jade a *Fodor's* Guide and proceeded to detail his time in Austria. Min Jade could tell it would be a long-winded, colorful speech, so she jumped from her perch, pecked him on the cheek and quickly headed for the door. "I have to meet one of my Ph.D. students," she said, tactfully excusing herself. Though Min Jade was no card-carrying bearer of America's racism, race talk banal at best, she laser-focused her efforts on women. Many of her Ph.D. students were indeed women of all shades and backgrounds. Clanking to the door, she left her mentor's office. Min Jade despised *Fodor's* Travel Guides. What was the purpose of traveling, if not to discover on one's own the joys of the unknown world?

Winful watched as she bounced out of his office. He loved Min Jade. He'd miss their daily tea and chatter about everything under the sun, from the meaning of the universe to techniques of cooking a leg of lamb. More than colleagues, they were friends. Their families spent time together. She knew his dreams, and he knew hers. He was like her academic father and always wanted to protect her. Maybe he was pushing too hard. Austria would indeed be an excellent place for her.

Back in her office, Min Jade googled The University of Innsbruck's Physics department. The University, established in 1669, had indeed produced an impressive list of Nobel Laureates in the sciences, mainly chemistry and physics. Stuffing the offending travel guide into her top desk drawer, Min Jade rested her elbows on her desk, cupping her face in her hands. Did she dare think of the possibility? A Nobel? It was her dream. Not the prize itself. Not even her impressive research in nonlinear optics, a field pioneered right at the University of Michigan, but that it would be the capstone, that final step to all she and her parents had endured, especially her mother. After Min Jade's "break," Jessica Jade had given up her career as a celebrated opera singer to devote her time to her daughter's well-being. Like the CEO of success, she ran Min Jade's life like a Fortune 500 company. "Process-sized" and focused. Jessica Jade had put all her effort, energy, and every fiber of her being into grooming her to be Number One, across race, gender, and culture lines and to keep her grounded from the plague of genius.

Min Jade's run to the Kerry Town farmers' market was the highlight of every Saturday morning. Boasting farm-to-table produce and staples, Kerry Town was a hub in the city. This morning, as usual, Min Jade would stop by Zingermans for coffee and scones with real clotted cream and jam, a leftover love from her time at Oxford.

The golden leaves of fall rustled under her feet as she moved at a nice clip down the jogging path on North Campus. A citadel itself, North Campus was on the other side of town and housed the schools of Engineering, Computer Science, Architecture, the sprawling Music school, and her home. Students and faculty trundled back and forth between campuses on shuttle buses. More residential than central campus, it was her favorite part of town. Min Jade especially loved running the path bordering the music school, often jogging in place to listen as notes caressed the wind. Many noted musicians had graced the campus: Jessye Norman and Bob James, for example, and even her mother. Ann Arbor was the place Min Jade had been the happiest, and God knows she'd fought every day for her happiness. Ann Arbor indeed was beautiful, and she loved it.

Real joggers shot past her, but Min Jade kept her steady pace. She was trying to build up her lungs for the Alps. If she did decide to go on sabbatical to Innsbruck, she would need stamina. For the first time in her professional career, she was excited to venture outside of her lab for any length of time and into the real world to explore other things life had to offer at a new university. Aware that her increasing restlessness included a yearning for something she could no longer find in her work, she'd been warming up to Winful's idea quite a bit. Whipping out her phone, she dialed her mom.

"Hi, Mom."

"Hi, honey. Why do you sound so out of breath? Is everything okay?"

"I'm jogging over to Zingermans. Want to come join me for coffee?"

"How coincidental. I was just heading over there."

"Great. I'll see you there."

Her mother was already waiting when she arrived. Min Jade ran over to her.

"Min Jade!" Jessica exclaimed, "honey, you look ghastly. What's with the circles under your eyes? What's going on?" Of course, Jessica Jade was impeccably dressed, even for the farmer's market, and eyed her daughter's psychedelic jogging suit.

"Mother, do you have to be so blatantly honest?"

"Min Jade…."

"I'm a little tired," Min Jade interrupted her scrutiny. "Been working long hours. Do you want your usual, Mom?" Min Jane asked, heading off to join the long, long coffee line.

"Yes. I'll have a piece of the key lime tart, too," Jessica said, leaving to find a seat on the patio. Something was up. She could tell.

"One key lime tart, a slice of pecan pie, a latte and an extra hot double espresso," Min Jade ordered. It took forever to get the order. "Thank you," she dropped a couple of dollars in the tip jar and padded over to the patio. Resting the tray, she sat across from her mother.

"What did you get?"

"Pecan pie and a double espresso."

"I've heard that pecan pie is delicious," Jessica lobbed off a corner of the pie, observing her daughter under her lashes. If there was one person in this life she knew to a T, it was her daughter. By the time Min Jade was three, Jessica had long known that her chubby-cheeked little one was quite different from other kids. The first clue was when Min Jade started making complete sentences at nine months old and became keenly interested in musical notes. When Jessica played the piano, Min Jade could always be found lying on the floor watching her feet work the pedals. The child could name every major and minor chord by three. At four, she would disappear from the house for long periods, sending her parents into fits of worry. Both day and night! During the day, they would find her in the garden consoling flowers whose friends had been picked for the vase, arguing vehemently that doing so interrupted the flower's life. At night, she'd be lying on the grass, counting stars, and pointing out patterns in the sky that no one else could see. Her little brain was always working overtime, so it was no surprise when she began experiencing insomnia. Despite it all, Min Jade had fought and won, and here she was, the youngest tenured professor at the University of Michigan.

She'd been a professor for seven years, tenured for four. Jessica felt proud but worried.

"Professor Winful thinks I should take a sabbatical," Min Jade spooned pecan pie into her mouth. "*Yum. That's good. What do you think, Mom?*"

"You know, I was thinking just the other day that you should take a break. You've pushed yourself hard, Min Jade, and you've accomplished a lot. Winful told your dad you were trending on something called Google Scholar. He said it was a big deal." Jessica's addled mind kept whirring. Maybe a sabbatical was just what Min Jade needed. A change. A new viewpoint. Some new challenge. Perhaps she might even find romance. Jessica often worried that at thirty, her daughter had not once fallen in love. Her work was her life, and her life her work. "I think it is a wonderful idea. What do you think?"

"I'm warming up to the idea. A change of scenery could be inspiring," Min Jade said, "and a sabbatical might just give me the motivation I need to spark some creativity. My mind has been feeling spent." True also was that Min Jade was petrified by her biggest fear—losing her mind again. Though it hadn't happened since she was sixteen, her ever-present madness was always lurking close by. Weeks of sleepless nights, which was what had preceded her first break, had shown up again. It was a sign she needed to change direction.

Jessica felt herself choking up. It hadn't been easy for her daughter. She knew better than anyone that, left unmanaged, her child's special gifts could have gone either way, and she also knew Min Jade worried about that a lot. In an attempt to protect her daughter's genius, Jessica had virtually become a one-woman force field against the world that pressed down on Min Jade because of her differences and because of her race. Jessica sighed and sipped her drink. She was glad her daughter was considering taking a break because she wanted Min Jade around for a very long time. What a blessing she was for her and Owen. "You must go, Min Jade. It'll be good for you."

Min Jade was approved to go to Austria, and before she knew it, the last day of the fall semester had arrived. Sigmund Fletcher would assume her classes in January, and she'd be on her way to the University of Innsbruck as an exchange professor in physics right after Christmas. It wasn't going to be easy because she didn't speak a word of German, but intellectual confidence was her strong suit. *Danke Schön* wouldn't get her far, but she had nary a worry, for kids the world over were studying English in grade school. It was, after all, the lingua franca.

Min Jade's Parents' Home, Ann Arbor, Michigan, Christmas Day

The Jades, Jessica, and Owen, lived in Burns Park, a posh neighborhood off Washtenaw, fifteen minutes from Min Jade's North Campus residence. It was the home in which she was born and in which she'd grown up. Too large for three people, her mother had insisted it was a necessity because of her love for entertaining. The lush gardens, wraparound patios and spacious backyard were the sites of many lavish entertainments. Every weekend, there was a "happening" at the Jades;' art exhibitions for friends, piano sing-alongs, summer barbeques and literary salons were just a few Min Jade remembered. Min Jade let herself in. "I'm here. Merry Christmas," she shouted up the stairs.

"Oh hi, honey, Merry Christmas to you, too. I'll be right down. Get yourself a drink," her mother shouted back.

A few minutes later, her parents came ambling down the stairs. "Dinner is ready. You're right on time, as usual." Always the precise, loving family sergeant, her mother's flair, influenced by both left-and right-brain harmony, had everything in its proper place. An older version of Min Jade in looks, though far more traditional in style, Jessica had been an artist of note in her time.

"Merry Christmas, darling," her father gave her a peck on the cheek. "I'm going to miss you, Scallywag."

"I'm going to miss you more," she said, kissing him back. Min Jade loved her father dearly. She loved her mother just as much, but in a different way. While her mother protected Min Jade's gift and fragility, her father was simply loving her and would have even if she'd been a dolt. Calm, logical, and highly sought-after, Owen Jade was considered one of his field's best attorneys. He was the balance in the Jade family.

"Let's eat before everything gets soggy," Jessica lit the candles on the exquisitely set table. The family of three would now sit down together for Christmas dinner and continue the festivities through Boxing Day as per her mother's country tradition, right through until the new year. The festivities would be cut short this year, as Min Jade would leave for Austria in four days.

"How long will you be gone?" her mother asked.

"Six months. Once I settle, you'll have to come over. We'll go to every music hall. Imagine us at the Vienna Philharmonic! It will be *beaucoup* fun, right?"

"Am I not invited?" Her father flopped down into his favorite chair and picked up the newspaper.

"Owen, why are you in that chair when I said, let's eat?" Jessica batted her eyes at her husband. She was still madly in love with him.

"What chair, dear?"

Min Jade smiled at their easy banter. They were, in this life, soul mates. They'd met at the University while attending a lecture on music. She'd thought he was a new music student and was charmed by his good looks and seemingly good manners. As it turned out, he was a law student who'd come to the concert because of a girl who was also at the music school, and it wasn't her.

"Would you come, Daddy?" Min Jade asked.

"It doesn't matter. Invite me anyway," he headed to the table.

"This is for you," her mother handed her a tastefully wrapped box. In it was a hat with tiger-print fur trimmed in green to fit Min Jade's eclectic taste and a pair of hunter-green leather gloves with a matching cashmere scarf. There were also ten nebulizers, a jar of tiger balm, Vicks VapoRub, and some EpiPens, not that Min Jade was allergic to anything. "Can't be too careful," her mother said. "Make sure you find a doctor as soon as you get there. Your asthma could act up at those altitudes."

"Thanks, Mom," Min Jade held her mother's hand across the table.

"Hurry home, sweetie. We'll miss you."

Min Jade sat, observing her mother. She was a good mother. A tough mother. A caring mother. Some might even call her a tiger mom with furry paws. They'd had their struggles, but Min Jade hated disappointing her mother, especially since she'd given up her career to hold space for her. Even with all her mother had done, Min Jade understood her frailty had created insecurities she'd tried hard to bury deep inside. Frailties that often were at the very edge of her reality, reminding her that her "gift" was as much a burden as it was an advantage. She'd miss her family dearly.

CHAPTER TWO

MIN LEE WOO/MIN JADE
AUSTRIA, SABBATICAL

MIN LEE WOO LEFT THE STAGE. Behind the curtains, he brought his arm down in a yes gesture. His grueling nine-month tour was over, and now he'd have three months to recuperate. Resting his tails over a chair in the green room of the concert hall, he poured himself a glass of whiskey.

"You were great tonight, as always." Ji-Joon picked up his jacket and hung it in the valise.

"So, what plans do you have for me for the next three months?" Min Lee asked, sitting on the burgundy couch.

"You said you wanted to go skiing."

"Yes, that's what I have in mind. How about Switzerland?"

"How about Austria?"

"No. *Ani.*"

"Min Lee, if you remember, we promised to play a concert in Innsbruck. It's a great place to ski, and we can kill two birds...."

"I thought you'd rescheduled it for when I teach there?" Min Lee didn't let Ji-Joon finish.

"Sorry, mate. It couldn't be changed."

"Damn it. When do we leave?"

"Tomorrow?"

Min Lee gave Ji-Joon a look of death. He was exhausted and had hoped to have a week or two in London before embarking on his ski trip. What a confounded nuisance. "No way in hell am I going there tomorrow. When is the concert?"

"Early January, but you need to practice and get used to the space."

"You go ahead, and I'll meet you there on the thirtieth. I'll take the train. I'll let you know my details so you can arrange my pickup. Let's get out of here," Min Lee drained his glass and walked out the door.

Ji-Joon knew better than to argue. Min Lee was a bear to deal with at the end of his tours. After sixteen years as his manager, he was adept at going with the flow.

*   *   *

Like no other country, Austria represented music. Vienna, home to some of the world-renowned musicians and composers, Haydn, Liszt—and Schubert, Min Jade's personal favorite—held a sort of magic for her. To top it off, weekend travel would be a cinch, as Austria bordered Switzerland, Italy, the Czech Republic, Hungary, and a few other countries with zero border control. For the first time in a long time, Min Jade felt truly alive.

It has been said that on every street corner, in every café, and in every opera house in Austria, music played. And played it did at the Vienna airport. Acoustically perfect, with its dramatic dome-shaped roof in what appeared to be a propeller-designed motif, the music, and the airport itself were a lovely welcome. Min Jade absorbed her surroundings.

There were symbols accompanying the words on the signs, so she pretty much got the gist of the next steps and joined the non-residents' line for passport control. The officer looked her up and down, took her passport, and then stamped it. Not much personality, she thought.

After clearing customs, Min Jade exited through massive sliding doors into the Arrival Hall, where she collected her luggage and checked the train schedule. With a two-hour wait, Min Jade went to an airport café and ordered a double espresso for her four-hour train ride from Vienna to Tyrol, where the University of Innsbruck was located. Following the signs to public transport, she found the taxi stand and caught a cab to the *Wein Westbahnhof* station. *Wein Westbahnhof* was an impressive, angular, and modern glass edifice with rows and rows of ticket lines, marble beams, and yellow neon-lit ceiling tiles. Red ticket kiosks dotted the hall, but Min Jade preferred to get help at the ticket counter. Trains departed to every direction in Austria and to bordering countries, and she surely didn't want to end up anywhere but Innsbruck.

From the cavernous and ultra-clean, well-lit orange-and-white track, Min Jade boarded the plush ÖBB first-class cabin. There were only two seats in each cabin, which pleased her. She tried hoisting her luggage into the overhead bin, only to have it fall back on her. The man sitting in the opposite seat offered no help. She felt like dropping the suitcase on his head. Finally, with the luggage in place, she took her seat opposite Mr. Ill-Mannered. He never looked up once from what appeared to be a music score. She studied him, starting from his feet. No socks. Blue corduroys turned up above his ankles. Legs crossed. White oxford peeked out from a burgundy sweater; his neck's butter color interrupted by a prominent Adam's apple. She stopped at his throat before glancing surreptitiously at his face. Taut jaw, slight stubble, jet black hair covering his left eye. His slanted eyes boasted long lashes. Every so often, they blinked. Min Jade could feel his confidence and sensed his musical competence by the way he turned the pages of his music book. He was obviously an artist, a musician, the kind who drove her to distraction with their *comme si, comme ça, que sera* outlook on life.

As was her favorite pastime, Min Jade was about to make up a story about him when the porter showed up and asked for their tickets. To her utter disbelief, he handed over his ticket without even looking up. Min Jade itched to say something. Bad manners were something she could not tolerate, but her better judgment decided her against it. Instead, she concentrated on the menu the porter handed her to order lunch. When lunch arrived, Min Jade clanked her knife and fork, slurped tea, trying to be as disgusting as possible to elicit a reaction. Nothing! This guy was not one to engage, much less make small talk. He was lost in his own world. She could only imagine what might have happened had she scolded him. For four hours, they rode in silence, him reading his score or gazing out the window, and she, eating lunch and reviewing her appointment documents. Every so often, she'd observe him, or inhale his spicy orange cologne, now and then dozing off.

The university driver recognized Min Jade right away.

"Dr. Jade."

Min Jade arched her eyebrows.

"A picture," he pulled a photo from his breast pocket. His English had only the slightest accent.

Good start. "That's me, alright."

"This way, please," he said, taking her luggage.

With the music calming her nerves, Min Jade followed her escort, relieved that a place where she could rest from her trip was close by. Incredible beauty came into view as they drove along the postcard-worthy scenery of the snow-covered Alps. Uniform buildings in different hues lined each side of wide, stately, tree-lined streets. A striking multi-colored building from which rose a blue marionette was breathtaking. Min Jade exclaimed aloud, "Gosh, that's magnificent."

"It's the Saint Anne's Column," her driver said. "It commemorates the defeat of the Bavarian invasion in 1703." Now winter-dark, the streets were lit with holiday lights that cast shadows on the imposing statue standing high in the center square. The statue appeared to be the Virgin Mary surrounded by priests.

"It truly is magnificent."

This prompted her driver to launch into a mini-history lesson as they drove through the old town of Innsbruck. The campus welcomed them through white and grey arches a short distance further. The architecture there was more modern, in stark contrast to the buildings on what Min Jade now knew to be *Maria-Theresien-Strasse*.

"This is the Hotting West Building," the driver said, pulling up to a grey stone structure.

"Thank you so much," Min Jade said. "What do I owe you?"

"Nothing, Miss. The University has handled this, and we cannot take tips." He removed her luggage from the trunk and put it on the sidewalk. "Will you need help?"

"No, it rolls well," Min Jade smiled warmly.

The driver bowed, got in the car, and drove off. Min Jade stood on the curb, rifling through her arrival instruction to see what to do next. Dragging her luggage up a few steps, she entered a long hallway and, following directions, began looking for room 454. She rapped on the door.

"*Öffnen Sie die Tür.*"

That had to mean to come in. Min Jade pushed open the door and was greeted by a sturdy-looking forty-something German woman. "Hello."

"Hello, I'm Dr. Jade."

"Yes, you are. Dr. Jade, we are pleased to have you with us. How was your trip?"

"Just great, and thanks for sending a car."

"Of course. I'm Haduwig Weber, Assistant to the Department Head. Would you like something hot to drink? It's pretty cold out there, huh?"

"I think Michigan is just as cold. It may seem colder since we don't have this picture-perfect scenery to distract us."

"We do have a beautiful landscape. Please sit," she said, pointing her to a chair. "I have a few documents for you to sign. Is now okay, or would you prefer to wait until tomorrow?" Haduwig offered hot apple saft.

"Now is just fine. You are working right up to the holiday," Min Jade said. "I hope that's not my fault."

"Not at all. Our visiting professors usually arrive about now every year. We are used to this." Haduwig said, searching through some files on her desk. "Ah, here we go. Take your time. I just need to dash into the Department Head's office before he leaves. It will be no longer than it will take you to fill out the forms. Sign at the yellow tabs."

True to her word, Haduwig was back just as she was signing the last document. Min Jade handed them back to her.

"Thank you. That's all for today. Please, let me get someone to take you to the faculty quarters. Get some rest. We'll have a New Year's party to welcome the visiting faculty tomorrow. At 9:00 a.m., however, we'll have a quick orientation, no more than an hour, just for the visiting physics faculty. I know.

I know. It's New Year's Eve, but we wanted you to meet each other and the Chair before the big party. Classes don't begin until the sixth, so you'll have some time to get acclimated and do some sightseeing. If you need anything, please reach out at any time. Here are my details." She handed her a card. "Email or text is the best way to reach me."

Like the University of Michigan, Innsbruck's buildings were spread across the city. The difference, there was no central hub, like State Street with the stately Hill Auditorium, the Literature, Science and Arts building, or the magnificent buildings of the Law School. However, unrivaled at Innsbruck were the Theology Building and the imposing library. Though she wanted to see more of the immediate surroundings, Min Jade decided to leave full exploration for another day, as she was dog-tired.

Conveniently, the staff quarters were located near Hotting West. Her escort opened the door to her flat, unloaded her luggage, and handed her a set of keys. "Thank you," Min Jade said, stepping into the small but comfortable apartment. Cedar smells greeted her as she entered her home for the next six months. Built-in paneled bookcases, practical and attractive, lined an entire living room wall. The sloped ceilings reminded her of a ski lodge at which she'd once stayed in Switzerland. The kitchen boasted modern conveniences, including a washing machine and a beautiful wooden table in the eat-in nook. Most important were the coffee pots: a French press and a Keurig. Min Jade opened the refrigerator. It had been stocked with groceries, as were the cupboards.

Walking down the narrowest hallway, she peeked behind door number one. An office. Then the other. A master bedroom, appointed with a king-size bed, rare in Europe and covered with a plump comforter. The two-bedroom flat was warm and quite welcoming. Min Jade toted her luggage to the master bedroom and unpacked the bare necessities. She washed up in the en-suite bathroom before making herself a sandwich and a cup of chamomile tea. It would be wise to stay awake until her regular bedtime, but she couldn't keep her eyes open. It was 8:00 a.m. the following morning when her eyes barely opened to the blaring alarm. Still groggy, she had a slow start. Her mother always teased her about being the quickest dresser in the west and, true to form, by ten to nine, Min Jade was on her way back to the Hotting West building.

Haduwig and six others were milling around in a great hall. A lavish spread for breakfast, *Semmeln*; rolls, cold cuts, cheese, honey, jams, soft boiled eggs, juices, coffee, and tea, welcomed them. After breakfast, the professors got a chance to get acquainted before the formal presentation began. The visiting physics faculty were from America, Russia, France, England, Nigeria, and China. They made up a veritable United Nations. From a Russian scientist family, Vadim was confident, as was Tunde, the Nigerian, who was rather kingly to boot. Anastase, as his name suggested, seemed resurrected from a bygone French era; Albert, the English chap, was stereotypically cherubic and witty, and Chin seemed well-bred and mystic, and of course, she as the American.

"Always the only woman in the room?" The Nigerian asked.

Min Jade observed him as an FBI agent would cold-assess a suspect. Cocky. Confident. Precise, mentally focused. She felt comfortable enough to banter instead of being her stoic self and a woman of little chatter.

"You have something against women?"

"Not ones like you!"

"Don't let my being a woman make you do something stupid."

"Ouch," Tunde noted she was no wilting flower.

"You deserved that don't you think?"

"Let me check in with the powers that be," he turned his eyes to the heavens.

"What on earth are you doing?"

"I'm joining forces with the all-knowing to get an answer to your question."

"And?"

"I deserved it."

Min Jade laughed. "I think our presentation is about to start."

Hans Wis, the Department Chair, had just strolled in. He was as she imagined: full mustache, receding gray hair, tall, a little wispy, and upright. He shook hands with the faculty, patting Min Jade's. "So happy to have *you* with us." All eyes turned in her direction. Wis gave a brief history of the university, proudly presenting short biographies of the Nobel Laureates the school had produced. The faculty then introduced themselves formally. The other visiting professors stared at Min Jade after she was finished with her biography. They now understood the hand-patting. A thirty-year-old tenured professor! Impressive!

After some housekeeping, their itinerary and projects were handed out. Wis apologized for the early meeting on New Year's Eve but said he wanted to meet them before the official welcoming party, which was for all the visiting faculty in each department, not just the physics department. Formalities over, Min Jade returned to her residence, dashing past Tunde, who was trying to get her attention. She'd rest up until the party. Her body was worn out.

Yellow with a bold purple slash. Not exactly the little black dress for cocktail parties, but Min Jade never wore black. The dress was nothing fancy, but it did make a statement. No one would care, really. After all, this was Austria, not Paris. Min Jade checked herself in the mirror. To any eye, she was a natural beauty, but she didn't seem to know it, nor did she do much to enhance it. Her hair, no longer pulled back in a scrunchie, was scattered around her face in curls, thanks to Miss Jessie's hair products. She gave her cheeks a quick dab of blush, her lips a deep reddish-purple burnish, and she was ready.

"Ah, Dr. Jade," Albert, her neighbor, was coming out of his residence as she pulled the door behind her. "Did you rest well?"

"I did. But I'm still fighting the time difference."

"Yes, that's a bugger, isn't it? Shall we head over together?"

"That'd be lovely."

"I must say, I am duly impressed with your resume. You are so young to be a tenured professor."

"Don't be. It's just one of those things."

"Still, I'm loving the progressive nature of the University of Michigan. At the Imperial College, you have to have one foot in the grave to get tenure."

Min Jade perked up. "You are at Imperial College? I must have missed that earlier. I'm very impressed with their work in quantum physics."

"Yes. The school is abuzz with hope for a breakthrough in creating matter from light. I'm into carbon myself, so I'm not up on the latest studies. Is that your specific interest?"

"Pretty much. Anyway, don't worry, your time will come. Tenure is not all it's cracked up to be."

"I'm not worried. My longevity is assured. No one in my family has died before the age of 95."

Min Jade laughed. She was going to enjoy Albert. They reached the venue. Albert opened the door and stepped back to allow Min Jade to enter. He offered to take her coat. She liked him even more. Then again, she always liked men in her field. They got it. The room was tastefully decorated. There were no gaudy turn-of-the-year goggles, iridescent tassel hats, or noisy blowers typical of American revelry. Cocktail tables, decked with beautiful floral arrangements, had Happy New Year stakes driven into their soil, the only giveaway that it was going to be a new year. Flat-mounted TVs, the volume lowered, were showing New Year celebrations around the world.

"This looks like a very sedate New Year's Eve," Albert said. "Drink?" He grabbed two glasses of wine from the waiter passing by.

"I rather like it." Min Jade accepted the glass he handed her. *Quite civilized.*

The dawn of a new year was when Min Jade came closest to full-blown doubtfulness. It reminded her of how much she had, yet not all she needed. She was glad to be away from home.

There were at least sixty visiting faculty across disciplines. Min Jade found conversation easy and was having a great time. She loved the international, intellectual gathering where banality was absent, and for once, she wasn't the odd person out. There were five other women, but she was still the only woman of color and the only one in the hard sciences.

"More wine?" asked a waiter, holding a tray. That was when she noticed him. The man from the train. He was standing in the corner, looking very uncomfortable. Min Jade knew the feeling only too well. Grabbing two glasses of wine, she made her way over to him.

"Here," she said. "This could help. Red or White?" Min Jade offered him one of her glasses of wine. A broad, understanding, and reassuring smile dotted her face and deepened her dimples as she looked at the man who towered over her by at least four inches. Spiced orange. She loved his smell.

"Help with what?" His expression did not change.

"I'm sure this wall isn't hugging you back, but with a few glasses of this, it just might. Believe me. I know how uncomfortable these things can be—been there. Freud's isolation theory states that by inserting an interval (glasses of wine)," she uttered, holding up the glass again, "said person will be distracted and not allow isolation to dominate thoughts. I usually down a couple of these, and then I'm fine. Unfortunately, it's only wine, but I'm sure the champagne will come. It's New Year's, after all."

The smile, again. Min Lee's eyes squinted. He finally recognized her. It was the loony girl from the train. Her loud attire had become even louder with matching eyeglasses to boot. What, he thought, was she planning with this introduction? He took the glass of wine from her hand.

"What are you here to teach?"

"I'm not here as a professor this semester. I'll teach in the summer. I'm here to perform. I think I was invited as a professional courtesy."

"I see. I'm Min Jade," she offered her outstretched hand.

"Really? That's an odd name." He did not take her hand.

"Odd? Why?"

"You don't look Korean."

"I don't? Are you sure? Try to be a bit more creative. You'll see everything in everything." She eased her hand back to her side.

"What exactly is it that you want, Miss? I take it, Jade?"

"I see. You're not a nice person, after all. My first impression was right."

"First impression?"

"Yes. When my luggage almost killed me on the train, you didn't offer to help. I was sitting opposite you. You didn't even look up…You…I can't imagine how you could ride a train for four hours and not look up. You didn't even look up when the porter asked for your ticket. I was thinking; you must be visually impaired or maybe…I thought I'd give you the benefit of the doubt, but…and here I am even after that trying to make you…."

"Well, one should always go with their first impression," he interrupted her.

"Generally, but I'll give you a pass. I'm like that. Well, sometimes, but next time, be more observant. It's good to know what's going on around you. To see the world in motion can be magic. Be more observant. And never decline to shake a woman's offered hand. It's just simply bad manners. Anyway, Happy New Year."

"And you always talk this much?" His free hand began mimicking the opening and closing of a duck's beak.

"Eh?" The question caught Min Jade off guard. She was aware she was blabbing, but only Winful would dare point out her coping trait when she was nervous. "Are you okay? I mean, are you having a bad day or something? I get those days sometimes, too, but I'm usually…."

"What does that have to do with you?" He interrupted again.

"I…was…."

"Are you in the habit of invading people's space and being so nosy? You must be an American."

Min Jade could not believe her ears. How incredibly rude! She was simply being a good company girl and trying to make someone feel included. She knew what it felt like to be the oddity in the room. "What makes you so hateful? Were you born this way? I can't imagine why you are this rude to someone…."

"How about who it is that makes me hateful? The answer is you. Barging in as my white knight." Another interruption.

He is crazy, Min Jade thought and decided to leave things as they were. Yet, she couldn't let it go. She just couldn't lose to such an idiot. "Too bad for you," Min Jade retorted. "I don't believe in fairytales. So that takes care of that." Min Jade spun on her heels, taking her hurt pride along to make a quick exit. Midway into her 180-degree spin, she paused, turned back to look at the mean man, his eyes laughing at her and said, "Why would you need a white knight?"

"What?" His thick eyebrows drew together like some Naturo comic character.

"I said, why would you need a white Knight? Aren't you, Korean?"

Min Lee watched the woman walk away, anger accompanying her every step. Who was this crazy woman? How dare she disrupt his evening? How dare she? Isolation theory…What poppycock! His thoughts stopped as she turned and flashed him a condescending smile. Suddenly, his heart skipped a beat. It was his mother's smile.

"What was that about?" Ji-Joon sidled up, handing him a whiskey.

"Beats me."

"So why are you staring at that woman in awe?"

"Ji-Joon, shut up and get me out of here!"

"Escaping the dragon?" Tunde, the Nigerian, slinked up, laughing. He was so impeccably dressed; Min Jade did a double take. Quite the distinguished one in a soft tan cashmere jacket and black pants; his umber skin, clean-shaven, glistened. He, too, smelled delicious. Strong, like oak. His sharp nose flared at the edges, and the dancing, steely eyes mocking her reminded her of the über-confident men from Gabon she'd danced with at *Kir Samba* in Paris. Tunde owned the room that night, and, she suspected, any room he entered, he'd stand out from the crowd.

"What's worse than a dragon?"

"A woman-eating dragon in yellow? I like it. You light up the room."

"You asked for it."

"I did. Please accept my apologies. After all, I did traverse the universe for an answer."

"Funny. So, do you know that jerk?"

"Not exactly know. What I do know is that he's one of the world's greatest pianists. A child prodigy. Min Lee Woo. Korea's answer to the Chinese Lang Lang. I hear he's playing a concert here."

"Ah, the quintessential, insufferable, genius artist! Well, I'll be sure to take a wide circle."

"Wise decision, even if your name is Min Jade. How on earth?"

"Don't start. It's a cosmopolitan world."

Tunde let out another hearty laugh. His face lit up, and his teeth were pearly white. "Even though your name should be Chidima, I'm sure I can get used to Min Jade."

"Well, if we're going to get specific, I suppose I should've been named LaShawn. I can even channel Sheniq'ua."

Tunde laughed again, and Min Jade couldn't help but join him. "Tell me about you," he said. He probably didn't even understand the African American reference!

"I'm a girl from Michigan."

"Bet not too many quantum physicists in the neighborhood."

"Are you always this banal?"

"Deserve that again. Can we start over?"

"One more chauvinistic or racial comment and you are dead."

"Why did you go over to Mr. Woo?"

"He seemed lonely and out of place."

"Feelings of solidarity?"

"You are incorrigible. He seemed sad, that's all."

"Distant, pensive, self-absorbed: maybe. Sad, no. But why do you want to defy gravity and race? Impossible love, my dear."

"Love? What on earth are you talking about?"

"You don't know? Okay, Okay. I'm sorry. I don't think I've said I'm sorry so much in my entire life."

"Let's not say it anymore tonight. Happy New Year." Min Jade left Tunde to join her other colleagues. What's with these men tonight? She mused. Smiling her way through the party and anxiously waiting for the right moment to escape. She'd forgotten just how much she hated togetherness.

Just after midnight, Min Jade slipped out. She could still feel the jetlag in her bones, and Min Lee's brush-off was pricking her insecurities. Thank God things would go into full tilt soon, and she'd do what she always did: drown out the noises in her head with work. She was genuinely excited about her class and wanted to be fresh and sharp on her first day as a visiting professor. With five days to go before classes began, she'd check out the town and fully acclimate. As much as she tried to forget the slight, Min Jade couldn't stop thinking of the dragon. What an ass! What a rude, colossal ass. She felt her anger rising as she exited the great hall.

"Not much of a party-goer, I see." Chin was outside smoking.

"Hey! Those will kill you."

"So, will talking to the enemy."

"Why is everyone cryptic tonight?"

"I saw you talking to Min Lee Woo. I'm Chinese. I have to root for Lang Lang."

"Ah. I see. I'll remember that. But no worries. I wouldn't talk to that horse's ass again, ever. Anyway, goodnight. I'm busted beyond busted."

"Me, too. I'll walk you back. I'll give you some ginseng. Drink it in the morning. Don't sweat over his behavior. It's not personal. Many people think of us physicists the same way, you know. Weird and difficult."

Unfortunately, the altitude change took some getting used to, so Min Jade spent the next two days in bed with her nebulizer. Her mother knew everything. At least she wasn't having an asthma attack! She'd find a doctor as soon as she felt better.

CHAPTER THREE

MIN LEE WOO
HOFKIRCHE CATHEDRAL,
INNSBRUCK
REHEARSAL

MIN LEE WOO PULLED OUT THE MUSIC SHEETS and stacked them on the table next to the piano, a habit. He didn't need them. Sixteen years on the stage, he'd memorized damn near all the classical works from Rachmaninoff to Bach, Schubert, Beethoven, and everyone in between. Most people were awed by his impressive repertoire, but it was just par for the course to him. Pouring a cup of coffee, he took a generous swig, placing the cup on a different table from the sheet music in case of spills—his OCD. Pulling a piece of paper from his jacket pocket, he looked over his tour schedule for the upcoming year.

Like every other year, it was going to be brutal. Torino, Italy, Stuttgart, Berlin, Vienna, Germany, Paris, France, Amsterdam, Netherlands, Shanghai, China, London, England, New York, the United States, and God knows where else Ji-Joon, his manager, would dig up. He'd cherish these few months. He'd practice for ten hours today and every day until he played his unexpected final concert at the Hofkirche. This could have waited. Ji-Joon was mercenary. Anyway, he could get in some good skiing before their contract jaunt to Switzerland. After his back-to-back tour with his last album, almost nine months nonstop on the road, Min Lee was adamant he'd be on the road no more than six months a year. In two weeks, he'd make that crystal clear to his management team. He'd also promised to teach Master Classes in piano and composition at Innsbruck in the summer, and if Ji-Joon had any sense at all, he'd have scheduled this concert then, Min Lee snorted. Well, it was all done, so he'd better get over it.

Min Lee placed a single sheet of paper on the piano, which listed the music he'd play on Friday, January 10th, here in the Hofkirche Cathedral.

1. Rhapsody on a Theme of Paganini: Variations 1-24 25 mins

2. Liszt Piano Concerto No. 1:20 mins

3. Hungarian Rhapsody 10:33 mins

4. Liebestraum 5:18 mins

5. Schubert's Ave Maria 7:04 mins

6. Schubert's Standchen Serenade 6:00 mins—One of his personal favorites. He played it every time he performed. It was a tribute to his mother. At the thought of her, tears pricked his eyes.

7. Finally, Partita No. 1 in B Flat 8:54 mins as an encore.

One hour, 22 minutes and 9 seconds. He never played for more than 1 hour and 30 minutes. It was just right.

He wished his mother could see what had become of her son. She'd have been pleased. *"Can you hear this with your heart, son? Close your eyes; let your heart guide your fingers."* Min Lee could still feel his mother beside him. He could still smell her shampoo as she reached over to guide his fingers, his on top of hers, gliding over black and white keys. *"Feel the music, don't just play the keys,"* she'd whisper. For hours she'd sit beside him and, together, they would play, his mother smiling, always smiling. True to Hofkirche's purpose, the air was filled with remorse and death.

Lifting the piano lid, Min Lee sat for a moment as familiar sadness crept in. Barely six months after his twelfth birthday, his mother had died. He'd thought his heart could never hurt more, but it was just the beginning of his painful life. Life had not been easy, but he'd carried on because of the unbroken connection with his mother through music. And he'd kept his solemn promise that her sacrifice would never be for naught by becoming a world-class pianist. His amazing, beautiful mother, even on her deathbed, had kept smiling. Smiling that he had been born, smiling because she knew he would not let her down, and smiling because his father had finally come. It was the last heartfelt smile that he'd seen in a very long time.

Min Lee ran his hand across the keys. He tried to warm up with scales, but his mind kept flitting to Min Jade. How dare she smile at him? That was his mother's smile. Min Lee pulled a tattered picture of his mother from his wallet. The silly woman in yellow, his mother's favorite color, looked exactly like his mom when she smiled, down to the dimples. Why had he lost his composure and responded to her kindness so vilely? Maybe, Min Lee thought, he'd been too unkind. Pushing the thought from his mind, he began with *Serenade*.

January 6th, Hotting West Building, Lecture Hall B, Innsbruck University Campus

"Good morning," Min Jade greeted her students: five undergraduate and ten masters' level. "Welcome. This is Applied Physics. If it's your major, you're in the right place. I'm Min Jade. I'll be your instructor for the next six months." Min Jade loved teaching and being in the classroom was where she felt most comfortable. "As you know, Applied Physics is a practical science. For those who have taken Applied Mathematics, you'll find the approach similar. We'll be focusing on lasers: Why? Because I'm from the University of Michigan, home to the award-winning, most powerful laser in the world–HERCULES, which, by the way, is not named after the strong guy in Greek Mythology. It actually has a meaning. High Energy Repetitive CUps LasEr System. Pretty clever, huh? It is a petawatt laser that can produce a focused laser beam in femtoseconds. Wrap your head around that! Currently, its maximum electric field, when focused down to the smallest possible spot, is ten volts to the fourteenth power per meter, four orders of magnitude less than the Schwinger field. We want to find a way to boost HERCULES's electric field to greater than three times that. If we can create that level of intensity, we can create matter out of nothing. Yes, matter from a vacuum! That, for sure, will answer all the creationists now, won't it?"

Laughter.

"We are going to try it, so it'll be – no pun intended –an intense six months."

Another chuckle.

"I'll have office hours every day from 3 to 5 p.m. You can make an appointment if those hours don't work for you. Any questions?"

"Professor, how old are you?"

"Old enough to give you a grade, so it's best to be on your toes. My youth makes me fast and sharp too, so watch out," she smiled. "Take a syllabus and pass it on. We'll meet tomorrow at 9 a.m. *Danke Schön.*" Thank goodness all her students were fluent in English, the civilized world.

Min Jade decided to spend the afternoon exploring what Innsbruck had to offer. She loved the narrow streets and pastel colors of the buildings against grey stones. The Golden Dachl, in the old town, was as impressive as she'd heard. The legendary Golden Roof was built with 2,738 fire-gilded copper tiles by Emperor Maximilian to mark his wedding to Bianca Marie Sforza. From their balcony, they allegedly watched festivities in the square. It was Innsbruck's most famous attraction. Strolling through imperial rooms and galleries with artifacts from the 1500s, she balked at the youth of her country, only five hundred years old! Min Jade was delighted to stop in cafés and museums and found her soul light and airy as she roamed. Her last stop was The Hofkirche. Min Jade bought her ticket and stepped inside the courtyard, where the most beautiful rendition of Schubert's *Serenade* filled the air. Who on earth had such a talent? What a fantastic gift! She felt her heart race at its inimitable beauty. The pianist's interpretation was sensitive, committed, and individualistic. Min Jade moved toward the music. There were few people in the world with a gift like that. Though just an okay pianist herself, she did have perfect pitch, and every note played was in harmony.

The music stopped. Min Jade heard footsteps and instinctively retreated.

"Who is there?" The voice reached her.

Min Jade stepped back from the door. Standing before her was the Dragon.

"You again! What are you doing here? I thought they were supposed to be closed to visitors today."

"Obviously not. I am visiting the cathedral," she said, holding up her ticket, "and heard the music. I was curious. I am a curious type. It was so amazing. I can't believe such beautiful music comes from a meanie like you." As though she had forgotten his insults, she smiled warmly. "You are truly gifted, even if you are a horse's arse."

"What?"

"You do know what a horse's arse is, I take it? The east end of a horse-headed west. In colloquial terms, a stupid and obnoxious person or, simply, a stupid son-of-a-bitch!"

"Well, I never. How much crazier can you get?"

"Much. I've seen crazy, and it doesn't scare me."

"How would you know if I am a great pianist? Are you a pianist, too?" His tone mocked.

"A pianist? No. I am a physicist, but I do have perfect pitch."

"Really? And I am right? You are a crazy American?"

"Yes. I'm Dr. Min Jade from America, and I've been called crazy on numerous occasions. I'm from The University of Michigan, here on sabbatical for six months."

"Ann Arbor, Michigan?"

"You know Ann Arbor?"

"I do and have fond memories. When I was at the Julliard, I studied with an instructor at the conservatory in Ann Arbor. North Campus."

For a moment, the man almost seemed normal. "How small is this world? I can't believe it. I'm glad you enjoyed it. I hope it was spring…I…." What were the chances that a Korean pianist in Austria had been to Ann Arbor? "What did I tell you about everything being everything?"

His hand started doing the duck beak thing again. "It was a lovely place, but if you could leave now, I'd like to get back to practicing. Remind them on your way out that this place is supposed to be closed until 3 p.m." he retrieved a sign that said, 'Do not go beyond this point.' "Have a great sabbatical," he placed the sign and abruptly walked away.

Min Jade watched him until he'd disappeared from view. How on earth could anyone be so boorish? Served her right for talking to the hideous man! He was way past rude. Still, she wanted to stay and listen to him play. Min Jade stood on the cathedral's cobbled stones' hedge labyrinth, flabbergasted by the Korean musician.

Back at his piano, Min Lee felt a little lost. Her smile unnerved him. Maybe serendipitously, he was in Innsbruck just to see that smile. To remind him of his "why."

"You have a call, you have a call," Min Jade's phone announced. She bolted down the path to the exit—no need having another confrontation with the crazy Korean.

"Hey."

"Hey, back to you. It's Albert. The physics faculty is out to dinner. Will you join us?"

"*Where?*"

"At *Der Pavillion* in the old town."

"I'd love to. I'm in the old town now. At the Hofkirche."

"Oh, you're close by. Ask someone to point you in the direction."

In fact, it was a very, very short walk to the modern two-story glass restaurant diagonally across from the cathedral.

"Over here," Tunde waved as she walked in. "How are you?"

"Good."

Tunde had never worked this hard to get a woman's attention.

"Just good?"

Min Jade stared at him. "Just good. Would you like a definition?"

"No."

"Good."

The restaurant was cozy and had a warm, welcoming glow. Ultramodern, it overlooked the future *Haus der Musik* under construction. All the tables were full, and the bar was packed—on a Monday night!

"What are you drinking?" Chin, who rarely spoke, asked. He was a completely different person with a few vodkas under his belt.

"Bourbon."

"Wow." Tunde chimed in but didn't get a chance to level his sarcasm as Chin continued,

"I think we physicists should teach the world a thing or two about harmony. Harmonic frequencies, progression, and the like."

"Meaning?" Vadim paused mid-drink.

"Look at us. We represent the world, right? All races, all cultures, all physicists, drinking in perfect harmony. "

"So very Paul McCartney and Stevie Wonder-ish," Anastase said.

"Ebony and Ivory, living in perfect harmony," Albert sang.

"Which one are you, Chin? Ebony or Ivory?" Tunde asked.

"Well, my friend, black is white and white is black. Black and white contain all other colors, so think of me as the balance. The reflection of every other color. On the piano, I'm straight down the middle. In musical terms, think of me as Middle C."

Everyone howled. Min Jade appreciated the comment more than most. All her colleagues were pretty much from homogeneous countries except Albert and her, where race, gender and every form of social and cultural divide permeated society. Worse, in America, far more racially lethal than England, she represented the embodiment of their irrational fear. Being black and a woman already made her an enemy of the state. Being in the so-called top five percent of the world's scientific minds—as had been written about her–doomed her to defending her inalienable rights to be.

"Let's make a pact," Tunde said. "Let's meet up once a year in some part of the world as the Perfect Harmonies Group. Talking about Middle C, maybe we could start a band. Who plays an instrument?"

All hands shot up.

"Drums," Tunde started.

Min Jade shot him a look, and he shrugged. "Bad, bad piano."

"Guitar," Anastase said.

"Violin." Chin followed.

"A mean voice." Albert did a falsetto.

"Ballet and bass, basically man in tights," Vadim said, rounding out the chorus.

"You'd actually wear tights?" Tunde asked.

"What else do men of the ballet wear? Consider me Baryshnikov with a bass guitar."

"That's it then. Tonight, is the birth of The Perfect Harmonies or the Mad Scientists. Take your pick," Chin said.

"The Perfect Harmonies," everyone said in unison.

"Let's drink to that," Albert said.

Chin somehow got the restaurant owner to come to their table. He explained their band formation and asked if he'd be game to let them play at the *Der Pavillion*. The owner thought it a grand idea. It was all in good jest. Min Jade, the maladaptive introvert she was, couldn't believe how she was blossoming into a new person with friends. She liked it.

"Look who's just walked in. None other than the Dragon himself," Tunde said, checking out Min Jade's reaction. Facing the door, Min Jade was in full view of the Korean.

Min Lee Woo walked over to the bar. Ji-Joon was nursing a drink, and the men greeted each other with a slight bow. "What do you want to drink?"

"I'll order at the table."

Ji-Joon nodded to the waiter, who escorted them to a table. On the way, Min Lee noticed the Duck Beak girl. He ought to apologize. He was prepared if the spirit moved him.

"Who is that woman?" Ji-Joon asked.

"A chatty physics professor from America," Min Lee scanned the menu. He could hear the laughter behind him and found himself wanting to know what made the odd girl laugh. He ordered and then got up from the table. "I'll be a couple of minutes," he said. Ji-Joon assumed he was headed to the WC, but instead, he bee-lined for the table of physicists.

"Enter the Dragon. Guess who is heading straight to our table," Chin whispered. "Whatever you do, don't bow."

"Oh, please," Tunde said and moved closer to Min Jade.

"Good evening." Min Lee said, nodding to the physicists.

"Mr. Woo, what a pleasure. Join us," Tunde offered, feeling a searing pain shoot up his leg from Min Jade's under-the-table kick.

"Thank you, but I can't. I'm dining with someone. May I have a word?" he said, directing his question to Min Jade. Tunde bristled.

The others looked in her direction, as did Ji-Joon, who wondered what on earth was going on between them.

Min Jade shot them a warning look, excused herself and followed Min Lee over to the bar.

"Have you found a heart or some manners along the way?" Min Jade queried.

"And you called me rude."

"Yup. Why do you have to be so rude?"

"Isn't that a song?"

"At least you aren't a prude."

A smile lit Min Lee's face, his eyes almost disappearing into the smile. At six feet one inch, he was a handsome man. Swoon-handsome, at that. And he was fit. Long, elegant fingers, perfect for a pianist, were well-manicured, and his smile was Kim Soo gorgeous, down to the lips that upturned at the corners. He annoyed her.

"I must be feeling the kinship of Min Jade. Letting my guard down," his smile broadened. "I'm glad we met again. I think I have been a little rude earlier today." *What was it about her?* He gave her a once-over. Red Glasses. Cute. Big Eyes. Nice. Lean body. Okay. Shoulder length, brownish curly hair, which complimented her acorn complexion. Nothing special. Nice eyebrows. Great lips. Exceptional smile. All adding up to an exquisite beauty, but not his type. Dimples, extra points. Attractive in a garish way if that moved one's needle. It didn't, except for the smile. His mother's smile.

"Well, don't bother. Keep being rude because all we have in common is the name Min."

"And you think I was rude? Think about it. You come up to a man you don't know and offer him a drink; it's not exactly…."

"Being culturally aware?" Min Jade interjected. "Okay, I can accept that, but regardless, don't you think your behavior was a little on the offensive side since I'd already explained the why of the situation. I truly thought you were feeling out of place. I know what that feels like. Really, I do. I think…"

His hand started to do the duck beak dance again. "Sorry for the misunderstanding. I'm glad you're here then. I wanted to give you these as an apology. Bring a friend." He cut her off pre-babble.

"How did you know I was here?"

"I didn't. Coincidence. I was going to leave them at your office."

Min Jade took the envelope and opened it. When she looked up to thank him, she was again looking at the back of Min Lee Woo's head. The confounded man was intolerable.

CHAPTER FOUR

MIN LEE WOO
THE CONCERT

MIN JADE WAS WEARING ONLY ONE COLOR: a pale pink, just above-the-knee chiffon dress with spaghetti straps and an empire waist. Loose curls framed her face, and her lips were glossed with frosty lipstick, the exact color of the dress. Even her glasses were changed to a pair of white rims. Black heels stretched her calves to advantage as she stepped into the Hofkirche. Min Jade couldn't believe how nervous she was; heart beating rapidly, hands jittery, and sweat beading her brows. She couldn't fathom why this brute of a man was having this effect on her. Already she felt irritated about her decision to show up–much less to dress up–but consoled herself with the civility of the situation. It was simply good manners if one accepts an invitation to show up. Nonetheless, she'd dragged Albert along for insurance.

The Hofkirche was packed to the rafters. The imposing white building, a Gothic church built by Emperor Ferdinand in 1553 to honor his grandfather Emperor Maximilian, was impressive. Min Jade made a note to return to explore the collection of Renaissance sculptures and galleries since she'd been forced to leave in a hurry last time. Like Westminster, Hofkirche housed the tombs of greats, including Andreas Hofer, Tyrol's national hero, and Emperor Maximilian's cenotaph, which sat atop the black-and-white marble floor. Entering the main vestibule, one's eyes could not help but be drawn to the ornately painted organ, one of the five best in the world, she'd heard. It was silent tonight. Instead, raised on a stage stood a fifty-foot Steinway, its full lid complement. The usher showed them to their seats. Min Jade was surprised at their eighth row-center seats, the best in the cathedral. At least the crazy man had class, she thought, sliding into the pew.

"This is impressive," Albert said. "Thanks for inviting me. I've always wanted to hear him play."

"You know of him, too?"

"Of course! You don't?"

"I'm afraid not before a few days ago."

"He is huge, particularly in England. Royal College prodigy. He's had an impressive international career for some time now. Sixteen years, at least."

"Sixteen. He can't be that old."

"He was sixteen when he went pro."

Right then and there, Min Jade texted her mother. "Mom, have you heard of a pianist called Min Lee Woo?"

"Of course. Why? Oh, don't tell me you're at one of his performances. I am *so* jealous. He's fantastic—the absolute best. Keep your mic on so I can hear. He is amazing. Keep the mic on, Okay?"

"Mom, you know I can't do that, but I'll take you to one of his concerts."

*   *   *

As many years as he'd been on stage, Min Lee still felt jitters before every concert. Opening and closing his fists, he felt calmed and still, and the beauty of the snow-capped peaks outside his window added to his serenity. Interlacing his fingers one last time, Min Lee stretched his arms over his head to dissipate the last bit of nervous energy.

"Ready?" Ji-Joon tapped on the door.

"As I'm going to be. Is that Min Jade character in her seat?"

"Who? Ah, the American. Yes, but...."

Min Lee held up his hand to halt Ji-Joon's question and headed toward the stage's holding area. It was, after all, his home. The lights dimmed, and Min Lee Woo in a black tuxedo entered from stage left. He bowed deeply to the audience, his eyes sweeping the room, resting for a moment on Min Jade. Then, without flourish, he sat at the piano, erect and obviously in no hurry to touch the keys. He seemed to be connecting with something otherworldly, and that otherworldliness spread to the audience who waited and waited. From the moment his hands touched the piano keys, Min Jade did not—could not— move. The mean man had transformed before her very eyes into the emotional content of the music itself. He was interpreting *Rhapsody on a Theme of Paganini* into a language so intimate, only a few could ever truly understand.

His long fingers, leaping and gliding, reaching across octaves, transmitted their intended hypnotic effect. He expertly conveyed visceral and gut-wrenching moods: joy, pain, disquietude, as inimitable, beautiful music spread through the audience with each note. He was in full command of the music, from swirling motifs turning back on themselves, never fully resolving before marching on to a resolute and stately conclusion. How simple he made it all seem. It was clear to Min Jade that what he lacked in empathetic language skills was poured into making the eighty-eight black and white keys on the piano express every feeling and color the universe had ever created. For an hour and twenty-two minutes, Min Jade sat enraptured, dizzy, and tense. When it ended, she wanted more. It was a magical evening.

Min Lee Woo rose, bowed deeply to his audience, and left the stage. The applause would not cease. He returned to the stage and obliged his audience with an ethereal rendition of *Partita No.1 in B-Flat*, stately, determined, and undulating, before finally leaving the stage. Min Jade, still dazed, watched as the line to meet him snaked out of sight. This could have been her mother's life, she thought fleetingly.

"Well?" Albert said.

"Masterful. One of the best, no doubt. Let's go," she headed toward the door, deciding to compliment the maestro the next time she saw him if she ever saw him again. Min Jade went home and programmed her iPhone with all the songs Min Lee Woo had played.

The K-Cup coffee maker made a sizzling sound. She really ought to save the earth and buy regular ground coffee Min Jade thought as she went over to the stove. Breaking two eggs into the skillet, she scrambled them, buttered two slices of toast, and then plopped down at the dining table. While pouring cream into her coffee, she found her mind straying to the man called Min Lee Woo—ill-mannered and disgusting, he was still a genius, and that made her soften toward him just a little. She, of all people, knew how hard life could be for "geniuses." Still, she couldn't fathom how someone so cold-hearted could interpret music with such passion? His playing was unarguably pure magic—no distracting Lang Lang theatrics to influence the emotions of the piece, just the enchanting music. Min Jade took a big bite out of her toast. Her heart was feeling something more sanguine than just the beauty of the music or the unforgettable evening. Whatever it was, she didn't care to find out. Certainly not eager to see him again, she would do all in her power to avoid the horrid man. Min hand-wrote a note of thanks, intending to leave it for him in the music department. And what the hell was up with his duck beak gesture anyway? She snorted in disgust as she headed to the shower.

The brisk morning forced Min Jade to pull her coat tightly around her body. Stepping out into the bitter bite of the Austrian morning, steady snowdrifts, she hastened her pace toward the Hotting West building. Picturesque or not, Innsbruck was unbearably cold, and she had to admit as she pulled her tiger hat over her ears that Mother knows best, making a mental note to call home after class.

"You didn't congratulate me."

Min Jade swung in the direction of the voice. Through the haze, she saw Min Lee walking toward her. She couldn't decide what to do. So much for avoiding the brute.

"You didn't like my playing?"

"Good morning, Mr. Woo," Min Jade said curtly, determined to use as few words as possible and to remain distant and unwelcoming.

"Good morning, Dr. Jade." He sized her up. Combative and smart. Direct eye contact. Confidence.

"Congratulations and yes, I loved your concert. I was going to drop this off," she whipped the thank you note from her purse with smug satisfaction and handed it to him.

"How classy of you."

"You mean for an ugly American?"

"I don't see anyone else around."

"Uh-huh."

"I'm calling a truce."

"Excuse me? Min Jade's eyes widened with disbelief. "*You* are calling a truce. You're a funny guy."

"Not really. I'm terrible with people, so this is a big step for me. As you so aptly pointed out, I am the poster child for the isolation theory you talked about. Please don't make me grovel too much. I am sorry," he outstretched his hand

Min Jade ignored it. "You take the cake."

Min Lee brought his face closer to hers. Min Jade backed up.

"At least give me the right to call a truce," he pleaded.

"Are you sure about that?"

"I'm sure."

"Okay, go ahead. Call it, but remember what Charles Swift says, a truce can create dangers that outweigh the peace intended."

"Peace is not my objective. Truce," Min Lee pushed his extended hand toward her.

Min Jade took his hand. He preceded to wrap his pinkie finger around hers and began tapping her thumb with his. *Yagsuk.* "I promise not to be a jerk anymore. I'm Min Lee Woo."

Min Jade looked up at the curious man. She couldn't read a single thought. "I'm Min Jade."

"Yes, I know. Did you really like the concert?"

"Very much. I just told you that. Despite your horrible manners, thank you for the tickets. I enjoyed the evening immensely, and to be honest, you are a super amazing pianist."

Min Lee brushed his hair to the side. His cheeks flushed an orange-red hue. "*Gomawo.* That's thank you' in Korean. "I guess it surprises you, I'm so insecure."

"Not at all. Most geniuses are socially maladapted."

"You?"

"I'm no genius, but I *am* totally maladapted."

They both laughed and fell in step. Min Jade doubled her steps as Min Lee's lope was long from his tall frame.

"Permission to speak?" *Where the hell did that come from?*

Min Lee's eyes disappeared into a smile. "We are going to get along famously. Speak," he said, chuckling.

"What's with the brusqueness?"

"My layer of protection. It's often necessary. As a public figure, to keep one's sanity, it's best to be curt. I often get excused for being a weird, quirky, eccentric artist."

"I see. And why did you change your mind about me?"

"Who says I have?" He'd never admit that he was hanging around her just to see her smile. His mother's smile. Somewhere he'd heard there were forty variations of faces the world over. Well, now he had proof of at least one. Min Jade, an African American, reminded him of his mother, a Korean. They were about the same height, too. Was it fate that he was in Innsbruck? Was it a reminder from his mother to keep going even when the road was steep? With no normalcy to his life, never being in one place made him even lonelier than usual these days. He indeed had been wearied lately. Was this his mother's way of reminding him never to give up?

"You. You just said, and I quote, 'I promise not to be a jerk."

"I did, didn't I?"

Unexpectedly, their ongoing exchange was pleasant and surprisingly comfortable. Parting ways at the Hotting West building, he grabbed her elbow. "Thanks for liking my work," Min Lee said.

There was a feeling of undeclared intimacy in their encounter.

Her students were dutifully awaiting her arrival. "Morning, Professor."

"*Guten Morgen*. Practicing my German."

"*Guten Morgen*," the students repeated jovially.

"Let's do this." This was going to be a fun class.

"When I decided to take a sabbatical to Innsbruck, it was because it has produced a few Nobel Laureates, so I know many of you are getting a top-notch education. Our work in this class is to create matter! Anyone who gets there first is sure to get a Nobel Prize, so why not someone at Innsbruck, since you are used to producing Nobel Laureates? What do you say?"

"I'm feeling godly," said a student, prompting laughter.

Another student raised his hand.

"Yes." Min, Jade nodded.

"This is an eighty-year-old problem. It's still very much theoretical. What has changed to make you think this can be accomplished now?"

"Well, a lot, of course. For one, T1: Sapphire lasers. Once they become less prohibitively expensive, I think we can solve the greatest mystery the world has ever seen."

"How close are we?"

"I believe very close. There's a lot of activity around this subject right now. Any other questions?" The class was focused and interested, and though Min Jade droned on for two more hours, not a single student seemed to have lost interest.

"More questions?'

"Where did you get these cool optics, you wear?"

"In a little shop in Birmingham, Michigan. I'll text you the name. If there are no more questions, be sure to get here at least ten minutes before the hour for our next lecture with Xi Lou, CEO of Technor Ltd., a leading firm in CO_2 lasers. He'll discuss how their work is being used to advance computer systems.

After the class left, Min Jade sat in her chair, legs tucked up under her. She closed her eyes and exhaled. For thirty minutes, she sat without moving. Min Lee, who had been waiting outside her door, observed the woman with admiration. She was the real McCoy.

"I'm impressed," he was standing outside the lecture hall when she emerged.

"Impressed? I like that word, but with what?"

"That you could sit for thirty minutes without moving a muscle. What was that about?"

"My student asked a question which prompted a thought. You can only hear answers in silence, away from the noise of everyday thought patterns. Why are you here?" Min Jade searched his face for a clue as to why he'd changed his mind about her. None.

"I concur. By the way, have you done any sightseeing?"

"Min, Lee."

"Yes, or no?"

"Not much." *Why am I allowing him to boss me around?*

"Good. Do you want to take a look around Innsbruck with me? Since you seem to be able to stand me, I think we can go sightseeing together without getting on each other's nerves."

"What are you doing right now? I don't know what's going on here. I think..."

The duck beak hand came up right away. "Don't think. I think, my dear, you do too much thinking. Overthinking can lead to analysis paralysis."

"Which can be better than the wrong decision," she sassed.

"Let me get my coat." *I am getting crazy here! Why does this man have such an effect on me?*

"I'll get the car. Stay inside until I honk."

And he was bossy!

Min Jade hopped into the warm car; glad he'd been dictatorial. They drove down *Maria-Theresien-Strasse* with its glittering lights. With the triumphant entrance to Innsbruck a-bustle, the numerous shops and restaurants overflowing, the winter landscape was indeed postcard-worthy.

The Alps, framing the streets as people strolled along, seemed a fairy-tale moment.

"Don't you think this place looks like a postcard?"

"It's beautiful, alright. But too bad, there's no water. I can't imagine living in a place that's landlocked."

"You love the water?"

"Can't live without it. I grew up near the water in Busan. If you're Korean, you have to love the water. We are a Peninsula."

"Busan is on the Southeastern tip of the peninsula. Big shipping port hosted the 2002 Asian games and FIFA World Cup. Great beaches. One of two cities not captured by the Japanese in the Korean War. Has the largest shopping mall in the world."

Min Lee spun his neck to look at the woman beside him. *Encyclopedia girl?* "Wow. I'm impressed all over again," he stared at her with new understanding. She was surely not provincial.

"What? Am I talking too much again?" She was waiting for the duck beak to come out.

"Yes," Min Lee said, a faraway look in his eyes. "But this time, I like it. How do you know so much about Korea?"

"I was once there for a lecture. A friend from high school runs a pretty big science organization there, and he invited me to speak at a conference. How long has it been since you've been back?"

"Seventeen years."

"Seventeen years. You mean you've never been back since you left?"

"Yes. At sixteen, I left Korea. At that time, I lived in Seoul, but I visited my hometown of Busan before I left."

He was thirty-three, Min Jade made a mental note. Three years older than she was, he seemed much younger, not in spirit, but certainly in looks. She snuck a peek at him. Min Lee's hand gripped the steering wheel hard, and he seemed lost in thought.

Sandwiched between Nandong and Suyeong rivers, Busan, the busiest seaport in Korea, was indeed beautiful.

"I spent much of my young life in Busan and never for a minute thought I'd ever leave. They were the happiest years of my life."

Min Jade could see sadness enter his eyes, and he looked away from her open stare. For a while, they drove in silence before Min Lee continued. "I'd hold my mother's hand so tightly as we navigated the overcrowded Jagalchi Market with its rows and rows of umbrella merchants, peddling their fresh catch. She was always worried she'd lose me. Mother would buy the freshest fish, and we'd make sushi together. My favorite part was rolling the seaweed over the sticky rice. On Saturdays, our shopping day, we'd take the jam-packed subway to Seomyeon for our weekly Lotte Department Store outing. Only later did I understand why my mother would visit Medica Street in Seomyeon so often. Busan was also where my happiness ended, but I still love being by water. I can't live without water," he said finally.

Min Jade struggled to find something to say but decided to remain quiet. Min Lee seemed content with the silence. As she took in the scenery, she pondered what his life was like now. At thirty-three, he could be married or for sure involved. Finally, she said, "London must be very different from Busan."

"Yes, but it's home now, and I still live by the water. What do you say we take the trolley around town?" He abruptly changed the subject.

"Great idea."

Min Lee parked the car. Grabbing her hand, they dashed across the street to catch the Fiaker trolley that was pulling up. "Come on," he said, "let's see what Innsbruck has to offer."

Min Jade hesitated before curling her hand around his. She was behaving, unlike the self she knew, yet there was no other place or no other person she wanted to be with at that moment. It all felt natural as she clutched his hand tightly and followed him across the wide street. Min Jade had never held a man's hand this way, except for her father's. Min Lee squeezed her hand in his and thought the change in them was imperceptible; it was there. Min Jade felt a strange sense of comfort as they tooled around Innsbruck on the bus, taking in sights like the Cathedral of St. James, the Imperial Palace, and even the famed Swarovski Crystal World. Min Lee was forever snapping pictures with the camera hanging from his neck. "Smile," he said, jumping into the frame of her selfie.

The next day, the Mins became constant social companions. Every hour away from her teaching or his music, they spent together. She began noticing the little things he did, like pushing her glasses up her nose, tucking a wisp of hair, or moving to her left as they walked down the street. Who would have thought from their rocky beginnings, they could become friends? Min Jade's mind would caution; *What are you doing? You don't need a friend.* In Min Jade's view, having friends was overrated, and she vibed better with the explanation of evolutionary psychologists: smart people are better off with fewer friends.

"How about we go skiing?" Min Lee said on their third day of hanging out. "Want to try the Bergisel Ski Jump?"

"Not on your life. First of all, I'm not a great skier. Second, I have night blindness. Bergisel is not exactly the place to snow-plow down the mountain. Let's just call it a day."

Bergisel, the Olympic facility designed by Zaha Hadid, was the high point of any daredevil snow bunny's trip. Eight hundred and twenty feet above the city, it boasted the most exquisite vistas of Innsbruck.

"You need more adventure in your life. Let's try it. It's only 2 p.m., so you don't have to worry about your night blindness. We have four hours before the lifts close. It'll still be light at 6 p.m. Come on. I dare you."

Challenge? Well, that was one thing Min Jade thrived on. "Okay. I'm in, but we should start with a more manageable mountain."

As a city that had hosted the Winter Olympics in 1964 and 1976, Innsbruck had over three hundred and ten miles of ski trails.

"Deal." Min Lee led the way to his car, dragging her behind him, her hand firmly clamped around his. They drove to Stubai Glacier, a nearby ski trail more accommodating to all levels of skiers. After parking, they boarded the ski bus that would take them to the actual resort. Everything was working like clockwork!

"I'll get the gear." Min Lee put himself in charge of renting the necessary equipment, and boy, was he meticulous. Her ski boots had to fit perfectly. He measured her pole for optimum support and fitted her goggles and cap. He was a bit retentive. "Let's fit your boots now," he eased her feet into Rossignol boots. Min Jade got the feeling they were more than hanging out. It felt like a real date, and she liked it.

On the mountain, Min Lee gave her hand warmers for her gloves. "Let's do a practice run," he said. "Just grab onto me from behind, but make sure you keep your poles under your arms and pointing outward. On this run, I'll be your eyes while you get a feel for the mountain."

"What's taking so long?" Min Lee turned to look at her.

Min Jade quickly pushed her goggles into place to hide the moisture gathering in her eyes. Every part of her body prickled. Curling her arms around his waist, feeling the strong muscles of his abs, her face resting on his shoulders, her body fitting perfectly into his, Min Jade somehow felt like she was home. This was unacceptable, but what should she do?

"I'm ready." She could hear their hearts synchronizing. When her body molded to his, the surge in her heart felt like a shot of adrenaline directly into her veins. The feeling was over-powering, and suddenly, Min Jade froze. This was unfamiliar territory for her, but from all the sappy movies she'd watched, she recognized that the tricky and treacherous serotonin hormone that plays havoc on common sense was at play.

"Here goes," Min Lee took off down the mountain, powdery snow flying everywhere and forming swirls of white cloud behind their heels. It was a moderate slope well-suited for beginners, and Min Lee was careful not to go too fast. Min Jade tightened her grip around his torso, not because she had to, but because she wanted to.

"That was awesome," Min Jade said as they reached the bottom of the hill because it was not quite a mountain. They trundled back to the lift, and Min Lee helped her onto the chair.

"Good. This time, you do it by yourself. But I'll be right behind you."

At the top of the hill, Min Jade and Min Lee jumped off the chair. Moisture blurred her vision as the snow dust swirled. She had the urge to sit in the snow and wail–for what reason, she had no idea. She'd never had a 'friend,' and Min Lee was beginning to feel like a friend. Maybe she should quit while she was ahead, for this was not exactly the perspective she'd hoped to find in Innsbruck. After their last run, the Mins made their way to the restaurant atop the mountain.

"I should ski like this all the time, especially while holding on to you. I like doing no work."

"Yeah. You were almost asleep back there," Min Lee flapped her with the hat he'd pulled off. "But you can sleep on my back anytime."

Min Jade could feel her cheeks tinting. In the short time they'd spent together, every defense she tried to put up came tumbling down like dominoes in free fall. Wide-open and venturing into dangerous waters, her heart racing like a horse in the Preakness, she was trying even harder to act normal as she flopped down into a chair.

"Let me guess. A chai latte."

"It'll do. But I'm famished," she said, attempting to hide his effect on her. Min Jade needed to know what to do. She thought of texting her mother, but that would be downright stupid. She was thirty years old. As Min Lee stood in line waiting to order, Min Jade fished her phone from the backpack next to her chair and texted her mother, although she didn't say anything but hello. Inserting an action into obsessive thoughts would stop the craziness going on in her head. Min Lee returned ten minutes later with two chai lattes and two hamburgers.

"Very American, right?"

"Yup. You're *so* thoughtful."

"Are you being rude?" Min Lee sat in the chair opposite Min Jade, his eyes mocking her.

"You never cease to amaze me," Min Jade bit into her burger.

Min Lee didn't sip his latte or try to eat his hamburger. Instead, he sat staring at Min Jade, who was engrossed in devouring her burger. *Was he having some sort of breakdown? He'd never felt this natural with a single soul in his entire life, except his mother and, of course, Ji-Joon, but that didn't count. Was he being a little too sick with this Oedipal complex thing?* As he took in the woman in front of him, he realized she was cute, and he loved that she was a loner like him. Being brain-empowered was a major plus, as Min Lee did not stomach fools easily. *Could they—two maladaptive—be soulmates?* Just as he was about to avert his eyes, Min Jade looked up.

"Why are you staring at me? Is there something on my face? I'm a very messy burger eater," she grabbed the napkin from her lap.

"No reason. What else do you like to do, other than teaching?" Min Lee asked.

Min Jade stopped chewing; her mouth stuffed with food. She cocked her head to the left, a habit when she was thinking. *What else did she like to do?*

"You're taking too long to answer."

"No, no. Give me a minute," she pointed to her stuffed mouth.

"*Cham-kkan-ma-nyo.* Wait a minute," he reached over and wiped the corner of her mouth with the napkin she'd placed next to her plate. Their faces were dangerously close, and when Min Lee leaned backward, he pinched the tip of her nose.

Min Jade almost choked. *Who is this man? Where was the gargoyle of a few days before?*

"One, two, three…."

"Okay, okay. I like puzzles, going to the farmers' market, music, reading, singing and my research."

"All activities you do alone."

Min Jade immediately felt self-conscious and exposed. She quickly sipped her latte, avoiding Min Lee's curious eyes.

"You don't have to hide from me." Min Lee patted her hand, noticing her retreat. "Wanna know what I do? I play piano for twelve hours a day. I travel to play concerts for which I practice twelve hours a day. I get on and off airplanes, sleep, eat, and start all over again. I do that pretty much alone. Except for Ji-Joon."

"Who is he?"

"My manager. Since I went pro, he's been my manager, but he is more like a brother – an annoying one at that. We are two peas in a pod. So, see, your life sounds far more exciting than mine. I really, really envy progressive maladaptives like you," he flashed her a smile.

Min Jade smiled back. *Were they too two peas in a pod? She certainly felt so. And she certainly liked this nonsense feeling, but scientifically she knew this was all ill-fated, a camouflage, a mirage.*

"What do you want to do tonight?" Min Lee asked.

"Collapse in my bed after I rub my aching body with Bengay."

"Shall we do that together?"

Min Jade spat out a mouthful of hamburger. "What?"

"That didn't come outright. What I meant was, I'll make you dinner, and while I'm doing that, you can relax and lather your body with Bengay. Something tells me we should get to know each other."

"Something tells me that you're a little nuts."

"We established that already. But if I heard you right, crazy, don't scare you, and something tells me you don't know how to cook. That hamburger won't be enough for dinner."

"And you do?"

"Yes, of course. I am a great cook. I told you. I always cooked with my mother, and she was the best cook on earth."

"You are so clichéd. Are we going to fall in love over dinner?" She watched enough Korean Drama to know what came next.

"I wouldn't go that far. But what's wrong with falling in love?"

"There is no such thing as love. I rather fancy the theory that says that which we call love is nothing but an irresistible cocktail of physiological chemicals to entice the brain into limerence—necessary steps, of course, for the purpose of procreation while making us believe that we've chosen. What has happened is we've become victims of nature's plan for perpetuating sturdy DNA. Don't you just love the perfection of nature?"

"Nature or no nature, we still choose. We don't just walk around, falling in love. The cocktail's ingredients have to be right. Sorry, no pun intended. Take us, for example. On New Year's Eve, it took you ninety seconds to decide you liked me. In fact, it took you less."

"You are more arrogant than I thought."

"I'm speaking your language. Research supports this, Miss Encyclopedia Girl."

"Why do you know this?"

"Because I, too, am an expert at steering clear of love. I'm very much the poster child for maladaptation. But seriously, here are some stats for you to chew on fifty-five percent of love is conveyed through body language. Thirty-eight percent is in the tone and speed of one's voice." His duck beak hand went up. "And only seven percent is from what you say. It's not what you say but what you do that counts. So, based on your tone, I'd say you were as good as gone in sixty seconds."

"Don't count on that flawed research. I'm a real scientist. I know how to control experiments and mix chemicals. I'll accept dinner, but the stats don't bode well for you beyond that. Forget the love potion number nine mix, my friend."

"Well, let's go find out," he pulled her up from her half-eaten burger.

"I'm still eating."

"I'm making you dinner!"

Min Jade took another bite of her burger. "One should never waste food. Look at yours, not even touched."

"You're right. My mother always said that. The food you're wasting could feed the children in Biafra. I didn't even know where Biafra was. Shall I have them wrap it, Miss America?"

"You are crazy," Min Jade donned her hat and scarf and followed Mr. Overconfident. She never lost at anything.

CHAPTER FIVE

MIN JADE
WOMANHOOD

MIN LEE'S FLAT WAS THREE TIMES THE SIZE OF HERS. Like hers, it was cedar-paneled and practical.

"I guess they had this installed before you came," Min Jade ran her hand along the lid of the ebony Steinway baby grand. "My mother loves playing."

"Yeah? She has perfect pitch, too?" he mocked. "Do you play?"

"Not very well."

"Go ahead, play something for me."

"Never."

"Oh my. A chicken physicist with perfect pitch, a full of stats nut, no fun. How about I play, and you sing. You say you like singing."

"I only play and sing for people I like," Min Jade returned the dig. "What about you? When did you start playing?"

When no acerbic response, Min Jade turned around from admiring the piano to see Min Lee standing near the kitchen counter, his face again masked by sadness. Did she say something wrong? Min Lee proceeded to the icebox and began pulling things out as though he hadn't heard a word she'd said. Removing a knife from its holder, he started chopping carrots, onions, and snow peas with such speed, he could have been a Ginsu chef. Min Jade pulled a stool up to the counter and sat. "Did I say something wrong?"

He suddenly leaned into her, his face inches away from hers. "Do you like me?"

"What! No! Absolutely NO," Min Jade jerked backward.

"Why do you want to know? Sharing emotions is the beginning of creating memories."

"I'm sorry. I didn't mean to be nosy."

"But do you want to create shared memories?"

Min Jade thought she'd had it all worked out, but this Min Lee Woo was a real challenge to her sanity. When she didn't answer, he began his story.

"Music for me is bittersweet," he eased back and began heaping vegetables into a smoking wok. "My mother was a great pianist. One of the best in Korea. When she stopped playing, she wanted me to become her successor."

"Well, you did a good job of that."

The sadness deepened in his eyes. "That's because she was relentless. '*Min Lee, stop playing around and practice,*' she'd say, rapping my knuckles," he mimicked his mother's voice. "My feet could barely reach the floor, but she would bribe me with my favorite cream-filled bread. It was my reward for playing well. At five, I rather preferred running around the garden with my school friends, but I loved that bread, too. '*Oma,*' I'd beg, '*if I play well for one hour, may I go out and play with Bon-Hwa for a little while and get the bread, too?*' His voice was now childlike. "She'd tussle my hair and say, '*You are my precious son. You are going to be great one day—a great pianist. You have to practice to be great. The effort you put in will be the results you get out, okay, Min Lee? Let me hear your scales, and we'll see.'* Mother would smile at me as she patted my sore behind and sent me out to play. I always got to play outside, and I got the bread too. My Mother was always smiling. I loved her smile very much. The way the little holes appeared in her cheeks and deepened, the broader she smiled. I'd stick a little finger into her dimples, which would make her smile even more."

Min Jade unconsciously touched her cheek.

"Because I loved my mother, I became a great pianist, ultimately fulfilling my destiny and hers."

"And why did she not want to play anymore?" Min Jade asked.

"My *Eomeoni*, Yu-sun-ah, grew up in Seoul, the only daughter of a well-to-do family. Korean society is hard to fathom. Just be glad you don't have to navigate our arcane customs. Classes don't mix. At a young age, she was a promising and gifted pianist and an only child doted on by her parents and grandparents alike. She always said she never believed life could get better for any child, but the heart wants what the heart wants. At the prestigious Seoul National University-College of Music, to which few were admitted, she met a gifted cellist named Hy Soo. Hy Soo was on scholarship and would never have met with her parent's approval. Life with him was not the life her parents envisioned for their only daughter. But mother could find no greater happiness than with Hy Soo, so she secretly continued to see him." He paused for a moment, an indication to Min Jade his story would have no happy ending.

"When she found out she was pregnant, she disappeared from his and her parent's life. Such news would have killed her parents and derailed Hy Soo's most promising career. Already he had caught the eye of the best conductor and was producing his first solo album. *How could she?* She always asked.

What right did she have, she said, to change his destiny? But Mom could not bring herself to get rid of me, which is what her mother would have insisted on, dragging her by the feet, if necessary, to a private hospital where silence could be bought. She decided that the child she carried—me—was a gift from her and my *Abojie's* deep love, and I was their crowning jewel. She said my dad would have been ecstatic to have me, but she couldn't burden him. Dad, she said, would have insisted on *doing the right thing*, which meant giving up his career, so she ran away to Busan." *What was the matter with him, he'd never told that story to a single soul?* "I'm sorry," he finally said. "That was selfish of me. I'm sorry."

"No, it wasn't." His overwhelming sadness moved Min Jade "She must be so proud of you today."

"I hope so," he half-smiled. "She died when I was twelve and a half," he handed her a napkin because tears were rolling down Min Jade's cheeks. "I guess all the visits to Medica Street could not delay the inevitable. I'm making a traditional Korean meal. Pork Belly and Perilla leaves."

"I've had that before." Min Jade said.

"Good," he nodded.

Minutes went by in silence. Finally, Min Jade said, "Mothers do so much for their children, don't they?"

Min Lee nodded again, the muscles in his jaw taut. "Hungry, hungry or just hungry?"

"Hungry, hungry," Min Jade answered.

"Uh, where do you put all the food?" He gave her body a once over. Once the food was cooking, Min Lee set the table and opened a wine bottle. "Sit," he ordered, pouring her a glass of wine. Soon the food was ready, and Min Lee spooned rice into Min Jade's bowl and placed a strip pork belly on top of it. Unaware of the meaning of that gesture in Korean culture—total acceptance—Min Jade, still hungry from leaving her half-eaten burger, shoved the food into her mouth. "Mmmm. This is delicious."

"As I said, I am a good cook," he added more food to her plate.

"We do have a lot in common, it seems," Min Jade said.

"How so?"

"I think you can tell I wasn't a normal kid."

"Or adult," he said, his mouth stuffed with food.

Min Jade grimaced. "Fine. I don't have to talk to you at all. I can just eat and run."

Min Lee rubbed his hands together in a gesture that asked for forgiveness. "How so? Why do you think you're not normal?"

"Well, I talked to trees."

"I see. So, what did your mother have to do to keep you "normal"?"

"My mom had to give up her career for me, too." Pain tainted her voice, and Min Lee stopped eating to look up.

"When I was younger, I had a tough time. I was not the most popular girl in school; in fact, I was the least. I was bullied a lot. I was also a sickly child with asthma attacks in and out of the hospital. After a particularly brutal confrontation with some students in my senior year, I was so upset that I couldn't sleep for ten days and nights straight. My friend Raymond Hue, the one who invited me to Korea for the conference when I learned about Busan, finally called my mother, and she came to get me."

Ah. The Asian association. He got it now. He was her Raymond. No wonder.

"Turned out, I'd had a psychotic break. I spent two weeks in a psych ward. My mother never called it that. She said my brain had gotten a bit muddled and needed a rest. After my 'rest,' she marched me back to school to face reality. I was glad I was graduating in a few months."

"You graduated at sixteen?"

"Uh-huh. Many RAIN graduates do."

"Go on." Min Lee's face was cradled in his hands, listening.

"As I got older, I realized what had happened to me. I truly believed my mom, or maybe I needed to believe my mother when she said my brain was special and just needed to rest. From that day, however, she gave up her career and devoted her entire life to me. I've spent my whole life feeling guilty because my mother was a great opera singer who was becoming a household name." Min Jade looked around at the man standing behind her, encircling her in his arms.

"We are the lucky ones then, aren't we?" He patted her back. "A mother's love is why we are here. That's what a mother's love is for."

"But it's unfair. So very unfair." Min Jade said.

"You know what?"

Min Jade shook her head.

"I think we are creating shared memories. I've never spoken of my mother to a single soul in this way, not even Ji-Joon."

"And I've never as much as whispered about my life, not even to myself."

"Well now, Miss Encyclopedia Girl, can you entertain the thought that love is maybe more than just for procreation? Could it be about finding our healing soul counterpart on whom we can unconditionally depend and grow as we endure life's challenges? Everyone in this life endures something. No one gets a pass. Maybe we are each other's shelter," he tightened his embrace.

Min Jade tried to wiggle out of his grip. He was not going to use this moment to bamboozle her.

"It's okay." Min Lee raised her to her feet. "It's okay because I think maybe you are the kind of person I could love. Maybe my crack fits yours. That's what we're trying to find out, isn't it?"

What. Did she hear that, right? "I doubt that." Min, Jade quickly answered. Struck by how fast things were moving, she excused herself to the powder room. *What was she doing? What on God's earth was she doing?* She put a hand over her constricting chest. How could he *maybe* love her? She was all but losing her wits. And even if she could entertain the idea of love, how was she going to tell him she was a thirty-year-old virgin. She had no idea what to do with the crazy feeling taking over her body. *Breathe. Breathe.*

"Hey, are you alright in there?" Min Lee knocked on the door.

"I'm fine." When she finally pulled open the door, Min Lee was standing in the doorway. He backed her back into the bathroom.

"Trust me," he whispered against her ear. "Trust me with your heart."

"I can't, and I won't."

"What if I said I think I might be falling in love with you, Min Jade?"

It was unmistakable, the swelling that began in her heart and radiated through her body. The measured breathing of love's eternal cocktail. As he leaned into her, their lips so close, she could find no strength to resist.

"Min Lee. I don't know what you think you're doing right now." Min Jade tried to get around him.

"Do you want me to stop?"

"Yes. Well…maybe…well, yes. I don't even know what I'm feeling."

"What are you feeling?" Min Lee pressed.

"Flustered, flushed, crazy…."

"You've never felt this before?"

"No. Why would I?"

"Are you a virgin?"

Min Jade almost died of shock. Wilting to the floor, she began to weep. He'd never maybe love her now. Not a man like him. He must think her a right weirdo, and he'd no longer maybe love her. That would be okay with her head, but in her heart, she knew it was not. As if he could read her thoughts, Min Lee got down on the floor beside her and said. "It only makes me want to love you more." He kissed her forehead. At the thought of her being a virgin, his carnal desires rose decibels. For him, too, it was the first time his sexual longing had reached such a fever pitch.

"Can you trust me?" He kissed her on the forehead again, moving slowly to the tip of her nose, and then he stopped just as their lips met.

Min Jade felt it. The heaviness in her belly, the twitching of her thighs. She felt the physical reaction of the secretion of desire. Yet, it was she who brought his head down to her lips and, from where she did not know, slipped her tongue between his lips. When he began to pull off her turtleneck and unclasp her bra, she was ready for this thing called *maybe* love.

You are beautiful," Min Lee touched her perfect brown nipples that sprung from behind lace. He flicked his tongue over her left areola, gently coaxing her still uncertain emotions to degrees above boiling point.

"I…I don't think…."

"Don't think." Min Lee kissed her again. Deeply. His hand slipped into the waist of her pants and slid them down her long legs. "Just feel," he pulled her into the shower and, from behind, cradled her body like a spoon. "You are safe. I feel safe for the first time in my life, too."

The water sprayed down on them. Min Lee's dripping white shirt clung to his taut abs. He squeezed orange spice shower gel into his hand and began lathering her body. Lifting her arms over her head, he reached around and kissed her again.

Min Jade leaned into him, her back against his abdomen. They fit perfectly, entwined in the heat of desire. Min Lee abandoned his clothes and swooped her into him in one quick move. He felt her resistance. It made him crazy in love. He gently pushed, soft, warm, and spellbindingly beautiful. He felt her body twitch and grab hold of him as he moved gently with her. The air smelled of orange spice.

"*Ah.*" Min Jade's head fell backward as the pleasure-pain shot through her. She was in total surrender and, although in pain, she didn't want it to stop.

"*Aisheeee.*" Min Lee cradled her close as their bodies moved in unison. "Min Jade," he cried out, his body shuddering. "*Sa rang hae.*"

She had no idea what he said, but for her, too, it was, *Sa rang hae* as she watched the virginal blood swirl down the drain. She had lost her virginity at last.

Min Jade woke with an arm wrapped around her. *What had she done?* Nocturnal seduction, as only the night and unbridled emotions could unleash, had blotted out reason. It was never her intent to be so vulnerable, to be so stupid, to be so crazy to admit to a perfect stranger she was a psycho and then lose her virginity to him. Now he must really think her crazy. Min Jade gingerly eased her body out of the offending arms. She had to disappear before he woke up. She'd be too embarrassed to face him. As Min Jade tried to untangle herself, Min Lee's arms tightened around her. "Stay still," he commanded. "You lost to love potion number nine."

"Well, I wouldn't say I've lost." She tried to save face and turn the uncomfortable event into a battle of wits. "I'll have to do some research to determine exactly what happened. I suppose there could be more to love than meets the biology, but I'll get back to you."

Min Lee pulled himself up against the headboard. "I love that you're a virgin," he said bluntly.

Min Jade got two shades darker. "Was a virgin," she proffered boldly.

"Now, you can never love anyone as you'll love me."

"Min Lee Woo!" She sprung off the bed. "You are a…you are…"

"Not in denial?" he finished her sentence. "That's another scientific fact. First love theory says a woman will never forget her first love."

"Well, I never! Really. Aren't you the one here in denial? Aren't you scared about what I told you? What if I'm psycho?" Min Jade pulled the cover off him to cover her body, quickly averting her eyes from his…oh dear.

"Scared?" He stretched his arms above his head. His chiseled abs made her look away once again. "I personally adore psychos."

"Are you sure?"

"You don't have an ax, though, do you?"

"Yet to be revealed."

"I'm famished," he rose to his full height from the bed, walked over to her and took her back to bed. To her utter surprise, the morning sun had brought no clarity, but more desire and nowhere in her mind was the thought that she wanted him to stop. On and off again, they made love, slept, made love again, all morning. She could not get enough of his warm hand roaming her body. She was possessed.

Min Jade finally, literally, went to the bathroom. She bolted the door and stared at herself in the mirror. She looked the same, but she was no longer the same. What a new perspective she'd found in Austria! When she reappeared, Min Lee was making breakfast.

"Scared?"

"Yes."

"Don't be. I am your new protector."

Wanting to get off the subject of her possession, Min Jade said as she slipped into a seat at the counter, "Will you tell me what happened next in your story so I can see if I can trust you?" She cradled her face in her hands. Just this once, she thought, let it be love…maybe or real.

"Ah, you don't want to hear that long story. Let's do more of what we did last night," he placed a coffee cup in front of her.

"Min Lee Woo!"

"Okay, okay. But I much rather talk about how it was for you for the first time."

"Min Lee Woo!"

"Okay, fine. Fine…but…."

"Min Lee Woo, do you want me to leave now?"

He sighed loudly, none too pleased, and continued his story. "To be honest, after a while, I began to love playing the piano. I became good enough to get invited to competitions, and soon I began to win a few. The more I won, the more I played, and the happier my mother got. I loved the audience's adoration, but the real reason I wanted to keep winning was to see my mother's eyes light up with joy. Oh, she was so happy when I was offered a scholarship to the prestigious KMC Music School at twelve, the same one she and my *Aboeji* had attended. But I didn't want to go. My mom and I would play Serenade, Schubert's Serenade, every night before bed. To me, that was sheer happiness. All I ever needed in this world was my mom by my side. I couldn't—or rather didn't—want to imagine being without her."

"When I was eleven, she began feeling poorly, but for over a year, she tried drinking ginseng and taking other medicinal herbs. Finally, she went to the doctor, who said she had cancer in her pancreas. That was when she finally called my father. I never imagined why, but my father told me it was because she wanted to make sure I always had someone who would love me. That's how I learned of and met my *Abeoji*." Min Lee was pensive, and she could tell he'd drifted into memory. '*You have both our talents in one, my son,*' she'd said. '*Go out and claim your world.*' I am all that I am because of my mother's faith and love. Barely six months later, she was gone."

"We are lucky. To be loved is a special thing."

"I thought you didn't believe in love?" he poked her in the head.

"I'm talking about *agape* love, not *eros*. Even with the kind of love that holds my space, and my parent's wide wingspan, I'm scared all the time," Min Jade said. "I've lived in fear for fourteen years, thinking my break was not just stress-related, but genetic. I've been waiting and waiting for it to strike again."

"I'm no expert here, but I think real psychosis onset happens in the late adolescence or early twenties. You were only sixteen. It seems to me yours was situational, brought on by stress. I have a feeling you're just a normal, loony-toon maladaptive. I hate to break this to you, but I knew you were mad from the moment you stepped onto the train."

"What?"

"All you had to do was ask for help, Miss Independent. Do you think a man like me would not notice everything around him?"

"You are insufferable! I just can't believe you're such a jerk," she said. "I can't believe I let you sucker me…."

"Hey. Don't even think about it. Statistically speaking, we are right on track. Third date…love grows. In my country, there is a saying; if you run into someone three times, destiny is afoot."

"Shut up," Min Jade threw a lettuce leaf at his head. "Be glad it's not an ax!"

"So, do we want to try and find out how we feel about each other for real? Would you like to be my girl?"

"I think I've proven I'm no girl." Min Jade sassed.

*   *   *

"Oh hell," Min Jade let out a loud groan as she climbed out of bed the following morning. Her body ached something fierce, like that of an eighty-year-old woman. How long had it been since she'd used the muscles needed for skiing and for—she blushed! She pressed her palm on either side of her back and pushed herself backward, which only led to another yelp. Jumping in the shower, she allowed the hot water to beat against her sore muscles. When she got back from class, she'd take a proper soak in an Epsom salts bath, and she'd call her mother. How on earth would she tell her mother she was a woman now? Maybe it was best not to tell her at all. With effort, Min Jade zipped up her boots and threw a blood-red scarf around her neck. Gingerly, she stepped out the door and bumped right into Min Lee.

"Careful," he grabbed her by the elbow.

Min Jade blinked twice to clear her eyes. "Why are you up so early if you don't have anything to do?" She straightened up somewhat, letting out a yelp as she strode off to get a head start.

"Too much activity?" He laughed, earning him a cutting of the eye. "Early morning is a great time to practice. But more importantly, I wanted to give you this," he caught up to her and handed her what looked like a photo album.

Min Jade took the album and quickly flipped through it. There were dozens of casual pictures of their time on the mountain and at his apartment. The Album was entitled, Creating Memories. *How sweet.* "You know, it's not cool to take pictures of people without their permission," she said, chuffed as all get out but not wanting to give in too easily to his seduction.

"Sue me. Shall I pick you up after class?"

"I have office hours today."

"Okay. I'll come to your place later," he said. "I'll bring a jigsaw puzzle."

Min Jade burst into laughter. "You are really something."

"I know."

Again, they parted ways at the Hotting West building.

For the next week, Min Lee waited for Min Jade on her doorstep every morning at 8 a.m. He'd walk her to class; video call her at lunch and then pick her up after her lecture. They'd dine and walk the old town, him always grabbing her hand if the street was too crowded or if they had to cross to the other side. "Look," he'd say, "we are doing things together. How does it feel?"

"Like a dream."

"Let's not wake up."

That night as they cuddled in bed, Min Lee said, "Look what I have," he pulled a book titled, *How to Fall in Love* from under the pillow. "I've never been in *maybe* love before," he handed it to her, "so I bought this to learn how to transform maybe love into true love so I can love you forever."

"Forever is a long time," Min Jade said, flipping through pages.

✓ Shower together
Slow dance
Go on a picnic
Take a bike ride on a two-seater bike…
✓ Make love in the wee hours of the morning

After scanning the book, she shut it and looked at Min Lee. "Love is something which grows for sure, but it takes time. Let's just say…we need time to find out."

"Thought you were a physicist. Isn't time relative? I still believe it only takes 3 seconds, but time, I'm willing to give it a try. Talking about time, I have to leave Innsbruck soon. I'll be gone for a while, but I think it'll be fun for us to meet up wherever I am on the weekends. Since I'll be in Europe, nothing will be too far. Until then, don't even think about hanging out with anyone else, and read this entire book so we know how to love each other forever. I bought two."

That weekend, as they spent time together, Min Jade realized that indeed she'd fallen hopelessly for Min Lee. Instead of being anxious, she felt a sense of peace. There was no denying now what had been missing in her life. Love. For the entire weekend, they'd barely left the bed but to make breakfast and dinner, skipping lunch for a better afternoon delight. On Sunday night, Min Lee's phone rang. It was Ji-Joon. Min Lee was then forced to leave her to discuss his upcoming trip to Switzerland. "Parting is such sweet sorrow," he kissed her passionately. "I'll pick you up in the morning."

CHAPTER SIX

MIN LEE WOO
DEPARTURE

"WHAT THE HELL DO YOU THINK YOU'RE DOING?" Ji-Joon accosted him as he walked through the door.

"I'm tired. What do you want to tell me?"

"Why are you playing house? You know this can't go anywhere. Plus, you've been neglecting your music since you met Miss Glasses."

"And?"

"And there are a few things we need to discuss before our trip to Switzerland."

"This could all wait until tomorrow. Don't tell me you're jealous? I know you've had me to yourself all these years, but I think Min Jade is going to become a major competitor." Min Lee winked at his friend. "I like her, Ji-Joon. Maybe even love her."

"*Aigoo*," Ji-Joon dropped some papers on the table. "It's time to come up for air," he snapped.

"*Oh…*my jealous boyfriend. I'm gonna take a shower and hit the sack. It's been a strenuous weekend," he winked again.

"*Daebak.*" Ji-Joon shook his head and walked next door to his flat.

Before retiring, Ji-Joon retrieved all their travel documents. "Oh shit!" he said. "We leave tomorrow. Why did I think we were leaving on Tuesday?" He went back over to Min Lee, who was fast asleep. *Damn. He must have been doing some work.* Ji-Joon went back to his flat. He'd just have to wake him early in the morning. Since everything was already packed for their departure, all he had to do now was call a cab. Ji-Joon arranged their transportation, set his alarm, and sprawled out on his bed. He'd never seen Min Lee like this, and he wasn't sure he liked it. At 2 a.m., he let himself into Min Lee's apartment and woke him up.

"Bad news, bud. We're leaving today."

"Today. We leave today?" A sleepy Min Lee threw off the covers.

"Yeah. Sorry bloke, I thought it was tomorrow."

"I've gotta tell Min Jade." He reached for his phone but decided against it. It was too early. He'd just leave her a note and call her when he got to Switzerland. At the airport in Geneva, Min Lee reached into his coat pocket for his phone. Min Jade would be up by now, and he didn't want her to wait for him to pick her up. He dug deeper into his pants pockets, then into his jacket and breast pockets. His phone was missing.

"Ji-Joon, do you have my phone?" He kept searching.

"No."

"I can't find it!"

"When did you last see it?"

"I don't remember. Give me your phone. I need to call Min Jade."

"I don't have a number for her on my phone."

"Then I'll call the school."

"Right now, we have an appointment," Ji-Joon tapped his watch.

"Give me your damn phone," Min Lee grabbed the phone and googled the Innsbruck Physics Department's main number. He dialed the number and asked to be transferred to Min Jade's office. The phone, which rang without answer, was transferred back to the receptionist. "Please leave a message for her along with this number," Min Lee instructed. "The confounded thing about cell phones," Min Lee scoffed, handing the phone back to Ji-Joon, "is that no one remembers people's numbers anymore." Rarely had he needed to dial Min Jade's number, she was I on his speed dial, and she was right next to him most of the time when they were not working, so her number was nowhere close to being imprinted on his photographic mind.

A day later, when he still hadn't heard from Min Jade, Min Lee decided he'd fly to Austria. His phone, which had been left in his flat, had arrived broken, even the sim card had been destroyed. Buying a new phone was useless since he'd not backed up his old phone to the cloud after arriving in Austria. Min Lee instructed Ji-Joon to call every hour on the hour.

"Did you call?" Min Lee asked Ji-Joon right after one of his meetings.

"How could I? I was sitting right next to you!"

"Did you book me a flight for this weekend?"

"No can do," Ji-Joon informed him. "No time in your schedule for that. Zero. Be patient. She'll call."

"I'll send an e-mail to her office."

"Good idea. Let me check if I can find her address on the school's website. Ah, here it is," Ji-Joon wrote the address down and handed it to Min Lee.

Another day went by, and nothing! Min Lee checked to see if she was on social media by chance, but he had a hunch even before checking that it would be a no. Though he had a social media site, it was professionally managed by his management company. Unless it was urgent, neither he nor Ji-Joon even cared what was on it. After four weeks, Min Lee was furious. The coward of a girl. Why hadn't she returned any of his calls or responded to his e-mail? Didn't she care? She must have been furious about his sudden disappearance, but he was sure she'd have understood. Being the considerate guy he was, he'd even left a note on her door at 4 in the morning! Maybe their togetherness meltdown had been too heavy for her. Perhaps he shouldn't have brought up the love word. It was probably way too soon, but Min Lee, a man who knew the difference between lust and love, was sure what he felt for Min Jade was heading toward love. He was willing to give it time to develop her feelings for him, but he knew it was love in his heart. Frustrated, Min Lee decided to call her office for the last time. If he didn't hear from her, he'd move on. He'd been so looking forward to their weekends together.

"We've ironed out your contract finally," Ji-Joon informed him, coming into his rented flat as usual unannounced and handing him a document. "I'll make arrangements for you to fly back to Austria now."

Min Lee grunted something. It was all Ji-Joon's fault. Had he not made an error in their departure date, he'd be a happier man right now. "I really ought to kill you," he slapped Ji-Joon on the back of his head.

"It was a mistake, Min Lee. Everyone makes them sometimes," Ji-Joon said, rubbing the back of his head, a scowl on his face.

"Mistakes are costly. Let me know what arrangements you make." Min Lee went to his studio and slammed the door. Still, why had Min Jade chosen to hide behind their separation? *Coward*, he thought again, as he banged the piano keys.

CHAPTER SEVEN

HOTTING WEST, INNSBRUCK
MIN JADE
DISAPPEARANCE

MIN JADE, WHO HAD BEEN TAKING EXTRA CARE of her appearance, had found her heart racing as she'd waited for Min Lee the Monday morning he'd disappeared. She'd waited and waited well past her allotted time, having to rush to class. That day she'd felt worried, but when Min Lee didn't show up after her class either, the worry turned to panic. She must have dialed him a thousand times throughout the day, but all her calls were directed to voicemail. Min Jade, heart hollowed out with worry, had sprinted over to his apartment after class, only to find Min Lee had left Innsbruck. A jolt of debilitating disappointment descended, and she'd been filled with fear of abandonment. How could someone who *maybe* loved her discard her with such callousness?

Min Jade checked her phone messages a hundred times a day for a week. Nothing. She checked her e-mail. Nothing. She never thought of checking her spam, which could number thousands of messages. She called Michigan to see if any messages were left there for her. Nothing. A week later, Min Jade, her mind in a quandary, almost bumped into a rushing student. "Sorry," she said, floating down the hall on automatic pilot. *Had he orchestrated all this? Was this his M.O.? That sly, no good predator. If not, why hadn't he said he was leaving? Why hadn't he even said goodbye? Twelve days. Twelve unforgettable days they'd spent together, and now he'd disappeared into thin air. How could she have been so stupid? Served her right for falling into the trap called love.* Min Jade hastened her steps to the lecture hall. She'd never felt this naive, used, and stupid, but coping was familiar territory, and she knew just what to do. She was, after all, a master at compartmentalization. Over the next few weeks, Min Jade wavered between a desire to give Min Lee the benefit of the doubt and fury. A month went by with no call from Min Lee. Min Jade finally called on her well-developed compartmentalization skills. She removed the photo they had snapped on the mountain from her iPhone, hid the photo album she'd looked at every night, and emptied her brain's data bank of anything to do with Min Lee Woo. Life would go on.

Band practice was beginning for their shindig at Der Pavillion. As she headed to the lounge for their practice, Tunde was approaching from the opposite direction.

"Well, if it isn't our long-lost professor. Where have you been?"

"Working."

"And where are you off to now?"

"The lounge. Chin sent a text that we have to begin band practice. Isn't that where you're going?"

"That's correct." *The poor love,* Tunde thought, not feeling an ounce of guilt about his covert plan to be the only man in her life. As they approached the Physics Lounge door, she could hear the posse debating one topic or the other, most of it inconsequential, to say the least.

"Trying to explain femtoseconds to laypeople is like trying to explain evolution to Christians. Impossible," she could hear Chin was saying from the hallway.

"But we should at least try. With all the emphasis on STEM these days, we have to attract more people into the program. That means we have to find a way to explain the language of physics in layman's terms," Albert was insisting.

"Maybe physics is not for laymen," Anastase said. "Plus, that's not our job. It's the recruiters. We just have to be physicists, plain and simple."

"Elitist," Vadim said. "Very."

Tunde entered the room, and Min Jade followed him in. "Hey, everyone. Look who I found wandering the hallways."

"Hey, stranger. Long time no see," Albert said.

"Perfect timing. We were just about to start discussing Perfect Harmony's rehearsal schedule and where we'll meet after our sabbatical is over," Chin said.

True to their word, they had started an ad hoc band, and Min Jade couldn't wait to see Vadim in a tutu! The following month they would play their first gig at *Der Pavillion*. Min Jade, an introvert by nature, was nervous about such a public performance. She wondered what her mother would think of the shenanigans and frivolity she was engaging in in Innsbruck.

"Min Jade, sweetheart," Tunde sidled up to her when the conversation about rehearsal was over. "Why are you making kimchi instead of fufu?" he whispered.

"Oh, Jesus, Tunde. Not again. Aren't we the perfect harmony?"

"But you don't answer to the beat of the drum at all? Where have you been lately? Are you deliberately being antisocial?" He was smiling, but Min Jade got the distinct feeling he was being irascible.

She whacked him with her purse. "You need to quit."

"Seriously. What's going on with this Woo guy? "

"I don't have a clue! Do you?"

Tunde cleared his throat. He felt a little guiltier now about his memo-snatching activities. He'd never seen Min Jade this flat and wondered if he should fess up. "Well, I'm glad you're here and that you didn't fall in love and run off on us."

"Love! You are completely trivial. Love," Min Jade snorted.

"Why is that impossible? Love doesn't take long. I fell in love with you in three seconds. I am throwing my hat in the game of love, but remember, I play to win! I am, after all, a game theorist."

"Get away from me," Min Jade pushed him into a nearby chair. *Love. She had fallen hopelessly in love with a con man named Min Lee Woo.*

Tunde swung his feet over the arm of the chair and stifled a smile at how Allah had unexpectedly helped him. Tunde, whose mail slot was next to Min Jade's, was rifling through his mail when he realized he'd accidentally retrieved Min Jade's mail. The first piece of mail he looked at was a transcribed phone message from the Korean Dragon. He'd dutifully returned all the mail except for the message. For about a second back then, he felt a bit like a cad, but before he could get to the end of the thought, the feeling had long passed. What the hell, out of sight, out of mind. The Dragon was all wrong for her, anyway. Daily, Tunde would race to the mail slot the moment the postman arrived, rifle through Min Jade's mail, and purge it of Min Lee's numerous messages. Man was the guy an obsessive type! Finally, after a month, the messages stopped coming. Tunde, who felt he had far more to offer Min Jade, had used the opportunity to shake her infatuation with the pianist. Clearly, Tunde could never understand how on earth she could pass him up for Min Lee.

Tunde Oghenekohwo, the only son of an infamous Nigerian oil baron and heir to his father's enormous wealth, was the catch of the century. Who in their right mind could resist him? Educated at the best schools, he was one of the most brilliant researchers in quantum physics, with a hobby in game theory. To his great pleasure, he had to spend very little time as the CEO of his father's London offices, as he was merely a figurehead. Tunde had the world at his fingertips, and he, the Lion, was ready to be tamed the moment Min Jade had walked into the room on their first day in Innsbruck. The thought that she wouldn't recapitulate and come to him never crossed his mind. It was just a matter of time, and he smiled some covert memo snatching activity.

Tunde watched Min Jade from the chair he occupied. She was still sad after an entire month, and he wanted to find a way to cheer her up. This moping around had gone on way too long, plus there was no question they'd be better together; they understood each other, he felt at home in her presence, she was his intellectual equal, a far cry from most of his women, and he really liked her. For darn sure, he offered much more than the Dragon. Excited to put his plan in action, Tunde jumped up from his chair and went to stand by her side once again. She pushed him back into the chair.

"Sit there and don't move," she warned.

Tunde wasn't used to waiting for women, nor was he a patient person. He would have to develop his EQ muscles with this Min Jade.

The day of their gig had arrived. Min Jade peered at herself in the mirror. Who was she? How she'd changed in Austria. Had she slept with a man she hardly knew and agreed to be a part of these musical shenanigans? Bizarre! She should've opted for insomnia. Min Jade rummaged through her closet for "the perfect gig" attire, settling on a red skit, white blouse, and blue go-go boots–a proud American. She was glad to have the Perfect Harmonies in her life. It was a good distraction and made her life bearable. They were backstage in the manager's cramped office, listening to Chin cracking his knuckles and watching him pace back and forth in the small room.

"How is everybody feeling?" Anastase asked, primping in the mirror.

"That's irritating," Tunde said to Chin, pushing Anastase aside and hogging the mirror. "I'm parched. Any libation around here?"

Vadim handed him a bottle of vodka. The band had a drink to loosen up, even Min Jade. Finally, it was time to hit the stage. Crowded in the wings, they watched Christophe, the venue owner, tap on the mic.

"Tonight, we have a special treat," he announced. "We have some visiting Innsbruck physicists whose band, the Perfect Harmonies, will perform for us tonight. He went on to explain the origin of their name. "It's all in good fun, so no heckling!" he warned. "Help me welcome the brains and the brawn of Innsbruck. The *PHs*…The Perfect Harmonies!"

The stage went dark, and the room was silent. The guitar played a progression of chords, and then the purple-tinted spotlight illuminated Anastase. Except for Vadim, the rest of the band joined him on stage, and the entire stage lit up. The crowd let out a woof-woof chant and went wild when Vadim, dressed in a white t-shirt and black tights, leaped onto the stage, strumming his bass. Min Jade, in a fit of laughter, almost missed her cue. They played five songs, a mixture of pop and classical. Then a song with beats they called *The*

Revolution. The crowd went wild for *Revolution* and began throwing euros. Oh, what a night! How she wished Min Lee had been there.

With their gig now over, Min Jade was left with evenings that dragged on and on. She couldn't deny she missed Min Lee terribly. Why had he chosen to disappear from her life without a word? Was their confession too cataclysmic? Were they too volatile and destined for combustion like the couple in *Like Water for Chocolate*? She was trying hard, but her lines were blurred, and her compartments were bleeding into one another. He would not leave her mind.

* * *

Tunde couldn't stand the change in Min Jade. Months of moping, in his book, was enough. He wondered if he should give her the messages from Min Lee to cheer her up, but he didn't want to, and how would he explain he'd been hacking her mailbox? He needed a fail-safe plan to woo Min Jade in earnest. On Monday, after her class, he waited for her outside in the hallway, the way Min Lee always did. "Take a walk with me," he grabbed her by the hand and led her to a secluded spot on campus.

"What are you doing?" Min Jade pulled her hand from his.

"I bet you didn't know this place existed," he said. "Sit down."

"Why?"

"Sit down," he pushed her onto a bench. "Stop trying to be brave and nonchalant."

"I don't know what you're talking about."

"For months, you have been moping around like a lost puppy. I know it's because Min Lee has left. Just admit you miss him. That would be a start."

"I miss him. I miss him. Now what?"

"Now trust that if you were meant to be, you'd find each other. Min Jade, even the end of the earth as we know it can't change a love that's meant to be. In the meantime, keep living and see what's in front of you."

"It's just that…."

"It is what it is. Have a good cry and let it all out. All you need is someone to stand by you. I'll stand by you, Min Jade. So, go ahead," he pulled her head to his shoulder. "Cry your heart out."

Min Jade allowed herself the vulnerability to lean on the shoulder he offered. "I never understood what that saying meant."

"It's primal…crying releases pent-up emotions, so we can go on."

Min Jade didn't cry, but she did rest her head on Tunde's shoulder. Tunde straightened his spine and gloated. He was such a master, in every way!

Time flew by. By February, Min Jade had settled into a new distraction pattern. On weekdays she taught and sequestered herself in the lab, leaving only time for sleep. On weekends, she traveled with the Perfect Harmonies to nearby countries. Tunde, who loved to be out and about, was especially attentive to Min Jade's every need.

"I hear from a little birdie that someone is having a birthday," Tunde cornered her as she left her lab late one evening.

"Yup. Aging fast." As they grew to know each other, Min Jade realized that she and Tunde fit professionally, and it was easy to be with him. Tunde understood her. To her band of physicists, she was just one of the boys.

"Let's do something fun for your birthday."

"Like what?"

"Leave that to me."

But when her birthday came in March, nothing special happened. The group brought her a cake shaped like an atom! On the following Saturday, there was a persistent knock on her door. Min Jade poked her head from under the covers. What kind of mad person was up at 6 a.m. on the weekend? She dragged herself to the door to find Tunde all dressed up and raring to go. "What's going on here?" Min Jade left the door open and was ready to climb back into bed. "Make your own coffee," she grunted. It was Tunde who had taken up her guardianship now. He'd dropped by in the evenings to have dinner and often met her after labs for coffee.

"Heck no," he pulled off the cover she'd already drawn up to her chin. "Go and take a shower and get ready. We have to be somewhere by 10 a.m."

"What do we have to do?"

"Min Jade, can't you, for once, just do as you are told?"

"Okay…okay," she threw off the covers and went to the bathroom.

When she returned to the dining room, all dolled up in a red beret, chartreuse pants, and a coat with multi-colors, with her neck wrapped in a matching scarf, Tunde handed her a cup of coffee. *How biblical,* he thought when he saw her attire, but he'd need more than the patience of Job to deal with Min Jade and a full appreciation of Joseph's coat to deal with her dress style. Yes, he was Muslim, but he wasn't small-minded. "Perfect! You are perfectly dressed," he squinted. "Drink up, and let's hurry. We need to be somewhere soon."

That somewhere was Paris. Min Jade was beside herself, giddy. Tunde had tickets to the private opening of the Botero exhibit at the Louvre. They had an early dinner at La Coupole where she overdosed on goose pâté and Osso Bucco, and then it was off to the Palais Garnier to see *Giselle* in two acts. Min Jade spent as much time admiring the *Chagall* ceiling as she did watching the ballet. She'd never enjoyed a birthday as much as she had her thirty-first. Normally, she'd spend her special day with her mom and dad. Tunde was a good distraction from all that ailed, but if she got too enamored, she wouldn't even be able to pronounce her own last name! Oghenekohwo. Nah! That in itself was a barrier, but she was grateful. The months continued without a word from Min Lee. She'd never have pegged him as such a man, but alas. It was now June, and the Alps shaped up to be as spectacular in the summer as they were in winter. These six months in Innsbruck had been the best and the worst time of her life, but she wouldn't trade the cross-cultural immersion that had shaped the new Min Jade even to save a broken heart. She'd wanted perspective, and by God, she got it. This kind of experience should be required for every human being.

Though Min Jade loved the University of Michigan, she wished her sabbatical had been for a year, but it was time for her to return to Ann Arbor. Min Jade had never been so sad to leave a place. Except for Albert, all of The Perfect Harmonies were going back to their respective lives, as apparently Min Lee Woo had. When Min Jade boarded the plane to Ann Arbor, she was downright sad. She'd come to Austria without one person whom she could call a friend, except Winful, who didn't count, and now she was leaving with five friends and, for twelve days, the indelible memory of a man called Min Lee Woo. And, in Innsbruck, she'd become a woman.

CHAPTER EIGHT

MIN LEE WOO
DETOUR ON THE WAY TO AUSTRIA

"JI-JOON WAS ABOUT TO CLICK THE BUTTON TO BOOK a flight to Austria when his phone rang. "Yes. This is Mr. Lee's assistant. Who? Ah yes. When? In two days? I don't think that is possible. I'll check with Min Lee and call you back. I understand. Yes, he does indeed love his father." Ji-Joon hung up the phone and broke out into a sweat. Min Lee was sure to kill him, but what was he to do? Maybe he could approach the entire thing from a different angle. He crossed the hall and knocked on Min Lee's door. His knocking without just letting himself in would be a clue that something was wrong, Ji-Joon hoped.

"What?" Min Lee, still icing Ji-Joon, pulled open the door. "Do you have my flight info?"

"Umm…well…not exactly. Something has come up."

"Are you trying to piss me off, Ji-Joon? Forget it. I'll do it myself." He was about to slam the door.

"I just got a call from Korea," J-Joon said calmly.

"Is something wrong with your parents?" Min Lee was now more concerned than angry.

"No. It was a request for your father."

"My father? And he called you instead of me?"

"His agent. They are willing to pay a lot of money for you to come to Korea."

"We don't need more money, do we? I won't do it. I thought you said, my father?"

"Yes. It was his agent who called on your father's behalf."

"And what did he want?"

"Your father's last concert is coming up, and he wants you to play it with him." Ji-Joon prattled on.

"Ji-Joon, is this a request from my father or his agent? Be clear and stop beating around the bush."

"Your father expressed his wish, and I think the agent took it upon himself to ask. I am not sure if your father is aware that he's asking. But is that too much to ask? Think how happy this would make your mother, Min Lee. The people she loved the most in life doing what she loved the best–playing music."

"I'll call father and find out what the situation is." Min Lee said.

"It would be such a gift. Your father was your foundation before you left."

"Indeed, he is a good father, and yes, he was a lifesaver after mother died, but does that mean I should go back to Korea to play a concert? I'm sure we can create and play a special engagement later, even after he's retired. *Shireoyo*. I don't want to. I want to see Min Jade."

"What about if this is your father's request? You owe him that much, don't you think?" Ji-Joon did not mention everything the agent told him. Somehow, he had to get Min Lee to Korea. He didn't need regrets in the future if he never saw his father again. He, of all people, needed no more regrets.

"What about it, Ji Joon? What?"

"Min Lee, he's a good father and deserves your loyalty. Think how happy your mother would be." He repeated.

Min Lee eyed his friend. Ji-Joon was a scoundrel. If anyone knew his Achilles' heel, it was him. Although Min Lee had never told Ji-Joon the full story of his life, Ji-Joon knew enough to know how much he'd have respected his mother's wishes. The wishes that still drove him from beyond her grave. Min Lee walked to the far corner of the room. Yes, his mother would be pleased, but how could he forget the pain of Korea? His father had been his savior, but that had not stopped him from giving in to his battle-ax of a wife who was dead bent on separating him from his only blood relative. In-Tak Hyun refused to acknowledge Min Lee when his father had brought him home, continuously calling him a bastard, she was spiteful, evil, and made his life a living hell. And she did not stop until she'd figured out how to get rid of him. "When are they asking us to come?"

"Now. The concert is in a week, and you'll need to practice. We'll only be there for a week, and you can fly directly to Austria from Korea. But you know I've had a lot of requests for you to produce a Korean album, but that would require us to be there for a month and…."

"I won't do that. What about Min Jade? She must be worried to death. Ji-Joon she's very important to me. If she has moved on, at least, I need to know. I need to see her."

"Right after this. I promise. Okay, forget the Korean album…but *jebal,* please," he rubbed his palms together in cultural emphasis, "let's do this for your father."

"One week, take it or leave it."

Ji-Joon tapped out a number on his phone. After seventeen years on the road with Min Lee, he knew just how to handle his enigmatic artist.

Min Lee was none too pleased with the news, but Ji-Joon would not insist unless he thought it was vital. Was there more he wasn't telling him? When Min Lee first came to Seoul, he'd met Ji-Joon at Seoul National University-College of Music. Ji-Joon was a young prodigy and his only real competitor until an accident claimed his talent. Depressed and ready to leave the music scene Min Lee had encouraged him not to give up. Although he could not regain his previous greatness, Min Lee had brought him back to being a good pianist. Ji-Joon had decided not to go back to the stage but insisted on remaining by his side as Min Lee's manager. They were closer than brothers and each other's strength. He wouldn't insist unless he thought it important. Like brothers, too, at times, Min Lee wanted to strangle his *Hyung*. This was one of those times.

"Make sure it's one week. Less if you can get away with it."

"*Aigooo*," Ji-Joon pointed to the phone, waving him out of the room.

Min Lee was about to say something else when an apparition of Min Jade's face came into view. She was smiling, smiling just like his mother. A little shaken, he immediately went to the bar and poured a whisky. Such a coward of a woman. He would set her straight as soon as he got to Austria. She was nothing like his mother! She was cold and callous for not responding to any of his calls. He'd been grateful for his crazy schedule, which had left him little time for his mind to wander. Still, not a day had gone by that he hadn't thought of his duck beak girl.

It was not without trepidation that Min Lee Woo returned to Korea. One would have thought him a K-pop star from the fuss they made over him on his arrival at Incheon Airport. True, he was one of the top pianists in the world, and Koreans were proud of their homegrown talent, but he was no pop star. Ji-Joon hurriedly moved him to a waiting car, two burly men, one on either side, keeping the press in check. Min Lee ducked into the vehicle while Ji-Joon stayed behind to set up press interviews.

The driver had been given his destination, and as soon as he was secured, he pulled off. Folding his hands on his lap, Min Lee looked out the window during the entire ride into Seoul. With early morning haze hovering, the water of the Hangang River, Min Lee wondered how his mother had been. Her ashes here, in the waters of the Hangang River. Seventeen years before, he'd stood on its bank, acting brave as he sprinkled her ashes in the river. He'd felt like jumping in with her. Later at the ossuary ritual, he'd met his maternal grandparents for the first time. Together, they had assembled his mother's–their daughter's–Remembrance Wall in Seoul. Min Lee would rather it had been in Busan, but he had no say. After that day, he never saw his grandparents again. They had little to do with him, blaming him for ruining their daughter's life. As tears had streamed down his face, his father, whom he'd met only days before his mother's death, stood close, steadily holding onto his shoulders. It had been reassuring, and though reluctantly, he was glad he'd come.

The driver pulled off the main drag onto a side street. Min Lee pulled out the photo of his mother that he kept in his wallet, along with one of his fathers. His father, who had hastily come to Busan after his mother's call, was indeed a good man.

Min Lee passed a finger under his eyes. He'd promised his mother to be strong, and she'd promised she would always be in the music. Forgiveness, she reminded him, was a gift from God, and she'd pleaded with him to trust his father because, like her, he loved him very much. Ji-Joon was right. He should be there for his father. Still, he felt nothing but anger as he got closer to his once adopted home. Min Lee watched the skyline pass by before closing his eyes for a moment of meditation and calm.

The house was as he remembered it. Maybe even more opulent and intimidating in the early morning fog. It was 9 a.m. Korean time. His father seemed to have been waiting for them. He opened the door and immediately held his son in a tight embrace. *"Adeul,"* he tightened his grip around Min Lee, "It's been way too long. Let me look at you, son."

"Abeoji." Min Lee, though uncomfortable, allowed the embrace. "It is good to see you."

"Thank you for coming, son. I know it's a sacrifice, but I am selfishly glad you're here."

His father, now nearing sixty-five years old, was still very distinguished. They'd kept in communication over the years but had only seen each other on the rare occasions their tour schedules intersected, usually only for a few hours at a time.

"I am glad to be with you, *Abeoji*, and honored you want to play with me."

His father nodded. "I am thankful, son. Really thankful."

Ji-Joon walked in as the men were about to sit down for a drink. "Dad, do you remember Ji-Joon?"

"Yes, of course. Great to see you. Come join us for a welcome drink. Hy Soo greeted Ji-Joon with a firm handshake and a pat to the back of his hand. "Thank you for bringing Min Lee home."

Min Lee noticed his father seemed a lot frailer than his years, and there was a weariness about him.

"You should both get some rest after this. We have a big party planned to welcome you home."

"Abeoji, you know I hate parties."

"I know, but Korea wouldn't forgive me if their precious son came home, and they weren't invited to meet him. You can't imagine how proud Korea is of you."

"I thought they were all at the airport already." Min Lee finished his drink and rose. "No worries, *Abeoji*, we've booked a hotel nearby. We'll be back well before the party."

His father's face drooped. "A hotel? This is your home. How can you stay at a hotel?" Hy Soo's crestfallen look made Ji-Joon hastily correct his oversight.

"I'll take care of that," Ji-Joon said quickly. "I'm sorry, *Abeoji*."

Min Lee flashed him a look of death. Ji-Joon ignored it. Hy Soo escorted Min Lee to his old room and Ji-Joon to one just down the hall.

"I didn't move a thing," Hy Soo said proudly.

Indeed, nothing had changed about the room. His miniature planes, a favorite hobby of his as a boy, were still on display. He was surprised that In-Tak Hyun hadn't disposed of any reminders of him when he'd left the house. He supposed he could stand this for four days. Thank God his stepmother and brother were not there on his arrival.

"Get some rest," Hy Soo again embraced his son.

As soon as his father left, Min Lee texted Ji-Joon: *Jackass!*

Ji-Joon texted right back: *It's the right thing to do.*

Min Lee: *Jackass!*

Ji-Joon: *Bray…aaaaayyyyy.*

Min Lee thought of settling in for a nap before the confounded party. He wondered if it was a good idea, given that jetlag would surely set in, and it might just be better to stay up until his usual bedtime. Pulling a bottle of water from the small refrigerator, best to keep hydrated, he sat on the bed, the very same bed he slept in when he first came to Seoul. It seemed only yesterday in Min Lee's memory that he'd met his father instead of seventeen years before. Apart from being older, he looked the same. Closing his eyes, he allowed his mind to go back to the first day they'd met. Today they were the same height.

The man in front of him seemed to go on forever, and it took a while for Min Lee's gaze to reach the top of his head.

"Ahn-nyohg ha-se-yoh." Min Lee had bowed deeply.

"Hello," the man returned, "You must be Min Lee," he'd smiled and knelt before him.

"Who are you?" Min Lee asked, matching his English.

"I am your father."

Min Lee stepped back and again bowed deeply. "Ahn-nyohg ha-se-yoh, Aboeji"

His father smiled again. "I am glad to finally meet you. You are all grown up."

"Yes, I am twelve and a half years old. It is good to meet you, Aboeji."

"Will you take me to your mother?"

His mother, who'd refused to be admitted to the hospital, was at home when his father had arrived. Min Lee allowed his father into the modest room his mother occupied.

"Hy Soo." His mother's eyes had brightened when his father walked into the room. Min Lee felt his anger rise. How could she be so happy after he had abandoned her? The man had touched her face, tenderly staring into her eyes, tears glistening. For a long time, his father sat, holding his mother's hand. Min Lee had watched them from the doorway. They were whispering. He couldn't hear what they were saying, but whatever it was, his mother just kept smiling and, in her dimming, eyes were still very much the love she felt for the man at her side. She was so young and beautiful. How could she be dying? Before his father's arrival, his mother had never told him the story of his father. That day, while his mother lay dying, she had invited him into the room and told him the story he'd relayed to Min Jade. On

the day his mother was laid to rest, Min Lee had drawn strength from the father he'd only just met, who was as unwelcome at his mother's funeral as was he. In-Tak Hyun, his father's default wife, had held on tightly to his father's other arm as though scared his mother would rise from the dead and reclaim Hy Soo.

Comforted by the memory Min Lee drifted into a fitful sleep.

By 7:00 p.m., the house filled with people. Min Lee descended the stairs, coming face-to-face with In-Tak Hyun. She hadn't aged a day. Not a single sign of evil lined her face. Fashionable as always, she paused with flair.

"Well, well, the bastard son has returned," she said, raising a glass, "I can't say I've missed you much, but you have become quite the star, haven't you?"

"Good evening, *Eomeoni*," Min bowed. "I hope you have been well."

"Well enough, but I am not your mother and not glad to see you. You are still not welcome in my home."

"It seems so, but you are still married to *Abeoji*, right? How is Seung-Le?" She was as evil as the day he first came to Seoul from Busan. He remembered the journey as though it were yesterday. *On the way from Busan with the ashes of the woman they both loved, his father and Min Lee had stopped for lunch. "Your mother loved this place." Hy Soo pulled up to a modest little shop. "We used to stop here every time we traveled this way," he said. "She loved their ramen."*

"Ah, Mister." The proprietor had remembered him, even after so many years. "Where is your beautiful wife?"

His father bowed his head.

"I am sorry. I'll bring her favorite dish," the man said, later returning with his mother's favorite ramen. Min Lee had sat staring at his father, trying to comprehend why his life had

changed so drastically. His mother was gone, and here he was with a father he was meeting for the first time in his almost thirteen years. His father had cried, his tears mixing with the broth of the noodles. He must have loved his mother very much, Min Lee thought, as he spooned the tasty ramen into his mouth. It was good.

Before continuing their journey, his father told him he had a brother and stepmother. "They might not understand," he said, giving him a heads up, "but I will always be by your side. I will never let you be alone. I promised your mother," he'd tousled his son's hair then, looking deeply into his eyes. "You are my firstborn and as precious to me as your mother. Do you understand, Min Lee?"

"Yes, Abeoji."

Four hours later, they'd reached Seoul. His father pulled up to a massive black wrought-iron gate and pressed some buttons on a keypad. Min Lee had never seen a house like this. It was large and imposing. His father held his hand as they walked up the driveway. Min Lee's head kept spinning. He and his mother lived in a modest flat in Busan. His father lived in a mansion. They entered a foyer inlaid with a diamond marble pattern. "No matter what anyone says, this is your home," he'd tightened his grip on Min Lee's hand. Two or three people came from nowhere to greet them, bowing deeply. They were the help. His father told them to take him to his room for a nap and prepare him a snack before dinner. The room was enormous. It was a palace, as far as he was concerned. He had his own desk and a wardrobe to boot! At dinner, he would meet the rest of the family, and all the joy in Min Lee's life would begin to seep out. Though his father loved and protected him, he was on the road touring too many weeks of the year to protect him from his vicious stepmother, In-Tak Hyun.

As the story goes, Min Lee later understood that In-Tak Hyun was his mother's rival. Although his father had rejected her repeatedly, once his mother had disappeared, she had done everything in her power to be his support. Min Lee's younger brother, Seung-Le, influenced by his mother's hatred, was no less evil. When Min Lee left Seoul at sixteen for study at the Royal College of Music, he simply did not return and never intended to return. It had now been seventeen years. He wasn't even Korean anymore.

In-Tak Hyun glared at him and kept walking. He felt smug satisfaction that he was one of the top solo pianists in the world. That had to irk her. He knew how much she'd wanted to be on stage if only to prove she was as good as his mother. But she wasn't. Not even by a stretch, which deepened her hatred for Yu-sun-ah. In-Tak Hyun had even tried to make Seung-Le into his competitor, but Seung-Le's talent was marginal like hers. Min Lee Woo was one of the greatest pianists alive, and the Evil Queen had not been able to stop him because his mother's love had combated her evil.

Min Lee proceeded to the great room where the party was in full swing. Immediately he was swarmed by people who, no doubt, would later brag how well they knew him, regaling their listeners with fabricated stories from their one-minute conversations. There wasn't anywhere to hide. Min Lee ceremoniously shook hands, smiled, and bowed as his father introduced one person after another. He had offers to relocate to Korea that would keep him working until he was 110 years old. Ji-Joon did his best to keep the line moving. Finding the room more and more claustrophobic, Min Lee was ready to escape the charade after an hour. Usually, he never stayed anywhere for more than fifteen minutes, but this was his *Abeoji*. As he was about to take his leave, someone caught him by the arm.

"I have been waiting to say hello. Please don't leave."

Annoyed.

Min Lee removed her hand from his arm.

"I've heard so much about you. I am a great admirer of your work."

Bored. "Thank you. I appreciate that."

"I hope you'll stay a bit and chat. I would love to work with you sometime."

Impatient. "Meaning?" *Really annoyed. Suggestive?*

"I am a violinist. I'd love to record some work with you."

The impertinence!

"The name is Choi."

"As in Choi Shin?"

Slightly impressed – only slightly.

"I am flattered. You know me."

Patronizing.

"Are you being modest?"

Fake.

Choi Shin was a rising world-class musician. A violinist featured with just about every notable philharmonic. They were bound to meet in time. In their rarified air, their paths would undoubtedly have crossed. Gifted, beautiful, seductive, and manipulative. He'd met her type too many times to count. His radar said to stay away.

"I'll let you go tonight if you promise to lunch with me tomorrow. There's much I'd love to talk about. Deal?"

Insufferable!

"I don't make deals, but I'll have Ji-Joon arrange lunch. Call this number in the morning." Min Lee excused himself.

Choi waited until he was out of sight before going back to the party. He was a lot colder than she imagined, which piqued her interest even more. Choi brought a perfectly manicured

red fingernail to her lips as she strolled back into the party whose guest had left. How exciting.

"*Hyung.*" Seung-Le was walking toward him as he was about to climb the staircase. "How can you leave your own party? Dad did a lot of work here, you know. Sorry, I'm late."

"Seung-Le. Wow. You're all grown up."

"I hope so. All those baby steps add up to time, my big brother. It's been way too long. I've missed you a lot."

Seung-Le was eleven years old when Min Lee left for England. It was the best option for family harmony. At twenty-eight, Seung-Le was almost unrecognizable. "It's great to see you," Min Lee said. He wouldn't lie about missing anyone but his father, and even that was a modest miss. "What have you been up to?"

"Wasting my life on women and wine. At least that's what I'd been doing until I met the love of my life. Come on back to the party, and I'll tell you all about it. She should be here. I'll introduce you."

"Seung-Le, I'm exhausted. Let's have breakfast tomorrow."

"I can imagine. What about all those TV appearances?"

"They don't start until the day after tomorrow. Ji-Joon is meticulous like that."

"Okay. I'll pick you up at 9:00 a.m. Digits?"

Min Lee gave him the number. "You're not at home anymore?"

"*Hyung,* it's a new day. Remember. Baby steps add up to time. I have a flat close by. Is it okay if I ask my lady love to join us? She'd love to meet you."

Seung-Le, it seemed, had indeed grown up. At least he wasn't the hostile kid who didn't want to share his dad. He'd see what the morning brought. Min Lee continued his ascent.

He didn't sleep well that night: the house, the memories, the pain. Up at 7:00 a.m., Min Lee made his way to the dining room. If memory served him right, breakfast began at seven, but usually, no one showed up before eight. When he pushed open the door, his father was pouring a cup of coffee.

"Need one?"

"Yes, *Abeoji*. Thanks."

His father handed him a cup. "Did you sleep well?"

"Like a baby, *Abeoji*, I slept very well," he lied.

"It is good to see you, Min Lee. Thank you for granting your old man's wish. Let's sit for a minute."

"*Abeoji,* you are not old. Sixty-five is *not* old."

"I feel old."

"Well, we'll have to change that. Let's go to the gym while I'm here."

"Gym," Hy Soo laughed. "That will be the day. So, how does it feel to be home after all these years?"

"To be honest, I don't know, *Abeoji*. It was a hard decision, but I really couldn't pass up the opportunity to play with you,' and I wanted to visit Mom. It's tough for me to be so far away from her and you."

"I understand. Shall we visit your mother today?"

"Would it be okay if I went alone the first time?"

"Sure, son. We'll go together another time."

"*Kamsahamnida, Abeoji.*"

"No, thank you, Min Lee," his father paused. "It's true. I've wanted us to play together for a long time. It's been my dream. Now that I am playing my last concert, I had to ask."

"Why is this your last concert? Are you just tired?"

His father sat in a chair opposite him. I wanted you to come home for my concert, but full confession, I want you here for more than just playing with me. Can you imagine how pleased your mother will be when she hears us? I bet our song will reach her in heaven. Do you think she'll know immediately that it's us?"

"I bet she will, *Abeoji.*"

His father leaned in, and his voice was soft. "She's the only woman both you and I have ever loved in this life, isn't it? I'm sure she'll hear us. I know she will. Next time, I'll do better by her, son."

Tears pricked Min Lee's eyes.

"I had another reason to ask you to come home. A few."

Min Lee composed himself. "I'm all ears."

"I want you to consider coming home for good."

"What? Father! *eotteoke?*"

"I know, I know. Things got a little complicated. I have been trying to deal with all the changes by myself, but I need your help. I have cancer. Brain cancer. I waited too late to get checked out, and now it's gone too far. I need you to help me sort things out. Would you consider it?"

"*Appa!*" Min Lee jumped up from his chair, using the word father, indicating his love for the man who sat before him.

"It's life, son. You win some; you lose some. I've had a great life so far. I think your mother misses me," he winked.

"Dad, don't joke about this. You'll come back with me to England. There has to be something that can be done. After that, we'll figure out the rest."

"Ah, you know I can't do that, son. Rest assured; your uncle is making sure I get the best care. He has every specialist on the case."

"How long have you known this?"

"It's been over six months now.

"And what are the doctors saying?"

"Who really knows? They think a year, but it could be tomorrow, or I could miraculously recover. No matter how long, it's inevitable. I won't be around too much longer, and I need you here to help me wrap things up. I've made a will and set up some trusts. Help me to figure out the next steps."

"That right belongs to Seung-Le, father."

"Your brother isn't yet up to the task. He's still young at heart. As my first son, you will have to take responsibility for my estate and this family. I need you to take care of your brother and stepmom. I know she's been awful to you but try to forgive her."

"Father, how? I travel nine months out of the year. Seung-Le, from what I see, can rise to the occasion. He should be your rightful heir, anyway. Plus, I don't want to talk about this. I'm only here for a week. Let's have a meaningful time together." *He would never forgive In Tak-Hyun, no matter that it was God's gift.*

"I don't mean financially. Seung-Le is well taken care of, and his mother will leave him everything. She is one of the wealthiest women in Korea, you know. He'll want for nothing. But he'll need you, emotionally and directionally, son. His mother has spoiled him a great deal, and he'll need some help finding his own way. You have to promise me you'll be there for him."

"Do they know about your illness?"

"No. I wanted you to hear it first. In-Tak Hyun is not going to take it well. I feel so much regret toward her. I couldn't love her the way I loved your mother, but she had tried her best and has been a good wife, except when it came to you."

Min Lee felt sudden compassion even for In-Tak Hyun. For the first time, he could appreciate what it must have been like to love someone and not have that love returned. He never thought he could love any woman besides his mother, and though he came close with Min Jade, he was far too rational a man for excessive drama. *Appa*," he said, holding his father's hand, "I'll do as you ask, but it does not make me happy."

His father patted his hand. "Thank you, son. I need one more favor."

Min Lee grimaced.

"I promised your mother I would never leave you alone. I swore to her I'd always make sure you had someone in your life who loves you. You're thirty-three now, Min Lee. Are you thinking about settling down? I'd like to see you married, and it would be great if you'd consider returning to Korea for good, not just temporarily. Could you do that for me?"

"Father, that's impossible."

"Nothing is impossible. Please think about it."

"Father. I cannot and will not come back for good. When the time comes, if the time comes, I will honor my filial duty as promised, but I cannot come back to Korea permanently."

"Don't make a hasty decision, son. Give it a few days. Please promise me you'll think about it. It would be nice to have you around in these last days."

Min Lee felt sorrow about his father's illness, but not like the pain that had crippled him when faced with losing his mother. He leaned over and touched his father's forehead with his. "Okay, *Abeoji*, I will do my best to be here for you as long as you need me but not permanently, and I'll do my best to find a girl." It was the least he could do. Should he tell his father about Min Jade? He decided against it, as even he had no idea where that love was headed at the moment.

"That's my son. By the way, I have a lovely girl to introduce you to," he winked.

Min Lee's cell rang just in time.

"Are you ready, *Hyung*? I'm in the driveway. It's a thirty-minute drive to the place I've chosen for breakfast. Are you having coffee with *Abeoji*? I know he's up."

"Yes. *Abeoji* is right here. I'll be out in a sec."

"Great. Tell him I'll see him later. I have good news."

"That's Seung-Le, *Abeoji*. Let's talk again when I get back. For what it's worth, I'm glad I came."

CHAPTER NINE

UNIVERSITY OF MICHIGAN
MIN JADE
ONWARD

ANN ARBOR WAS GREEN AND LUSH as she made her way from the airport. Summertime, in her special city, was her favorite time, and Min Jade was happy to be home. For two days, she'd rest up, and then on Sunday, she'd contact her mother, who insisted she come to dinner. Min Jade couldn't believe how much they missed each other. On Monday morning, she decided to surprise Winful and stopped in at his office. She wondered if he'd recognize her footsteps. His secretary looked up as Min Jade entered. Min Jade brought her index finger to her lips and tip toed into Winful's office.

"Anybody home?" She sang.

"Min, Jade! What a delightful surprise," Winful rushed over to greet her. "How I've missed you. You will never imagine just how much." He enveloped her in a bear hug.

"I've missed you too," she pecked him on the cheek.

"I'm telling you now. You can never leave me again."

"I won't," she kissed his cheek. "This is for you!" she handed him a gift, flopped down in her usual chair, and tucked her legs up under her as usual.

Winful noted that the sabbatical had not altered her style: her shoes tinkled as she tucked them beneath her. "I didn't hear those bells earlier," he said, opening his gift. "Oh, a Nobel replica," he chuckled at the souvenir.

"I tip-toed," Min Jade said.

"So, are we any closer to creating matter?"

"I'm not sure about all that. I had more fun than I did physics," she told him all about the Perfect Harmonies.

"Young people are not serious anymore. Can you have dinner tomorrow night? There is someone I'd like you to meet and maybe mentor."

"I'm not ready to go back to work, but sure. What time and where?"

"Let's say 7:00 p.m. West End Grill?"

"This must be someone important. Who is it? National Science Foundation (NSF?")

"No, a visiting professor from London. We'd like to attract her as a staff member. She's here for a few months to look around, and we want to put our best foot forward. Which, of course, is you."

"And if I hadn't come back?"

"Stop talking nonsense," Winful said, going off to brew iced tea.

Min Jade was the first to arrive at the restaurant. She abhorred lateness, which she considered an aggressive power play. As usual, she was ten minutes early. "I'm sure reservations are under Professor Winful's name," she said, approaching the hostess at the restaurant. The woman scanned her list.

"Yes, here it is—a party of three. You're the first? Would you like to be seated or wait by the bar for your party to arrive?"

"Seated, please."

Min Jade followed the hostess to a table near the window. Good, she thought, she'd see Winful approaching. But she'd barely sat down when he came wandering back. No sooner had he taken his seat than a woman was being shown to their table. Min Jade felt a sudden chill and began rubbing her arm. The woman was about ten years her senior but seemed younger. Her blonde hair, slicked back, had not one strand out of place. She wore a pea-green knit suit that hugged her petite frame. As she came closer, Min Jade noted her eyes were the exact color of her suit, which gave an even chillier feeling. *Who dresses like that in academia? She looked like she belonged in Corporate America.*

"Dr. Kessler, meet Min Jade. Dr. Kessler is from The Imperial College of London. She is a visiting professor who will be with us for the next three months. She is a great admirer of yours, and I promised to introduce her to you." Winful said, retaking his seat and flapping a napkin onto his lap.

Kessler's smile stretched her lips but did not reach her eyes as she held Min Jade's hand in a vice grip. Min Jade smiled back and hurriedly released Kessler's hand from the bone-crushing handshake.

"It is good to have you with us," Min Jade said.

"I am very much looking forward to my time here." The woman's eyes traveled over Min Jade, plumed feather headdress in her curls and all. Today Min Jade wore combat boots, an orange ruffled skirt, and a brown top with sequined "fusion is everything" written on it. "It is, isn't it?" Dr. Kessler frosted the room with another smile. "Fusion is indeed everything," she said, gliding into her chair. "Dr. Jade, Chair Winful speaks highly of you, and your research is very impressive. I'm glad we had a chance to meet and hope your sabbatical was productive."

Min Jade scowled at Winful in a way only he'd recognize. *Tattletale.*

"I hope you'll have some time for lunch." The eyes didn't blink once.

"I think you guys in London are doing a good job. I'm sure you could give me a few pointers."

"I can't. I'm actually in EE. But like you, I am one of few women in the department. I hope we can exchange war stories sometimes."

Min Jade had no idea why Winful wanted her to meet Dr. Kessler. The woman needed no mentoring, so Min Jade figured she was a part of Winful's wooing plan. "Yes, indeed. Women like us must have a war chest full of stories." Of course, Min Jade did not.

Back at the University, life went into full tilt when Min Jade came back to learn she'd been awarded an NSF grant to further her research. Julian–her student lab associate–and she burned the midnight oil to fast track their research. Jade burst into her office only to find Dr. Kessler sitting in her lab with Julian.

"I hope you don't mind," the annoying woman rose. "You've got quite the star here in Julian."

"Dr. Kessler, I do mind." Min Jade's annoyance could not be tempered. "I would prefer that you call me beforehand if you'd like to visit my lab. It's just protocol here at the University. We don't just show up at our colleagues' labs without an appointment. What is it that you'd like to observe?"

Kessler's green eyes narrowed. "I'm sorry if I offended you. It was not my intent. Please forgive me," she said, and though she was apologizing, it sounded like a reprimand.

"No problem, but please don't do it again."

Kessler, face stoic, left the office.

In her office, Min Jade checked her e-mail. Every so often, she'd get a Google alert about Min Lee Woo, from whom she had not heard a single word. She wondered where he was and what he was doing. Glad she was too busy to pine away for her lost love, she decided to end her cyberstalking. It wasn't healthy. *Still,* she hit the delete button; *he could have said goodbye.*

Min Jade kicked off her shoes and sighed at the state of her pedicure. Too many hours in the lab rendered her comatose every night. Today was her first day home at a reasonable hour, and she was looking forward to dinner night with her parents. Wiggling her toes, affirming she'd definitely get a mani-pedi tomorrow, she flopped down on the hall bench to flip through the dog-eared, week-old mail that had been crammed into her mailbox. She'd also brought home mail from her office, which she didn't get a chance to get to. *Trash, trash, trash,* she began throwing junk mail into the garbage until she came across a beautiful linen envelope with a London, England postmark. It was addressed to her at the University, and Min Jade's heart did a flip. Min Lee lived in London. Min Jade put the rest of the mail on the foyer console and opened the envelope with shaky hands.

Dear Min Jade,

Long time. I can't believe we haven't been in touch since our time in Austria. We have been remiss.

Min Jade's heart skipped a beat. She hastily continued.

The demands and chaos of our lives. I suppose, and since you didn't encourage me to sweep you off your feet…sad…sad…sad…I had to lick my wounds for a while. Anyway, the door is still wide open, but promises must be kept. We finally found common ground on times and wanted to make sure the Perfect Harmonies remained perfect. That's why you're getting this letter—reaching out to keep that promise. I am in charge of invitations and Chin is in charge of booking our gig. Don't ask me why when Albert and I live here. Democracy. Make sure you brush up on the ivories. Though it's not a year, we thought Christmas in London would be an excellent place for our meetup. Who can pass up a Charles Dickens Christmas? So, are we meeting in London over the holidays? Are you up to it? You have to be, so ignore the question and consider the invite a command (smile). Weird to get a letter rather than a text or email, huh? I'm classy like that. Next week, I'll ring you to make sure you don't fink out.

Tunde

P.S. By the way, the other Min is playing at The Royal Albert while you'd be here. Don't know why I'm even telling you this, except I think you'd like that. I hope not, but I'll get tickets. You are over him, right? Remember 30 seconds, and one look is all it took.
♥♥♥♫♫

P.P.S. I can't wait to see you.

Min Jade was disappointed the letter hadn't come from Min Lee, but she was happy to hear from Tunde. She reread the letter and laughed out loud. The man was unbelievable. It would be great to see her friends again, though, so for sure she'd go to England. The off chance she could see Min Lee also spurred her quick decision and set her heart racing. So much for compartmentalization. Min Jade scrolled through her iPhone and sent a text to Tunde.

Ping: *You're still a funny guy.*

Immediately her phone pinged: *See you got my letter. Classy, right?*

Ping: *Didn't expect less. Some courtier you are, though! You gave up after a few months. Fickle man. Why haven't we been in touch?*

Ping: *Life, time, research, time difference, travel, work, family...forlorn, unrequited love. But friendships survive all that. Are you coming? You'd better. A promise is a promise.*

Ping: *I'm definitely coming. Bring me up to date on everyone.*

Ping: *I see Albert all the time. We've become best buds. I'll fill you in on the others as soon as I get the 411. Promise. Remember 30 seconds...That's all it took...just one look and thirty seconds. I'm still feeling it.*

Ping: *Some kinda love, that is. You mean forgotten in 30 seconds, don't you?*

Ping: *Love is perpetual. Follows the sinus rhythm of life.*

Ping: *Crazy Nigerian.*

Ping: *Crazy like a fox...but only for you.*

Ping: *Bye.*

Min Jade felt light. A feeling she hadn't had since returning from Austria. She'd channeled her loneliness, as always, into her work. The Perfect Harmonies. What a hoot they'd been on stage. She smiled at the memory of their makeshift band and went to the bathroom to shower before dinner with her parents. The thought of seeing Min Lee was tempting, but maybe she should not go to his concert and open old wounds.

Then again, her mother loved Min Lee Woo, and bringing her along could be an excuse. Nah. She'd take her to see Min Lee Woo when he played in New York. She was sure he would.

Professor Winful summoned Min Jade to meet him at his office. She couldn't imagine what he could want again. Their morning meeting had only been a few hours ago! Daydreaming about another sabbatical was a pipe dream, as the university only allowed sabbaticals every seven years, but she still liked the idea. With her research in high gear, time away was impossible anyway. Min Jade hurried across the quad, dashed into the physics building, and sprinted up three flights of stairs. It was just too damn hot, but then again, it was the end of July in Michigan. Her exercise was paying off for sure as she was not out of breath when she reached the top of the stairs.

"Morning, Professor." One student, after the other, greeted her as she made her way to the Chair's office. She could never be annoyed with Winful, no matter how demanding he was on her time. Relentless with his demands and high standards, his mission was admirable, but his approach was tiresome. Min Jade entered the office suite and was greeted by his competent assistant.

"Professor Jade. Go right in. He's expecting you."

Min Jade entered the office. Winful was watering his orchids. "They don't need as much in the winter, you know, but I had to move them from the windowsills. They don't like the cold or direct light."

"They are as beautiful as they were this morning," Min Jade said, intending to be obvious.

"Yes. Good to see you again, Professor Jade. Would you like some hot cocoa? Better for you than that designer coffee you always drink. Do you know chocolate had a soothing effect on the brain?"

"That would be lovely," Min Jade said. "Soothing is also welcomed."

"How are things going all around? What are your feelings about Dr. Kessler?"

"I don't like her much. She is a bit presumptuous."

"She told me you scolded her about being in your lab without your presence. Good for you."

"I'm not quite sure why she is here. And why she would be in my lab. I just don't seem to be able to warm up to her. Do you think she is snooping for London?"

"Don't let your imagination get the better of you. London is not that kind of institution. Plus, she is not a fusion physicist."

"If you say so. So, what are we meeting about this fine day?"

"Well, two things. I got a call just now. NSF is extending your grant indefinitely, and they will give us as much as we need to keep your research going."

"I'm glad to hear that," Min Jade went to make the cocoa he'd offered since he seemed to have forgotten he'd offered it. Winful, when it came to anything that got him closer to winning a prize for the university, could be quite forgetful. More money from NSF would be one of those things.

"You know why this is happening, don't you?"

"We do good work?"

"Min Jade, your last research paper has been cited six hundred times. Do you know what that means?"

"Yup. I do good work, and I'm working too hard. What does it mean to you?" She sensed Winful was going to do something unacceptable.

"Second, remember the conference the Dean wants to create around your work?"

"*No. No,* Dr. Winful, no. Not yet. Not right now. I'm too busy. Really, I am."

Winful paused. "You, my dear, really don't have a say. Think, Min Jade, what this will do for the department, and the signal we'll make to those cronies in London. The Dean is ecstatic about this. Your peer recognition is right up there with Higgs Boson! Do I have to remind you they are still using the acid test for citations to compare your work?"

"But it's not a good time for a dog and pony show right now. When is the Dean thinking?"

"Now. Right now. I'm not supposed to tell you this, but he thinks you could be a contender for the Nobel. That's why he wants to do it now. Min Jade, can you imagine? This could happen."

Min Jade appreciated that Winful wanted to keep the physics department in the top tier of all universities, a place it held for years, but she was not happy she was carrying this burden.

Min Jade covered her ears. "I don't want to know anymore. Dr. Winful, it's too much pressure. You know what this kind of pressure can do to me. Can you try to get the Dean to push this back a bit?"

"No. Absolutely not. I want this more than he does. I want a Nobel Prize."

"Dr. Winful, you aren't serious, are you?" Min Jade felt the room heating up. "It's not up to any of us who gets a Nobel."

"I am very serious. Your nerves are rested. You just returned from a sabbatical. That's why you went in the first place, remember."

"But…but…the Nobel is such a long shot in the dark."

"Professor Jade, you are too modest. You are thirty-two years old, am I right?"

"Thirty-one. Thirty-two in March. That's a whole five months from now."

"You are one of the youngest tenured professors in physics in the entire United States, if not the world. You know why?" *Rhetorical question.* "Because you are brilliant. Do you know how many questions I field about you daily? Thousands." *Overstatement.* "Do you know how many people would love to steal you from this University?" *Poppycock.* "But you are mine. Please help me get this University to the number one place for physics globally. Do you know what that means?" *Another rhetorical question.* "It means everything. Think about it. I don't mean to be obvious or trite, my dear, but you are black and a woman. You have made history already. Think about it, Professor Jade. The conference is a ticket to the stratosphere. Step into your greatness."

Hyperbole.

"Let's do this," he said.

"You don't care about my sanity?"

"Your sanity is fine. Let's do this," he repeated, "for all of us. Let's do this for Jessica."

That was downright overt manipulation. Winful knew more than anyone, this kind of recognition for Min Jade's work, would be her mother's greatest glory.

"The world could be righted by this, Min." He never shortened her name. This was serious.

What malarkey, Min Jade thought. Nobel? She would be dishonest if she said the thought hadn't crossed her mind. Sure, it was on her bucket list, the one you make before pushing up daisies. "I…I…don't know what to say."

"Say yes!" Winful pulled up a chair in front of her. "What's the downside here? Eric will do it anyway. Claim your greatness, Min Jade," he repeated.

Min Jade began rubbing the side of her head. "I'm feeling crazy already, but okay, Dr. Winful. After the holidays."

Winful stood and pulled Min Jade to her feet. He cupped her face in his hand. "You deserve this and more. I'm proud of you and so grateful that you're in my life."

"I hope you feel the same way when you have to visit me in the looney bin," Min Jade batted his hand away. Min Jade left Winful's office in a daze. She wasn't a drinker, except socially, but she needed a drink. She rubbed her arm, pinching it every few minutes to make sure this wasn't a dream. Was the Nobel really in her realm of possibility? Min Jade shook her head, trying to clear the cloud. What a bunch of hogwash! In her office, Min Jade booted up her computer. She rarely checked her work's performance, but the number of times her work had been cited was indeed off the charts. Still, it didn't mean much unless her peers nominated her. Min Jade pushed all thoughts of a Nobel from her mind and made her way to her lab.

"Julian," Min Jade called as she entered her lab, "are you here?" He was not. She pulled a key from the safe installed in a hidden drawer in her desk where her secret notebook was stashed to study once again the equation that was causing all the frenzy:

$$E_S = \frac{m_e^2 c^3}{q_e \hbar} \quad 1.3 \quad 10^{18} \text{ V/m}$$

She had been working on the premise that Nobel Prize Winner Julian Schwinger had predicted. Schwinger convinced that when the electric field associated with an electromagnetic wave like a laser beam exceeds certain volts per meter, it creates a vacuum itself that acts as a nonlinear material. For months, she'd been colliding intense laser beams, hoping to be able to create electrons and positrons out of empty space! She'd gotten sporadic results, which was the basis of the paper she'd written that was now causing all the hoopla.

"Dr. Jade," Dr. Kessler pushed her head around her lab door. "Do you have a moment?"

Min Jade hurriedly stashed the notebook back into the drawer and bade her in. *Didn't she tell that woman to call?*

"I wanted to apologize again for barging in a few weeks ago. I am told you are an all-rounder and wanted to discuss an idea with you. Would you be open to that?"

"You're in optics, right? I haven't been focused on that for a while. Maybe Dr. Shapiro in electrical engineering might be a better fit, but I'll take a look. Let's have lunch tomorrow. The Red Dragon, say 1 p.m.?"

"That would be lovely. Thank you so much. As a woman, I'd feel more comfortable talking to you."

"Most of my colleagues don't see me as a woman. Just a physicist."

The night found Min Jade restless. For a moment, she basked in imagining the news headlines: *University of Michigan Professor awarded the Nobel Prize in Physics!* Did she hope to dream that far so soon? It would never happen, she thought, as she switched off her lights. Still, she wished it would.

CHAPTER TEN

SOUTH KOREA
MIN LEE WOO
TRAPPED

THE CITY HAD CHANGED A LOT. In the years since Min Lee had left, Seoul had emerged on the world economic stage as a real player. It was modern, chic, educated, young, and vibrant. K-Pop and Korean dramas were taking over the world. The face of many *Hallyu* stars were now household names, some internationally recognized. The faces of Rain, Min Lee Ho, Kim Joon Hyun, Kim Soo, Park Shin Hy, and Han Ye Seul adorned neon billboards dotting the skyline, plugging some brand or the other. Giant LCD screens broadcast news non-stop, and Min Lee felt like a man from another planet. He'd never heard of these new idols.

After answering a million questions, Seung-Le finally asked, "*Hyung*, have you been under a rock?"

"I think so."

"Don't you miss Korea?"

Min Lee looked out the window. "No."

"Not even the food?"

"No. I don't miss anything."

"Not very patriotic. Sorry, *Hyung*. I'm sure that's partly because of me. I was a bad brother, but I intend to make up for that now."

They arrived for brunch at "A Story" in Gangnam-gu, a snazzy venue with outdoor seating. Seung-Le, treated like royalty, was immediately seated. Min Lee, whose picture was all over the newspaper, got many glances as the two headed to their table. "Koreans love celebrities," Seung-Le said.

"I'm hardly that," Min Lee replied.

"Not according to the news coverage."

Just as they were seated, Choi Shin entered. The men rose as Choi approached. Min Lee was utterly taken back. It was the woman who had accosted him at the party.

"You've heard of her, right? Isn't she a beauty?" Seung-Le said. "Our lunch guest and my new fiancée, Choi Shin."

"What?"

"Well, well. I guess breakfast is as good as lunch," Choi directed her gaze at Min Lee.

Seung-Le looked puzzled.

"I met Mr. Woo last night," she proffered.

"You did? Brother, you never mentioned." Min Lee had kept his mother's surname, so it made sense she would not have known. She'd thought the party a social gathering for a celebrated pianist, as In-Tak Hyun was always the socialite with first dibs on celebrities.

"Brother? You are brothers?"

"Yes. My long-lost brother is the world-famous Min Lee Woo."

Choi was none too pleased. "How could you not have mentioned that?"

"I wanted to surprise you. Are you surprised?"

"Completely," she smiled sweetly.

"*Hyung,* seems you already met my fiancée."

"Yes. It seems like it. Congratulations to you both." Min Lee was careful not to betray his emotions. He now understood what his father meant by Seung Le's immaturity. Why did he not see this girl was taking him for a ride? By the time breakfast was over, Choi and Min Lee, much to Seung-Le's displeasure, exchanged contact information to discuss a possible collaboration. For a moment, he felt like Min Lee was taking everything from him again: his father, his home, his girl.

Choi was ecstatic she'd pulled off a coup until she noticed the number he'd given her was once again for his manager, Ji-Joon. *Naughty boy,* a sardonic smile dotted her face. This, however, was hardly a bump in the road to her intent. Collaboration between them could be a great move for her career, and she intended to realize that win. Two Koreans on the world stage could be interesting. Her smile turned sweet and grateful. Her charm always worked, and she'd work it on the gatekeeper, Ji-Joon.

"I'll walk you to your car," Seung-Le said. "Wait here a minute, *Hyung.*"

Min Lee leaned against the car.

Choi nodded. She knew how Seung-Le felt about her. Unfortunately, she didn't feel the same, but it was hard to resist his enormous wealth. She twisted the ring on her finger. Her talent had brought her far, but there was a long way to go, and Seung Lee's money had opened doors. It would be a challenge being In Tak-Hyun's daughter-in-law, especially since the woman pretty much despised her. Min Lee Woo seemed a far better catch, and their worlds meshed. She could go further if he took her under his wing as his protégée.

"Nice to formally meet you." Choi outstretched a hand.

Min Lee respected Choi Shin's work, but he had no interest in playing with someone like her, not in music or any other form of "play." Women like her boiled rabbits. He could sense that in his bones. How could she have flirted shamelessly with him when she was his brother's fiancée? Min Lee felt he should warn Seung-Le but thought better of it. It was none of his business. *Take care of your brother, his father's voice rang in his ear.*

"Back in a sec," Seung-Le said to Min Lee.

A few people came up to Min Lee for autographs or to take selfies, an indication he needed to be less conspicuous. Donning shades, he got in the car and lowered the seat to a reclining position.

"I told you, you were famous," Seung-Le said, laughing at Min Lee's disguise as he slid into the driver's seat. "What'd you think of my girl?"

"She is a beautiful girl. How long have you known her?"

"About six months."

"That's not long. Are you sure about marriage?"

"As sure as I need to be. How about you? Anyone special?"

"No time."

Min Lee had Seung-Le drop him off at the Sejong Chamber Hall, where he would play the concert with his father. Ji-Joon was already there when he arrived. Together they checked acoustics, piano tuning, lighting, and even the height of the piano stool, ensuring all the details for his performance were handled. Min Lee was a stickler for details.

"Is everything good, sir?" the hall manager asked.

Ji-Joon gave him the thumbs up and a list of Min Lee's requests for the green room.

"Your *Abeoji* will be sharing the green room with you," Ji-Joon said as they walked back to the car.

"Nice touch." Min Lee slipped into their waiting car, and Ji-Joon slid in next to him.

"Have you met Choi Shin?" Min Lee asked.

"Yup. A looker, right?"

"And I dare say a black widow."

"Yeah, I got that impression. Why are you asking?"

"She's Seung-Le's fiancée."

"You're kidding."

"Wish I was."

Min Lee had the driver drop Ji-Joon off in Samseong-Dong to visit his family. It had also been at least five years since he'd seen them, and they deserved to spend some time with their only son. When they arrived, Min Lee quickly paid his respects to the family, promising to return for a longer visit before leaving Korea. They had been like second parents to him. Min Lee then directed the driver to his mother's Remembrance Wall. Would his mother forgive him for not visiting all these years? By the time the car pulled up to their destination, Min Lee's emotions were raw. Conveniently, there was a nearby flower shop, and he crossed the street and bought the most beautiful arrangement of calla lilies, his mother's favorite. He approached the well-kept building that housed his mother's memory with a heavy heart. Beautiful lighting, grand architecture, and its pristine condition gave him comfort that his mother was resting well. Min Lee took a deep breath before entering her sanctuary. Immaculately kept, there were the photos and memorabilia he remembered inside the glassed cubicle. There was a picture of his mother, smiling, one of him, one of his father, and one of her parents. Vases held fresh-cut flowers, ones he'd seen in his father's garden. He arranged his bouquet in an empty vase. "*Eomeoni*. It's Min Lee. Have you been well?" Min Lee paused as though expecting an answer.

"Sorry, Ma, that I am only just coming. I hope you're not too mad, but I kept my promise. I am a world-renowned pianist now. Do you hear me play our *Serenade* just for you? Are you proud, *Eomeoni*?" Two hours later, Min Lee was still sitting in the room with his mother. He missed her now just as he had when he was twelve and a half years old. Emotionally drained, he made it back to the house and went straight to bed.

Min Lee had no idea Korea had so many reporters and media outlets. The hall was packed for his press conference. To his chagrin, he still had to do a few private interviews after this, and he was working on a severe headache. Ji-Joon handed him two painkillers and a glass of water.

"How many private interviews?" Min Lee rubbed his temple.

"Six."

"Are you trying to kill me? When do I practice?"

"Tomorrow and before the concert. You got this."

Min Lee crossed his eyes. "I hate this."

"Yeah, I know. Just another hour and a half. Just keep thinking we are one day closer to leaving. We are ready," Ji-Joon announced, pushing the mic closer to Min Lee.

"What took you so long to return to Korea?" a reporter asked.

"When are you going back to London?

"No idea," he lied.

It turned out his one-week stay had dragged on for more than three months. It was now July, and Min Lee Woo returned to Innsbruck to teach his master class. Upon returning, he'd fully expected to see Min Jade and was determined to have it out with her. Depositing his luggage, he went straight to her apartment. She was not there. He went to her office only to find out she had returned to Ann Arbor at the end of June. He was shaken at the thought that their love had meant nothing to her when it had meant the world to him. Well, *c'est la vie.* He dejectedly left the physics office, vowing to move on, but that was far from how he felt. He wanted to see his Duck Beak again. He thought fleetingly of going to Ann Arbor, but his pride would not let him. At the end of his time in Innsbruck, he returned to London.

CHAPTER ELEVEN

DECEMBER, LONDON
MIN LEE WOO, MIN JADE, TUNDE

TUNDE PULLED UP TO THE CURB AS MIN JADE EXITED baggage claim, perfect timing as usual. He tapped his horn, and she saw him and waved. How he'd let this gorgeous creature slip through his hands was unfathomable. He jumped from the car to help with her luggage. Today she was wearing a tan shearling lined with fur and ecru riding pants tucked into knee-length brown boots, matching her scarf and gloves. She looked like a woman who should be on his arm. Her hair was longer now, the curls falling shoulder length. The glasses were now purple. Tunde opened his arms. Min Jade set her luggage down and embraced him. He planted a kiss on each cheek then pushed her away to look closer at her flawless beauty. "How did I let you get away from me? I'll never make that mistake again!"

"Hi, Tunde." Min Jade's smile was disarming. "You look fantastic in your natural habitat."

"You'd look fantastic in my natural habitat, too, Min Jade," Tunde was beaming like a lovesick schoolboy. "Let's fall in love right now," he said as if he was asking her for a cup of coffee.

"Fall in love?"

"Why not? Why couldn't *we*?"

"I didn't know love was a will. Isn't it just nature's nuisance to trip up humans?"

"Love. Love," Tunde repeated, "is a will of the head and, okay, maybe a bit of nature's prank to get us off our self-absorbed butts. Love can grow. Think of all the arranged marriages in the world, my country included."

"Move it along. Move it along," a bobby said, tapping on the car. Tunde turned.

"Oh, sorry, sir." Tunde was a constant fixture at Heathrow. Grabbing Min Jade's luggage, he loaded it into the boot and proceeded to open the passenger door. "Get in," he said. "Where to?" He leaned over to buckle her seatbelt.

Min Jade, thinking he was going to kiss her, leaned back.

"Kensington. Give me a minute. I'll get the address."

"I guess you didn't take me up on my offer."

Min Jade, who'd declined his offer to stay with him, had rented an Airbnb flat in Kensington, which Tunde thought unconscionable. As much as she'd protested him picking her up at the airport, he had brushed her off. This man, she realized, did exactly as he pleased. Under normal circumstances, an overbearing man like Tunde would give her the heebie-jeebies, but she'd come to appreciate his directness. He'd been the one to help her over her heartbreak when so long ago he'd comforted her and taken such care of her after Min Lee's duplicity. He was a good man despite his enormous ego and arrogance.

"I can't understand this. Why not just stay at my place? It's big, it's fabulous, and you'll be pampered."

"We are going to Kensington," Min Jade insisted.

"Then how exactly will we find time to fall in love?"

Min Jade couldn't believe he'd blurted out that they should fall in love so casually. Why with these men and their maybe love confessions! Min Jade inwardly smiled, noting that her months of deflection hadn't dissuaded him one bit from his nonsense talk! She supposed there was some logic to his line of thinking, though. Maybe love as a will was indeed a much better choice than love as the heart's irrational call, which always seems blind to its emotional and psychological consequences. *Let's fall in love! Love as a will of the head.* This was rational thinking. Love, whether as a war between the heart, the head, or nature's prank, now held very little interest for her.

"Remember, it only takes thirty seconds," Tunde laughed, his autocratic face taking on a softer look. "Really," Tunde said as he pulled the car from the curb. "It's been way too long. How on earth could you have gotten prettier?"

"Flattery, Flattery, Flattery. Tunde, you haven't changed a bit. Can you believe it's already six months since we parted? Tell me, how have you been?"

"As you see, fine and as usual, fabulous," he steered his sleek black convertible, the top now secured against the inclement weather, expertly into traffic. It barely purred as he accelerated to fifty kilometers per hour in zero seconds.

Kensington had always been Min Jade's favorite part of the city when she studied at Oxford, and she'd be happy there as she knew her way around. Over the years, on her periodic visits, she'd watched its transformation. "I can't wait to see everyone. Everyone's here, right?" Min Jade asked.

"Yes. Everyone is here."

They chatted away until Tunde groaned. "Here we are. 456 Riverton. Min Jade, must you? This is yuck," he didn't jump out of the car to open her door, hoping she'd change her mind. "Can you imagine how many people have slept in that bed?"

"It's fine. Just like a hotel, right? Anyway, anything in Kensington can't be all bad."

"Point, but…"

"Shush," Min Jade opened the car door.

Tunde took her luggage from the trunk and set it by the doorstep. "I'd love to come in, but I've got a few errands to run. Get some rest. I'll fetch you at 8:00 p.m. Shall I get groceries or anything?" He immediately regretted asking that. Being too eager was not a good strategy for her.

"Thanks, Tunde. The place is stocked with essentials, part of the deal. I did good, right?"

He winced.

"See you later," Min Jade said, pecking his cheek.

Tunde stalled, wanting to tell her something. He finally touched her arm. "Min Jade, I'm thrilled to see you. And I really mean it. I want to be your boyfriend. Just say yes, okay?" There, he'd said it, but maybe he should have stopped at the groceries. He hoped he hadn't scared her off.

"Thinking about it," Min Jade said, tapping the side of her head. "Love as a will. It's quite rational, you know."

"Yeah. It is,"

Punching in the secret code for the lock on the door, she waved from the doorway as he pulled away. How sweet of him to offer to get groceries. He wasn't anywhere near the gargoyle he likes to portray. Tunde watched as she entered the flat. His heart was doing unimaginable things in his chest, and his…. Ah, well, no point going there. He pulled his jacket close. She was the woman for him. Operation Min Jade was about to commence all over again.

They met at the One Aldridge, a beautiful minimalist hotel in the heart of Kensington with a great bar and dinner spot. Everyone was there when they arrived, hanging out at the bar.

"Min Jade," Albert rushed forward. "You look sensational."

"Nice new glasses," Anastase said. "Neon purple. Very French Chic."

Vadim nodded his head as usual, and Chin gave her his signature smile. Everyone high-fived, exchanged hugs, and then ordered food and drinks. They took turns sharing what had transpired in their lives over the past six months and were glad they didn't have to wait an entire year to see each other.

"How did all this come about, anyway?" Min Jade asked.

"It appeared all of us were going to be in London except you and Vadim...so we thought, why not," Chin said.

"You mean everyone has been communicating, except with me?"

"Not exactly. That's not how it happened. Chin was going to be here at the University giving a lecture. While he was here, Anastase happened to call. He said he was going to be in London for the Christmas holidays. That's four of the six of us. Tunde said, why not see if everyone can make it?" Albert explained. "Vadim said he'd make it, and so did you."

"And guess where we are playing?" Chin announced, poking out his chest. "The Pig and Swine."

"The what? Is there really such a place?" Anastase asked. "How very British!"

"Ah, ah, not allowed. We are in perfect harmony, remember?" Vadim wagged a finger at Anastase. The French were always taking a dig at the Brits.

"There is, and it's a real hot spot. We will likely get booed."

"When is this shindig?" Vadim asked. "I brought just the tutu."

"Saturday night," Chin said.

"Oh, good. On Friday I'm taking Min Jade to see the Korean Dragon: Min Lee Woo's in concert. Any takers?"

"Ah…no. Got tickets for West End…Hamilton." Vadim shook his head.

"Dinner with Mom." Albert looked sad to have to miss a concert by Min Lee.

"Party with my host," Anastase said.

"Finalizing details for rocking the joint! Plus, solidarity with Lang Lang." Chin smiled.

The rotund Albert Hall was breathtaking. In the heart of South Kensington, the spectacle maintained the opulence of a time of high art. The 5,272-seat venue, with red chairs, mahogany panels, and curtained boxes, was alive tonight. Well-dressed patrons milled around in the lobby, waiting for ushers to seat them. There was a general air of anticipation, and for Min Jade, subdued excitement. Unconsciously, she was twisting her hands.

Tunde reached for her hand. "Pleased?" He asked.

"It feels a little surreal."

"He still makes you feel that way?"

"What way would that be?"

"Have you guys been in touch since Austria?" he ignored her question.

"No. We haven't." She allowed her hand to remain in Tunde's as a sign of having long gotten over Min Lee Woo.

"Good," he curled his fingers around hers. Now he could let himself off the hook. The least he could do, before sweeping her off her feet, was to allow her to see her love one more time—from a distance. Spotting Min Jade in the darkened room would be like finding a needle in a haystack. Tunde was immaculate, as usual, in black tuxedo pants, a white jacket, and an ascot. Min Jade, no slouch in a jade crepe dress, looking like a princess. Tunde handed their tickets to the usher who led them to center stage's main floor, eight rows back from the magnificent pipe organs now bathed in blue and green lights. Min Jade took her seat. She'd been to Royal Albert Hall countless times, but tonight was different. She was expectant and jittery, though it would be quite unlikely Min Lee would know of her presence. She wanted to keep it that way.

As they waited for the Maestro to make his appearance, a tastefully choreographed laser presentation lit up in the background. How uncanny. When the crowd began a low murmur, she turned as Min Lee Woo walked on stage. Min Jade felt her heart stop. The man was beyond distinguished in white tails with black lapels, and he was unbearably handsome. He didn't seem to have missed a beat from their breakup. Angry as she felt, her memory of those very fingers holding her close was vivid, and she closed her eyes to remove this force of nature of a man from her mind. Unlike other venues, the great hall allowed the audience to surround the artists intimately. Min Lee bowed deeply in her direction, and when he turned to her section, she lowered her gaze and brought the program up to partially cover her face. There was no single sign of the nervousness he must have felt playing to over five thousand fans in the round. Min Jade eased her hand from Tunde's. Entirely focused on Min Lee, he didn't seem to notice.

Min Lee bowed one last time, flipped his tails, and sat at the piano stool. He touched the keys softly, his fingers creating the lyrical sound of crystal swaying in a soft breeze. Min Jade, who had grown up listening to the piano's magic, was no stranger to its hypnotic and healing powers, but no one in her entire life had poured their very soul into the music the way Min Lee was now doing on stage. It was magical. As the syncopated rhythm rose and fell to tempo, Min Lee transmitted the full harmonic sonority and an improvised melody that spoke directly to the soul of his audience.

Crystals gave way to polyphonic counterpoints, clashing, demanding and dissonant with melancholy crescendos, rising and then fading to codas. As always, Min Jade was spellbound by his talent. One hour and ten minutes later, Min Lee rose from the stool.

Min Lee Woo, who rarely addressed his audience; a part of his mystery, began speaking. "If you have followed my career, you will know I play Schubert's *Serenade* at every concert. Many people have asked me why I do that; tonight, I will answer. This is the first time in my seventeen years as a concert pianist, I have played a concert on this day. Today, you see, would have been my mother's sixtieth birthday. *Serenade* is the song we played together every night until the night before she passed away. Today, I will again play *Serenade* for my mother on her special day."

Min Jade felt the tears cradle her eyelids. A powerful feeling of love was coursing through her body, and all she wanted to do was to climb onto the stage and encircle him in her arms. With a feeling of warmth and familiarity, her anger began to fade away, and the love she'd felt for this man jolted her resolve. A night like tonight was when maladaptives had to work extra hard to be brave and forgiving.

The well-behaved British audience was focused and rapt, but she could hear sniffles as Min Lee again sat in front of the piano. Staccato notes immediately bounced off the walls, spreading out and enveloping them. An accompanying laser light show interpreted the notes as he played, rendering the evening pure magic. The standing ovation, when he was done, lasted fifteen minutes. Min Jade sat still, mesmerized. Tunde, who'd been observing her the entire time, used his thumb to wipe away a threading tear. "I'm here. No need to cry," he said as he pulled her into an embrace.

"The music was moving," Min Jade rested her head against his broad shoulders. How could anyone be this remarkable? "Music and physics, together in synchrony."

"But not harmony," Tunde said.

Finally, the crowd began thinning. "Is something wrong?" Tunde asked when Min Jade didn't rise from her seat.

"I just need a moment." Min Jade said.

"I'll wait for you in the lobby."

With the show over, Min Jade categorically knew that opening old wounds would be the wrong thing to do. Until her heart could finally release Min Lee once and for all, she could not see him. After what seemed like an eternity, she made her way to the lobby and headed straight to the restroom to repair her make-up. It was the proper thing to do before facing the ever-gracious Tunde, who'd given her the space she needed to grieve. She did not want to seem ungrateful.

"Min Jade? Hey, Min Jade! Is that you?"

"Ji-Joon? I can't say I'm surprised to see you here, but what's the chance? It's good to see you again. Have you been well?"

"Yes. Quite well. Does Min Lee know you are here?"

"Why would he?"

"You have to see him. You must…come with me."

"I'm afraid not before I use the restroom. Go on over, and I'll be there in a minute." She was categorically not going to see Min Lee. Why open wounds she'd work so hard to heal? Min Jade took a deep breath and exhaled, walking to the ladies' room as steadily as she could. She truly wanted to leave things as they were, but her heart was pulling her under. "Get a grip," Min Jade said to herself. When she walked back into the hall, Ji-Joon was waiting.

"I couldn't chance it and risk your leaving. Min Lee would never forgive me."

"He doesn't have to know. Ji-Joon, I think I want to leave things as they are. Please just pretend you didn't see me."

"He would never forgive me. You just don't know."

Tunde, wondering what was taking Min Jade so long, walked toward the women's restroom. His smile faded when he saw Ji-Joon walking toward him, Min Jade by his side.

"Hello." The twerp bowed, annoying Tunde even more. "Would you mind terribly if I asked Min Lee to meet with Min Jade? There was a misunderstanding back in Innsbruck; I think they need to be cleared up. You are with Min Jade, am I correct?"

"Yes, I am." Tunde looked over at Min Jade. Her eyes said it all. What a mistake it was to have brought her here. Out of 5,000-plus people, how in the hell did they run into Min Lee's Tonto?! "Do you want to meet Min Lee?"

"It'll only take a minute. Let's go together."

The line of patrons waiting for their CD to be signed was long, and it took a half-hour before she was finally standing before him. Her heart did somersaults while her stomach did knots.

Min Lee took her CD without even looking up. As he handed it back to her, he looked up and smiled and then let out a gasp. "Min Jade? Min Jade?" Min Lee's eyes widened.

"Hello, Min Lee."

"*Daebak,*" he clasped her hand as though he'd never let it go again. "Oh, Min Jade, I can't believe you are here. How good of you to come!"

Min Jade ogled him. Her heart mamboed. "You were all that and more tonight," she said simply. "Congratulations."

"How long are you here?"

"I leave on Monday."

"Do you mind staying back a few?"

"I really can't. I'm here with someone." Min Jade released her hand from Min Lee's as Tunde stepped closer. He bowed to his nemesis.

"Do you remember Tunde?"

"I can't say I do, but it's my pleasure. Forgive me if I am remiss."

Tunde bristled and threw his shoulder back in a kingly stance. Their path had only crossed twice, at the welcome party and at the restaurant, but Tunde considered himself an unforgettable guy! He was insulted.

"I'm sorry we can't stay. *We* have a previous engagement. It's great to see you again, Min Lee." He stressed the "again." They held each other's gazes. The dragon and the lion stood facing each other, one looking down slightly at the other. "You were superb tonight."

"Thank you." Min Lee bowed.

Tunde preened. He was proud of Min Jade's grace.

"Congratulations again on tonight. You truly were remarkable tonight," Min Jade said. "We truly wish we could stay."

"Let's go, Min Jade," Tunde took her elbow. "We'll be late for our reunion rehearsal."

"Rehearsal?" Min Lee looked from one to the other.

"While in Austria, the Perfect Harmonies, a wonderful musical ensemble of the visiting physicists you met at the restaurant *Der Pavillion*," he stressed, "was formed. I dare say we are physicists with style. We're playing tomorrow. You should come by and hear us," Tunde said, making sure not to tell him where they were playing.

"Oh, no. I don't think so," Min Jade butted in. "We are just having a bit of geeky fun. Nothing worth it at all. We are pretty terrible. No need to pollute your ears."

"I'd like that," Min Lee said to Tunde. "I believe you must be pretty good." He didn't miss the dig, and of course, he'd remembered the arrogant man, but who cared.

"We are," Tunde said.

"Min Lee, Ji-Joon, it was great to see you both," Min Jade said, signaling her readiness to Tunde, who was only too happy to oblige. She was about to hyperventilate, and she had to get outside.

Min Lee bowed deeply. "Same here."

As they walked away, Min Lee pulled Ji-Joon aside. "Get her details. Discreetly. Don't you dare let her leave this building without getting her details," he turned back to the next person in line and smiled. Ji-Joon found his moment when Tunde decided to make a quick stop in the restroom before they left.

"It's good to see you, Min Jade. Where are you staying, anyway? If you give me your address, I'll messenger over with Min Lee's latest CDs. And your number, in case the driver needs to call."

"Thank you," Min Jade wrote her details on the card he handed her. "I'd like that."

Ji-Joon waved goodbye and disappeared.

"You were good back there," Tunde said as he rejoined her.

Min Jade nodded.

"I'm proud of you."

"Me, too."

"Splendid," he took her hand, and they walked down the stairs to his waiting car. She did not resist because she needed his steadying hand.

The following morning, Min Jade found herself in a much better emotional shape than she'd have imagined or thought possible. "Yes!" she said aloud as she served up her bangers, beans, and eggs breakfast. "Compartmentalization in full force." She pulled out a chair and plopped down, fork in hand, ready to enjoy her English breakfast. *You have a text,* her general ping tone announced. Min Jade had special texts and ringtones for the important people in her life. Her mother's, *Your lovely daughter is calling,* and her dad's, *Scallywag, I'm tracking you down.* Winful's was, *I give my all to fusion.* Min Jade rested her fork on the plate and checked the message. *It's Min Lee Woo. I'm at your door.*

Ping: *My door?*

Ping: *Yes. Come to the door.*

Min Jade looked through the peephole, and indeed Min Lee was standing there.

"Hey," he said when she opened the door.

"Go away. Right this minute," Min Jade tried to shut the door.

"Really?"

"Yes, really. How dare you come here and say, hey? Is that all you have to say to someone you abandoned?"

"I think you are the one who should have something to say to me, Miss Coward."

"Well, I never," she tried to shut the door in his face, but this his foot was in it. "How did you know where to find me, anyway and get this number?" She was trying to be as casual as she could muster.

"Ji-Joon, of course." Min Lee stood miffed. "Is that all? Don't *you* have anything else to say to me?"

"You are interrupting my breakfast."

"You are kidding, right?"

"Why would I kid? Do I look like I'm kidding?"

"Well, I think you'd better be because you'd better *have* some things to say to me."

"Why? Aren't you the one who left without saying goodbye?"

"I did say goodbye. I left a note on your door because I didn't want to wake you at four in the morning."

"You left a note?"

"And called you a million times and sent as many e-mails to your office, not to talk about the months' worth of messages I left with the physics department."

"Boy, you really are something." Min Jade relented and let him into the apartment. "Was it a million, a thousand or NO calls at all! Min Lee, you should be ashamed of yourself for being so two-faced. No need going this far to explain the obvious. You won. Okay. Clever man you are. Love potion #9 worked. Tell a maladaptive soppy story, and then bed said subject. I was a good target. I can see that now. It was a good story, too, and it did the trick-got me into your bed. You proved your point, and I'm okay with that. Really. We are grown. No commitment is necessary. We never said anything about a permanent relationship, did we?"

"Yes, we did. I even asked you to be my girlfriend, and you reminded me you were a woman. For god's sake, I even bought a book on love!"

"Too bad it didn't teach you anything, especially how not to lie."

"But I'm telling the truth, Min Jade. I lost my cell phone on the way to the airport the morning I left. I hadn't memorized your number, and since I didn't back up my phone to the cloud after I'd arrived in Austria, I had no number, so I couldn't call your cell, but I left a thousand messages for you at the physics department. You never responded to one. Not even to my e-mails? I'll even tell you something fun…I looked to see if you had a social media account anywhere. That's how desperate I was to connect with you. Why then should I have to be the one to say something? I thought we meant more to each other than that. I even thought I loved you, Min Jade. I said that didn't I? Doesn't that imply a permanent relationship? I had good reasons to think it did. Didn't you imagine something was wrong? Are you only book smart? Do you think I could have done that? Do you think I randomly tell women I love them? I almost went mad there for a few months."

"You said *maybe* you loved me. I figured you found out otherwise and went back to your normal life. I called and texted you a million times too. Did you answer?"

"I couldn't get your messages. I just told you I lost my phone. I had a temporary number in Switzerland, that's why you couldn't reach me. Stupid me, as I said, I hadn't backed up my phone, so even when I got a new phone, I still didn't have your number. I explained all that in the thousand phone messages I left with the physics department and through e-mail. They knew me by name after my millionth call! Why couldn't you at least answer your e-mail? Do you know how hurt I was?"

"I can only imagine," Min Jade's voice dripped sarcasm. "I got no email from you." Min Jade thought back to the countless times she'd checked. Why didn't you try harder?"

"How could you not get my e-mail. Did you ever check your spam?"

It had never occurred to Min Jade back them. She never, ever checks her spam before hitting the delete button. Could he be telling the truth? "If I'd been that important to you, you would have tried to find out what was going on. Austria isn't far from Switzerland. Even if you were crazy busy and couldn't make it back, I can accept that; you know where I work in the United States. I, on the other hand, could only call a non-working cell phone number!"

"I was planning to fly over the weekend my father called. I swear. Ask Ji-Joon. Unfortunately, I had to go to Korea, and what was to have been a week turned into three months plus. When I got back to teach my master's class, you were already gone. But why didn't you call me? I got my old number back after I got back to England."

"Why would I do that when you'd declared your hand? I was too upset at the time to forgive you, and as they say, life goes on. We're not kids anymore, you know, even if you were my first lover. I have been married for a very long time to my work and to be frank, that's good enough for me. I honestly never got any messages from you. That's why. What else was I to think other than you'd declared *your* hand."

"That's impossible. Impossible."

"Fine. Whatever you say. I think you should just leave. Now we both understand the snafu that happened. It's probably nature's way of telling us we were on the wrong track, anyway."

"I will not. I will not leave this flat until you hear me out and you give me some answers."

"I'm being civil here, Min Lee, so don't push your luck." Min Jade said, walking toward the kitchen. Suddenly Min Lee spun her around and pulled her into his embrace. "We are made for each other. Nature is wrong. From now on, I will never let you be."

"Stop that," she slapped his arm. "Don't you think we have timed out?" She released herself from his embrace.

"Not ever," he pulled her back into him and held her closer. "My schedule *was* brutal, but believe me, if I'd known that Ji-Joon had made a mistake on our departure day, things would have turned out differently. We'd have made plans. But I didn't know, Min Jade, not until he banged on my door until 2 a.m.

I thought I was being considerate by sticking a note on your door so as not to wake you up. I figured we'd sort things out when we spoke."

"Okay. Let's say all that's true," her voice still dripped with sarcasm. "It's passé now. We've moved on. Why are you here?"

"First, as Ji-Joon's messenger. This is yours," he handed her a CD. "And because I have to know if we are still very much in love." *Maybe he could make his father's dream come true after all in the wife department.*

"It was *maybe* love," Min Jade pulled out of his embrace once again, took the CD, and studied the cover photo of Min Lee. He was so incredibly handsome. "I'm not cut out to go through the roller-coaster emotions of maybe love, much less real love. I don't even believe in love, remember? So, let's leave things the way they are and just chalk Austria up to a fluke. Two flawed people seeking a moment of solace. You don't have to feel any guilt about that. I've moved on. You should too."

"Stop lying."

Min Jade averted her eyes from his stare, but her interlaced hands gave away her true feelings. She opened her mouth, and he quickly clamped his fingers over her lips. "Don't say it. You are right. I should have known something was wrong. Min Jade, I'm sorry. *ottoke?*"

"I'm sorry, too, Min Lee, but I have more than I can handle right now. I'm glad it wasn't as we both thought. Let's be thankful we got a chance to explain."

He moved in even closer to her. Min Jade struggled to release his hold, but there was no question she felt the magic. He'd been right after all. She belonged to him. Her first love. Still, she turned her face away from his kiss, his lips landing against her ear. "I've missed you," he murmured. "Every minute of every day, I've missed you."

"How can I believe you?" She was saying while her face had turned toward his lips. He backed her up into the bedroom, and she found her hand pulling him close into her... rather than pushing him away. "I don't think...."

"Shush, don't think," he said, slipping his hand beneath her robe. So deep had been their connection, Min Jade had no will to resist the hand that flickered her now awakened desire. Her body on fire, Min Jade frantically pulled at his shirt. He helped her, quickly easing out of his clothes, and then he undressed her slowly until she was stark naked and trembling with desire before him. Then as slowly, he took her until she cried out his name over and over again. They must have fallen asleep, drained from hours of insatiable carnal desire.

Now awake from the physical and emotional drain of their love and lovemaking, Min Jade circled her hand over Min Lee's smooth chest, his skin tingling red as she drew her hand downwards. She was bold and decisive as she made him stir once again. Min Lee watched her closely and felt a moment of insane jealousy. She was no longer his timid bird. Has she? He pulled her up along his body and kissed her hard, her moist lips parting to receive his. Laying claim with that searing kiss, Min Lee vowed to his woman that he'd never let her go ever and then he took her again and again. This last time they fell apart, he cradled her head in his arms and, without trying to seem obvious, casually said, "The man with you last night? Do you need to explain him?"

"No. I don't. He's a dear and cherished friend, one of the visiting physics professors in Austria."

"Truce?" he kissed the top of her head.

"No truce."

"The next time we meet...."

"I don't think there will be a next time," she cut him off.

"Then what are we doing?"

"Farewell sex. Finishing what we started. Conclusion, so to speak."

Min Lee left the bed and went to the bathroom. On his way out, he brushed past her and went into the bathroom. She followed him.

"I'll never let you go," he said with finality. "Believe that."

Min Jade felt the melt, her walls tumbling down. She wanted to believe him, yet she was sure it was another ploy to get him to more afternoon delights. "I am not as brave as you think I am. I can't go through the pain I felt when you left. It's debilitating, distracting, and it's truly not who I am. People like us are selfish. Work is our master, and you know that, too. Everything, all this, will have to take a backseat to our real lives, and I'm alright with that. Really, I am. Since we've both managed to move on, let's just keep our precious moments and not taint them with expectations and empty words anymore. Look, Min Lee…"

He formed a duck beak with his hands. Then, out of nowhere, he smiled and pulled her close to him. "I have never moved on. I will never move on. We belong together. You, my love, cannot control destiny or fate."

"Stop this right now!" Her voice commanded.

"I can't, Min Jade. I can't. Let's give it time. Let's take it slower."

He was doing it again, this time tugging at her strings. God help her.

Now washed and dressed, Min Lee went to the kitchen, opened the refrigerator door, and guzzled a bottle of water. He handed her a bottle. "Sex requires hydration. I'll see you tonight. Where are you playing, again?" his gaze penetrated her very soul.

"Stop staring at me like that." Min Jade said.

"I can't help it. People in love can't help staring...our *maybe* love is no longer maybe, right? Where are you playing tonight?" he asked again.

"No! Please don't come tonight. We'll meet before I go."

"Where are you playing?" he repeated.

"Someplace called the Pig and Swine." *He was still bossy.*

"How very British. Permission?" he said.

"For what this time?" Min Jade was emotionally exhausted.

Min Lee pulled her tightly to him. "For this," he seared her lips, and then he was gone.

Behind closed doors, Min Jade struggled with her emotions. Her heart thumped inside her chest. She could barely stand. Why was she such an idiot? She threw her bangers, beans, and eggs into the trash.

Ji-Joon," Min Lee bellowed, slamming the door to Ji-Joon's apartment, which was, as usual, just across the corridor. "Arrange for me to go someplace called the Pig and Swine tonight."

"The what?"

"Pig and Swine."

"What the hell is that?"

"Min Jade and her band are playing there."

"Min Lee, do you still have feelings for Min Jade?" Ji-Joon's voice was cautionary. "If we are going home, why not just let this remain where it is? You've cleared the air. Let this go. It'll be too hard for her."

"Meaning?"

"Korean society will never accept her. She is a foreigner. An independent woman, and she is not going to walk behind you. Do you want her to live through all that? Right now, you have the benefit of disruption. Let it be."

"What if it's my one chance at love?"

"Min Lee…"

"*Araso.* Okay. No preaching."

Ji-Joon sighed again.

"Quit with the sighing already, okay?"

Unable to help himself, Ji-Joon sighed again. Tapping the Google app on his phone, he set out to find the Pig and Swine. Tonight, he was feeling uncertain about this relationship. Never in life would Min Lee be caught dead in a place called the Pig and Swine.

Noticing his whirring mind, Min Lee said, "Ji-Joon. Relax. We are, as Min Jade would say, a couple of maladaptives trying to figure out life. So, cool it. I'll let you know if we decide to run away."

Ji-Joon clenched his jaw and summoned the maids to pack for their trip to the Netherlands.

Min Lee, who had been no saint in the women's department, never wanted to change his ways until he'd met Min Jade. He suspected Ji-Joon, who knew him firsthand, was left to clean up the mess after each teary heartbreak, didn't want to clean up this mess, but there would be no mess. He'd always been clear about his intentions, but as only women could, they chose to ignore them. He was clear, very clear about his intention for Min Jade. He wanted her in his life.

CHAPTER TWELVE

LONDON PIG & SWINE
PERFECT HARMONY

PIG AND SWINE WAS ROCKING. Pulsating with debauchery and abandon.

"So?" Tunde said as they got dolled up for their gig. "Are you going to make kimchi again?"

"Did I ever tell you how much I hate cabbage?"

"I rather like the sound of that. How do you feel about yams?"

Min Jade sneered at him as they headed for the stage door. How on earth could she get involved with two crazy people?

The crowd got louder as Perfect Harmonies took to the stage. Min Jade scanned the room, praying Min Lee wouldn't show up. As far as she could see, he wasn't there. She felt relieved. The bawdy crowd roared.

"One, two, three," Anastase counted down.

Tunde began with a rhythmic drumbeat. Bodies swayed and jerked. The place went wild when Vadim took the stage in his checkered tights. Min Jade riffed on the piano to "Revolution," and Perfect Harmonies held sway. Midway through the show, Albert explained the reason behind the origin of their band and why the world needs to be progressive, educated, and as culturally diverse as their band. Then out of nowhere, Tunde announced Min Jade, their pianist, had the most heavenly voice, "And if you aren't convinced," he blabbered, "encourage her to sing. You won't regret it."

Min Jade almost fainted.

"Come on," Chin egged her on. "It's all in good fun."

"Min Jade, Min Jade, Min Jade," the crowd kept repeating.

Min Jade rose. She'd show that Tunde.

"Yes. He's right. I sing. Badly. I play the piano even worse, but I can put on a mean laser show," she said. "Are you sure now you want me to do all that? This is your last chance to save the night."

"Min Jade, Min Jade, Min Jade," The chant got louder and louder.

"All right." Min Jade spoke to the band and then took the mic.

Albert took over on keyboards, and the intro bell riffed to: *Say something, I'm giving up on you. I'll be the one if you want me to. Anywhere I will follow you…And I,* Chin joined in, *am feeling so small…*

The room became quiet. The crowd began looking up from whatever they were doing to check out the woman in the purple glasses with the voice of the century. They wanted more. "Min Jade, Min Jade," the crowd chanted.

Min Jade sang "Thinking Out Loud" as a tribute to Britain's rising star, Ed Sheeran. When they wouldn't let her off the stage, she sang Rihanna's "I'll Drink to That." *Cheers,* she began. The place went wild, chanting along *to the freakin' weekend I'll drink to that.* Patrons were singing along, clinking glasses, snapping fingers, and they were under Min Jade's spell.

"Cheers." The manager flew onto the stage, waxing. "Applause for smart people. Tonight, not only did we bring sexy back, but we made brains, culture, and togetherness sexy. Did you have fun?"

Stomping. Fingers snapping and glasses clinking.

Min Jade swatted Tunde when she got off stage. "I should kill you."

"You should thank me. You came out tonight, Lady Jade."

The band joined the patrons. Min Jade took a drink some-one handed her. The room was sardine packed as she tried to maneuver her way to a place where she could breathe. Some-one leaned in, brushing her ears. She was about to punch the drunken sod's lights out when the voice whispered, "You are a star all around, Min Jade. If by any slim, and I mean minuscule chance, you don't get a Nobel, go for a Grammy. I loved *Revo-lution,* and I love that you'll follow me anywhere."

She couldn't even turn around in the crowd. "*Gomawo,*" she said. "Thank you for coming."

"You remembered your Korean. Good."

"I always remember what I want to."

"Since you're so fluent in my language, I'm making you an honorary Korean. Confession," he was pressed up against her, rising in the small of her back. Heat radiated from her body, and it was not from the crowded room. She could feel the thump of his heart. "Confession?"

"Yeah." Min Lee nodded, his lips resting against her ear as though they belonged there. "You're not so bad on the piano, and your voice is heaven-sent," he nuzzled her neck.

Min Jade scrunched her eyebrows together. "Friends don't lie."

"Feel me," he pushed closer, "I'm not lying."

Min Jade guzzled her drink. "So, what do you want to do about it?" she let the alcohol speak for her.

"Can I stay the night with you?" he pulled her toward the door.

Over breakfast, the Mins caught up with each other's lives since their hiatus. "Tell me everything." Min Lee said.

Being with Min Lee, even for the short time they'd spent together, was like plopping down in an old comfy chair that knew every curve of her body. What if he was her soul mate, and she let him go? But what if she sat down and couldn't get up again? It was too much of a risk. Their timing was all wrong, which was enough of a sign they were not meant to be. Her life's purpose was unfulfilled, and love was a choice she could not make. Min Jade stared at Min Lee. "I don't know where my life will go over the next months. This coming year, I must work hard."

"Why?"

"My Chair has some hair-brained notion I could be a contender for the Nobel."

"That's no surprise. That's pretty realistic from where I sit. It'd be fantastic."

"Well, it's not fantastic yet. It's not that easy to get a Nobel Prize. I think it's a pipe dream."

"Dreams, pipe or not, are the seedlings of reality. Believe him?"

"I don't know why I'm telling you this, but I need you to understand who I am."

"You're telling me because that's what we do. Only maladaptives understand each other. You've fought demons for this opportunity, as I have for my music. I know what that feels like, but we can find our way together. I know this," he patted her shoulder like a parent comforting a child. "I have a good feeling about this and us," he continued. "Please trust me with your heart."

Min Jade felt a strange comfort again. "What about you?"

"I was in Korea for over three months, as I told you. I went because my father was retiring from music and asked that I play his last concert. When I got there, I found out he was doing poorly— cancer of the brain. I couldn't leave him. But the good news is that I got to see my mom for the first time in seventeen years." Min Lee's mood changed. He paused for a moment, acknowledging his love-hate relationship with the country of his birth. His visit had been bittersweet, but undoubtedly, a part of his soul was some-where there. His allegiance to the Great Republic of Korea ran deep, even if he could never go back for good.

"How was that experience? Was it hard?"

"Visiting with mom was comforting. It was hard to see my dad being ill. Overall, I wouldn't say my visit was amazing, but it was good, not nearly as bad as I'd imagined it would be. I'm thinking of going back to be with Dad for a while."

"You mean leaving the stage?" Min Jade's eyes widened.

"The world stage for a bit, but I will still perform in Korea. I need to do this for my father." He was encouraged by her concern.

Would he give up his career to be by his father's side? How admirable. "Min Lee, you should do it. I can't pretend understand all the dynamics, but family is family. If your father needs you, you should go. We should show the people in our lives how much we care about them when they are living… And if he's doing…."

"What about the fact that I need you in my life, Min Jade?" he interrupted.

"I was never really in your life, Min Lee. I was just a passerby."

"Do you think I am that frivolous? Love's not easy for me. I've never said those words to a single soul on this earth, except my mother. I love you, Min Jade, no, maybe. *I love you,* and I'm sorry I disappointed you. How am I supposed to find another you? Let's try. Let's try to work out our life together. Come to Korea when I am there. See where I come from, and then you will better understand who I am."

The moment felt warm and heart-wrenching. All Min Jade wanted to do was stay by Min Lee's side, but she had a master bigger than even than herself. In their two-hour-long breakfast, before he had to leave for the airport, she'd traversed the gamut of emotions: anger, understanding, yearning, and a deep desire to be with the man who could very well be her soul mate.

"Let's give it some time. I am willing to try," Min Jade said. "Tomorrow, I leave England, and we go back to our realities. We'll see how long these feelings hold up once we're apart."

"I wish we had more time together. Can you take a few more days and come to Amsterdam with me?"

"I wish I could. Unfortunately, I can't."

CHAPTER THIRTEEN

MIN JADE
LEAVING AGAIN

TUNDE WAS PISSED. He should never have bought tickets to the Korean's show. Idling outside her Kensington flat, his mind couldn't blot out the image of the Mins pressed close at the Pig and Swine. But when they left the club together, he'd spun out of control into a tizzy. Albert had to calm him down by plying him with a few glasses of hard liquor. For him not to get what he wanted was an unfamiliar and maddening feeling, but worse, he had fallen hard for Min Jade. Tunde had decided then and there he'd fight to the bitter end for Min Jade's love. He wanted, no he needed, no matter how difficult it might prove, this woman by his side always. He impatiently blew the horn.

"Coming," Min Jade said, throwing the door open. Today one couldn't miss her if they tried. A bright red coat perfectly paired with a red and black tam squelching the baubles of curls, topped off with green studded boots. A purple scarf matched the glasses.

Tunde met her at the steps and grabbed her luggage. He'd insisted on driving her to the airport because they had to talk. "Got everything?"

Min Jade nodded. "Thank you for doing this. Did everyone get off okay?" She slipped into the passenger's seat.

Tunde nodded and reached over to buckle her seat belt. Familiar with his habit, Min Jade sat still. "Did I ever tell you I learned to drive in England? On a Mini Cooper."

"I see you've always been careless with your life," he slammed the passenger's door much harder than necessary. The confounded woman began rummaging through her bag to find her ticket, wondering how she could look so unfazed by her debauchery. He slid into the driver's seat. "Are you deliberately trying to drive me crazy?" He started the engine, staring straight ahead.

Min Jade stared at him through her mop of curls. "What are you talking about, now? Love again?"

Tunde, the one-evening wonder, not the type to miss or want anyone, was having a meltdown. He'd miss her though it was clear it could be in vain as Operation Min Jade hadn't gone as planned. Maybe this was his punishment for all the broken hearts he'd left behind. Tunde was racking his brain on how best to win her affection, which noticeably favored Min Lee Woo. "I am serious, Min Jade," he said as the car came to a stop. "I want to be your boyfriend."

Min Jade stuffed her ticket in her coat pocket. "I am not looking for a boyfriend, Tunde." She watched as his jaw tightened, and he lapsed into silence. She wanted to be honest and tell him about Min Lee but thought better of it. When the car pulled up, curbside Min Jade jumped out and quickly got the luggage the porter was taking from the trunk. "Don't get out," she said as Tunde yanked open his door. "I'll make my way, and I promise I'll give much thought to the boyfriend thing," she kissed his cheek. "I had the best time ever. Truly. Thanks, Tunde. I'll call you when I get home."

He waved goodbye and watched as she disappeared into the terminal. The moment she was out of his sight, he wanted her right back beside him. Tunde sat at the curb for ten minutes, his heart heavy.

Amsterdam, Netherlands

Min Lee paced, coffee in hand. He drained his cup, grabbed his coat, and went for a walk along the Prinsengracht. He'd hardly slept a wink, and his body ached for his duck beak girl; he was sure he could hear it breaking. Nothing seemed right this morning, either, and the emotional blankness he could pull down in any given moment was out of reach. Walking briskly along the canal, he thought of Ji-Joon. Was he correct? Should he leave well enough alone? He couldn't tell which was worse, loss or love. Back in his hotel room, Min Lee went to his desk and flipped through his datebook. His finger traveled down each page and stopped on March 6th. He'd be in New York then. Three months away was way too long, though it'd go fast with the busy quarter ahead of him. New York would be his last performance of the year as he had decided to return to Korea to be with his father. Min Lee pulled his phone from his pocket and scrolled down to Min Jade's number.

Min Jade was sitting in the Delta Sky Lounge when her phone blared, "You have a text, you have a text, you have a text." She fumbled in her bag, looking apologetically at the person next to her. "So sorry," she grabbed the phone and clicked the silencer. Min Lee. If they were going to be "friends," she'd have to make a special tone for him. What? Deserter? Heart-throb, Handsome Pianist? White Knight Korean, Unfathomable Pianist, Duck Beak, Crazy Korean? Asshole? She decided on Crazy Korean.

Ping: *Min, Jade.*

Ping: *Anyoung. Yes, it's me—your Honorary Korean.*

Ping: *Where are you?*

Ping: *In the Delta lounge, waiting on my flight. How is Amsterdam?*

Ping: *Lonely. I miss you.*

Ping: *At least you didn't lose your phone this time. Dig.*

Ping: *Funny. You are so refreshing in my life.*

Ping: *Refreshing? How are you defining that?*

Ping: *Do you want the explanation as an adjective or a verb?*

Min Jade laughed.

Ping: *Both.*

Ping: *Verb: Refresh: revive, enliven, vigor. Stimulate. Adjective: Refreshing: the power to restore vitality. I felt stimulated when I saw you.*

Ping: *Blush.*

Ping: *Really, Min, Jade. I love the way I feel when I'm with you.*

Ping: *It's an illusion. She touched her lips. His kiss still lingered there.*

Ping: *I'll be seeing you soon.*

Ping: *Is that a promise?*

Ping: *Pinky swear…stamp…Put it up.*

She didn't believe a word of it. Back home, not a day had gone by since their meeting in London that Min Lee hadn't called. She especially loved when he face-timed her. To her, he was the most handsome man in the world. Still, she hated having to always be dolled up for this Facetime thing as she wasn't ready to show him her tatty red pajamas.

By mid-January, the conference had been fully organized. It would take place on January 21st at Hill Auditorium. Who in their right mind would want to come to Michigan in January? Min Jade had never seen Winful so excited.

"Consider it an early birthday gift," he nudged her. The Dean is over the moon."

"What do I need to do right now?" Min Jade asked.

"Just show up and let your brilliance shine. Your phone is ringing," Winful pointed at the contraption vibrating on her hip.

"Ah, yeah. Hello," Min Jade answered the cell.

"Hey, it's Tunde and Albert."

"Hey, guys. To what do I owe this pleasure?"

"Your conference just came over the wire. Thought we should congratulate you," Albert said.

"We're thinking of coming over," Tunde added.

"Don't be daft. It's not all that."

"It kinda is," Albert chimed in. "This is pretty impressive, Professor Jade."

"Trust me. There is no need to come all the way here. I'll probably be too busy to entertain you, and I'd feel bad if I couldn't be as great a host as you guys were. You know I'm competitive that way. I'll send you a video."

"Okay, if you say so. Congrats, Min Jade, truly. You are one helluva woman. You'll probably be hearing from the other PHs. They've been blowing up our inbox."

"Thanks, guys. I appreciate the call. I'll send the video. Promise."

"It's a good thing, Min Jade," Tunde said.

"Yes, it is pretty special," Min Jade proffered before hanging up.

Winful was waiting expectantly. "My friends from my sabbatical. They saw the conference announcement."

"Why did you discourage them from coming?"

"Come on, Professor. It's not all that."

"I beg to differ. We have registrants from over sixty countries. Now," Winful said, "let's have cocoa."

The number of reporters around Hill Auditorium was baffling. Why would they show up for a science conference? A physics conference was a far cry from reporting what Kim Kardashian wore to the Met Ball, though Min Jade's outfit could be fodder for conversation.

"Professor Jade. Professor Jade," reporters swarmed, pushing microphones into her face as she climbed the stairs to Hill Auditorium.

"What's this all about?" She paused.

"How do you feel?"

"About what?" Min Jade asked.

"That this conference is all about you?"

"I feel great, but why is a science conference such big news? No scandal here, just protons and neutrons colliding."

"Well, a black woman has never been so decorated in the sciences. That's news. Doesn't it make you…"

"Ah, I see. You are interested in my blackness. Well, I don't think that's any concern of mine, never has been. I am a scientist, and whatever labels you want to put on it be my guest, but I have nothing to say on that score. Now I am already late," she pushed through the crowd.

"Are you saying it doesn't matter to you that you are black?"

"Why would it matter to me? I've been black my whole life. The question is, why does it matter to you? But that's your question to answer, isn't it? Not mine. For the record, I never engage in race conversations that's prosaic so, if my blackness is what's of interest…take out your checkbook. I can give you an expert lecturer on that too…but I never work for free."

"What about…."

Min Jade left the reporter mid-sentence. When she walked into the conference room, she was blown away by the number of people who had shown up and the number of countries from which they came. It was highly unusual for a mere science conference. Was her blackness so weighted, or was her research groundbreaking? As Min Jade climbed the steps to the stage, right in the front row were members of the Perfect Harmonies. What the hell?

"Surprise," Albert mouthed as she took her seat.

Min Jade acknowledged her friends with a nod. Right behind them sat Dr. Winful, Dr. Kessler – who'd extended her stay, and the Dean. Winful spent the entire time preening, and the Dean was only slightly more modest. This kind of attention, they'd said, would attract significant funding to the University. Min Jade hadn't realized that the conference was being live-streamed, too.

"So," the interviewer began, "your work has received impressive reviews and citations. Can you share with us what it all means?"

"It could mean nothing and everything," Min Jade said. "The controversial nature of quantum physics is that it's impossible to predict with certainty the outcome of a single experiment on a quantum system. So, we are talking probability, of course, and making comparisons between theory and experiment. Over repeated experiments, my results have been encouraging."

"There's a lot of debate about what, exactly, this quantum physics wave function represents."

"There's an active effort in the quantum foundations community to find a way to derive the Born rule from a more fundamental principle; to date, none of these have been fully successful, but it generates a lot of interesting science."

"And so, what does your probability research suggest?"

"That we are onto something special."

After many questions and answers, someone from the back of the room asked, "Professor Jade, how does it feel to be a black woman in the sciences?"

"I can't answer that. I have nothing to compare it to. You see, I've always been a black woman in the sciences, and personally, prosaic questions like this bore me to distraction," she rose, unclipped her mic and left the stage. The topic of race in America was one that bored her to tears.

After the seminar concluded, Min Jade approached her friends. "I can't believe you guys came all the way here for this! I bet this is Tunde's idea."

"What do you mean, 'for this'?" Chin said. "This is our life. How could we be first-class scientists and not be here? We are learning from one of the best, not to mention our fabu pianist, too."

To her surprise, Tunde was not the first to take control. He was hanging back, just observing.

"Come, let me introduce you to my Chair. Dr. Winful," she beckoned him over.

Winful excused himself from a conversation with Dr. Kessler, ambling over. Instead of joining him, Dr. Kessler hurriedly went in the other direction.

"I'd like you to meet my Austrian posse." Min Jade said

"So, you're the posse that kept Min Jade too busy to do science in Austria," he chuckled. "What did you think?" Winful said, puffing out his chest.

"Brilliant. You surely have a star here." Tunde said.

Winful nodded. "That I do."

"Dr. Winful, would you care to join us for dinner?" Min Jade offered.

"Ah, shucks. Tonight, I have a date with my wife. But I'm certain I'll see you all again, in Sweden," he laughed, his belly moving up and down as he did.

"Geez," Min Jade cut her eyes at him. "Give it a rest, already."

"I think I'll be able to do that soon," he winked.

"Okay. See you tomorrow for debriefing." Min Jade pecked Chair Winful's cheek and watched as he ambled away with a pep in his step.

Albert liked the University of Michigan. He'd never as much as shook his Chair's hand, much less kissed him.

"What do you fancy for dinner?" Min Jade asked her friends. "I'll take you to my favorite place. The Red Dragon."

Close to the physics building, the Red Dragon was a haunt for physics professors and students alike. It was a little kitsch with its red plastic booths and spinning lantern, but the food was good and reasonably priced. When Min Jade wasn't eating lunch with her beloved Winful, pontificating on the meaning of everything, she was at the Red Dragon. "Stay open-minded, Tunde," she warned. "It's not fancy, but it's good- and easy for us to visit from here."

"Maybe we'll play there when we come to the United States. Sure, wish we had time to do a gig," Ansel said.

"Me too," Albert chimed in.

"But we're missing the tutu?" Tunde said, taking a position next to Min Jade. "He's on a trip but sends his apologies."

Tunde leaned into Min Jade and whispered, "You, my love, rock in so many ways."

"By the way, Min Jade, who was that woman talking to Chair Winful?" Albert asked. "She looks so familiar to me."

"She could be. She's one of yours on sabbatical here for six months. Dr. Kessler," Min Jade informed.

"Huh."

"So, how long are you staying?" Min Jade asked her posse.

"We leave early tomorrow morning," Tunde said.

They spent the next few hours together discussing everything, including the race problem in America.

"I am still surprised," Chin said at the insistence of that reporter trying to force you to comment on being a Black woman in Physics. Bizarre."

Right after the conference, Min Jade went full throttle. She sequestered herself in her lab and spent hours in the library. She'd written ten drafts of a new abstract and suspected she'd write another ten before it was ready for submission. Over and over, she repeated her experiment and then over and over again, controlling different variables. Min Jade hadn't seen her parents in way too long. It was now March 2nd and her birthday, and she was feeling every bit of the always-present madness. At noon, she decided to have an early day and to take the weekend off. She'd plan to return numerous unanswered calls, drop by her parents to celebrate, and then have an early night. After a long bath, a glass of wine, and some rest, she'd treat herself to a Korean drama before heading to her parents for dinner. After all, it was her birthday, and one way to feel close to Min Lee was watching soppy Korean dramas. Her phone bleated, "Crazy Korean, Crazy Korean." How was that possible? She thought of Korean drama, and the Korean called.

"Can you talk?" Min Jade loved when he did that. So conscious. Min Lee's face, all smiles, loomed on the video screen.

"I was just thinking about you."

"As you should be."

"Where are you? That's another thing he did. Always asked where she was.

"I just got home for a day of rest."

"Good. I can wait to give you a proper birthday present," he said, donning a party hat and holding up a cupcake with a candle. "*Saeng-il chu gha, ka hamida,*" he sang, blowing a party whistle.

"Ah, thank you. Can you blow the candle out for me?" She was all atwitter.

He did. "Want my other gift?"

"Yea, send it through the phone." She mocked

"I can show you through the phone. Are you in bed?"

"Yup."

"Are you naked?"

"Min Lee! Don't you dare! This is the internet! I can see the headlines now after your phone is hacked. But don't tell me we were going to have phone sex!"

"We are. Why not? What could be better on your birthday, old lady? You should be glad you can still turn a man on."

"Dirty old man. Let's see thirty-five, right?"

"Never ask a man his age."

"Sheesh."

"So, what are you doing on your birthday? I wish I could be there with you."

"I'm having dinner with my parents. Then I'll do something inspiring, like watch a Korean drama. It'll make you feel close."

"Then, I have great recommendations. *Five Fingers, Beethoven's Virus, Baker In-Tak,* or something like that. Wait, *Boys Over Flowers,* that one takes the cake for drivel."

"Ah, ha. You watch Korean dramas?" Min Jade hooted.

"I have reason. I've decided to move to Korea for a few months to be with my dad. I really have no idea what goes on in that country, so I thought I could catch up…that's all."

Min Jade felt her heart drop. *He was leaving her again.* Still, she said, "I'm so glad you made that decision, Min Lee. Your father will be so happy. It's the right thing to do."

"Okay, Duck Beak. I hear you. Do you think you can make time to come while I'm there? I want you to meet my father."

Thirty minutes later, Min Lee wondered why she hadn't brought up the tickets he'd sent for her birthday. His surprise for March 6. He'd give her until tomorrow to acknowledge his gift.

"If I'm going to get anything done today, I have to get off the phone."

"*Arasseo*. Happy birthday, my special Duck Beak. Can you at least tell me the color of your knickers?"

"Red."

Min Jade felt herself blush. She was becoming quite the trollop. She fluffed her pillow and turned on Vicki. She scrolled through to see what to watch. She, too, had heard *Boys Over Flowers* was indeed entertaining. Min Jade's phone chimed again just as the opening titles came on screen. Damn it. She didn't know that many people…who the hell…"Hello."

"Where are you?" Tunde asked

"Home. What's up, Tunde? I'm in a rush, so can I call you later?"

"You can see me later. I'm in Ann Arbor."

"Ann Arbor? Are you kidding, as usual?"

"Nope. I'm in Ann Arbor. I'm back at the God-awful Campus Inn Hotel on Huron Street. Is this the best Ann Arbor can do in the accommodations department?"

"You can't be serious."

"I am."

"What are you doing here?"

"I've come to visit you. It's your birthday, isn't it? I remember."

"You're kidding, right?"

"Min Jade, I am in Ann Arbor at the Campus Inn Hotel. There's a foot of snow outside my window. How would I know that unless I'm here? A guy coming to visit his girlfriend on her birthday is a good thing. You will be my girlfriend since we fell in love in London, right? Can you have dinner?"

Min Jade was stunned. Did he come all the way from London just to visit her for her birthday? She looked at her watch. It was just 12:45 p.m.

"I can't believe this. I'd planned to have dinner with my parents at seven, but I'd love to have dinner with you. I'm sure they'll understand…." *And I'll set the record straight while I'm at it. I would never be your girlfriend, Mr. Almighty Chauvinist.* "I'll pick you up, say at 7:30 p.m. Does that work?"

"I'll pick you up," he countered.

"But you don't know your way around?"

"Why would I have to do that? I have a driver. Give me your address."

"When did you get in?"

"About noon."

"I wasn't aware there was a flight that got in from London at noon."

"I flew myself in."

"Excuse me?"

"Well, not exactly. My pilot did."

Min Jade was trying to pick her jaw up off the floor. She knew Tunde came from wealth, though he never flaunted it, typical for those born into wealth, but she never imagined this kind of money. A private plane!

There was no way to get her planned activity in, so Min Jade called her parents. She'd visit at 3:00 p.m. and ask to celebrate her birthday the following day, as she'd be stuck in the lab all night. A little white lie, but what to do? She couldn't tell the truth. Her mother would not quite understand why Tunde was here and explaining it would get too complicated and most likely get her an earful.

At 7:30 p.m., a black Mercedes pulled up. Min Jade was agog, not because of the Mercedes, but because Tunde stepped out of the car. "Hey," he greeted her with a kiss on the cheek. "Happy birthday."

"I'm thinking you are crazy right about now!" She hugged him. "Really crazy."

"That's a byproduct of our profession. I made reservations at the Chop House on Main Street. The concierge told me it was the best restaurant in Ann Arbor. Is that good?" Ann Arbor was a bit too provincial for his taste.

Min Jade was shaking her head up and down. She'd forgotten how spontaneous Tunde could be. When they arrived at the Chop House, there was no one else at the restaurant because Tunde had rented it for the next six hours.

"I'm sorry I can't stay longer. I have to fly back right after dinner. I just wanted to spend some time with you."

"What if I wasn't here?"

"You think I wouldn't know that? I called your office, of course, to find out your schedule. I knew you were in town, and I'm glad you're not mad."

"Mad about a stalker friend. I'm not mad, but there's something we need to discuss."

"Good. But let's have some wine first. I have a lot to tell you, too."

Without consult, Tunde proceeded to order what turned out to be a 1953 Chateau Margaux to go with the dinner, which had also been pre-selected, a variety from the menu, so it didn't matter if she was an herbivore, carnivore or pescatarian.

The waiter poured the wine, and Tunde raised his glass. "To surprises," he said.

"Tunde, I'm a physicist. I don't like surprises."

"Ah, there is that. Next time, we'll make plans."

"How is Albert?"

"He's good. We've been busy since the conference, so we haven't seen much of each other, but I see from the write-ups that the conference was a huge success."

"It was. I think everyone was pleased."

"And you?" His eyes searched her face.

"It was neither here nor there for me. I did it for Winful, and since then, I've been, like you, busy and crazed. This is my first weekend off in a month."

"Really?"

Min Jade paused. She didn't want to go into detail with him. "Yup. It's a hectic time."

"Are you taking care of yourself?"

"Why? Do I look awful?"

"You? Never!" Tunde said, nodding to the waiter to serve the first course. "But you need to feed all of you," he looked at her over the rim of his glass.

Min Jade smiled and sipped her wine. Feed all of her? She brushed her ear, remembering Min Lee's lips and their naughty conversation earlier.

After dinner, Tunde placed a royal blue box on the table. "Happy birthday to you. I hope you like it."

Min Jade couldn't believe four hours had passed since they'd sat down for dinner. She opened the box. An Asscher-cut diamond bracelet. "Tunde, I can't accept this."

"It would be an insult to give back a birthday gift. Please accept it, Min Jade. Look, I'm not a man who beats around the bush. I want to give you so many things, most of all, me. I want you to be my girlfriend," he declared matter-of-factly, as though telling her the sky was blue.

"Tunde," Min Jade began.

"Don't say anything. Don't even try to understand it now. Just sit with it. I can give you everything you desire in this life. I don't need an answer today. In a few months. Give me a few months to make you believe."

"Tunde," Min Jade said again.

His index finger touched her lips. "We won't speak of this for two months. Let's just enjoy your birthday. But I need you to be my woman, so give it some real thought."

"Why?"

"Because I can't imagine being with anyone else."

Min Jade was quiet. She didn't have that kind of feeling for Tunde, but she cherished him as a friend, and she didn't have the heart to tell him she was Min Lee's girlfriend. If she were honest, though, the attention was flattering and made her feel girlie. It was nice to have two men pursuing her for a girl who didn't even have a best girlfriend and whose only intimate contacts were her parents and professor. *Really* nice, in fact. She thought of Min Lee. Why wasn't he the one sitting before her?

"So," Tunde said ruefully. I must go. I have an important meeting in London, but I just wanted you to know how much you mean to me."

Min Jade remained silent. When she got home, Min Jade googled Tunde. As his story unfolded, she felt more and more like she was living on the pages of a storybook.

The following morning, Min Jade was sitting at her desk when Joan, her secretary, handed her a FedEx envelope. "It came yesterday, and Dr. Winful would like you to come to his office, pronto."

Placing the envelope on her desk, she headed to her Chair's office. When she entered, Winful, as always, was fussing with his orchids. She wondered if he did anything else.

"Look at this," he handed her a letter. "What did I tell you. The conference did wonders for our program."

Min Jade slipped on her glasses and read the letter. "Oh, my God. Oh my God!" she said, looking up at Dr. Winful. A look of satisfaction was spreading over his face.

"I can't tell you what you mean to me. Thank you, my Min Jade."

The letter was a multiple-year funding award for the physics department, with twenty million dollars earmarked for Min Jade's research. Min Jade walked over and held Winful in a grateful embrace, and he held her right back. "I have something to tell you."

Winful looked stricken. The conference boosted her profile, and now he was fielding, even more calls from poachers! *She wasn't leaving, was she?*

"I think I'm onto something big. This is going to help."

"Something like what?" Winful whispered.

Min Jade handed him a printout.

Winful's eyes widened with each line he read. "Have you told anyone else?"

"No, of course not."

"Don't say anything!"

"You are the only one I'm telling. The thing is, can *you* keep it a secret?"

"Not even the Dean?"

"Not even the Dean." Min Jade said.

Back in her office, Min Jade opened the FedEx envelope Joan had handed her earlier. Inside was another envelope with two tickets to Carnegie Hall for March 6th and a note.

Happy birthday, Sweetheart. Time to get you out of the foxhole and into my bed. I need refreshing... adjectives. The other ticket is for your mom. You said she thought I was good, if not better than Lang Lang. Flattery will get her everywhere with me. Longing to see you. Happy birthday, my one and only girl. See you soon?

Sarang he.

Min Lee Woo.

Min Jade let out a loud woo-hoo that brought Joan running to her door.

"Dr. Jade?"

"I'm fine, Joan. A bit of good news today."

Everything in her life was looking up. A whopping grant, and now this! Min Jade slipped the tickets back into the envelope. In three days, she'd see Min Lee. Was he longing to see her? Could this relationship work? Dare she speak his name to her heart? In an instance, Min Jade felt, without a shadow of a doubt, that Min Lee held her heart, though her head was still trying to be in control. Quite honestly, she believed it had lost to her heart! Min Jade left her office and drove directly to her parents' home. Feeling even guiltier about ditching them for Tunde, she could think of no better way to make it up than Min Lee's invitation. Her mother would be so happy. She dropped by the wine store on the way and brought her dad a bottle of his favorite red wine. What a way to bring in her thirty-second year. Guilt, surprises, fear, joy, achievement, and hope. Life in its full contradiction. Min Jade unlocked her parents' front door with the same key she'd had since she was a child. "Mother...*Mo-therrr.*"

"Happy birthday to you, happy birthday to you, happy birthday!" Her mother sang; her father, dancing right behind her. They did their best, Stevie Wonder imitation, head movement and all. "Happy birthday, darling," her mother said, pulling Min Jade by the hand into the kitchen where a cake and wine glasses were set.

"You sang that yesterday, and you had a cake yesterday, too," Min Jade laughed at her parents' tomfoolery.

"Well, your dad wanted us to do it all over again, and we'll have another cake at dinner. Come blow out your candles. We've made reservations at The Gandy Dancer for 8:00 p.m., so let's eat cake. By the way, how was the rest of yesterday? Did you accomplish what you needed to? So sorry you had to work on your birthday darling, but *c'est la vie....* We'll celebrate in style tonight."

"Yes, Mom," Min Jade stared at the cake to avert her inability to lie, "but every day is my birthday with you." Looking at her parents and feeling every bit of their love, Min Jade suddenly burst into tears. She'd never lied to her parents before.

"Oh," her father said, pulling her into his arms. "Why is my lovely, beautiful Scallywag crying?"

"Oh, Daddy," Min Jade sobbed. "Thank you so much. Thank you so much."

"Min Jade," her mother was now hovering next to her. "What is it, darling? Are you okay? Darling, don't cry."

"I can't help it, Mom. I made it to thirty-two years old only because of you and Dad. And today I've got news. Excellent news."

"Good news? What's the good news, darling?" Jessica spun to face her daughter head-on.

"Today, we got news. Our department got a multi-year grant; twenty million of it was earmarked for my research. Dr. Winful is beyond himself. The old coot foolishly thinks I could be in the running for the Nobel."

"He said that? Oh, dear God. Oh, dear God!" Owen Jade said.

Her mother was now crying louder than Min Jade. "Is it possible, Min Jade?" Her mother's eyes glistened.

"Anything is possible, Mom…but I doubt it."

By the time they were done hollering, the women had to go and repair their make-up before leaving for dinner.

"That's not all, Mom," Min Jade said when they were in the bathroom. "We have tickets to see Min Lee Woo in concert. March 6th at Carnegie. He sent you a special ticket."

"Oh, happy day…Oh, happy day," her mother sang. Jessica Jade grabbed her daughter and turned her to face her. "You are my joy and my pride. I am so proud of you, Min Jade."

"Mom," Min Jade hugged her mother. She wanted to confess but instead said, "I love you."

"I know that, darling."

That night when Min Jade got home, a package was awaiting her. An Asscher-cut diamond necklace to match her bracelet. *"Happy Birthday to you, again, my darling-to-be. You are this precious to me. And you can't get mad because I've never been happier in my life. Want to share that joy with you.*

Thank you for sharing your birthday with me. Can I take it as a sign? Are we in love?"

Min Jade shook her head. Cocky damn Nigerian.

I'll wear it to your funeral, she texted.

Her phone rang.

"Now, is that a way to treat a guy trying so hard?"

"Thank you, Tunde. But it's a little extravagant. I'm sending it back—no need to woo me with stuff like this. I'm a physicist, not a Hollywood star. Where would I wear something like this? Let's make a pact. No gifts."

"Don't use that word 'woo' around me. I don't have to worry, do I?"

"Worry about what?"

"Keep it that way. And please don't send back the necklace. It's a bad omen in my culture. It matches you; don't you think?"

"No more gifts. Got it?"

"You are no fun. But okay."

Over the next five days, roses arrived on her desk at 10:00 a.m. with a note. *Thank you for being so gracious. These are categorically not gifts.* Then nothing for ten days. Then a sable. A sable! Was this man crazy? *I am still shivering from Ann Arbor. I'd like to keep you warm, if not in my arms, with this. I saw it while I was in Russia. Don't think what you're thinking—last gift. Scout's honor*, read the note. A few days later, he sent her a master recording of their gig at the Pig and Swine. *Not a gift, just memorabilia*, the sticky note said.

Min Jade went crazy. Did he understand anything? Did he understand her? She was a professor, for God's sake. What did money and things like a sable and diamonds matter? Her heart didn't feel settled. No wonder she'd steered clear of love for so long. Had she any sense, she should have crossed it altogether out of her life. Though it would never happen, it was clear that having Tunde as a lover would consume her. She dialed his number, which went straight to voicemail.

Ping: *If you send me another gift, I will stop talking to you! You don't get me, do you? At this rate, you won't ever qualify as a boyfriend!*

A text immediately came back.

Ping: *Done. Scout's honor. I'll get you because I have to be your boyfriend.*

She added a ringtone: Cocky Nigerian Physicist.

CHAPTER FOURTEEN

NEW YORK
MIN LEE WOO
MOTHER'S NOD

"MOM, WE ARE ONLY GOING TO BE IN New York for the weekend. Why do you need this much luggage?"

"Dear, I might still be recognized, you know. Carnegie was my home stage."

"And?"

Jessica Jade blinked her eyes. "And? What's that supposed to mean? We'll have to dress for breakfast, lunch, dinner, concert, shopping, and who knows what else. I might run into old colleagues or even set up lunch with a few. Do you want me to wear the same thing every day? From the looks of your luggage, you'll need something from mine!"

Min Jade, none too pleased, hoisted the oversized suitcase into the trunk of her Mini Cooper Roadster. They'd probably have to check the damn thing at the airport. Unlike most people, New York was not a place that excited Min Jade. Arguably, it was the world's most exciting city, with a level of kinetic energy rarely found elsewhere, if at all. A weekend visit was always enjoyable, but more than that had Min Jade scampering back to Ann Arbor.

Arriving at LaGuardia, they hopped a cab to the Viceroy on 57th Street somewhere between 6th and 7th avenues. With Carnegie Hall practically across the street, negotiating New York traffic was nonexistent, which is a relief. With Fifth Avenue a block away and Nobu almost next door, leaving the block was optional. The moment they'd decided to make the trip, Min Jade had made reservations at Nobu, her favorite restaurant. In London, she'd stayed at the Metropolitan in Hyde Park and had discovered Nobu there. Every night of her stay, she would dine there, so much that the chef began sending new menu items for her to try before putting them on the night's menu.

"I'm excited," Jessica Jade stood admiring the edifice she knew so well. It had been years since she'd performed in the Hall. Tonight, walking through the doors will bring back great memories. "It looks the same," she said. "I can't wait to hear Min Lee Woo play. You know it has one of the best acoustics of any concert hall."

"Let's check-in and then have lunch, Mom."

"Sounds good to me." They checked in and then went directly to the hotel restaurant.

"What would you like to do this afternoon, Mom?" Min Jade asked at lunch.

"I think I should take a little nap. I wanted to look good for old times' sake and for when we go to hear Mr. Woo," Jessica said, wondering why all of a sudden, she felt as though the wind had been knocked out of her. "I want to be completely alert."

"Great idea," Min Jade was relieved. Traipsing up and down Fifth Avenue would be *the* dreaded activity. After lunch, both women retired to a bedroom in their two-bedroom suite.

Min Jade, propped up in bed, was itching to call Min Lee, but distracting him before his recital was a bad idea.

At 6:00 p.m., when Min Jade came from her room, Jessica was already dressed to the nines, maybe even twelves. Min Jade hurried back inside to dress. Returning to the living room, she said, "I'm ready. Let's go a little early and miss the crowd."

Her Mother scrutinized her up and down, a disagreeable look on her face. "Min Jade, don't you have something more interesting to wear?" she asked as she looped diamond earrings through her lobes.

"What's wrong with what I have on?"

"It's lovely, dear, but it has no oomph. Let's see," she said, rummaging through her jewelry case. She pulled out a double strand of pearls with matching earrings. "This will bring it up a bit. The perennials," she clasped them around her daughter's neck. "Your Grandma's."

"Mom, I don't want to wear those old lady pearls." Min Jade said. "It certainly doesn't match my dress. The above the knee, fitted, squared-neck contraption with some kind of wings looked like a spaceship. It was blood red.

"But dear, that dress is—well—so you." Jessica could never fathom where the child's fashion sense came from. Of course, it could only be from the patterns in her head no one else could see because it certainly was not from her. "Let's see what else we can find," she searched through Min Jade's sparse closet. "How about this?" Jessica held up a chartreuse satin dress flared from the waist and had a wide black patent leather belt. "This is better. Let's see. I think this will go well with it," her mother handed her a thin gold necklace with a pearl teardrop pendant. The diamonds Tunde had given her would've been perfect. Min Jade slipped into the dress and kept on the gold necklace. It was close to the time for them to leave, and there was no point arguing with her mother and making matters worse. Now both women dressed to the nines exited the Viceroy and crossed the street to Carnegie Hall. The concert was sold out. Min Jade handed her tickets to the usher and was led to the center parquet, again eight rows from the stage.

"How classy of him," her mother whispered. "These are the best seats in the house. Do you think he'll meet us afterward?"

"I am sure of it," Min Jade said.

The Orchestra intro rose in fanfare. Min Lee Woo, in white tails this time, entered stage right. He bowed deeply to the audience, scanning the room as he always did. He knew precisely where Min Jade was, and when he bowed to the center aisle, his eyes rested on her, almost closing with his smile.

"It seems he is looking for you," Jessica nudged Min Jade.

"I doubt that, Mom."

"Yes, he is!"

The evening began with Bach's *Partita No.1 B-flat major,* followed by *Nocturne op.9. No 2,* then Chopin and Beethoven. Finally, it was time for his signature Schubert's *St*ändchen. Tonight, Min Jade heard something new in his playing; introspection, letting go, healing, reconciliation, and hope. The staccato opening of *Serenade* gave way to lyrical melodic legato. Min Jade found herself floating on calm waters as the work trilled into angelic beauty, then forte demanded a new emotion before again melting away to coda. By the time Min Lee reached Serenade's end, both her mother and she were choked with emotions. As always, Min Lee outdid himself. Critics often described his calmness, flair, verve, technique, and complete mastery of the piano as the "maturity of a great pianist and a sight to behold." Min Jade held her breath. Was it possible to love someone more?

"He is amazing. Simply amazing. Thank you," Jessica mouthed.

"He is, isn't he? Thank him when you see him," Min Jade noted the rapt look on her mother's face. She belonged here in this hall—every part of her being said so. Min Jade felt a stab of guilt for being the reason her mother was no longer on that stage.

"Mom, do you think you could go back to the stage?" Min Jade whispered.

"No, dear. Not after all these years." She was clapping enthusiastically.

The crowd's response, entirely different from that at The Royal Albert, drowned out her next question. It was wild and thunderous. Love, American style.

"We're going to meet him now?" Jessica asked as they stepped into the aisle.

"Yes. I think so."

Ji-Joon was waiting at the end of the row. "Min Jade," he bowed. "Min Jade's Mother, I presume," he repeated the bow. "We are so happy you made it. Min Lee would like me to take you to his green room. He has a couple of interviews. Is that okay with you?"

Jessica's hand tightened around her daughter's. "Of course, it is," she blurted out.

"Thank you, Ji-Joon. It would be an honor for my mom," Min Jade added.

The green room, set up with finger foods, spirits, wine, water, and juices, was quite plush as far as green rooms go. Ji-Joon entertained by answering a gazillion questions from her mother while waiting for Min Lee to join them. "How long have you been with him? What was it like playing for the Queen?" Min Jade nudged her mother to no avail. "How old was he when he started playing? Is he married?" This time there was no subtlety to Min Jade's jab! Ji-Joon was gracious and seemed to enjoy regaling her nosy mother with stories.

"Don't believe much of what he tells you," Min Lee stood just inside the frame of the door. Min Jade's heart skipped three beats; she counted them. Jessica Jade rushed over to Min Lee, enveloping him in a big embrace before planting a red lipstick kiss on his cheek. "Thank you. Thank you so much for tonight. You are the best pianist in the world."

Min Lee hesitated only for a minute before folding his arms around her. No one had embraced him this way since his mother had passed. *He could get used to this.* Min Lee settled into the embrace, now understanding the light this woman had passed on to her daughter. Over her head, he smiled at Min Jade, who seemed lost for words. "I am so grateful you came. Thank you for accepting my invitation and for your kind words. Are you sure you're not Min Jade's sister?"

"Oh, say that again," Jessica patted his hand.

Moving over to Min Jade, he clasped her hand warmly. "Happy birthday, darling," he whispered, and then in a normal tone, "I am delighted you came. You look amazing. How have you been?"

"Great. Really great. You look dashing yourself." Min Jade's heart skipped five beats this time and then began a mambo.

"I have made reservations at Nobu. Would you and your mother care to join us?"

"Wow. How coincidental. I've made reservations there, too."

"The minds of maladaptives," he winked. "Let me change and meet you there."

Ji-Joon escorted them to the waiting car.

"It's a block away, isn't it?" Min Jade said.

"Yes. But it's cold, and the car is waiting."

Jessica stepped into the car with flair, for a moment wondering just how far she might have gotten as an artist. Could she go back to the stage? It was only a fleeting thought, and she knew the answer. She had chosen her path, and there was not an ounce of regret. At the restaurant, Ji-Joon took their coats. "Go on up. I'll be there in a New York minute," he grinned.

"Oh my, Min Jade," Jessica held on to her daughter's hand as they climbed the stairs. "This is very special. These men are so cultured, and that Min Lee is such a handsome devil. What a stately man in person. What do you think of him?"

"He is a little unfathomable but very nice most of the time, except when we first met."

"Really? What happened?"

Just as Min Jade was about to give her mother edited details, Ji-Joon was headed over to the table. "Is this seating acceptable?"

"Everything is perfect." Jessica cooed.

They were settling in when Ji-Joon said, "Oh, here's Min Lee," he rose as the hostess escorted him to the table. Min Lee took a seat next to Min Jade. Ji-Joon then spoke to the waiter, and before long, plates of food began arriving. "Hope you don't mind. I thought a sampling of everything would be okay. Min Lee especially loves the Miso Chilean, Sea Bass."

It also happened to be Min Jade's favorite.

The dinner conversation centered on Min Lee asking Jessica Jade as many questions about Min Jade as Jessica had asked Ji-Joon about him. "You have to be very proud of your daughter."

Jessica Jade beamed. "She is our pride and joy."

Min Jade felt herself flushing. They were talking about her as though she wasn't there—some rare specimen in a museum.

"I have a burning question," Min Lee said. "Why Min, and why does everyone address Min by her first and last name?"

Jessica Jade was only too happy to answer. "I named her after a Korean pianist, Min Kim Ye-Kwon. Can you believe that, and here you are, another Min? When Min Jade was young, she had a habit of disappearing. We were always shouting, Min Jade, Min Jade, where are you? It stuck."

Next, the conversation turned to dreams. Had Min Lee fully realized his dream? Jessica wanted to know.

"I have accomplished a lot," he answered. "But there is always more to do. I dream of opening a music school and making classical music more accessible to everyday people." Then he did the unthinkable. "Min Jade gave me a great idea. I haven't told her yet, but when her band played at the Pig and Swine in London, I loved what they did with their song, *Revolution*. A classical number with beats. Really good. I've been experimenting with her idea."

"What band? Min Jade, you are in a band?" her mother asked.

Min Jade felt her spine rattling and shifted her position. Her little secret was exposed. What to do? "Not exactly, but sort of. It was just a lark we started in Austria. All the visiting physicists could play an instrument, and so we got together to play for fun."

Jessica Jade eyed her daughter. "Really? Then you should ask all of them to come and play for my charity. What is your band called, dear?" Her mother was asked.

"The Perfect Harmonies." Min Jade went on to explain the name.

"And that they are. The Russian physicist," Min Lee said, seemingly determined to laugh at her expense, "looks great in tights."

Min Jade glared at him and swallowed hard.

"Min Lee, would you consider my request, too?" Jessica asked. "I host an event every year for an organization that supports gifted children. They can be so fragile. I started it when Min Jade was six. Twenty-six years now, we've been up and running."

Min Jade gulped her wine. Not only was her mother freely giving away her age; worse, she made it seem like Min Jade was some kind of fragile freak! She'd murder her. What the hell did she mean by fragile! Gifted, maybe, but fragile?

"I hear you are a pretty good pianist, too," Min Lee said. "If you promise to play with me, I'll definitely do it."

Jessica did not hesitate. "Of course," she said with confidence, "I can always explain away my flaws when I mess up as really, I was an opera singer who played piano."

"Somehow, I doubt you'll mess up," Min Lee said. "Just a feeling."

You got that right. She'll be practicing every day from now until the event, Min Jade thought.

"I just can't imagine how proud your mother must be of you." Jessica took his hand across the table.

"I hope so. She passed away."

"I am so sorry dear one, but don't worry, Min Lee. Your angelic music reaches her in heaven. I'm sure of that."

For the first time, Min Lee looked forlorn. He pressed his lids together quickly to hold back the tears that threatened. "*Kamsahamnida*," he raised Jessica's hand to his lips. "Thank you so much."

"I hope you'll come and see me soon," Jessica Jade said.

"This will be my last concert for a while. I am moving back to Korea to be with my father for a while. He is not doing well, but I will make a special effort to see you the first opportunity I get. If you come to Korea before then, I'll take great care of you."

"Of that, I am sure," Jessica smiled, squeezing his hand. She adored him. "Anyway, it's been a long day for me. Do you mind if Ji-Joon escorts an old lady back to the hotel?"

"Mom, we can call it a night." Min Jade rested her napkin on the table.

"No dear, you visit some more with Mr. Woo. You don't see each other often, right?" It sounded to Min Jade like a fishing question.

"Not often enough," Min Lee said.

"Then stay and have dessert for me." Jessica beamed. *Did he like her daughter?*

Ji-Joon helped Jessica from her chair and escorted her down the stairs. Once Ji-Joon and Jessica left, Min Lee pulled his chair close to Min Jade, poured more wine, and handed her the dessert menu. "Your mother is amazing. I see where you get your warmth, and…" his hand did the duck beak dance. "Let's drink to our great collaboration for gifted, fragile children. Can you imagine what ours will be like? Love shot?" he lifted his glass.

"I hope Mom wasn't too inquisitive. She means no harm. She is so honored that you invited us," Min Jade allowed him to intertwine their arms as they drank from each other's glasses.

"Are you kidding? I am the one who is honored. It was like a memory for me. Warm, kind, loving memories, like being with my mom. They are hard to come by for a guy like me. But if you marry me, I can get another mom."

Min Jade sipped her wine. She didn't trust herself to speak. *Did he just say marry me?*

"You're not going to answer that, are you? I was hoping to convince you tonight, but I suppose since your mother's here,

I can't find out how love plays out tonight, can I?" He leaned over, and with not an ounce of public caution, kissed her. "I miss seeing you in my shirt."

"That was a while ago."

"Indelible memory. Since I can't have you for my dessert, shall we spend the day together tomorrow and find out? Will your mother let us?"

"She'll be more than glad to spend the day shopping without me, complaining every five minutes. I hate shopping. I'll see how she feels and give you a call."

"Ji-Joon's favorite pastime is shopping. The two of them would get along swell. Then we can be alone to see how close you are to marrying me."

Min Jade could see he was exhausted. "Let's call it a night. Tomorrow will speak for itself."

Min Lee pushed back his chair and pulled hers out as she stood. It was evident that credit cards had been given upon arrival, as no one came with a bill. Downstairs, he helped her into her coat, and as they walked the block back to her hotel with the car trailing behind them, he reached for her hand.

"Where are you staying in the city?"

"Tribeca."

"I love that part of the city."

"You can see it tomorrow," he kissed her passionately.

Min Jade looked at him, love beams shooting from her eyes. She'd never be able to say no to him as long as she lived.

Jessica Jade was nowhere near tired. She was propped up on the sofa, waiting expectantly for Min Jade.

"Min Jade," she said, as her daughter walked in, "you must marry this man."

Min Jade continued to hang her coat. This was the opportunity. "Does that mean I can spend the day with him tomorrow?"

"Of course. I don't need anyone to entertain me. I'll go shopping. Maybe I'll call a couple of my friends for dinner. Don't worry, and don't come back without a ring!" Her mother laughed. "He is such a catch, and he likes you."

"Mom, I have never heard…."

"I know. It's a feeling. Marry this guy."

"We're just friends."

"Then do something about that. And stop lying to yourself."

"Sure. I'll try. By the way, Ji-Joon will accompany you shopping tomorrow."

"Oh, my! This weekend is shaping up to be a memorable one."

Sunday Morning, a glorious, brisk, sunny day, Min Lee woke with a smile on his face. He was confident, with nary a doubt, that his maybe love was now really love. He wanted to take Min Jade to the jewelry store. He wondered if that would scare her. Was she as ready as he was? He paused, looking at the drip coffee splashing into the beaker. He was leaving soon, and he didn't know how long he'd be gone just yet. Maybe he should wait.

"Are you up," he said into the receiver.

Stretching like a cat, Min Jade felt alive and happy. "Yes, I'm up."

"Well, get dressed. My driver will be there in an hour. He'll drop Ji-Joon off to accompany your mom shopping and bring you here to me. I'll make you breakfast."

The loft was stunning. Blanched heated herringbone floors throughout and entirely surrounded by glass walls, boasted three bedrooms and the most fantastic kitchen. Min Jade walked around, noting every little detail. If this was his four times a year home, she wondered what his London apartment looked like!

"You like?" He encircled her from behind.

"I love, but why do you need all this when you only visit a few times a year?"

"Why not? I hate hotels! New York is one of my most frequent stops on tour."

"Indeed." Min Jade said, walking into the kitchen. "Shall I make breakfast?" She asked.

"Will it be edible?" Min Lee laughed. "No, darling, let me do the honors for you. On second thought, come over here and help me." Opening a closet, he pulled out an apron and slipped it over her head.

Out of nowhere, Min Jade began to cry.

"What's wrong? Did I do something wrong?" He was now standing in front of her, wiping her tears. *Uljima.* Don't cry," he pleaded.

Min Jade shook her head.

"Then, why are you crying?"

"Because I never believed I'd ever be this happy." Min Lee pulled her close to him, and she rested her head in the crook of his neck. "I was just waiting on the day when I would probably go mad again. That's why I've worked so hard…just in case… and now here you are."

"I told you silly. You had a stress-related break. You are not mad, mad. Just a little ole maladaptive. Just like me."

"Why did you become one of those?" she sniffled.

"It's the only way I could survive. After my mother died and I moved in with my father, my Stepmom really hated me for some reason I didn't understand. I tried so hard to please her, but I never could. Father was away very often, and though my brother and I were in the same house, my Stepmom always fostered a spirit of anger between us. At times we would hide away and play together, but mostly I had to entertain myself. I learned to love my own company and shied away from people, so my social skills were lacking, which I didn't mind at all. To be honest, I am petrified about going back home to be with Dad. In-Tak Hyun was unkind to me when I was there, and it seemed, after so many years, she's only gotten more bitter. But I have to put up with it."

"Why do you have to?" Min Jade pulled back to look at him. "No one should ever put up with abuse."

"Even though I was born out of wedlock, which in itself is an affront to Korean society, I am a love child, my dad's first child. I have to honor my filial duties. It's hard to understand, but as Korean culture dictates, it's a must. I thought I wasn't Korean anymore, but I guess I am."

"I see," Min Jade went from weepy to jovial. "Then make me a Korean breakfast, and we will figure out the best way to handle being home."

Min Lee laughed at how suddenly the tears had disappeared, and the problem-solving physicist returned. He walked by her toward the kitchen, kissing her lips lightly as he passed.

"So, Min Jade said, "Do you want breakfast now or after?"

"Definitely after," Min Lee swept her off her feet and carried her to bed.

CHAPTER FIFTEEN

LONDON
MIN JADE
TROUBLE

TUNDE'S OFFICE AT O. ENTERPRISES OVERLOOKED the Thames. He spent as little time there as possible. The business his father set up for him to run, a conglomerate of aviation, retail, and oil, was a royal pain. His title as chairman was fluff at best. With his father's imminent arrival, Tunde needed to be briefed on what was going on in the company, so, as usual, he'd called a meeting of his CEOs and senior staff who pretty much ran the business. With strict checks and balances, Tunde had little to worry about any shenanigans. He would be, as he always was, impressive when he gave his father a full report.

"Welcome, sir," Renee Offew, his assistant, greeted him. Renee was smart, educated, and efficient beyond words. A Nigerian expatriate who never seemed to have left Nigeria, she took his coat and valise, returning with a pot of tea she placed on his sideboard. "Everyone is assembled in conference room three. Your agenda," she said, handing him an iPad. "I'll let them know you'll be down in ten minutes."

"Thank you," Tunde said as he flipped through the report. "Is everything ready for father's arrival?"

"Oh, yes. The maids have been sent, the grocer will deliver on Friday, and the cars have been inspected. I got tickets for *Mama Mia* and arranged for them to have lunch with MP Abbott."

"What would I do without you, Renee?" Tunde buttoned his jacket and checked his cell before heading down to his meeting. Tunde, since early morning had been incessantly dialing Min Jade's number. Each and every time, it'd gone to voicemail. Impatience and annoyance sparked the headache he was now nursing. *Why have a damn cell phone?* Tunde collected his valise and headed to his office. He'd wanted to introduce her to his father, who was arriving Sunday. Should he just fly over to pick her up? She would be livid if he showed up on her doorstep again. What to do? What to do? He racked his brain. He looked at his phone, again. No call. No text. He tried Min Jade once more as he walked down the hall. His impatience was at a ten.

Three hours later, Tunde emerged well-versed on the latest projects of O. Enterprises. Alongside him was his old friend and CEO, Olganki Nimbutu. "Let's meet in my office around four today if you can fit it in. If not, I'll be in the office all week, so please keep me abreast of everything."

At 7:00 p.m. that night, his phone pinged: Is everything okay?

He texted back: Where have you been?

Ping: Oh, I was in New York for the weekend. Min Lee was here playing at Carnegie. I am going straight from the airport to my lab. What's up?"

Tunde was fuming.

Min Jade waited a few minutes for a return text. Instead, her phone announced Cocky Nigerian Physicist, Cocky Nigerian Physicist calling.

"Tunde. What's up?" she answered.

"Min Jade. One carries a cell phone so that they can be reached at all times. I have been calling."

"That's why I'm calling back. There were so many missed calls. I was in flight. Is everything okay?" She asked again.

"Everything is fine," Tunde huffed.

"So, what's with the twelve calls?"

Twelve! Tunde paused to calm himself. He didn't want to seem overly possessive or obsessive. "I called twelve times. Must have been pocket calls. Anyway, I want to see you. Can you come over?"

"Over where?" Min Jade asked. If he were in Ann Arbor again, she would not be pleased.

"To London. For the weekend."

"You're joking, right?"

"I am not. My father is coming, and I'd like you to meet him."

"Tunde," Min Jade said.

"I'll send my plane for you Friday after work. You'll be in London Saturday morning, and I'll send you back Sunday night. How's that?"

Min Jade couldn't believe her ears. What on earth was this man thinking?

"Tunde," she leveled her voice. "Why do I need to meet your father?"

"Don't act daft, Min Jade. Why does an able-bodied man want a woman to meet his father? Aren't you thinking of being my girlfriend?"

Min Jade sat on the sofa. She had to choose her words carefully as Tunde was a man used to getting what he wanted. The rare collector watch, the chalet in Switzerland, the private jet, the desired woman? Min Jade cleared her throat. "Tunde. I'm so flattered, but when did I become your girlfriend? I am afraid I can't...."

"There is no such word as can't. Can't or won't? You just went to New York to see Min Lee Woo!" He threw a cushion across the room.

Min Jade redirected the conversation. "My mother wanted to see him."

"Can't or won't?" he snapped.

"Can't," she said calmly.

As soon as he hung up from Min Jade, Tunde dialed his phone. "Renee," he said, trying to keep a leveled voice, "I need you to locate the pianist, Min Lee Woo. Find out where he lives and when he's back in London."

"Yes, sir."

Keep your enemies close, Tunde thought as he grabbed his keys. Why was she lying to him? This woman was driving him crazy. He needed some company tonight. Who would pleasantly fill up sometime? He scrolled through his phone. To be honest, he didn't feel enamored by anyone, so he called up Albert, and they headed to the pub.

"So, you're telling me you really like Min Jade?" Albert's cheeks were red from one too many whiskies.

"Like I've never liked anyone before."

"So, what's the problem?"

"I think she likes Min Lee."

"She said that?"

"No. She said her work was her priority, but I get the feeling he's competition."

"And what do you want to do about it?"

"What should I do?"

"If she likes Min Lee and not you, nothing."

"If I arrange to work on a special project with her, we'll be together all the time. I can woo her away from that, Woo?"

"Bad idea. I don't think you want to be in a competitive environment like that with Min Jade. If you're not as good as she is, which you might not be, you'll get your feelings hurt. Plus, you have no reason to think she likes Min Lee Woo."

Tunde stiffened. Him, not as good? Was Albert crazy? He was a man used to victory in everything he did! Not good enough? The thought irked him in a big way.

"If I were you, I'd just let it all play out," Albert continued.

Tunde thought he'd have a coronary. "Do I look like someone who gives up on what I want?" he gruffed.

"Just saying." Albert downed the rest of his drink.

Tunde texted Renee: Where the hell is Min Lee Woo's details?"

Ping: "Sir, we have been unable to complete that task."

Min Jade needed to have a heart-to-heart with Tunde, but she couldn't interrupt her blissful moment with that conversation. Trundling to her bedroom, all she could think of was the incredible weekend she'd just spent with Min Lee. Their relationship had reached a new level, and in the magical moment, she'd given herself entirely to him. Her Mother's consent had given their love even more vigor, and they'd officially declared themselves coupled. Min Lee had been right all along. Never would she be able to forget the man who'd taken her virginity and now who wanted her to be his wife. Min Jade undressed and headed to the shower, her mind filled with the memory of Min Lee Woo's body, making her lose reason. Did they have a chance of making it? Min Jade hated the distance between them and feared that all she'd have to look forward to for a while was their never-ending parting. Her work, her first love, would take care of that, she was sure. Still, she wanted it all.

Soon enough, as she expected, life intruded on her obsession. On Monday morning, when Min Jade got to her office, she was greeted by a morose Julian. He was avoiding eye contact as he wrung his hands together and gave her the news, she was sure he dreaded telling her.

"Dr. Jade, I have something I need to discuss."

"What is it, Julian?"

"I need to take some time off."

"Now? Julian, why would you do this now? You are so close to graduating?"

"I just need a break. I really do. I've been climbing the walls lately, and I can't sleep."

Min Jade understood. She had been there a dozen times. She wondered if Julian had someone to hold his space. Had it not been for her mother's constant watch and care of her 'gift of madness,' she too might have quit. But how could he quit when they were so close? What would it mean for their progress? Julian was her ace, and she had no one in mind to replace him, but she had to let him go. It might have been all her fault too. They'd been pushing hard, working overtime, sometimes not even taking lunch breaks.

"I tell you what. Take the semester off. Going on sabbatical was great for me. It gave me such a new viewpoint on life. Go backpacking around the world. Think of nothing or no one but you. I'll hold your space, Julian. I'll handle it with Chair Winful, and we'll pay your stipend for the semester. Don't worry. I'll cover you."

"Thank you, Professor Jade. Thank you so much."

It was the most inopportune time to lose her trusted assistant. The closer they came to what Min Jade thought could be a breakthrough, the harder they'd worked. She should have been more mindful of his mental state. Min Jade dragged herself to Winful's office.

"What's with the maudlin state?"

Flopping down into her favorite chair, she said, "I think Julian is having a break. I think he needs to take the semester off without penalty. Please."

"A byproduct of genius, I suppose."

Julian was indeed a budding genius, Min Jade concurred. He'd been the only person to last in her lab.

"What will you do now? We are so close?" Winful eyes twitched ever so slightly. He wanted this prize, but he could not say no. Min Jade would never forgive him!

"I'm not sure but…but he needs to rest."

"Okay…okay…." Winful offered her his calming tea. His portly body swayed from side to side as he paced. Abruptly he stopped. "Why not have Ansel's protégée fill in. What's his name again? He's pretty good. He's been working over at his lab and putting in some time with Yanovsky."

"Chambers. No way. That man gives me the creeps."

"Min Jade! This is not like you."

"I'm just tired. Maybe I should take a break, too. Let me give it some thought, and I'll get back to you, but I'd rather like to have a woman. There is Sarah Lightly."

"I can't give up on this prize. You know that, right?"

"What prize is that?" Min Jade said, hugging her relentless professor. It was a weary Min Jade who slumped into her bed at 8:00 p.m. No sooner than her head hit the pillow, her phone rang. She debated answering but finally gave in to its insistence. It was the Cocky Nigerian Physicist, and he'd only call back until he reached her. "Yupp Tunde."

"Why do you sound so tired?"

"Because I am. What's up, Tunde?"

"So, I have a few days off. I think it's a perfect time for us to take a trip to Noumea."

"You mean New Caledonia?"

"Yup. Whatcha say?"

"I say I can't go to New Caledonia, or for that matter, any-where anytime soon."

"Why is that?"

Tunde, I can't get into that right now. I'm too beat tonight. Let's talk tomorrow," Min Jade ended the call, turned off the phone and was asleep before she could raise her arm to put her cell phone on the nightstand.

CHAPTER SIXTEEN

SOUTH KOREA
MIN LEE WOO
BUSINESSMAN

"HY SOO, I'VE LIVED WITH YOU FOR thirty years, knowing I could never own your heart. Do you know how painful that is? All I've ever had of you, is our son. Seung-Le has been by your side all these years. Why? Why are you bringing Min Lee back? Do you still want me to compete with a woman, who even in death, controls your heart? How could you ask this of me?"

"In-Tak Hyun! Stop this rant. What do you want from me? I let you send Min Lee away. Wasn't that enough? Can't I be with my son in my twilight years? Is that too much to ask?"

"You have a son right here in Korea."

"I need to have Min Lee with me. I promised his mother on her deathbed; I would make sure he was not alone."

"What about me? I've been alone for thirty years!'

"Mother." Seung-Le's voice came floating up the stairs. "Are you up there?"

"This is not over," In-Tak Hyun said as she slammed the door on her way out of Hy Soo's study. Halfway down the stairs, she met Seung-Le.

"*Oma*." Seung-Le hurried toward his mom. "What's with the bad attitude?" He hated when his mother was in a bad mood. Now was not the time to tell her he'd gotten engaged to Choi.

"Your brother is coming home."

"And?"

"Seung-Le, I am warning you, don't get too close to him."

"*Eomeoni*, why do you dislike Min Lee so much?"

"Don't listen to me, and I'm sure you'll find out!" she huffed past him.

From the day Min Lee had arrived in Seoul, his mother had spent every waking moment creating a rift between him and his brother. He never understood why. He'd been a lonely child, and the truth was, he'd been overjoyed to have a big brother. When Min Lee left for London, he'd missed his *Hyung* a great deal, though he never dared breathe a word of it. Seung-Le followed his mother down the stairs, but she went into her bedroom and slammed the door. He wanted to know why his mother hated Min Lee so much. His mother, who loved him no matter what he did, must have a valid reason. Still, he loved the idea that Min Lee was coming back, but he'd watch his back, just in case.

As much as his father pleaded for him to move into the family house, Min Lee got a flat in Gangnam. Overlooking the Han River, the spacious flat boasted amazing views of Seoul's skyline. Gangnam, which was nothing but wasteland when he was a child, had sprung up as the cool and hip place to be after the 1998 Olympics. Now taken over by K-pop idols, it wasn't just Gangnam that impressed Min Lee; it was the fact that Seoul had transformed itself from a third-world country to one of the most prosperous in only a few decades and one of the most high-tech countries in the world. With a booming export economy and cultural power, it was a great time to be a proud Korean. His father lived on the north side of town where the super-wealthy Koreans, who'd seen their fortune grow exponentially with the country's success, looked down on Gangnam as vulgar and *nouveau riche*. Yet, it was their *chaebol* children who had created the Gangnam style. Gangnam was where change was happening, and Min Lee liked change. Well, moderate change. Yes, he was a classical pianist, but he wasn't a dinosaur. Maybe *Hallyu* culture could bring something new to his work like Min Jade's band did with *Revolution*.

Min Lee pulled a denim shirt from his closet. Living in the house of horror, as he'd called it, would've forced him to endure the slights and battles In-Tak Hyun was bound to wage daily. He was here for his father, and no matter how much angst that may cause her, he was as much his father's son as Seung-Le.

"Ready?" Ji-Joon asked.

"Yup." Min Lee looped his belt. He and Ji-Joon were setting out to transform their adjoining flats. The first order of business was a visit to Nagwon music. Ji-Joon, far more interested in checking out girls than pianos, insisted on taking the train. As they headed to Jongno 3-ga Station, Ji-Joon kept jabbing Min Lee in the side. "Isn't she's a looker? Man, I feel so at home."

The fool was bowing in every direction. Min Lee couldn't help but burst into laughter. But he understood cultural identity. No matter where people find themselves on earth, home is always home. Here, he and Ji-Joon were part of the middling crowd. In London, they were two guys from Chinatown!

"Hey, are you checking out the babes?" Ji-Joon elbowed Min Lee again.

Min Lee ignored him. Thirty minutes later, they pulled into their stop. The aroma of food smacked them in the face.

"Hungry, boss man?"

"Whatever they are cooking smells delicious," Min Lee nodded.

"Ramen, mate. Let's go," Ji-Joon pulled Min Lee into one of the many noodle shops.

"Are you trying to kill me with MSG?"

"Why not die happy," Ji-Joon pushed him into a chair and ordered two ramens. Two steaming bowls arrived post-haste. Ji-Joon shoved chopsticks after chopsticks of hot noodles into his mouth, now and then lifting the bowl to his face to slurp broth. Min Lee followed suit.

"This is good," Min Lee said, thinking of the ramen shop his mother had loved.

"What did I tell you?"

They each ordered another bowl before heading to Nagwon. Nagwon Music Hall was massive and filled with every instrument known to man. They visited a few of the stores which specialized in pianos. Min Lee, now a local celebrity, was welcomed with fanfare.

"Try this one." A bespectacled proprietor pointed to an ebony Fazioli. Min Lee played a few bars on each of the instruments and was surprised by the sounds of the Japanese pianos. He was impressed with the vibrant sounds of the Yamahas and Kawais. They had sure come a long way. Naturally, however, he chose a mahogany Steinway Model B. Once his decision was made, Min Lee left Ji-Joon to haggle with the shopkeeper and arrange for delivery.

"*Oppa Gangnam style*," Ji-Joon, doing a whipping Psy movement, rejoined Min Lee outside the store. The silly song had taken the world by storm, and once started, would stay in the head for hours. "That was heady. Do you know how much we saved because I'm the best haggler on earth?"

Min Lee began heading toward the train station.

"No, No, No…," Ji-Joon said, grabbing his arm. "We've got enough dukas to get our Gangnam style on."

Humoring his I-am-really-happy-to-be-home buddy, Min Lee dutifully followed Ji-Joon from one shop to the next. "We can't live here looking like Brits," he was pulling clothes from racks, "they'll laugh us out of court. What about this?" he held up a god-awful outfit. "And, my friend, we'll need new haircuts to go with our new life."

With bags of new attire in hand, Min Lee again traipsed after Ji-Joon to a men's spa. Dear God, sometimes he couldn't tell if the men in Korea were men. They were as coiffed, pampered, and stylish as the women. When the stylist said they were done, Min Lee touched the spiky hair jutting from his scalp. It felt stiff and dangerous. What had they done to him?

Hy Soo's Estate

A slap landed across his face. Seung-Le stared at his mother in disbelief. "When are you going to grow up?" In-Tak Hyun said, rubbing the sting from her hand.

"*Eomeoni!*"

"Do you think I endured all these years with your father as a second fiddle woman because I wanted to? No! I did it for you, for you to take your rightful place as the head of Soo Industries and erase that bastard once and for all. Not only are you running around with a gold digger who you want to make your wife, but you're playing nice-nice to the child I got rid of, handing you Soo Industries on a platter. Now you are handing it right back to him. Not over my dead body. Don't you see what's happening, Seung-Le? He is taking what's yours – your father, your inheritance, and maybe even your lousy girl – who can't stop batting her eyes every time he is in the room. If you don't want to see me die, use your power for once. No one cares about a stupid, rich playboy."

When Min Lee walked in, Seung-Le's loud voice could be heard from his mother's study. Suddenly an irate Seung-Le, holding his cheek, barged into the foyer from the study. "*Abeoji* is in his study," Seung-Le said, brushing past Min Jade.

"Is he okay?"

"He's fine."

"So why are you so upset?"

"Nothing of concern. Just family drama. You know we Koreans love drama."

"*Hyung!*"

"Dad's waiting for you." Seung-Le bolted out the front door.

"But I thought we were going fishing."

The door slammed, and Min Lee heard Seung-Le's car engine roar to life. *What now?*

In-Tak Hyun was glaring at him from the top of the stairs. She was in an even fouler mood than Seung-Le. "Over my dead body," she shouted and disappeared back into her study.

Min Lee went to his father's study, which was also on the ground floor but at the opposite end of the house. *I guess they need distance between each other.* He knocked on the door. His father didn't look too well when he entered. "*Abeoji.* What's going on?"

"Hello, son. *Anj-a.* Sit down."

Min Lee took a seat opposite his father. There were papers and a signature stamp laid out before him. "In-Tak Hyun is upset about some decisions I've made."

"I see. What decisions did you make?"

"When your mother and I were at Seoul National University-College of Music, we often dreamed about creating an industry for young artists. So many people didn't have the opportunity to be where we were. In fact, only a few could hope, even on scholarship. Your mother always felt it was unfair, so I built Soo Industries because of her. In-Tak Hyun has always opposed the idea, but she supported me despite her objections when the business took off. I have decided to leave you in charge of Soo Industries, and this has upset her very much."

"But surely you can understand that, *Abeoji?*"

"I do understand. I understand that I let her manipulate me into sending you away. I want you to return to your rightful place, *Adeul,* and I want to do right by your mom. I'm sorry that I didn't protect you better, son, but it's time for things to be righted. I don't care how mad In-Tak gets. This business was built for your mother, and you are its rightful inheritor."

"Me? *Abeoji,* I have no clue how to run a business. I'm an artist!"

"Don't worry. It wasn't easy for me at first, as I, too, am just a musician, but I found the right people to stand by me, and sure enough, In-Tak was one of them. She feels I should make Seung-Le the head of Soo Industries. It's not that I don't want him to be involved. I very much want that, but he is immature and spoilt, and I can't run the risk of having what I spent years building as a temple to your mother destroyed by frivolity. Son, I don't know how much longer I have, but I'd like you to take over Soo Industries now." His father seemed weary. Fighting with his wife was not helping.

"Father, I'm flattered you think so highly of me. I'm even more grateful that you honored my mother in such an auspicious way, but I'm simply a musician. I know nothing about business. Soo Industries has gone way beyond a shrine to

Mother. It requires expert leadership. Rightfully, *Abeoji,* Soo Industries, belongs as much to Seung-Le, not just to me. I am good knowing your noble intent, and that, Father, makes me happy and grateful. Why cause all this for no real reason?" Min Lee hadn't known the story behind Soo industries. That his father's intent was for him to run a business was entirely out of the question. How could he say no to his mother's legacy, but how could he say yes?

"Soo Industries belongs to Seung-Le as much as it does to you, that's true. Seung-Le can hold any position at Soo, but you must be its rightful heir. You can see for yourself he is not ready. Please grant me this request, Min Lee."

"*Appa.* I can't give up my career. Moreover, I don't want to. The life I want to choose for myself does not include Korea or Soo Industries."

"You can continue your life any way you want. As you see, we have great people working for us, so you don't ever have to give up your career. Just be involved as the figurehead and in the strategic end of the business."

"That would be very hard for me. I travel nine months out of the year. You know that."

"As I said, son, it's strategic. Please. Please, let me be at rest. When I meet your mother, I want to tell her I kept my promise."

"*Abeoji.*"

"Please, son."

Everyone, it seemed, knew his weak spot.

After much back and forth, the paperwork was done. Hy Soo opened a bottle of whiskey. "We must drink to this," he handed his son a glass. "Thank you for coming back, Min Lee."

Min Lee raised his glass, none too pleased with this coercion. He knew it was the right thing to do; it honored his father and mother, but he was downright annoyed with Korean filial responsibilities. If only he hadn't listened to Ji-Joon about coming to Korea in the first place.

"Promise me one more thing?" Hy Soo slyly added. "Your mother would scold me if I didn't try."

"What now, *Abeoji*?"

"You are thirty-five. Isn't it time to think of a family? About having an heir?"

"You've had your wish for today, Dad." Min Lee said.

Soo Headquarters

Against his better judgment, Min Lee reported to Soo headquarters. As his car pulled up to the massive glass building with *Soo Industries* emblazoned in silver, there was a line of employees waiting. He had no idea why. As he alit, everyone bowed at a forty-five-degree angle.

"Welcome, sir," they said in unison. Min Lee looked behind him to see who they were greeting. There was no one but his driver and him. They were bowing to him. "*Kamsahaminda.*" Min Lee bowed, hastily moving toward the revolving door. The expanse of his father's holdings was unknown to him.

"Good morning, sir," the greetings now came from bowed men and women lining his path to the elevator. While waiting for the elevator, Min Lee took in the opulence. When did all this happen? He couldn't wait to tell Min Jade about this. It felt like a scene from a Korean drama. He stifled a smile. Min Lee pushed the button to the 35th floor, where his father's office was located. Walking into the massive, well-appointed reception area, he approached the receptionist. She immediately rose, bowed, and dialed the phone. "Straight ahead, Sir." She knew who he was, not surprising since his face had been plastered all over the media.

Min Lee tapped on the glass door of his father's office and entered.

"Min Lee," his father rose to greet him. "*Anj-a.* Sit."

An assistant he hadn't seen appeared out of nowhere with a tray of tea.

"*Aboeji.* I have no idea about all this. It's a massive operation."

"It'll take some time to get used to all this, but you will grasp everything soon enough. I promise. A few people from senior management will be here soon to explain things. In the meantime, take a look at the stack of papers on my desk. Let's talk about them when I get back. I have a doctor's appointment." Hy Soo had been increasingly nauseous the past few weeks. He'd tried to ignore it, but today he felt especially poorly.

"Is everything okay, *Abeoji?*"

"Yes, yes. Fine. Just a routine check-up," he lied.

Min Lee felt genuine distress. Did his father think he'd be able to take over the business? He wasn't even planning on being in Korea long enough to learn the ropes! Flipping through the papers on his father's desk, there were several artist's contracts to be reviewed, including Choi Shin and his eyes glazed over at the gibberish. As far as Min Lee was concerned, appeasing his father had been a bad idea. As soon as humanly possible, he'd put a team in place and return to London.

"*Hyung,* busy?" Seung-Le pushed his head around the door. His office, which he rarely visited as Min Lee understood, was next to their father's. "I heard you'd be here this morning."

"Come on in. Dad went to a doctor's appointment. He said a few suits will be here to explain everything. I'd like it if you stuck around for that. I was just looking over some contracts, and I can't make head or tails of them." Min Lee said.

"There are lawyers for that."

"I didn't realize your fiancée was signed with us." Min Lee handed Seung-Le a contract.

"Yeah. I have big plans for her. She is new to us, and we're getting ready to do her first album. She really wants to do this gig with you, so that's why I'm here. I think it would be great for her debut. Would you do that for your brother?"

"Seung-Le."

"She is amazing. Really, she is."

"I know her talent…."

"Please, *Hyung*."

"I've been giving this some thought. I've decided to do a Korean Album with Dad. She could play with us on that."

"Don't think that's what she had in mind, but it's a start. She's having a party soon. Come through and let's discuss it," he handed Min Lee an invitation.

"Aren't you going to wait for the suits?"

"No. I have other plans right now. Have fun."

As Seung-Le headed for the door, Ji-Joon walked into the office. "Ji-Joon," Seung-Le said, slapping hands. "Good to see you again. How are you, *chingu*?"

"Great. You, my friend?"

"Glad big bro is here to let me off the hook. If you're not careful, your star musician might become CEO of Soo Industries."

"Could be."

"Let's get together over drinks soon."

"You got it." Ji-Joon stepped aside to let Seung-Le exit.

Min Lee handed the tedious contracts to Ji-Joon. He'd never read a contract in his life, not even his own. "What does this say?"

"It says contract."

Min Lee was about to swat him when the suits came in. They bowed and proceeded to explain what his job would be.

The thing was, they were mostly addressing Ji-Joon. "Seems like Dad recruited you, too?" Min Lee whispered to Ji-Joon.

"Yup. I'm afraid so. I'm to be your right-hand man. Lucky you."

For about two hours, they were briefed, and then they reviewed contracts of upcoming artists. Min Lee comprehended less than before they started.

CHAPTER SEVENTEEN

MIN JADE
ANN ARBOR, MICHIGAN
SPARK

IT WAS 6:00 P.M. IN ANN ARBOR. Min Jade dialed Tunde's number.

"Hello."

"Hey. Sorry about the other day. I was a wreck."

"How come?"

"My lab researcher is taking a break. Just when I think I'm onto something real—such a bummer. There aren't too many people as good as Julian or whom I trust. The whole thing wiped me out. Anyway, what's up?"

"What's your Chair saying about that? He seems gung-ho on having you running the race for the prize."

"Dr. Winful isn't saying it, but I know he's having conniptions. I never listen to him much about his prize obsession, but I, too, wanted to get to the finish line. I believe we are so very close. Ah well, I'll get there, but it'll be more definitely challenging working on my own."

"Can I offer help? I don't love Ann Arbor, but as I told you, I'll be there for you always. With me, you will never be on your own."

"Don't even joke about it."

"Who's joking. I'm not joking. I mean it."

"Wouldn't that be great if you did? Unfortunately, I don't think the university will allow such a thing."

"Why not if they want to be first? You and I, as a team, are a definite first. You do realize how brilliant I am, right?"

"You are one cocky, brilliant man, I know."

"I told you, Min Jade, I'd move heaven and earth for you. I'll come to Ann Arbor and help you. *I* can certainly be your assistant researcher."

"Really, Tunde. You are such a joker!"

"Min Jade, I'm deadly serious. In a week, I can clear my calendar. I haven't done anything exciting in a while. It'd be electrifying, no pun, to be in a lab again. We could knock this thing out in a jiffy and make matter from nothing!"

"Thanks, Tunde. That's sweet of you. I'll check with Dr. Winful, though it's doubtful."

"Let me have the conversation with Dr. Winful. He won't say no, I promise."

"Sure, I'll ask him to get back to you." Min Jade humored him.

"That doesn't sound convincing, Min Jade. All joking aside. I can really help you."

Min Jade felt choked up. He was serious. "But I truly don't know how that would be possible. Winful would have to…."

"Everything is possible. Just let me talk to Winful."

And so it was. A week later, Tunde didn't just arrive in Ann Arbor. He arrived with an entourage. His cook, his dresser, and his housekeeper! The house he rented in Burns Park was big enough for a family of twelve. Min Jade doubled over in laughter as she watched him instruct his staff where to put things. "You're funny beyond words," she was shaking her head in disbelief as the movers changed around the bed for the fourth time.

"Why?"

"What's with all this?" She gestured, her hand sweeping the room.

"We are going to be working tirelessly, aren't we? Who needs to think about clothes and food, and housekeeping? Maybe you should move in with me so they could take care of you, too."

"Thanks. I'll manage." She couldn't stop laughing.

"You won't be laughing soon. I *am* no joke."

Ming Jade was all choked up. His irreverent and persistent friend always seems to be there for her in her crisis moments. This, though would not earn him a boyfriend status, would earn him her eternal loyalty and her friendship for life.

To Min Jade's surprise, Tunde, the wealthy, frivolous, and seemingly charming man was gone the moment they entered the labs. Incredibly focused, detailed, and a quick study, he became so relentless that Min Jade felt incompetent in her own lab. When he took to bossing her around or scolding her for some reason or the other, she had to wonder whose lab it was! Tunde grasped things at such lightning speed that within days, it felt as though he'd been in her lab for a lifetime. Min Jade loved the feeling of kinetic energy that swirled between them. They were superb together—professionally.

"It's not that your experiment isn't showing pairing. It just needs to be more detectable. Let's try calculating every variable in the hohlraum under different conditions before we release the photons."

"That could take weeks," Min Jade protested.

"So?"

"So, time is not on our side."

"Neither is stupidity."

For weeks they worked side by side, countless hours. Min Jade found herself staring at Tunde more often than she cared to. He was dazzlingly brilliant. Why, she wondered, was he not actively pursuing experimental physics? He would have been a formidable contender. Feeling closer to him, Min Jade invited him to her home on their one free Sunday, and they sat around after dinner doing puzzles. On their first free Saturday, he accompanied her to the farmer's market, where they guzzled coffee and ate pecan pie.

Tunde felt good having Min Jade by his side. This, he thought, could be enough for him. This simple life he was experiencing with Min Jade made him feel more alive in every way. He'd never done a puzzle in his life!

Winful, who had taken quite a shine to Tunde, began inviting him to his office as much as he did Min Jade. They were sitting in his office when the professor announced, "Today, you both need to take a break. You are making great progress, no?" He couldn't hide his glee. "No need working yourselves to the bone."

"But we're close." Min Jade's excitement lit up the room.

"Exciting indeed," Winful rubbed his hands together, "but Min Jade, your mother, has been calling me to find out why she hasn't seen you in the past few weeks. You know what that means."

It was true. She had neglected her parents, not even a phone call for the first two weeks when they'd worked at a frantic pace. That he could only be with her for a month, and his imminent return to London was drawing nigh, he wanted them to have a real breakthrough before his departure though he'd promised to return after attending his business.

"I second that, Professor Winful. We could use a break, and I think it's time for me to meet the Jades, anyway."

"Jessica has instructed me to have you both at dinner tonight," Winful slyly slipped in. "And you know what'll happen if I disobey Jessica."

Min Jade groaned. "I sure do."

"Well, old girl," Tunde said, rising, "seems we have a free afternoon. Freedom, he sang Freedom. Come on. I'll take you home. What time is dinner, Dr. Winful?"

"7:00 p.m. sharp."

"Yes, sir," Tunde saluted, and Min Jade felt a little peeved he and Winful had become such friends. "Shall I pick you up on the way?" Tunde asked Min Jade as they walked to the parking lot.

"Nope. I'll see you there and, Tunde, please don't start with any craziness about girlfriend this and that. My mother is a Tiger Mom, and Jamaican to boot, and my father is a very conservative lawyer."

"*Chu*," he sucked air between his teeth. "I am from Africa, man. What's the address?"

Tunde dressed with casual flare. It took him over one hour to put his "casual outfit" together. Aware he needed to make an impact but appear laid-back at the same time, he lightly dabbed his throat with Eros, not too over the top. Checking his whiskey collection, Tunde chose two bottles of Glenmorangie Signet, also not over the top. For Min Jade and her mother, Tunde chose a Min Lee double CD for Jessica Jade; he'd heard he was her favorite. And for Min Jade, he chose a one-thousand-piece puzzle of Innsbruck. Satisfied he'd covered all bases; Tunde even drove himself to the Jade's lovely house. Cursing up to the lengthy driveway's brick entrance, Tunde checked himself in the rearview mirror one last time.

He was a rather dashing man. Tonight, for sure, he needed to kill his competition.

An older Min Jade answered the door to his knock.

"Hello there, Professor Tunde. Welcome. I'm Jessica Jade." The woman looked him up and down, her wheels of judgment working overtime.

"Mrs. Jade. It's a great pleasure to meet you. Thank you for inviting me to your home."

"You didn't have much trouble finding the place, did you?" The man was impeccable, and Jessica Jade knew good breeding when she saw it.

"Not at all. I'm an Ann Arborite these days, Mrs. Jade."

"So I hear. It is a lovely place, isn't it?"

Tunde begged to differ, but he vehemently agreed. Ann Arbor was a yawn.

Entering the beautifully appointed house, noting it was lovely but too small, conservative, and English-chintz for his liking, he removed his shoes. It was a far cry from his world, but he did not feel out of place.

"Min Jade is in the kitchen with her dad and Professor Winful. This way."

Tunde followed.

"So, you are the man keeping my daughter enslaved?" Owen Jade, a broad smile on his face, hand outstretched, approached Tunde. Tunde clasped it in a warm but solid embrace, returning a megawatt smile. "Thank you for being here. We are most grateful. Min Jade is so very complimentary of you. A first, I must say."

Min Jade blushed. "Dad, stop with the nonsense!"

"That compliment is not an overstatement," Winful said.

"It's an honor for me to work with your amazing daughter, all thanks to Dr. Winful here."

Winful nodded, then ported himself over to the bar. "Would you like a drink, Tunde?"

"Ah, yes, thank you," Tunde handed the bag of gifts to Min Jade. "I hope you like them."

"We love gifts, don't we, Winful?" Owen Jade chuckled.

"Without a doubt."

Min Jade shook her head at the two old friends who always carried on like this when they were together. From the bag, she pulled out two bottles of whiskey. "I can only imagine who these are for. Dad. Professor," she handed them each a bottle.

"Well, my, my," Owen nodded to Winful in apparent approval.

"Thank you, young man. You nailed it. Didn't he, Owen?"

"He sure did. And since you were offering drinks, let's drink yours first."

"Drink?" Winful chortled. "It's way too expensive to drink."

Amid hearty laughter, Min Jade pulled out a double CD of Min Lee's Korean recordings. Her heart fluttered for a minute. *Why would Tunde buy her such a gift? Wasn't it a bit cruel?* She flashed him a look, and he hunched his shoulders, a mischievous look on his face.

"Ah," Tunde took the CD and handed it to Jessica. "I understand he is one of your favorites. It's his new work. It's experimental."

"How amazing is this? Did Min Jade tell you we went to see him at Carnegie Hall? Isn't he incredible? I'm glad you're a fan."

"I hear you are not so bad yourself on the ivories." *I am no fan of that Korean Dragon. I am his biggest rival for your daughter's heart.*

"I can hold my own," Jessica said.

What a snake oil charmer, Min Jade thought as she reached into the bag for the last gift. She was floored by this thoughtful

Tunde, who was not such a bad guy after all. As he was chatting away with her mother, who seemed taken by the God of Good Looks, Min Jade observed him. Was her heartwarming up to him, or was it the energy of working together? How can anyone be so confident, charming, rich, and brilliant simultaneously? "Drink?" Min Jade repeated, interrupting her unsettling thought, as well as the mutual admiration society who were rapt with Tunde's story. Winful, who had forgotten he'd offered drinks in the first place, piped up. "Yes, please, of course."

"I'll help," Jessica dragged Min Jade behind her. "He is delightful. So cultured," she whispered. "I guess when it rains, it pours. He likes you. I can tell. What are you going to do? How will you choose?"

Min Jade pulled glasses from the cupboard. "I won't."

"Well, there is a saying, love the one you're with or be with the one you love!"

"Mother! You are so fickle."

"I'm joking, dear. It's just nice to see two wonderful men in your life. Two worthwhile men. I think it's high time we developed those skills in you, don't you? The other glasses, dear. Right cupboard."

Who cares about glasses? Min Jade huffed as she fetched "proper" glasses from the right cupboard.

Monday morning, Min Jade arrived at the lab very early, only to see Tunde already working. "Feeling the vibe this morning?"

"Yup. But what are you doing here so early?" Min Jade asked.

"Today feels like a breakthrough day! The ancestors were restless last night."

"Huh?"

"Never mind."

"Funny, I felt the same vibe this morning. Something kept saying we were going to have good luck today."

"Maybe it's the power of kinetic love?" Tunde winked.

"There you go again," Min Jade rose from her chair and went to look at the experiment setup.

"Really, Min Jade, you are no fun. Anyway, I couldn't sleep last night. I kept thinking of the 'what if'? I kept going over the results of the past few weeks' experiments and thought, what if we hold the proton release?"

"What do you think that'll do?"

"Dunno, but what can it hurt?"

Halfway through the day, a spark in the gold tube had Tunde and Min Jade looking at each other in awe. "Did you see…?"

"I did. Do you think…I mean, you saw that, right?"

"Let's repeat this exactly."

There was another spark.

Min Jade took off her safety glasses and stood looking at Tunde. Did they really? Did he really?

"You really saw that…You really saw that, right?" Tunde said.

Min Jade shook her head up and down, and her body shimmied. "I saw that. I really saw that."

Tunde lifted Min Jade into the air. "Maybe we got this," he lowered her to the ground, and as she slid down his muscular torso, there was another spark.

The following week proved exciting times for Min Jade and Tunde. They confirmed their experiments repeatedly and decided to keep the news to themselves for a couple of days.

"Min Jade," Tunde said as they finished the dinner his chef had prepared. Handing her a brandy, he sat beside her and looked her dead in the eyes.

"Yes, Tunde." Min Jade answered, putting a little distance between them. She was absolutely sure she loved Min Lee, so why was Tunde making her sway. She'd heard about this kind of thing when people worked on a shared goal. Could love be a will? Over the month, she'd appreciated Min Lee even more. He'd been understanding, and she felt guilty she'd chosen not to tell him about Tunde's presence in Ann Arbor. She didn't doubt their love, but she also didn't have time to explain, and she was sure he'd want to know why. Now she, too, was wondering why. Love the one you're with, her mother had said. Min Jade caught herself and was shocked at the thought.

"Let's take the weekend off and go somewhere. Put some distance between this confounded lab and us. Let's not think of protons and neutrons for a few days. I bet we'll see with clearer eyes once we repeat the experiment next week. Would you consent to letting me whisk you away?"

"Tunde, I, I…," Min Jade suddenly stopped. It was the least she could do. "Getting away sounds tempting."

"Then let's do it. While we're there, you might give some thought to being my girl!"

"And what happens if we don't fall madly in love? Will you stop being my friend?"

"Don't ask silly questions."

"I want our friendship to last forever, Tunde and I don't want to do anything to jeopardize that. I can't begin to tell you how grateful I am to you. This love business muddles things. Friendship is far more certain, and I want to be certain you will always be my friend."

"Yes, yes," he interrupted. "I get that. Let's just see how we feel with no pressure, no obligations, and no expectations. Let's just take a well-deserved break."

"But…."

"But me no buts," he rose from the couch. "I'll take you home."

Min Jade was silent on the way home. Her heart was unsettled. How could she say no to such a decent, loyal man, but how could she say yes and mislead him when she loved Min Lee? She should come clean and tell him they were a couple, but something made her hold back. Why had she decided against telling Min Lee that Tunde was with her in Ann Arbor and telling Tunde she and Min Lee were a couple? Was Tunde shaking her resolve?

On Thursday at noon, they boarded Tunde's private plane.

"So, where are we going?" Min Jade asked.

"Well, since New Caledonia is too far, I think to one of my next favorite place, Martinique."

"I've never been to a French Caribbean Island."

"Well, welcome to paradise."

With the chill of winter still in the air, a Caribbean Island vacation was welcome. Min Jade was glad it was not one of the usual suspects, and indeed she'd never been to a French Caribbean Island. Buckling up, she sat back and relaxed. With dinner, movie, and Tunde's chatter, the five-hour flight swiftly went by, and before long, they were landing at the Aime Cesaire International Airport

Martinique's French heritage was unmistakable. Whisked away by car to the Marina, they boarded a boat which delivered them to the majestic shores of the Vauclin Bay and later, in the early evening, to the incredible Le Domaine des Bulles hotel and spa resort. Nothing could have prepared Min Jade for its beauty. On the Caribbean Sea and nestled into a secluded, eco-friendly enclave were clear bubble houses. It boasted bedrooms that made one feel they were sleeping under the stars. The wraparound veranda led to other living spaces overlooking the Caribbean Sea's calm, aqua blue water. It was completely private, and Min Jade sat in awe of the wonders of human imagination.

"*Bonsoir.*" Her housemaid met her.

"Ah, *Bonsoir*," Min Jade was preparing to coax out her college French when the greeter spoke to her in fluent English.

"I will unpack for you and turn your bed down for the night. Mr. Tunde asks that you join him for dinner once you have refreshed. Do you have questions?"

"No. But might I ask if you have recommendations on what's best to do on the island?"

"Oh, you don't have to worry about that. Mr. Tunde has it all under control."

Min Jade wondered just how far Tunde's power reached. Happy to be in Martinique, she wondered too if she was being duplicitous by accepting this trip when she knew she'd never answer the question Tunde wanted. Over their past month of working closely, she'd come to regard him highly, and indeed that was the reason she hadn't said no to this trip. She was beyond grateful for his support, but when he'd said he'd move heaven and earth for her success, she couldn't help but open her heart. He was a much better match for her than Min Lee, but her heart knew where it belonged from a professional perspective. Clearly, she'd be lying if she said she didn't derive some twisted pleasure from being pursued by two men, but she had to make the right moves.

The following day, after lunching at the resort's restaurant on very French cuisine—cheeses, crepes, wines, baguettes, pates, and sweets—Tunde summoned their driver so they could explore what the town had to offer. Taking the short boat ride back to the city, Min Jade and Tunde darted in and out of boutiques and artisans' shops. Min Jade felt like they were actually in France. Inside a store that sold everything from wine to refrigerators, an older woman—who seemed to have been watching her since she'd entered—beckoned her over when Tunde had wandered off. Min Jade looked behind her to see who she was beckoning.

"Come," the woman said, "I have something to tell you."

Min Jade pointed at herself.

"Yes. You, pretty lady," she said. "Where you from?"

"America," Min Jade said, a little disappointed. Too bad there were tricksters on such a beautiful island.

"No worry. Come," she urged Min Jade over to her counter.

"How may I help you?" Min Jade asked.

"No, Luv. It's how may I help you! Your spirits are asking me to give you some information."

"My what?"

"Spirits."

Min Jade wanted to laugh out loud but did not. Was this woman a spiritualist! "I am a physicist." Min Jade said.

"No matter to your spirits. You have two men in your aura. You have to choose right."

"Excuse me?"

"You must choose right," she said. "Your sanity depends on it."

"Oh, there you are," Tunde came strolling up, and Min Jade was relieved.

The woman returned to what she had been doing, shelving t-shirts of Martinique.

"Shall we buy some?" Tunde asked.

"No," Min Jade said hurriedly, turning away.

Back at the hotel at dusk, when the sunset had turned the Caribbean sky golden, they dined in a thatch-roofed French restaurant on stilts in the middle of the sea. Floodlights illuminated the crystal water, and the magic was complete when underwater life put on their flawless show. Min Jade felt she was in a dream. This was what life would be like as the woman of a billionaire.

"Feeling relaxed?" Tunde asked.

"Completely. I have never been anywhere like this, ever. Sleeping in a bubble should be possible every night. Do you see how bright the stars are? "

"It is amazing. This place is like being in a parallel world. Min Jade," Tunde was saying when Min Jade's phone trilled. She looked at the number. Korea. Thank God, the speaker was off.

"Excuse me. My mother," Min Jade lied, walking to the distant part of the terrace. *Why did she lie? It was the opportune time to come clean.* Tapping the call answer button on her iPhone, Min Jade said, "Hey, can I call you in about an hour?"

"What's wrong with now?"

"I'm at dinner."

"With whom?"

"Tunde."

"Who?"

"You remember my friend from London. At the Royal Albert."

"Why?"

"Min Lee, allow me to call you in an hour. I'll explain everything."

"I was in love once," Tunde said when she returned to the table. He was sure it was not her mother on the other end of the call from her body language. "I know lightning doesn't often strike twice in the same spot, but the moment you walked into the great hall in Austria, I fell in love with you. All you have to do now is tell me you want to be with me, and I'll choose love. Nothing else will matter."

When she looked up, Tunde's eyes were burning a hole through hers. "What have you decided?" He said simply.

"Tunde," Min Jade said. "I'm incredibly flattered by your attention and your genuine heart. You are brilliant, rich, confident, and drop-dead gorgeous. I'm not blind or made of stone, you know. To have you open your heart up to a girl like me makes me feel like a winner. I can't even fathom why a man like you find me interesting, but I've been thinking and thinking ever since you first asked me in London to be your girlfriend. Why would a man like you want a woman like me by your side? The only thing we have in common is that we are both physicists. You are rich. I'm a college professor. You are a Muslim. I have no religion. Your father wants you to marry a Nigerian girl. I am American...you're...."

She was speaking the truth. It wasn't going to be easy to convince his family that he'd like to make her his wife as she was neither Nigerian, Muslim nor was she of equivalent financial stature. In a culture like his, yoke with your own kind partnerships is far more important than love. An even bigger problem was that there would be no way in hell Min Jade would ever acquiesce to playing the role of a Nigerian wife to a man in his position. But she was the woman he intended to marry, and he intended to find a way to convince her and his family. Min Jade, he knew, still had no idea of his lineage, though, in his opinion, some things couldn't be hidden. His unmistakable air of entitlement, charm, and unquestionable manners, which made people look at him cock-eyed, was hard to hide. Regardless of the obstacles, Tunde was keenly aware she had to be the woman in his life. "How about love? Does that count for anything? I can do anything for love."

"And then what, Tunde? As physicists, we are the most practical people on earth. Our lives are polar opposites."

"Min Jade. How much closer must I stand, and what else can I do to convince you that I love you, and I will move heaven and earth for you. I'll become the kind of man you could love?"

"For how long could you go against your nature and culture? Why would you want to twist yourself into a pretzel for love?" Min Jade sat with the words Tunde had uttered. She didn't feel she had to make sacrifices to be with Min Lee though they too would be fighting an uphill battle. Korea was the least multicultural country in the world…and it wasn't a black thing. It was an every foreigner thing, including people who looked like them. China, Japan, you name it. Min Lee or Tunde. Neither of these relationships would be easy. *But why did that woman say choose when she had already chosen?*

"Is it the Korean?" Tunde asked.

"It's me." Min Jade said.

Tunde rested his hand on hers. "I can make you happy, Min Jade. I'll truly will move heaven and earth for you. Isn't it better to marry a man who loves you than to marry the one you love? Let's just give it some time because I don't think I can live without you." When he took her hand as they walked back to the villa, she allowed hers to close reassuringly over his. He'd said exactly what her mother had said. And the woman in the market had scared her witless. *What did she mean by two men and choose right? Were these men Tunde and Min Lee Woo? Who then was she supposed to choose?* Min Jade, a true loyalist, was for the first time in a quandary. Was he shaking her resolve? Tunde had indeed stood by her through all her trials and tribulations; Min Lee's disappearance, Julian's crisis and the confounded man had shown up on her birthday.

Min Jade was in bed, looking up at the stars through her transparent bedroom bubble. Why was she wavering? Why would she need reassurance? Had she, in the back of her head, been thinking Min Lee would disappear again? She rolled over and texted Min Lee.

Ping: *Sorry about earlier.*

His ping was immediate: *Where are you?*

Ping: *Martinique.*

Crazy Korean: *What? With that man?*

Ping: *I'm calling you now. Too much to text.*

Crazy Korean: *Right now!*

Min Jade dialed Korea.

Min Jade awoke to the sunlight, dancing on her transparent walls. Just as she'd finished donning a pastel print dress, sandals, and a floppy hat, there was a knock on her door.

"Coffee," Tunde handed her a cup. "Black, right? Seems you need it. Why do you look so tired."

The morning sunbathed his umber skin, and his handsome face was aglow. He'd been the consummate gentleman during their difficult conversation, and he had not forced an agenda. She found herself appreciating him more and more, but she had to tell him…she had to.

CHAPTER EIGHTEEN

MIN LEE WOO
MAD AS HELL

WHEN MIN LEE HUNG UP THE PHONE, he was shaking with anger. "Stupid girl. Stupid, stupid girl," he roared, grabbing a bottle of scotch on his way to the living room. He didn't like this entire thing one bit. He should pay Min Jade a surprise visit and shore up his status as her boyfriend. Then again, Tunde was her friend, and there was nothing wrong with him helping her out. Still, she should have told him about it a month ago! After all, they spoke or texted each other every night, so there was ample opportunity for her to tell him. Min Lee poured scotch. Why didn't she mention any of it, but especially the trip! He gulped his scotch and poured another. Did he have a right to be angry? Probably not, yet, something in him was unsettled. There was no way he would let that pompous Tunde weasel his way into her heart. "Stupid girl," he banged the table. This love business was uncharted territory, and he didn't like it one bit. The more discomfort he felt, the more alcohol he drank.

"Min Lee," Ji-Joon wafted the air, which smelled like a distillery. "Min Lee," he called again when he saw his friend sprawled out on the sofa. "What the hell," he shook him, but Min Lee was passed out. Ji-Joon had never seen Min Lee sloppy drunk. He was way too controlled for that. Lifting him to the bedroom, he deposited Min Lee into bed and pulled the blanket around him. Ji-Joon tried to ease himself from his grip. "Don't leave me, don't you dare leave me," he kept pulling Ji-Joon back toward him. Ji-Joon sat on the bed until Min Lee had fallen back to sleep. Something terrible must have happened with his family. He should check with Hy Soo but decided against it. Whatever it was could wait until morning. *Damn, this was such poor timing*, Ji-Joon eased out of Min Lee's grip. Work on his album began the next day, and any distraction was unwelcome.

At 8:00 a.m., Ji-Joon went to check in on Min Lee. He was dressed and at the piano. Min Lee looked up as he entered the room.

"Shall we? I think Hy Soo will be excited about today. What do you think he'll say about playing on the album?" Ji-Joon handed him a bottle.

"Are you making small talk?" Min Lee took the bottle of hangover tonic.

"Well, you…."

"Do you want to ask me something, Ji-Joon?" Min Lee held his gaze.

"No. You're grown. You can drink yourself into a stupor."

"Liar."

"I've never seen you drunk, that's all. Any particular reason?"

"Korea."

Hy Soo looked a bit under the weather when they arrived home.

"*Appa. Gwaen-cha-na?*"

"Fine. I'm fine. *Anj-a.* Sit."

"Coffee?" Min Lee offered, pouring himself a cup.

"Yes."

"You, Ji-Joon?"

"Yes, sir," Ji-Joon answered.

Hy Soo rose to help Min Lee with the coffee. He faltered and was a little off kilter.

"*Appa,*" Min Lee quickly grabbed his father, his face showing grave concern. "*Gwaen-cha-na?*" Min Lee helped him back to the chair.

"I'm okay," Hy-Shoo, prostrated, sat down with some effort. *Was that a stroke?*

"Are you sure everything is fine? What is your doctor saying about all this?" Min Lee had sensed a change in his father weeks before. It was a now-or-never feeling.

"*Adeul*, I am fine." Hy-Soo patted his son's hand. "Don't make such a fuss. You said you had something to ask me. What is it?"

"I've been thinking a lot about doing a Korean album before I leave. I want to dedicate it to Mom. I'd love it if you played with me on the album. Are you well enough to record an entire album with me? What do you think?"

His father perked up. "Yes. Yes. Your mother would love that. If you sign a music contract with Soo Industries, I'll definitely stay around for that, son."

"Our first planning meeting is today. Are you up to that?"

"Think we could postpone today?"

"Yes, *Appa.* Ji-Joon will reschedule."

"Thank you, son."

As they headed back to Gangnam, Ji-Joon said. "That went well about the album, I mean. But I'm a little worried that he seems to be getting frailer."

"Me too. We need to get started right away. He seems to be having more bad days than good days. I'll see his doctors later today and get the real story. I think Dad's holding back."

"I'll check in with Choi at her party if she'll do the album too. It's tomorrow night, you know."

"I'm not going, so can you take care of it," Min Lee asked.

"You have to go, Min Lee. The young Korean music scene will be in one place. It's good to reconnect with them if you are serious about doing beats," Ji-Joon pleaded. "Trust me for once, and remember, I am your manager."

Min Lee snorted. *Min Jade wouldn't always doubt him if he'd trusted Ji-Joon less.* "*Arraso.*" Min Lee nodded. It was better than staying at home sulking about Min Jade's omission.

At five p.m. on Saturday, Ji-Joon sauntered into Min Lee's flat with stacks and stacks of bags. "Our party digs," he pulled out a few gaudy outfits. "What do you think of this?" he held up a god-awful skinny-leg pair of jeans with torn knees and patches.

"Hell no!" Min Lee said.

"Part of this new music world is their style. Gangnam style. How about this one?"

Min Lee shook his head.

"This?"

Min Lee grimaced.

"Try it on. Please. This you have to see on."

Min Lee grabbed bags and went to his room. He tried on a few of the kitschy outfits before deciding on the best of the bad lot! Pulling at the crotch of the pants, which were way too tight, and made his long legs look like sticks, Min Lee began to walk back to show J-Joon before quickly shedding the clothes.

"Stop!" Ji-Joon let out a whistle. "That's the look."

Min Lee looked at himself in the mirror and gasped. Fitted shirt–he did have a great body–skinny leg pants rolled up to mid-thigh, no socks and laced up crepes, in orange, Min Lee could hardly recognize himself. His prickly hair could have been mistaken as a weapon, and he looked like an overage, androgynous K-pop idol. "You can't be serious," he looked at Ji-Joon, eyes wide as saucers.

"You look fab. Really you do."

"Seriously? I feel as stupid as *you* look."

"I look hot," Ji-Joon said, walking out the door. "Let's rock, baby!" he pretended to strum a guitar. Min Lee, constantly pulling at his tight pants, followed him.

Choi Shin's place was *très* chic. Pulling up under the art deco glass building's portico, overhung with modern chandeliers that illuminated ivy trellises in blue luminescence light, Ji-Joon handed the keys to the valet. Inside, the ultra-modern brass and glass apartments overlooking the river, the buildings were even more spectacular.

"There you are," Choi reached out to hug Min Lee as though they were long lost friends. Min Lee drew back and outstretched a hand. Taken back but not skipping a single beat, Choi graciously shook his hand. She welcomed Ji-Joon with a handshake, too. "You both look amazing," Choi flattered.

Naturally, Ji-Joon beamed.

"Let me introduce you around," Choi said, leading them into a spacious living room all decked out in white. The party was not just for classical musicians because Hallyu stars were everywhere. Min Lee fit right in dress-wise but felt entirely out of place and like a right idiot.

"*Hyung*," Seung-Le greeted his brother, then snaked his arm around Choi's waist. "What do you think, huh? Nice party, right?"

"Seems nice. Good to see you, *Hyung*." He bet Seung-Le was footing the bill for this party.

"So, did you two get a chance to talk?"

"Not yet. They just arrived." Choi smiled warmly.

"I'd just as soon we chat right now," Min Lee said as he was out of there.

"That's fine with me," Choi said, leading the way to her music room. It, too, was decked out in all-white. On the right wall, several violins were mounted. "Thank you for considering my request to do an album. I am looking forward to working with you."

"Why do you want to work with me?" Min Lee asked, examining the row of violins.

"Because you are the best. I want to learn from the best. Drink?" Choi offered.

"I'll pass," Min Lee said, taking a seat on the sofa. "Play something."

Choi went to the rack of fiddles. She chose a Jacob Stainer instrument and tuned it in record time. Poised bow, she began playing Bach's *Air on the G string*. Even without orchestral accompaniment, her skillful use of legato, vibrato, and rubato' elevated the piece to mastery. Min Lee relaxed on the sofa and closed his eyes. Choi was, without a doubt, an amazing musician. Suddenly, he was jarred by her change from straight classical to classical pop. Min Lee opened his eyes and sat upright. This was magical. He reclosed his eyes and was blown away, his excitement rising. When she was done, he gave her enthusiastic applause. "I've been toying with the idea of modernizing classical music."

"Me too," Choi gushed. "There's a friend coming tonight. I'd like you to meet. Collaboration among us could be innovative."

"Play that again." Min Lee walked over to the wall-to-wall windows overlooking the twinkling Gangnam skyline. This was the kind of music he was interested in exploring as Min Jade played on *Revolution*. When the music stopped, he did not turn from the window. Choi was gifted, no doubt.

"Seoul has changed quite a bit, hasn't it?"

"It has," Min Lee turned around. She was standing so close; he had to step back.

"Are you really considering my request, or is this just a favor to Seung-Le?"

"Well, I like the idea of collaboration. I have a proposal for you. I am recording a Korean album with my dad. Would you consider playing with us?"

"What about my album? Are you considering my debut album?"

"We'll see how well you do. After this recording, I shall." Min Lee headed for the door. He didn't want to be behind closed doors one minute longer than necessary with this black widow.

"There you are. Been looking all over for you."

"Rain. I'm so glad you could make it. How are you?"

"This is quite some party. I love the vibe," The man kissed Choi's cheek.

"Crazed, but good. I'd like you to meet a friend. He's interested in learning about your kind of music. This is Min Lee Woo." Choi introduced the men, and Rain bowed deeply. "Don't think he needs an introduction. Hey," Rain said, turning to Min Lee. "Been checking you out on the news. Welcome home, man."

"Thanks," Min Lee returned the bow.

"Rain is our biggest K-pop idol. He's amazing."

"Really," Min Lee said. "I'm fascinated by this music."

"Just a derivative from masters like you, but it's cool. Drop by and hear us in the studio. Maybe we could do some work together."

"I'll do that."

They exchanged info, and Rain went off to chat with a group of people.

"He is really popular." Choi leveled Min Lee with a look.

Min Lee could tell she knew more about Rain than she was letting on. A right vixen this woman, but he could truly see why. Choi was beautiful. With her flawless porcelain skin, jet black, waist-length hair, a model's body at 5'8", bright eyes with the coveted double lids and a face to rival Song Hye Kyo, the most beautiful woman in Korea, Choi was indeed stunning. Her swan's neck, like her namesake, the actress Choi Ji Woo, made her seem ethereal as she floated about. Min Lee clearly understood the spell Seung-Le was under, but he knew danger when he saw it, and Choi Shin spelled trouble. It didn't escape him either that she played an Austrian instrument and looked like a woman with the last name Woo.

"I'll call him. I'm very curious about K-Pop."

Seung-Le, who'd had a little too much to drink, stumbled into the kitchen. "Brother, you do know that this is my woman, right?" he slurred, holding up Choi's left hand with the prominent bauble on her third finger. "Mother is furious."

"She'll get over it." He could feel Choi's displeasure. "Choi was just telling me about Rain. Classical music and K-pop could be an interesting combination." Min Lee switched the focus of the conversation.

"That could be nice. Just don't try those moves he does. You might break your back. So, when do I get an invite to your new pad?" Seung-Le slurred. So, Min Lee confirmed what he suspected; this was his brother's pad, after all.

"Is next week good?" Min Lee asked.

"I'll come with him, too. *Oppa*, I'll get the housewarming gift," Choi said to Seung-Le.

"You do that, my sweets." Seung-Le pulled her close. Her eyes never left Min Lee.

Min Lee made his escape. On the way home, Ji-Joon said, "That Choi sure is a looker, but she is Danger with a bolded D. Stay clear."

"Nothing to worry about in this department. I'm probably the least of Seung-Le's troubles."

Min Lee and Ji-Joon looked at each other. Years together gave them telepathy. "She likes you, though," he whispered. "Danger zone."

"Not for me. I'm not interested, plus I've got a girl, I think."

"What do you mean by that?"

Min Lee was only too happy to solicit his opinion on Min Jade's trip with Tunde.

The Following Week

"This is awesome." Seung-Le walked around Min Lee's apartment. Very high ceilings for Korea. An excellent instrument," he played a scale then walked over to the bar where Min Lee was fixing a drink. The living room, overlooking the Han River, was dominated by the ebony Steinway & Sons. "Is this place soundproof?"

"It is," Min Lee handed him a gin and tonic.

"Really nice."

"Where's your fiancée?"

"Ah, last-minute gig. She'll come next time. So, what do you think? Will you work with Choi?"

"Yes. I'll work with her on the Album Dad, and I will do, and then I'll see. She's terrific."

"One of our best…like you. How long will you be staying this time, *Hyung?*"

"I hope no more than six months, but it depends on Dad's health. I'm hoping things will improve faster."

"Will you take over Soo Industries?"

"As for Soo Industries, I have zero interest in taking it over. You should come to work more often and learn the ropes from Dad."

"I'm not cut out for suits. I think Dad knows it, and that's why he wants you here. Can't say the same about Mom, though. Why does she hate you so?"

Min Lee sat on the grey leather sofa and crossed his legs. "Because of my *Eomeoni*. She and Dad were college sweethearts. I guess your mom liked dad, but he loved my mom."

"*Aishheeee*. That explains a lot," Seung-Le rubbed his cheek unconsciously. That's what his mother always meant by second fiddle. The dreaded love triangle. "I suppose you remind her of her rejection."

"I guess so." Min Lee said.

"To be honest, I always wondered why they were married. I don't think Dad has ever loved Mom that way, but she adores him. I'm sorry, *Hyung*, we got the fallout. So," he said, changing the subject abruptly, "what did you think of Choi's shindig? Some party, huh?"

"It was a very nice party. Very eclectic. She's stunning, and her friends were nice."

"Yeah. Lots of those kids might not be around tomorrow. These stars are killing themselves like flies. 59% of young Koreans think of committing suicide, you know. Gangnam is not as glamorous as it looks."

"Is that real?"

"Yup. Look it up. It's a national crisis. I think we grew up too fast. Too much money and too much excess. New money vices. Choi, of course, is not one of us. It hasn't been easy for her. I worry she likes hanging out with them too much. Since we plan to marry next year, I'm trying to move her in another direction. That's why I'm asking for your help. If you keep her busy with her album…."

"Seung-Le, I can't promise that. Let the cards play out."

"Fine. Shall we stop by home tomorrow and see if Dad wants to go fishing? He seems to be trying to beat this thing now that you are home. He's so brave, but I don't think he's winning."

"Yeah, he'd love that. Let's pay him a visit. How about 10:00 a.m.?"

Ji-Joon rapped on the inside of the door. "Hey, Seung-Le. Good to see you again in our neck of the woods."

"You, too, *Chingu*."

When were they ever friends? "Min Lee. Need a word."

Seung-Le feeling a teeny bit jealous of Min Lee, excused himself to pour another drink. He and Ji-Joon seemed close. The guy even had a key to his apartment. On the other hand, he had been forced to grow up in a fishbowl and had to endure his mother's scorn for being a failed musician.

"Your phone," he handed him the cell phone he'd left in his apartment. "Min Jade called."

"Who's that?" Seung-Le asked.

"A friend from America."

As soon as Seung-Le left, Min Lee dialed Min Jade. He was routed to voicemail.

CHAPTER NINETEEN

MIN JADE
BAD NEWS

"IS THIS A BAD JOKE? What the heck is going on, Winful?"

"You've seen the papers; I take it."

"How could this happen? How on earth could this happen? What is Dr. Jade saying about all this?" The Dean was furious.

"Knowing Min Jade, she probably hasn't heard the news. This is very disappointing."

"Get her on the phone right now."

Winful had been staring at the paper all morning. He was shaking with anger. *London Scientists declare they have cracked the 80-year-old problem of turning light into matter. Scientists at the Imperial College describe their process as the most spectacular prediction of quantum electrodynamics.* Winful threw the paper into the trash.

It wasn't Winful who called Min Jade first. It was Albert. "Isn't something fishy to you?"

"Like what?"

"Have you seen the Physics Gazette?"

"No. Why?"

"The Imperial College has announced that it had cracked the code of making matter from nothing."

"What?" Min Jade stopped buttering her toast. "No way."

The Imperial College had been working on and actively publishing their findings in the *Nature Photonics Journal*. From those findings, as far as Min Jade was concerned, they were further away from a solution than she was. But what could she do except take it in stride? Min Jade walked to her home office and logged on to her subscription to the journal. There was no mistake. What to do but accept it and put on her big girl panties?

"Didn't you tell me the woman I saw at your conference name was Dr. Kessler? Her name is on the paper as part of the team of scientists."

"She must have made some contribution. But she isn't exactly in the field."

"That's why this entire thing is so puzzling."

"It's not unusual. I often work with my electrical engineering counterparts. It could be a coincidence. Albert, just a moment. I'm getting a call from my Chair. I can only imagine why. Let me call you right back." Min Jade clicked over the line.

"Professor Winful."

"I guess you haven't heard the news," Winful said.

"I did. Just now. One of my physicist friends from Austria just called. He's at The Imperial College."

"Min Jade, I'm so sorry." Then hurriedly, "What did he say?"

"He said Dr. Kessler is listed on the actual paper."

"How could this happen? This is all my fault." Winful lamented.

"How is it your fault? It's very disappointing, of course, but I told you a million times not to get ahead of yourself. To begin with, it was a long shot as QED is the hottest thing in physics right now. We have to expect anything."

"But their work was not nearly as cited as yours!"

"But they got to the finish line first. It's only a paper. They'll have to prove it. Really, Dr. Winful, I'm okay. Are you okay?"

"No, I am not, and neither is Eric."

"I can't help that. You were both too optimistic."

"Well, it isn't over until it's over."

"That's true. I suppose I need to see the Dean."

"Yup. Will you come down?"

"Of course."

Min Jade hung up the phone. She felt as though the wind had been knocked out of her. She thought of her mother and how disappointed she was going to be. "I'm sorry, Mother. I tried," she whispered. Min Jade crossed the Diag, none too pleased about the subject of the forthcoming meeting with the Dean, but she had to remain detached. Winful and Eric were huddling when she entered the Dean's office. Eric, an intense man, had a noticeable grimace on his face.

"How are you, dear?" Eric's approach was dramatic.

"Fine." Min Jade's confidence was shaken but not obvious.

"What can we do…what should we do…what will we do?" He rambled.

"Dean, look. There is danger in trying to do a one-upmanship. We have solid work, and the only thing we can do is publish our paper. Let the chips fall where they may."

"You are too democratic." Eric scolded.

"I am a University of Michigan scientist. I stand for all the things you've both instilled in me. If they get there first, they get there first. They just made a statement. They still have to prove it. I'm not happy about this either, but as professionals, we know luck could be on anyone's side." Unlike Winful and Eric, Min Jade had not been counting on winning a prize, though it would've been nice because it was her life's work. Her work was solid, and that was enough for her.

"Yes," Winful chimed in. "Let's release our findings and see where we stack up."

"Are you sure that's the right thing to do?"

"I think you already know the answer to that, Eric," Winful said. He would never give up on the idea of his physics department bringing home a Nobel.

Min Jade left the meeting with a feeling of setback. She felt the need to talk with someone completely removed from the situation but who would understand. She was about to dial Min Lee, who was still mad she'd gone to Martinique, then realized the thirteen-hour time difference would make it 2 a.m. in Korea. She sighed. They were never on the same schedule.

It was Tunde, as usual, who saved the day. "Min Jade," his face loomed on FaceTime, "what is this Albert is telling me?"

"Seems your adopted country is ahead of me on QED."

"Have you completed the paper?"

"Pretty much."

"Then publish it right away. Shall I come back?"

Too quickly, Min Jade said, "No. I can manage, plus I have a new assistant."

"I see," Tunde deadpanned.

A few weeks later, Min Jade's paper was finished. She'd worked around the clock, and she was exhausted. It was 10 p.m. when she finally headed to her car. Getting behind the wheel, this tired was not advisable, but what to do. Thank goodness she didn't have to go far. She was about to start the engine when her phone rang. Fishing it from her bag, she plugged it into her hands-free device. "Hello."

"What took so long to answer the phone?" Min Lee admonished

"I was getting into my car."

"So late. How are you right now?"

"Good. Exhausted. You?"

"Is it done?"

"It is."

Min Lee could only get one syllable answers out of Min Jade. He could only imagine how exhausted she was from the long hours devoted to getting her work published. Still irked that she'd gone off with Tunde, he'd lightened up when he heard the news about The Imperial College. The idea of Tunde working alongside Min Jade still made him cautious because he'd seen too many times how the energy of shared goals transforms nothing into something. He was sure, also, that Tunde's intention hadn't been to be there as just her assistant.

"Min Jade," Min Lee said. "As soon as my album is done, I'll come to Ann Arbor. I guess your coming to Korea is out of the question right now."

"Yes. I'm afraid so."

"Anything I can do to help?"

"You can be more patient and understanding. But Min Lee, I'm a little tired right now, and I just need to get home."

"I miss you, Duck Beak."

"I miss you too. So very much. This will all be over soon," Min Jade said, starting the engine. "I'll call you before I go to sleep."

"Don't. I'm heading into a rehearsal, so get some rest. I'll call you in the morning. *Sarang-hae.*"

Min Jade hung up the phone and sat with the car idling. She needed to be sure that her love for Min Lee was unshakable. Tunde's generous gift to her research had caused her pause. Love of the head or the heart. She sighed loudly before heading out.

CHAPTER TWENTY

SOUTH KOREA
MIN LEE WOO
MUSIC FOR MOTHER

MIN LEE WAS ADAMANT ABOUT FAST-TRACK-ING the album for his father's sake, and as important, he needed to be by Min Jade's side. Pocketing his phone, he got ready to head over to the studio. His poor Duck Beak. He needed to be by her side.

Ji-Joon had arranged a discovery session for his K-Pop/classical music composition vision. Opening the door to the studio, the glare from the stage almost blinded him. The music was loud, the stage glowed, and the bodies on stage defied gravity. Every inch of Rain glistened, including his exaggerated eyelashes that sparkled with glitter. He was thrusting his pelvis to a song called "Hip Hop Night Tonight." At thirty-three years old, Min Lee never imagined bodies could contort the way the men did on stage. He hoped they weren't expecting him to do anything like that on stage. Rain saw Min Lee, waved, and jumped down from the stage.

"We're just wrapping up here. What'd you think?"

"It's loud and dynamic," Min Lee laughed.

"That it is," Rain smiled, then turned to his backup dancers and musicians, "Thanks, everyone. See you tomorrow." Rain turned back to Min Lee, "Beer?" he opened the icebox in the corner of the room.

"Not before I play."

"It loosens up my hips," Rain laughed. "Ah, here comes Choi."

Choi Shin was the violinist on the album. Min Lee nodded as she came into the room.

"So, what did you have in mind? The producer will sample a few beats." Rain said.

For an hour or so, they experimented. Min Lee played a chord when he heard a beat he liked. "What'd you think?" he asked. Most of the instrumentalists on the record played classical music, so they would quickly get a feel for Min Lee's vision. The producer sampled more beats. Choi matched on the violin. The drummer's beat was hypnotic and rhythmic, and Min Lee waited.

"The piano should come in about here," the producer shouted over the din, "Go."

Min Lee began a fast arpeggio, and before long, the world of K-pop and classical music was jamming. Min Lee felt alive and engaged. This was going to be breathtaking.

"That was dope," Rain said, and Ji-Joon couldn't stop clapping.

Filled with satisfaction, Choi gushed. "How was it, *Oppa?* Is this what you imagined?"

"It was better than I imagined." Min Lee appreciated anew, the gifted musician. "It's definitely raining, and the G string was talking."

Choi blushed.

At 3:00 p.m., his father walked into the studio to begin recording their album, closely followed by his faithful secretary carrying his cello. "Dad, this is Rain. He is going to help us with the beats for the album."

'I know who he is." Hy Soo said, winking. "Let's do this. Min Lee's Mom is waiting."

Min Lee didn't like the sound of that, no matter which way it was intended. Had his father reconciled his death?

"Yes, sir." Rain said, jumping on stage.

The session, which lasted three hours plus, was fantastic. Choi Shin shone like a bright star against his father's mastery on the cello. Min Lee wondered why she thought her talent wasn't enough to stand on its own. His father had the time of his life and was, without question, one of the best cellists, bar none.

"It's a wrap." The sound engineer was ecstatic to be working with such professionals. Nevermore than two takes made his life pleasant.

"*Adeul*," Hy Soo took his son by the shoulders, "you are truly gifted. Thank you so much for this."

"Thank you, Dad. You were amazing. Wish we'd done this before. Are you tired? I'll take you home," Min Lee offered.

"My driver should be here any minute."

"Call him and tell him I'll take you home. I want to discuss something with you. "

"Okay. Let me go to the men's room," his father said, punching a number on his speed dial.

Choi walked over to Min Lee as soon as his father left. "I have a couple of compositions I've been working on; if you'd like, I can let you hear them."

"I'd like that. Why don't you bring them over tomorrow? I've been thinking maybe we could work on that album you want."

"Really? *Kamsahamnida. Kamsahamnida*," she threw her arms around Min Lee.

Lunch with Dad

The following day, Min Lee allowed himself to be talked into lunch with his dad and Ha Yun Hye, the daughter of one of his father's oldest friends and his doctor. Apparently, she was going to help redecorate his office, or that's the excuse his father gave him.

A woman rose and moved toward Hy-Soo as they entered the restaurant. "*Appa*," she embraced his dad in a tight hug and kissed his cheek. "Are you doing well?"

"Better than expected. Your dad is keeping me from kicking the bucket."

"He'd better. We can't do without you," she escorted him to a nearby chair. "I'm Ha Yun Hye," she said, turning to Min Lee.

Min Lee bowed. "I'm Min Lee. Dad's been raving about your work."

"He is my most successful referrer and biggest collector. Aren't you, *Abeoji*?"

"That's because she pays me back in smiles."

Indeed, her smile lit up the room. About 5'5", Ha Yu somehow seemed taller, and like Min Jade, her personality was big, and her style was unique and eclectic. Hair clasped in a messy up-top style showed off the fine features of her face. She wore a red pair of glasses, and Min Lee again thought of Min Jade. Min Lee pulled out a chair, and she sat.

"How are you liking Korea?" she asked.

"I'm getting used to it."

"Quite different from when you left, huh?"

"That it is."

"Don't you remember me?"

"Eh…eh…."

"I used to make you pretty drawings at school. In art class. You called me Pigtails."

"Oh, my goodness. Is that you? The little girl who followed me around? You were but eight or so. I can't believe how you've grown up."

"You were all of twelve or so," she mocked. "I can't believe how you have grown up."

The laughter among them was refreshing. Min Lee couldn't tell the last time he'd laughed.

"Min Lee has a place in Gangnam. Your work would look great on his walls there too."

"*Abeoji*," Ha Yu said, squeezing his father's hand, "don't be so obvious."

"I don't know how he knows that. He refuses to come to my place."

"I can't hear myself think in Gangnam." Hy Soo covered his ears.

"That's because you are old-fashioned. What shall I order for you today, *Abeoji*?" Ha Yu showed him the menu.

Min Lee wondered if they often had lunch together. She took such care with his father.

"She treats me like an old man. Always fussing over me."

"I do no such thing," she elbowed him.

Lunch was pleasant. The old friends reminisced, and Min Lee made her promise to come to check out his blank walls. A twinkle appeared in her eyes. "I'd love to, but first, come down to my gallery," she handed him her card. "See if there's something you like. No pressure," she flashed him a radiant smile, then turned to his father. "*Abeoji*," she kissed his father's cheek again. "*Kamsahamnida*."

Min Lee held his father's elbow as they descended the restaurant steps. "Dad, would you go with me now to see Mom?"

Hi, Soo's shoulders drooped as he looped his arms through his son's. "I'd like nothing better, *Adeul*. Nothing."

At the ossuary, the men sat in reverent silence. It was Hy Soo who spoke first. "I loved her so very much. Your mother was the most unselfish person I'd ever met. But I'm still angry with her. She should have trusted me." He seemed at that very moment to age five years.

"What would you have done if she'd told you about me, dad?"

"I know why she didn't tell me, but she should have trusted me to find a way. I was a poor kid on scholarship at the most prestigious school. I found a way to get there, and I'd have found a way for all of us to be happy. You suffered so, my son."

"I never suffered with mom, dad. She loved me fiercely. It helped me make it through during the rough times. All I have to do is close my eyes and remember her smile."

"The smile of a Goddess." Hy Soo was nodding his head. "She had the most beautiful smile in the world. So," Hy Soo got to the real reason they'd gone to lunch. "What did you think of Ha Yun? You know I always have good taste in women," he winked. "Isn't that right, *yeabo?*" He picked up the picture of the love of his life.

"She is very special, dad."

"Would you consider her as a wife?"

"That, I will not do. Dad, no cajoling in the world will make me agree to that request. I can't marry without love. Plus, there is someone I'm interested in. That's what I came to talk to you and Mom about."

"There is?" His father's eyes brightened. "Why have I not met her? What family is she from?"

"*Abeoji*. I haven't lived in Korea for seventeen years. I don't know who the families are these days, though I suspect they haven't changed. I'm not even Korean anymore."

"What nonsense. Once a Korean, always a Korean. So, where is she? London? Is she Korean?"

"No, she lives in the U.S., and she is an American?"

"American?"

"Yes."

"American-American?"

"Yes." He'd save the bombshell for later.

"Son, I am not one to argue with love. But you know it will be hard. Are you serious about this woman?"

"Very. I'd like to ask her to marry me formally." He wanted to tell his dad about the woman with his mother's smile, but he wanted to wait for him to see it himself.

"Why don't you invite her to visit us?"

"I would like that, Dad. I'd like that."

"*Yobbo*," Hy Soo said, replacing his mother's photo behind the glass door. "I kept my promise, but she is not Korean."

Three days later, Min Lee showed up at Ha Yun's gallery.

"You came." Ha Yun ushered him in. This morning she was dressed in a wicked green and blue get-up. It made him miss his Duck Beak even more. To be honest, being with Ha Yun made him feel less lonely.

"Look around. Let me know what sparks your interest."

"This one." Min Lee immediately pointed to a bamboo painting of a mother and child sitting on a sofa in silence, yet together.

"It's one of my favorites, too. I would have imagined you were more into contemporary art."

"I am, but this touches me in a special way."

"I'll bring it over and see how it works. How about some tea?"

Min Lee found himself enjoying Ha-Yun's company immensely. "You remind me of someone." He did the honors of pouring the tea.

"Really? Thought there was only one of me."

"We all have a twin."

The wind chime jingled as the door opened. While Ha Yun was busy with a patron, Min Lee pulled out his phone, scrolling to Min Jade's number. He texted.

Ping: *I love you. I have good news.* His brows knitted with anticipation at her return text.

"Why the scowl?" Ha Yun asked as she came back into the room.

"Long-distance love," he sipped his tea. "Just missing my best girl today."

"Hmm. That's hard. Wanna have dinner? I'm a great listener."

"I need to get home and practice for tomorrow's recording, but I want a rain check – and a woman's ear, I could use." He was sure they would become friends.

Instead of going home, Min Lee went back to the ossuary to visit his mother's Wall of Remembrance. He added fresh flowers to the vase, then sat on a bench opposite his mother's shrine. "*Eomeoni*, I've missed you so much. I can't stop coming. Did you enjoy Dad's visit yesterday? He still loves you so very much. But Ma, I came to tell you something special today. The girl I love looks a lot like you. She even has dimples like yours, *Eomeoni*, and she likes yellow. I want to be with her very much, but Dad needs me here. What should I do? If I stay here, *Eomeoni,* I might lose the woman I love."

CHAPTER TWENTY-ONE

MIN JADE
HEART OR HEAD

TUNDE COULD NOT KEEP THE GRIN OFF HIS FACE. He was pleased. To his chagrin, even after a month in Ann Arbor, he'd not gotten to first base with Min Jade, but being in her life had been enough. He'd won some kind of affection after all, and he was going to wipe Albert's face in his quasi triumph. Operation Min Jade was inching ahead. He headed down to the squash court for his weekly game with Albert. Tunde hit the first squash ball so hard it split open against the wall.

"Crikey," Albert said. "What's up with that?"

"Frustration, mate. Frustration."

"Min Jade got those jockeys in a twist, huh."

"She is a cruel wench, I tell you. How long am I going to have to wait for her, do you think?" In general, he was pleased with their "friendship progress," but he was frustrated beyond words. He missed Min Jade and their daily routine in Ann Arbor. What else could he do to get her to give him her heart fully? Was their spark in her lab an illusion? He ached for the woman, and he didn't know how much longer his body could take this. He'd been waiting expectantly for her call since her paper had been submitted, and here it was three weeks later, and not a single call, still he was lingering in "afterglow." He hit another ball, which whizzed past Albert's head. After a half-hour of hard play, Albert threw a towel at Tunde. "Mate," are you trying to kill me?"

"Sorry, bud. I'm just uptight bout Min Jade."

"I do have to say you proved me wrong and found the perfect assignment to be by her side. I was convinced you'd be sacked, but you're the better man — and I hear — a darn great physicist."

"I can't see how you ever doubted that," Tunde caught the towel Albert threw his way and dabbed his face.

"What do you say we hit the pub later, mate? It'll take the sting out of the wait. Gotta get to my lecture by nine, but I'll see you later at Spirits? I'm sure it'll help."

Tunde nodded and headed for the shower. He whipped off his shirt and stared at his buff torso. *Who wouldn't want to rest her head on this shoulder?* His phone rang. He looked at the number. The lovable Ice Queen. He couldn't sound too excited, so he took a deep breath before he answered.

"Are you up?"

"Of course, I'm up. It's 8 a.m. Albert and I just finished a game of squash."

"Great. Can you talk?"

"I am talking, Min Jade. I just annihilated a squash ball, so I feel calm and collected. What…."

"I'm ready to listen to your reasons why we think we should be together." She interjected before Tunde could finish his sentence. She knew what he was going to say anyway.

"What? What?" Tunde was jumping for joy. People in the locker room were staring at him, but he could care less until he became aware that his towel had slipped to the floor from all the jumping around. He shrugged his shoulders, proud to bare his toned, fit body, all of it. Girding his waist with the towel, he headed toward the shower stall to have a bit of privacy. "Min Jade, you're not pulling my leg, are you?"

"Do you want me to hang up?"

"*No…*no. Wait a minute. What exactly are you saying?"

"I am saying that I want to find out why you think we should be together. I know this sounds strange, but I just want to be absolutely sure I am making the right choice."

"Can we take a real vacation and discuss it? I want to do that so we can be face-to-face."

"Yes, but there is one condition."

"Anything. Anything."

"We go to Korea."

"You're fuckin' kidding, right?"

"I've been invited to speak at a conference. It's only right that you should be with me, anyway. You know how much I love you as a friend and how grateful I am. You've confused me a bit, you know, and I'm wondering if it could be possible that love is a will. What better opportunity?"

"You mean you need to see how I stack up against the Korean Dragon? I think you know the answer to that already." He was curt.

"I'd like to sort out my feelings for you both and put them in the right place with no doubt about which is which. I love Min Lee, but I also love you for a different reason. Could this be a start? I think…I just think…I think…."

"You think what, Min Jade," Tunde loosened the swathed towel from his waist. God, he groaned at the sight of himself. *What the fuck?! If going to Korea was what was necessary to get her to Yes, he'd do it…but, this time, Min Lee Woo had to leave their lives for good.*

"I think it's the only way for me to hear the hum."

"The what?" *What the fuck is a hum. The woman was bonkers.*

"See you in about three weeks?"

"Come to London, and we will fly from here," Tunde ordered. He turned on the cold tap and shivered as the icy water hit his body.

Min Jade sat cross-legged on the bed. She closed her eyes and listened to the sound of her heart. What was it telling her? She felt enormous gratitude to Tunde for giving his time and energy to help her in her lab. He was great, brilliant, and easy to communicate with, and professionally they were on the same wavelength. Was it enough to will her heart into love? Min Jade tried to imagine what her life could be like with the two men. *Choose right*, the old woman had said to her in Martinique. Tunde, she listened closely. Did she hear a hum? She didn't. Then she shifted her thoughts to Min Lee. Her heart at once began to race. They certainly had less in common than Tunde and her, but there was no denying the hum that started low in her belly and kept rising. What would she decide? She already knew she believed, and it was only right to give Tunde an answer once and for all.

Life had settled down quite a bit after Min Jade's paper had been published. Winful was back to gloating as her citations had doubled that of the Imperial College. Min Jade needed a voice of reason, so here she was, sitting across from her mother at the Chop House. The last time she'd been there was with Tunde. She smiled at the memory—such a confident man.

"You've got something on your mind," her mother said.

"You know me too well," Min Jade said, looking over the menu.

Jessica was staring at her daughter. Involuntary muscles under her eyes were twitching, which meant she was in a quandary. From the dark circles, too, Jessica could tell Min Jade was not sleeping well. "What's causing this anxiety? Min Lee and Tunde?"

"Oh, Mom. How did you know?"

"It's only natural, darling. Love and guilt." Matters of the heart were out of her domain, but her daughter was in a predicament. "I've been there, you know. When I met your dad, there was someone else in my life. A great and wonderful man who supported me in every way. I felt so much guilt when I realized I was in love with your father, and there was nothing my heart could do to stop moving in his direction."

"So, you went with your heart."

"It's the only thing to do."

"But Mom, I've been thinking about Tunde a lot."

"It's natural. He is a marvelous man, and he seems to love you a lot."

"Min Lee seems so far away, and I'm not sure when we will ever be able to be together. Tunde has asked me to be his girlfriend, and we seem so evenly yoked when I think about it. His career and mine fit perfectly together, and…."

"I see," Jessica inhaled deeply. "Unfortunately, darling, the heart doesn't think. It simply reacts." Jessica wanted to see her daughter in a great relationship as any mother would. She wanted someone who could understand her quirks and whose wingspan was big enough to cover her in her times of need. Tunde had certainly done that, and he'd taken great care of her daughter. "Can you say categorically you are in love with him?"

"No. I think what I need to do is start a new project. I have too much time on my hands, and my thoughts are running rampant."

"When you think of Tunde, do you hear the hum?"

"I don't hear any hum, Mom, but what does the hum mean?"

"The hum is love. What about when you think of Min Lee?" Jessica saw the visceral change in her daughter. It was Min Lee who held her heart. "No matter how much we try, Min Jade, life is not a matter of head versus heart when it comes to love. The heart wins, hands down. Lucky for you, it's the heart that holds the hum."

"But how do you know if the hum is real love or if it's just an imitation of love? You know, activated receptors can pretty much mimic the real thing?"

"Ah, mimic. Therein lies the operant word. A door can't be opened with an *almost* key. The key has to *be* the right key. The hum of love is unmistakable. All I can say, Min Jade, is find the right key. It's the only way. To love somebody is a precious gift. I think I've raised a wonderful, well-adjusted human being, so my job is done here. I've done my best. Now the rest is up to you."

Min Jade nodded her head and reached for her mother's hand. "I'll order for you."

Back at home, Min Jade sat in a meditation pose. She needed to hear her voice without judgment or interruption. She plugged in her earbuds and then hit play. The Joy of Being introductory screen flashed on. She closed her eyes and began a slow intake of breath. For the next hour, she focused on letting go and tuning in. She had climbed one great mountain in her career; now it was time for love, so her mother had said. Was she brave enough to love without all the fear she was feeling? Min Jade unbuttoned her silk blouse and threw it across the bed. She stepped out of her skirt and went to the bathroom. She brought her hand up to touch her breast and imagined…a little embarrassed at her thoughts, she jumped in the shower and was soon settled into bed.

CHAPTER TWENTY-TWO

MIN LEE WOO
DOUBT

SEUNG-LE SAT NURSING HIS *SOJU*. Choi twisted the olive in her martini. "*Oppa*. I'm not asking for forever, but couldn't we push back the wedding? Min Lee's going to do the solo album with my compositions. It could mean I will be touring for months. How can I leave you right after our wedding? Min Lee thinks...."

"Min Lee. Min Lee. That's all you talk about lately!" Seung-Le could hear his mother's voice in his head...*and now he'll take your gold-digging two-bit hussy, too.* "I don't want you to push back anything, so cancel the album or just postpone it until after the wedding."

"*Oppa*. This is the chance of a lifetime. Isn't this what you wanted for me?"

"Choi, I said to cancel the album for now. You can do it after our honeymoon."

"I will not!" Choi jumped to her feet, twisted the ring off her finger and threw it on the table. "*Heeojida*, let's break up," she turned on her heels and walked out.

Seung-Le threw his glass at the restaurant's wall, which had the proprietor flying over to his table. His restaurant was a hot spot for unruly chaebol children whose bad behavior and abuses of power forced him to double the insurance necessary for any other restaurant. Seung-Le threw some bills on the table and left without a word of apology. Outside he demanded his car, and the valet went scampering. *Maybe his mother was right after all. How dare that woman break up with him? Who did she think she was to throw his ring in his face? He'd teach her a lesson.* Seung-Le straightened his red tie, got in his car, and roared off. He was, right this minute, going to take his rightful place at Soo Industries, and the first thing he would do was cancel Choi Shin's contract.

Wheels screeched as he pulled to the building. He threw the keys at the porter and marched into the lobby.

"Hold the elevator," Seung-Le rushed toward the closing doors.

Min Lee automatically reacted to the request

"*Hyung.* Just the person I want to see."

"To what do we owe this pleasure?" Min Lee's eyebrows shot up at seeing Seung-Le.

"I'm assuming my position at Soo. I know it's hard to believe, but when the fox is in the henhouse, one has to be vigilant."

"And who's the fox?"

Seung-Le looked up at his brother, who stretched him by two or three inches. "*Hyung,* I know I asked you to help Choi out, but I want to rescind the request."

"After all the cajoling?"

"She's given me back my ring. She says she wants to push back our wedding so that she can do this album with you.

Can you find a reason to cancel the album until after the wedding?"

"*Hyung*, if you have to go that far for love, is this the right relationship for you? Choi's career will take her away from home six to eight months a year. Are you ready for that?"

"Absolutely not. I'm expecting her to put our home first. Why would she want to go running around the world, anyway? I can more than take care of her and send her around the world a few times just for fun."

"Seung-Le, that's not the point. What should she do with her talent? Her career?"

"Play me lullabies and teach our children music. That should be enough."

Min Lee could see the conversation was going nowhere, so he listened as Seung-Le prattled on. He was glad when Seung-Le's phone rang.

"Now. Right now?" He was saying into the phone. "*Arraso*," he pushed the elevator button back to the lobby. "We'll continue later," he said as Min Lee got off on the floor to his office. "Gotta take care of something urgent but think about what I'm asking."

Choi was waiting in his office when Min Lee entered. Though his office was on a separate floor from his brother's, he quickly closed the blinds just in case Seung-Le decided to continue the elevator conversation sooner rather than later. He asked his secretary to hold his calls and not let anyone in. "What's going on between you and Seung-Le?" Min Lee got straight to the point of why he was sure she was there.

"*Oppa* is very unreasonable. How can he ask me to postpone the album when he knows you might leave at any moment?"

"That's a bit of an exaggeration, don't you think? How do you know when I'm leaving?"

"I still think it's unfair. What does he expect me to do, put my life on hold to be his wife?" Choi fiddled with a button on the sleeve of her cotton shirt. "Are you even listening to me?" Choi asked, noticing Min Lee was checking his phone.

"Seung-Le is just overreacting right now." Min Lee pocketed his phone. "Give it a moment."

"*Shireoyo.* I don't want to. I am not going back to him. I won't give up my career. Please help me."

"I can't get involved, Choi. I believe you have the right to any decision you make, but it's not up to me."

"Min Lee, you have to help me. I'll do anything," she grabbed his arm.

"That's enough." Min Lee pried her hand off him. "I said I won't get involved. This is between you and Seung-Le. I'm willing to do the album. The rest is up to you." Min Lee again pulled the phone from his pocket. He was expecting Min Jade to call.

"Is that phone more important than me right now?"

Min Lee, annoyed on all counts by Choi's whining and, more importantly, because he'd not yet heard from Min Jade, and it was their usual call time.

"But *Oppa*…you have to speak with your brother."

"Choi, I am not your *Oppa,* and as I said, I will not be involved in your and Seung-Le's affairs. Work this out with him and get back to me. *Chakaman,* hold on…hold on…" He was trying to wrestle his arm away from an insistent Choi. A ping sounded on his phone. It was from Min Jade.

"Is something wrong, *Oppa?*" Choi purred.

"Choi, I need you to leave right now. I am not, and I repeat, *not* getting involved in this matter, and please do not come into my office in the future when I am not here."

"But *Oppa*." Choi advanced.

Min Lee grabbed her by the hand, led her to the door, and pushed her out into the hallway. "Don't play games," he warned. "I am on to you."

Shocked, Choi kept spinning around like a top. He didn't just throw her out of his office! Korean men were impossible. Choi, who was not one to give up easily, collected herself and strolled down the hallway, a smile on her face. Boy, was she glad a convenient reason had shown up to end her engagement? It was no longer Seung-Le who interested her but Min Lee. *But Oppa*. She liked the sound of that.

Min Lee shut the door and looked at the message on his phone.

Ping: *Hi.*

Crazy Korean: *It's about time.* He typed furiously.

Ping: *You miss me…you miss me…*

Crazy Korean: *I do. I really do Duck Beak.*

Ping: *Does that mean you want me to come to Korea right now?*

Crazy Korean: *I'm calling you right now.* He looked at his watch. Pick up the phone immediately.

Ping: *I'll be waiting for your call.*

Min Lee called Min Jade. "Are you serious? Can you come to Korea?

"Yes.

"Would you rather I come to you. I'll be on the next plane!"

"No. I have been invited to speak at a conference in Korea!"

"Oh," Min Lee felt disappointed. "And I thought you were coming because you missed me."

"There may be that, too."

"When do you get here? I'll send a driver to pick you up."

"I'll be with Tunde, as he was a major supporter of the project. I'm sure he'll have a driver."

Min Lee felt the constriction in his chest. Silence. The long pause prompted Min Jade to ask, "Are you there?"

"*Wae?* Why must you do that? *eotteoke?*"

"How could I not? How could you even ask that?"

"Min Jade, you've spent years on your research. He was there for a month. Why is it so important that you bring him?"

It was Min Jade's turn to hesitate. "Min Lee, please don't get me wrong, but I need to say this. Tunde has asked me out. I know it's crazy, but I have been a little conflicted. Tunde and I understand each other. We work in the same field, and he has been enormously good to me. I have been struggling to get clear on my feelings. I want to believe what we have is special, but I keep thinking our time may have passed, Min Lee. I know it's irrational, but…."

"Are you being crazy right now?"

"Min Lee. Life can change in seconds. I keep thinking we belong in different worlds. I think you know that as much as I do. I'm not confused that it's you who I love and that we can create sparks, but is it enough? When the dust settles, will it be enough? I don't know if we can hold on to what we have. I need to know."

"What you're feeling for Tunde is not love, Min Jade. It's gratitude."

"Maybe. But I need to find out. When I see you, I think I'll know."

Min Lee collapsed onto the nearby sofa. His breathing was shallow, and no matter how hard he tried, he could not contain his anger.

"I'll tell you one thing, Min Jade," Min Lee's voice was low and rumbling. "What you feel is not love, and I will prove it to you." The bulging vein in his forehead pulsed as he disconnected the call. For the first time in his life, Min Lee had fallen in love, and here he was being cast aside for gratitude. Why had he allowed this woman to make him break a covenant with himself? What an idiot he was to think life could be so easy. Tunde would never win, but that Min Jade doubted her love for him was heart-wrenching.

"I am…" Min Jade realized she was now talking to a dial tone.

"*Yeoboseyo. Yeoboseyo.* Hello," Ji-Joon shouted over the din. He was at a bar across from the office.

"Where are you?"

"Across the street at Once in a Blue Moon."

"I'm on my way over there."

When Min Lee walked in, he spotted Ji-Joon right away. Trundling over to the bar, he hoisted himself into a highchair and ordered a scotch. Neither he nor Ji-Joon had noticed Choi, who was also drowning her annoyance in *soju*.

"What happened? Why are you here?" Ji-Joon asked.

"I'm going to get drunk." He guzzled the drink in his hand.

"Does this have something to do with Min Jade? Why must you get all worked up when you're upset with her? What now? The only time you get drunk is when you get angry with Min Jade."

"I may have no choice now." He ordered a double scotch this time. "She tells me the Lion has asked her out. That damn Tunde. I knew I should have been there with her in Ann Abor."

"Who is stronger, a Lion or a Dragon? Light the sky afire, man."

"Ji-Joon, how could she, after everything we've shared?"

"She is confused, that's all." Ji-Joon's eyebrows shot up. "That she discussed it with you is a good thing. You haven't seen each other in almost seven months. He's been there with her constantly. It's just transference, but that guy Tunde, I promise, is playing for keeps. He's making time, so you better up your game."

"Then make time for me to do so, Ji-Joon, or I'll quit playing."

"Don't be melodramatic."

Min Lee downed his drink and banged his glass on the counter for another, and another, and another. "Don't tell me what I can and cannot be! Damn it." The bartender kept refilling his glass with amber liquid.

Choi looked up at the commotion at the bar. When she saw Min Lee and Ji-Joon, she perked up. She ordered two cups of coffee, drank them both, and moved closer to where they were so she could be in earshot of their conversation. She took a shadowed booth so she wouldn't be noticed.

"You are the reason all this happened to begin with," Min Lee accused Ji-Joon. "If we hadn't left Austria early…."

"That's water under the bridge, and I thought you handled that in London and New York."

"And then you make me come to Korea. I should really…." Min Lee knocked back another glass of amber liquid. He continued throwing back drinks one after the other, and when he was sufficiently sloshed, and his words were nothing but a slur, he collapsed on the counter.

Huh, Choi thought. *Trouble in paradise. An opening.* Choi approached the men. "Hey there," slightly inebriated herself, but much better after downing the coffee, she smiled at the men.

"What do you want, Choi?" Ji-Joon immediately moved into a protective stance.

"May I join you?"

"No."

"Sure. Why not?" Min Lee said, flopping around on his chair. "Choi here is drowning her sorrows, too, I bet. Let's all drown our sorrows in alcohol. What are you drinking, Choi?"

"I think it's time we head out," Ji-Joon handed his credit card to the bartender.

"Don't worry, Ji-Joon. Go. Enjoy yourself. I'm not done drinking," he let out a loud hiccup.

Ji-Joon did not move.

"*Naga. Ga. Go.*" Min Lee waved him away.

"*Oppa.*" Choi climbed into the chair next to Min Lee. "Are you okay?"

"No, I am not okay."

"Let me buy *you* some coffee."

"I'll buy the drinks," he said, signaling the waiter. "Give her what she wants."

Choi sipped her drink, a ginger ale. What an excellent opportunity had fallen into her lap tonight. She was going to use it to her advantage to get what she wanted. All she had to do was figure out how to get his watchdog Ji-Joon out of the picture. Who, she pondered, was this woman who had the stoic Min Lee in a quandary, and where the hell was Ann Arbor? She googled it on her phone. Michigan! As in the U.S! This was fabulous.

"Min Lee, I think you should stop drinking," Ji-Joon said.

"*Shireoyo.*" Min Lee ordered another drink.

"Okay, man. I am outta here. I can't watch this anymore." Ji-Joon handed the waiter a card with his driver's contact. "Call me when he's had enough and put his tab on my tab."

"I think you should leave with Ji-Joon," Choi said, disingenuously, trying to help Min Lee up.

"No," Min Lee pushed her hand off him. "I am fine. Just fine," he said. "I can handle my affairs."

It wasn't long before Min Lee was passed out on the counter. The bartender pulled out the number Ji-Joon had given him, but Choi assured him she would help Min Lee out to his car. Instead of taking Min Lee to his car, she hopped a cab and then realized she didn't know where he lived. "Min Lee," she tried to rouse him. "What is your address?" He mumbled, but she'd heard every word. When they arrived, Choi went to the night-super and had him help her take Min Lee up to his flat. Good thing, too, because the man was zonked out, and there was no way she could carry him on her back. Plus, she had no idea which apartment. "He is in bad shape," Choi smiled, beguilingly at the super. "Can you override his code? I don't think I can get it out of him." She looked at the man slumped across the back of the super.

Once in the apartment, Min Lee roused and headed straight to the bar. "I'm not going to beg. If Simba wants her, he can have her!" he kept shouting. "The Lion King has won!"

"Let me help you to bed. You've had too much to drink." Choi offered. *Who was this Simba?* Choi wondered. *Lion King? Hmmm, all was not well on the love boat.*

"Go away. I'm okay." Min Lee dropped the glass.

Choi began dragging Min Lee to his bedroom. His room was, as she had imagined, very masculine. A plush quilted headboard in browns and black offset the grey motif. Most enticing was the smell of spiced orange. She like spiced orange. Choi dropped Min Lee across the bed.

"Where are you going?" He grabbed her wrist so tightly she thought he'd break it. "Don't go. Min Jade, don't you dare go," he pulled her onto his chest.

Who the hell was Min Jade?

"Okay. I won't leave you. I won't." Choi was only too happy to climb into bed with Min Lee.

When Ji-Joon entered the flat the following morning to check on Min Lee, he was all covered up.

"Min Lee," Ji-Joon shouted. "Min Lee," he shouted again. What the hell? He jumped back when Choi Shin's head popped out from under the covers.

"What's up?" A sleepy Choi rolled over, and Min Lee stirred. Min Lee began unwrapping himself from a tangle of arms and legs. "Don't shout," he eased himself into a sitting position, his hands cradling his pounding head. Choi stirred against him. Min Lee sprung from the bed when he saw the woman in his bed. "What is she doing here?"

"Oh Jesus," Ji-Joon threw him a robe. He was stark naked! "That's what I want to know."

Both men covered their eyes when Choi sat up, the sheets falling from her naked breasts. Ji-Joon was frantically gathering clothes from the floor and throwing them at her. He pulled Min Lee out of the room. "What the fuck?"

"What's she doing here?" Min Lee repeated.

Ji-Joon needed to get rid of Choi in a hurry. If this got out, there would be hell to pay. Seung-Le would never forgive his brother and, worse, there would be worse than hell to pay from In-Tak Hyun. Ji-Joon practically threw Choi out the door as soon as she was dressed.

By now, Min Lee had sequestered himself in the bathroom, scrubbing furiously at his body until it was raw. *What the hell was going on here?* When he finally came into the living room, Ji-Joon punched him in the gut. "What the hell is going on with you?"

Doubled over, Min Lee held his stomach and sunk to the floor. He should never have come back to Korea. "I didn't do anything. I didn't, did I?"

"Then why were you wearing your birthday suit in bed with that woman, whom I should point out, was buck naked and your brother's fiancée?"

"I don't know. I can't remember."

"You're such a fool! Jesus Christ!" Ji-Joon pushed a cup of coffee into his hand. "Are you trying to fucking kill me? Get dressed," Ji-Joon scorned, slamming the door as he left Min Lee's apartment.

When Min Lee got himself organized, he bolted across the hall to Ji-Joon's apartment. He'd need to fix this. How could Ji-Joon have left him alone with Choi Shin? Regardless of outward pretenses, the barracuda of a woman was no wilting flower. She would eat her own grandmother alive to get what she wanted. How did Ji-Joon let this happen? How could he have let his guard down? It was Min Jade's fault, too. She was holding all the cards to his sanity.

"What are we going to do?" Min Lee said sheepishly. If he had indeed slept with Choi, it would be the end of him. How could anyone so talented and beautiful resort to this kind of blackmail? He was sure that's what it was all about. Taking advantage of his drunkenness was sordid. "Let's leave Korea this minute. If I stay here, my life is going to be over. I can feel it."

"Why did you do that, man? Are you now having feelings for Choi? Her finger still has the impression of your brother's ring!"

"Give me a fuckin' break." Min Lee slammed his hand on the kitchen counter. "I have zero feelings for that woman. I'm not even attracted to her kind; you know that. Did she say I slept with her? Do you have proof? What did you find out, anyway? I really can't remember. Wouldn't I at least have some pleasant memories?"

"You, my friend, are crazy! How do you expect me to know that? I wasn't in your bed!"

"Ask the woman that."

"How?"

"I don't care. Find out."

Min Lee went out of his way to avoid Choi Shin from that night. Right after rehearsals for his album, he'd quickly leave the building. Now that Seung-Le had taken on the artist division of Soo Industries, her new contract would have to be negotiated with him. But there was nothing he could do to stop her recording her album, so he'd acquiesced. Min Lee refused to do the album. Realizing Min Lee would never forgive her, Choi put her engagement ring back on her finger.

CHAPTER TWENTY-THREE

LONDON, MIN JADE
THE LION AND THE DRAGON

"WHAT TIME WILL YOU ARRIVE? Tunde asked.

"Around eight in the morning. I'm taking the redeye."

"I can't understand you, Min Jade. Why would you choose to go through the hassle of a commercial flight when I can send my plane for you?"

"Tunde!"

"Just saying." He backed off. "This time, you'll stay with me, right? I insist. You now know how well-behaved I am, and I promise to be on my best behavior."

Min Jade, exhausted with this relentless man and his expectations, demands and desires, could find no strength to protest. "It's just for one night, so as long as you have two bedrooms, I'm okay with that."

"I have five."

Min Jade arrived in London seven hours after leaving Michigan. Tunde's chauffeur was waiting for her as she deplaned, quickly shepherding her through customs. *How did this man have so much power at an airport?* Min Jade smiled at her escort, handing him her luggage. "Mr. Tunde sends his apologies for not being able to come personally."

"He is forgiven," Min Jade grinned again, following the driver to the car parked right in front of the exit door. *Maybe his father was the Nigerian who'd bought Heathrow!*

Min Jade expected Tunde would undoubtedly live in Kensington, W8. Instead, he lived in Knightsbridge SW7, not a total surprise. It was where the ultra-understated rich lived.

Tunde greeted her warmly upon her arrival at his home. "How was the flight?" he embraced her.

"I slept all the way," she glanced over the house. It was not a house but a mansion. Too awestruck to try to describe it, suffice it to say, it had way more than five bedrooms.

"Sorry I couldn't pick you up. I had to be at the office for official business. Let me show you to your quarters so you can freshen up. I'll wait for you to have breakfast."

"Thoughtful Tunde," Min Jade said, patting his cheek. Min Jade was no country bumpkin, but suddenly, she was unsure. This kind of wealth was far removed from the world she inhabited. She had nothing to draw on to inform how the ultra-rich conducted protocol.

"You're in here," Tunde pushed open the door to a suite as big as her home's entire first floor. "The living room is through this door, the bathroom, and your playroom over there. Freshen up and come down when you are ready."

This was a mistake. Min Jade sat on the bed. At the knock on the door, she jumped up, feeling like she was Goldilocks stealing porridge. It was her luggage. Min Jade padded to the bathroom to freshen up. It was an experience all on its own. Back in the bedroom, she checked her e-mail and text messages. Maybe an emergency call would come in, and she'd have to head right back to Michigan. She laughed. There was rarely an emergency in her life. What the hell was she thinking? She should have just met Tunde in Korea. *Well, old girl, what's done is done.* A growl in her belly made her hurry downstairs to find the breakfast room.

"This way, Madam. Dr. Tunde is waiting for you." A housemaid met her at the bottom of the stairs.

Dr. Tunde? Yes, indeed, she supposed he was. This truly feels like the twilight zone. She increased her pace to match the very efficient, crisp Nigerian housemaid.

"Can I tell you how excited I am?" Tunde jumped up and pulled out a chair for Min Jade. "I couldn't wait for you to get here. I was like an expectant father…well maybe, boyfriend," he wrapped his arm around her shoulder. "Am I?"

Min Jade socked him in the arm.

"Ouch," he rubbed his arm. "Coffee, please," he instructed the waiting staff. "What do you want for breakfast?"

"How about braised kidney, baked beans and to-*mah*-to? I've missed that."

"I don't know about all that, but let's start with fruit and see what Chef comes up with," he nodded again to the staff. "Min Jade, I have a big surprise for you."

"Again?"

"Don't be sarcastic."

"Is it *really* a *surprise* or a surprise?" Min Jade asked. Tunde couldn't be trusted in the surprise department.

"My parents are here. We are having dinner with them tonight."

Min Jade's heart dropped. What on earth was wrong with this man? She had no interest in meeting his parents. It was clear from this decision he'd made alone that telling him about her relationship with Min Lee was the right thing to do. She would never be able to put a stop to Tunde's sense of entitlement and his persistence unless she was brutally honest. "Tonight? Here?"

"No, we are meeting them at the Araki. It's a sushi place. I hope you like sushi. It only seats nine people in total, so there will be just us. If you prefer, we could go to one of our family-owned restaurants, but I think it'd be too pretentious, right?"

"Entirely." Min Jade bit into the tangy pineapple.

Dinner in the Lion's Den

A kingly man rose as they entered the restaurant. Robed, he reached them with his long stride in what seemed like seconds. "Tunde, my boy, good to see you, son," he pulled his son into a bear hug. His booming voice echoing through the small restaurant was as intimidating. Unblinking, his gaze fell upon Min Jade, and his shrewd eyes traveled from her head to her toes. Releasing his son, he took a step toward her, a broad smile appearing on his face. He looked nothing like Tunde. "So, you are the lassie who has my son burning a hole in my ear," his laugh was thunderous.

Lassie? Lassie! A damn dog! Min Jade felt her arteries constrict. For some reason, the stifling environment of her high school popped into her head. "It's good to meet you," he said, patting her like a poodle. "I am Aba Oghenekohwo. Come, come. Meet Tunde's mother," he turned away, not even waiting for her to acknowledge him. It was clear women were an afterthought in this man's world. The woman sitting erect at the table was dressed in the finest threads, her head adorned with an orange silk headdress. She did not stand when Min Jade approached the table but extended her hand. "Lovely to meet you."

Min Jade shook her hand and slid into the chair beside her. "It's my pleasure." The woman's thoughts were imperceptible, and her blank emotions hard to gauge. Tunde's mother spoke very little throughout dinner, yet not for a second did she take her eyes off Min Jade. Min Jade kept dabbing her nose, thinking maybe she had boogers or something.

"Min Jade—see, I know your name—my son calls it so much." The booming voice penetrated her eardrum just as she thought she might outstare the woman beside her. "I hear you are a world-class physicist. Are you willing to give it all up to become my son's wife? And you're willing to convert to the Muslim faith?"

"Dad!" Tunde admonished. "You promised. Dinner. No inquisition."

"Okay. We will discuss all this later." Aba Oghenekohwo waved a hand, and the waiter brought the menu. "We try everything. Why not?" he smiled at Min Jade.

Did he just say, wife? Min Jade was rendered speechless. She felt the blood drain from her face, and she leveled Tunde with the look of death. What on earth was he telling his parents about them? Boy, would she let the presumptuous, cocky bastard have it? With the topic of their son's marriage off the table, the conversation turned to business between the men. Min Jade was too bristled to try to make small talk with his stone of a mother. In the middle of dinner, Min Jade's cell phone announced, "Crazy Korean calling." Everyone looked at her. Tunde seemed very displeased, and that pleased Min Jade. Served him right.

"Excuse me," Min Jade said, leaving the table. "I'll only be a moment." She felt the stares falling on her back like arrows intending to wound.

"She is beautiful," she heard Aba Oghenekohwo say, and she walked to the other end of the small restaurant.

"When are you getting here tomorrow?" Min Lee asked

"Honey, may I call you back? I'm at dinner."

"With whom this time?"

"Tunde and his parents."

That was it. Min Lee would kill the bastard when he got to Korea.

When Min Jade returned to the table, Tunde's eyes were like lasers burning a hole through hers.

"Crazy Korean?" His father's eyebrows raised, and a frown appeared on his mother's face.

"Yes. A good friend who I will see when we go to Korea. They just wanted to know when I was arriving," she stressed the word friend and Tunde frowned.

"Min Jade has been invited to lecture there. *We* are flying there tomorrow. That's why I wanted us to have dinner tonight." Tunde took his shot on the way to recovering his charm.

"I see. It's a lovely place." His father said.

For the rest of the evening, they made small talk. Aware she'd made a grave mistake, Min Jade wished she'd not invited Tunde to accompany her to Korea. Not soon enough for Min Jade, dinner ended.

"You must come to Nigeria." Tunde's father was saying as they walked to the exit. "We will talk more there," he pumped her hand up and down with gusto. Min Jade got into Tunde's car. Did they think this was some Coming to America drama? Min Jade, beyond irritated, gave Tunde the silent treatment as they drove back to Knightsbridge. Tunde finally spoke.

"I'm sorry about that. I bet you were shocked!"

"I don't think that's the word."

"I didn't know Dad would do that. I'd warned him, but he can't help himself. I didn't tell him anything about marriage. I simply told him I admired you and wanted him to meet you. He probably saw the chemistry between us and assumed…."

The Pianist and Min Jade

"The only problem is, Tunde, we are physicists, not chemists." Min Jade spat.

"I understand why you are angry, but please, believe me, Min Jade, Dad, does this with every woman he meets, even ones that were not girlfriends. He even asked my math teacher in high school if she'd give up teaching if she married me! She was fairly young," he hastily added.

"I'm not just angry, Tunde. I'm disappointed. The least you could have done was give me a heads up about your father's predilection for making every woman he meets your wife. For all I knew back there, your father seems to think I'll be walking down the aisle soon."

"He even promised when I told him I liked you that he wouldn't bring up his usual nonsense. It's been a bone of contention between us, but as you can see, my father does exactly what he wants to. He always breaks his promises." Tunde pouted like a disappointed child.

As you do, Min Jade looked over at him. She had never heard this kind of defeat from the overconfident man she knew. Before her very eyes, in the presence of his father, Tunde had become an *enfant*. Though she was fuming, Min Jade was glad to have seen this side of him and get to hear the ridiculous expectations of the woman who would become his wife. Back at the mansion, Tunde suggested they had a nightcap. And miraculously, he'd reverted to the man she knew.

"I'm exhausted, so I'd like to call it a night. Tomorrow, we have a long flight ahead of us." Min Jade declined the offer.

"Please, Min Jade, let's have a nightcap. We'll go to my private quarters."

"Not tonight. We'll drink and talk all the way to Korea."

"Can you at least answer this? What have you decided? Me or the Korean?"

"Tunde, to be honest, I truly wanted to hear your reason for my being your girlfriend, but after tonight, that's no longer an option. Did you hear your father tonight? I would be expected to give up my career to be your wife! You know I could never live up to that."

"He was joking. Really, he was. I'll change. I can change. Please, Min Jade."

"And then what, Tunde? As physicists, we are the most practical people on earth. What will you change into, and for how long?"

"Just hear me out. I need you to listen to me."

Min Jade had never heard this kind of gravitas from Tunde, who always made light of things, even when he was dead serious.

"Okay," Min Jade said. "You have one hour."

"Let's go up to my space."

Tunde's space was a house all on its own: a living room, game room, sauna, two bathrooms, a movie room, a dining room, and an exercise room.

"What will you drink?" He poured himself a whiskey.

"Coke."

Tunde handed her a glass of bubbly soda. "I'm not a cad, you know," he raised an eyebrow looking at the glass in her hand.

"I know that."

"Do you know why I wanted you to meet my parents?" He sat in a chair opposite her on the sofa.

"No, but I thought you knew me better than that."

"I do. But I want you to understand what I am about to say to you now. Remember I told you in Martinique I'd been in love once? When I was twenty-two, I fell hopelessly in love with a girl at Cambridge. It was the first time I had ever loved someone.

This woman had me at hello. She was so different from me, free, fun-loving, and beautiful. She made me laugh. Oh, how she made me laugh, and she taught me to breathe. Adaline was a simple girl with the most generous heart and a smile that lit up my world. She loved me as much as I loved her. It was a rare, and I believed an ordained love could weather any storm. I proposed to her, and she said yes. I was beside myself with happiness. I immediately introduced her to my family, though I knew it would be a fight. I was young and believed that I would marry that girl no matter what my family said. I was prepared to go against their wishes if they didn't give their blessings."

Tunde had Min Jade's full attention. She never pegged him as a man who could fall head over heels, madly in love, for anyone. Men's hearts, too, she began to appreciate, were deep oceans that buried lost love and broken hearts.

"In my culture, marriage is purposeful and about strengthening families. Love does not compete with family honor. When I introduced her to my father, and he had his talk with her, she was so distraught she disappeared in the middle of the night. I never saw her again. She never returned to school. I didn't think I would ever get over her or that I would ever care about another person in this life. I decided I would never marry if it meant being with someone I didn't love."

Min Jade looked at him curiously, clearly seeing him in a new light. She could hear the pain in his voice, reliving his heartbreak all over again.

"I became the player's player, but then you walked in for breakfast that first morning in Innsbruck. For the first time, my heart did something it hadn't done in years. I know lightning doesn't strike twice, but even filled with the scars of lost love, I wanted to try just once more when I saw you. You were so self-assured, funny, and brilliant. So easy to talk with and original. All kidding aside, Min Jade, I loved you the moment you walked into the room. I know. I know it's corny, but it's true. If you say yes, I promise I will protect you for the rest of my life, with my life if necessary. If my father interferes, I'm ready to be disinherited for the woman I love. All you have to do is tell me you want to be with me, and I'll choose love over everything else. Nothing else will matter." He had shed his usual humor and unmasked the vulnerable boy.

"I'm so sorry, Tunde. How did you get through the pain?"

"None of us get a pass from pain. It makes you understand who you are and what matters. I may seem all that to you, but in the end, I'm looking for love just like everyone else. I'm just a scared little boy who believes he will never find love because my culture does not value love."

There were no filters in his conversation. The wealthy, brilliant physicist had given way to a man simply wanting to be loved. "Love may be nothing but an illusion. Maybe your parents know best, Tunde. This love business can be great for a while until reality sets in—life changes after the chemistry wane. Unfortunately, moments don't replace lifetimes. Sometimes, they are just meant to be moments." Min Jade thought about Min Lee. She should take her own advice. Placing her glass on the sofa table, Min Jade rose, "One day, Tunde, you will have to go home and assume your position as head of household. What then?"

"Not if it means I can't love you, Min Jade. How much closer must I stand, and what else can I do to convince you that I deeply love you?"

"Maybe you should back up a bit." Min Jade said, taking her leave.

Min Jade sat in front of the bathroom mirror, removed her make-up. She stopped mid-action and began pondering

Tunde's words. He had been vulnerable and truthful tonight. She'd felt how genuine his confession was, and her heart softened. Min Jade pulled another infused wipe from the container, *but what would that change if she acted on his words?* She still could not hear the hum. Min Lee or Tunde. One represented the heart and the other, the head. Neither would be easy. With Tunde, she'd be indulging his one-sided fantasy, ignoring the emotional tax it carried and risking the loss of a friendship she valued. With Min Lee, she'd be opening herself up to a vulnerability that could destroy her, but if she walked away, she'd have to give up the love that had already nested in her heart. Min Jade, too tired to try to figure out what her next move had to be, slumped across the bed.

In his quarters, Tunde poured another whiskey. Something had shifted tonight. He hoped it was in his favor. Damn the Korean. And damn his motor-mouth father. If it weren't for them, he'd have this all sewn up. Tunde rested his glass on his bedside stand. "I can make you happy, Min Jade." He said aloud. "I will move heaven and earth for you because I don't think I can live without you. Please just let me come closer and show you that love is all." He emptied his glass and climbed into bed. Even the spirit could not stop his racing mind. What did he need to do?

Min Jade couldn't believe she had zonked out so quickly, but it had been a long and emotionally taxing day. The morning sun was dancing on her walls as she went to the powder room. Showered and primped, she donned combat boots, a sequined army top, and a bright orange skirt. If she met Tunde's parents again, she was ready to go to war!

CHAPTER TWENTY-FOUR

MIN LEE WOO, SOUTH KOREA
DECISIONS

MIN LEE'S STRIDE WAS LONG AND PURPOSEFUL. He must have been crazy to make this kind of commitment to his father. He was tired of looking around every corner to avoid Choi, tired of In-Tak Hyun's venom, Seung-Le's childishness, and even Korea. His father would have to understand it was imperative that he go to be with Min Jade. He could feel her wavering, and that could never happen. As he was about to enter his father's office, his phone rang. Duck Beak? His heart skipped a beat.

"Are you here?" He sounded too eager and pulled back his excitement a bit.

"We're leaving in an hour or so. I'll call you when we get there."

When Min Lee returned to his office, Choi Shin was seated on the white leather sofa.

"*Oppa*, why are you avoiding me?"

"Choi, didn't I tell you never to come into my office unless I am here?" He'd give his incompetent secretary the boot. "Get out! We have nothing to say to each other, and I am not in the mood for nonsense, plus I am no longer in charge of your contract. Go see your ex-fiancé for that."

"I'm not here to talk about my contract."

"I don't care what you're here to talk about. This is not a good time." He pulled her up from the chair and marched her to the door. Choi yanked her hand away and spun to face Min Lee.

"*Oppa*, but I so enjoyed our time together, but it seemed you didn't. I'd like to...."

"Choi, get out. I am not and will never think about any night with you, ever," he abruptly cut her off. "I know it looks bad, but I'm pretty sure nothing happened between us, right? It was a horrible mistake if it did, and I am very sorry. Let's just put it all behind us because I don't have one ounce of affection for you. I have a girl who will be here today. She is the woman I will marry, so there is no place in my life for you. And in case you have forgotten, you were my brother's fiancée. Don't do anything foolish. Now, if you'll excuse me." Min Lee was about to throw her into the hallway when Ji-Joon walked up. Min Lee was glad because he never ever wanted to be alone with Choi.

Choi leaned into Min Lee and whispered in his ear, "Think carefully about what I will be proposing," and for Ji-Joon's benefit, she kissed Min Lee on the cheek. "I'm good for you," she whispered.

Ji-Joon watched as she strode out the door. Min Lee was one crazy guy.

"*Annyeonghaseo*," Choi smiled at Ji-Joon as she passed.

"You are something else!" Ji-Joon went into Min Lee's office and shut the door. "Now you're trying to cause a scandal in broad daylight."

"That woman is crazy, I tell you," Min Lee wiped off the kiss with a handkerchief he whipped out of his breast pocket.

"Then stay away from her. What if Seung-Le had seen that? Your office is glass, you know."

"Quit with the lecture. Did I tell you Min Jade is coming to Korea?" For some reason, he'd kept Min Jade's visit a secret because he didn't want to hear Ji-Joon's babble.

"Min Jade? When?"

"Ji-Joon. None of that matters. Just tell me what to do!"

"I'll tell you what to do, all right. Let's get the hell out of here, out of Korea. You are becoming unstable here, and my life is fast going into a hell hole. I don't know what you'll do next. Naked woman in your bed, your brother's ex at that, and now you've lost all sense of reality. You are head over heels in love with a Black American!"

"What does that have to do with anything?"

"This is Korea, Min Lee. Koreans marry Koreans. Period. But don't mind me. Keep your head in the sand. This is not a liberal society. What are you planning now?"

"What the hell does any of what you just said have to do with love? People love people, period."

"Americans are off-limits, period, let alone a Black American."

"Stop while you are ahead," Min Lee warned.

Ji-Joon, of course, did not.

"Too late for all that anyway. She'll be here today." Min Lee tuned out Ji-Joon's jabbering. Deep in thought, his mind was turning like wheels. When Ji-Joon looked over at Min Lee, he was pacing back and forth, from the desk to the door, running his hand through his hair, his jaw locked in determination.

"I've got it!" He suddenly stopped pacing. "Why don't we have a party at my dad's place? That would take care of all this speculation. I'll introduce her as a friend I met in Austria who is visiting Korea. It's pretty much true. You think we're all wrong for each other anyway, so that should please you, too." Min Lee brightened at his clever solution.

"A party? You want to have a party?" Ji-Joon was picking up his lip off the floor. Min Lee hated parties. What Ji-Joon didn't know was that Min Lee had spoken about his love to his father.

Min Lee immediately called his father. "Dad, I have a friend coming into town. I'd like to have a small get-together at your place. I'd like you to meet her."

"The girl, huh?"

"Yes, Dad. But you can't let on."

Ji-Joon, gesticulating with his hand in wild fashion, tried to stop Min Lee from this madness. He *had to be* joking. "Are you trying to kill your stepmother?" Ji-Joon was mouthing, two fingers to his head.

"It can't be a party-party, *Abeoji*, but rather a musical evening," Min Lee ignored him and continued. "We'll play together, Dad. Just a small party, okay? Just family and close friends, so it's not intimidating. You know Koreans."

Ji-Joon flopped down on the couch. *The controlled, unflappable, reality-based Min Lee had turned into a complete half-wit. A party?* This was not going to be an easy love. Ji-Joon braced himself for what was to come. He shook his head and went to find some strong analgesics. He could feel the headache coming on.

Min Lee's plan to solidify Min Jade's heart pleased him. He texted her. She had agreed to the party. It was easier than he'd thought to convince her. It was good in another way, too, because he'd simply said he couldn't trust Tunde, and now the Lion would have to back down. Pouring himself a cup of coffee, Min Lee grabbed the morning paper. Every day there was some news or other about Soo Industries, speculating on its future with Hy Soo's retirement announcement. He'd been hopeful when Seung-Le showed some interest in the company; unfortunately, it was just to block Choi's contract, and Min Lee found himself often mediating clashes between the two. He wished Seung-Le would step up, so he could feel some loosening of the noose of big business and see his way clearly to Min Jade. He was a classical pianist, and he could live anywhere – like Ann Arbor, for instance – which would make his nomadic life more meaningful with a family to come home to. Min Lee smiled and turned the page to find something more palatable than news about Soo Industries.

University of Michigan's Min Jade guest lectures at KAIST. National University. Min Lee rested the paper next to his coffee cup. He had every intention of marrying her.

Incheon International Airport looked like a humpback whale. Impressive beyond words, the lattice-and-glass building proudly represented Korea's transformation and economic relevance. As they passed the Cultural Experience Center, men and women dressed in traditional Joseon attire, *Hanbok*, bowed deeply to the newly arrived as they strolled through the terminal. The Joseon era, which had lasted five centuries, still very much defined modern Korea: its etiquette, cultural norms, societal attitudes, and even its modern Korean language–*Hangul*. In the Millennium Hall, with its suspended colored globes, a musical ensemble played. Min Jade later discovered the airport, boasted a spa, an ice-skating rink, and a driving range. She was impressed. This was not the airport she'd seen on her first visit. Progress was afoot.

They were met at her gate by the long arm of Tunde's international prowess. Tunde's only aim was to get out of the building as quickly as possible. He wasn't exactly pleased to be in Korea in the first place. He hated the idea of even being on the same continent, much less in the same country as the Dragon Pianist. Tunde was still upset about Min Jade's ultimatum to vacation in Korea or nowhere, but he would've traveled to the end of the earth to be with her. The only high point of the damn nuisance trip was that he would face Min Lee Woo and set him straight man-to-man.

They headed to their passenger terminal, where Tunde had a driver waiting. Min Jade continued to be impressed by the power he wielded any and everywhere. "After the lecture, we can spend a week in Thailand, no?" he'd said. To swallow the whole bitter ordeal and somewhat save face, he'd insisted she fly with him from London, but even their time in flight made zero dent in her decision. Tried as he did to continue their conversation from the night before, Min Jade cleverly skirted the issue. He was not feeling confident. What else? He'd poured his heart out and laid it at her feet. Would she trample on his already-battered heart? Tunde was at wit's end with this woman. He didn't feel good about this trip at all, not one bit. As the car sped towards Seoul, he said, anger seeping into his controlled voice, "Why do we have to stay here after your lecture, anyway?"

"Oh, sexy lady, whoop, whoop. *Oppa* Gangnam Style," Min Jade did a Psy move.

"How cliched," Tunde was not in a jovial mood.

"Whoop, whoop," Min Jade jiggled in her seat.

"Min Jade, this is not funny. After your little shindig with Mr. Woo, let's just go. Why would he have a party to welcome you anyway? Isn't it a bit over the top?" Tunde asked

"Did you say over the top?" Min Jade stopped her jiggle and faced him. "You got to be joking! Tunde, everything you do is over the top. Do you have an exclusive on over-the-top-ness?"

"Stop being argumentative. You know what I mean. When exactly do we go to this party?"

"Tomorrow night," she said, taking his hand. "Let's go with this. I'm trying here."

"Do you think it's fair?" Tunde tried to keep his voice calm, but he was fuming.

"The universe..." she gave his hand a little squeeze. "You are getting worked up for no reason at all when the universe already has a plan."

"Fake physicist," he flung her hand off his. Tunde wished he could believe that. Gritting his teeth, he reminded himself to be more cautious with his outbursts. Not being in control irked him to no end.   An hour or so later, they checked into the Grand Intercontinental Parnas.

Min Jade called Min Lee.

Min Lee's Father's Estate – The Party

In-Tak Hyun had reluctantly organized the party for Min Lee's guests. She truly wanted nothing to do with it, but she couldn't displease her husband. Not now. In-Tak wanted to believe that one day before Hy Soo died, he'd fall in love with her. That bastard child was getting on her last nerve and making it harder for Hy Soo to forget his dead first love. At a time like this, when Hy Soo was trying so hard to get well, she needed to be a supportive wife. As much as she despised Min Lee, his presence had given Hy Soo hope, and she was grateful for that. "Over there...No...there." In Tak-Hyun barked at the help.

The party was on the north side of town, their driver informed Tunde. Dapper in a casual white dinner jacket, grey-and-white striped shirt open at the neck, and charcoal grey pants, he waited for Min Jade in the hotel lobby. He gasped as she approached him. *Good Allah!* He pulled his coat closer as he never knew how his other head would behave in her presence. How much more beautiful can this woman get? Decked out in a white A-line dress, cinched with an electric blue patent leather belt and matching shoes, a blue mid-waist cardigan draped her shoulders, she shone. Hair in an up-sweep, her dimpled cheeks aglow with just the right amount of blush complimenting the deep rouge of her lips, made her a sight to behold. She'd toned her style eclecticism down quite a bit, which aggravated him. Only her translucent green specs perched tastefully on her nose gave any inclination of her style. In Tunde's eyes, she was the most beautiful woman in the world, no matter what she wore.

"How do I look?" She took her place next to him.

"Divine!" Tunde could not take his eyes off her as they made their way to the car. What was the matter with him? What was it about this woman that had allowed him to swallow his Nigerian pride so readily? The combination of her brains and beauty, her disinterest in his mega-wealth, her fun side and her great voice were all real turn-ons. He wanted to lay her on the back seat of the car and make her call out his name. Just the thought forced him to cross his hands over his lap as they settled in the car. If she only knew what he'd had to do to tamper his sexual urge for her – the unthinkable for a man like him. He had to make this woman his – lock, stock, and barrel – tonight.

As the car sped along the highway, Tunde asked the driver, "Were the packages delivered?"

"Yes, sir."

"Good."

They pulled up to a tall, black, wrought iron gate. The driver buzzed, and the massive gate opened. The long driveway led to a large, airy, pagoda-style building, and they pulled up under the portico. The place was magnificent. Wealth expressed in gardens that rivaled any in Japanese was stunning. The driver opened the door for Min Jade and then Tunde. Tunde, uncurling his six-foot frame, exuded calm as he straightened to his full height. Min Jade noticed Tunde's demeanor had now transformed into a supremely confident man and one ready to do battle. "Ready?"

Min Jade nodded. What on earth was she doing? What was a simple physicist doing starring in this melodrama?

Min Lee himself greeted them. The two men stood facing each other, one just slightly taller, their eyes meeting, acknowledging what they already knew.

"How wonderful of you to come. Thank you for the thoughtful gifts. The best bottles of champagne the world has to offer are always appreciated," Min Lee extended his hand.

"Min Jade and *I*," Tunde emphasized, offering his hand, "are delighted to see you again."

Min Lee turned his attention to Min Jade. She looked wonderful tonight. "Min Jade," he said, almost whispering her name, "Welcome." *Tonight, he was going to ask her to marry him.* "It's great to have you in Korea." As per the tradition, he offered them footwear. Tunde, who seemed to be preening, offered Min Jade a steadying hand. *Why did she have to bring this man? Min Lee wished he'd said no when she asked.*

"*Abeoji, Eomeoni.*" His parents had gathered in the foyer. "These are my friends. Dr. Min Jade and Dr. Tunde Oghenekohwo."

"Welcome to our home. I am Hy Soo Woo. Min Lee's father. And this is my wife. In-Tak Hyun Woo." Bowing his head, he waved them in. Hy Soo was as handsome as his son, although shorter. He didn't look ill to her at all. Min Jade smiled at the charming man. In-Tak Hyun, who had reluctantly shuffled forward, her eyes wide and lips slightly apart, bowed. "I am delighted to meet you," her lips were tight, and the words barely slipped out. "Please," she said, "Let's join the party." The smile plastered on her lips stretched, yet her eyes were deadly cold. She, too, bowed ever so slightly. "We are so pleased you came." *Was Min Lee crazy? What would their friends think? Who were these people? Were they international musicians? That would make it easier to explain. Surely that had to be it.*

"The pleasure is ours," Tunde said. The way he said "ours" made Min Lee flinch and In-Tak Hyun relieved. In-Tak Hyun looked discreetly at Min Lee. Was this bastard child trying to bring disgrace to the family? Did he forget who she was? Tunde glanced at Min Jade with smug satisfaction at In-Tak Hyun's obvious forced greeting. She would never be accepted in Min Lee's world, and that's what life with the Dragon would be like.

"Come in, come in," Hy Soo said, leading the way to a great room. Walking into the great hall, Min Jade could hear a pin drop. The guests were unabashedly staring at her and Tunde and seemed at a loss for words. Maybe they had never seen black folks before, which was unlikely, but Min Jade suspected they had not welcomed them in their home. There were only about fifteen people.

"Are you musicians too?" In-Tak Hyun asked as she took her place beside her husband.

"They are physicists," Min Lee said. "We all met in Austria."

"Oh, how impressive," Hy Soo said.

"*Abeoji*, Min Jade is a tenured professor in the U. S."

"What? But you are so young. That is quite an accomplishment. Congratulations." Hy Soo took her hand.

Physicists. In-Tak Hyun was somewhat relieved. *That could make the night tolerable.*

"Hello." A young, stylish, artistic-looking woman approached. "I'm Ha Yun. A friend of Min Lee's. So pleased to meet you."

"Hello," Min Jade said. "I'm Min Jade, and this is Tunde." The woman was bubbly and genuinely friendly.

"Your *Oppa*?"

"I suppose of sorts," Min Jade laughed, looking at Tunde.

Min Lee did his best to stay composed.

Tunde was grinning from ear to ear. He could barely contain his joy.

"There must be a story behind the name Min Jade." Ha Yun asked.

"Min Jade's mother loved Min Kim Ye-Kwon. She named Min Jade after her," Min Lee hurriedly said. He was not about to be outdone in the 'I know all about Min Jade' department.

From Min Lee's jaw's tightness, Ha Yun soon surmised this was the woman Min Lee loved.

"*Oppa*," Ha Yun looped her arm through Min Lee's to help him save face, "Let's introduce Min Jade and Tunde to everyone."

"Yes," Min Lee said stoically. "Let's do that."

People began coming forward, many still with stunned looks on their faces.

"How do you know Min Lee? Are you musicians? From where? How did you come by your name?" Min Jade and Tunde were bombarded with questions. Finally, Hy Soo Lee rescued Min Jade. "Come with me," he took her by the elbow and led her to a small garden off the great room. "So," he said as they sat together on a wrought iron bench, "you must be the girl Min Lee loves. I am not supposed to know this," he winked, "but I've never seen my son like this."

"I think you have it all wrong, Mr. Woo."

"I don't."

"Why is that?"

"Min Lee hates parties, yet he asked me to host one for his friends. I suspect it was because he wanted me to meet you. He told me all about the woman he loved in the USA when I tried to fix him up with Ha Yun. He talks a lot about you – a lot." Hy Soo peered closely at the woman in front of him.

Min Jade felt the blush coming on. "Mr. Woo, Min Lee, and I are friends. I think he is a wonderful person…but we don't quite know if this will work."

Hy Soo nodded, but Min Jade didn't get the impression he believed her. "So, the gentleman with you is also a 'special friend.' He didn't bother to correct her about calling him Mr. Woo.

"Well, yes. He's a very special friend, but not the way you think."

"I see," Hy Soo patted Min Jade's shoulder and then changed the subject. "Was it hard for you just now? My wife is not good at hiding feelings. Our culture is quite closed, so please forgive her for being awkward earlier. Min Lee never said anything about you other than you were American. You caught us off guard."

"There is nothing to forgive. Most people can't wrap their heads around diversity in America, not even Americans, though we are the most diverse nation on earth. I do understand. There is no need to apologize. Next time, you'll know what questions to ask when he says he's bringing home an American!" Min Jade smiled warmly. She liked Hy Soo a lot.

Hy Soo's eyes crinkled with laughter. He couldn't take his eyes off Min Jade, for, indeed, as Min Lee had said, she looked like *Yun Sun Ah*, especially when she smiled. Hy Soo took her hand again. He could see why his son loved her. He wasn't wrong on any score. "Thank you for coming. You have set my heart and Min Lee's mother's heart at rest." *This woman was clearly in love with his son.* "So, what will you do if my son asks you to marry him?"

"I...I...you know," the blush was no longer willing to be staved off, and Min Jade's face flushed. "I'd be pretty surprised if Min Lee does that. He wants to be here for you. That's his only priority right now."

"I know, but he is very much in love with you, my dear, and don't be surprised – love causes all kinds of chaos. I don't think I can compete with love. Think about that. Love is, or it isn't – isn't it?" Hy Soo's eyes twinkled with wisdom. "Even though Min Lee's mother passed many years ago, I have not once stopped loving her. I'm afraid my wife has had to live with that fact for thirty years. Love is strange like that. It may take a second, minutes, or months, but it can never be ignored."

Tunde took the opportunity to corner Min Lee. "I hope you'll give us your blessing," he came right to the point.

"For what?"

"What do you mean? I'm going to marry Min Jade."

"Really? I don't think so. What exactly does Min Jade have to say about that?" Min Lee was calm and confident.

Tunde bristled but never answered the question. Instead, he said, "Min Lee, let's be clear about one thing: I never lose. If Min Jade had feelings for you, which I know she did, they are resolved now. And, if you have feelings for her, now is a good time to resolve them. It's better for her to be with me."

"And why not with me?"

Tunde paused. "It would be far less complicated. I think you know that."

"Why? Because you are both black? I think your culture may be less accepting than mine. First, we have the same religion. Second, her love for me was never out of gratitude. Third, she loves *me,* and *I* love her, but I will make it crystal clear tonight. I know it's been tough on her. With me being here and you being there for her in Ann Arbor, she was confused for a minute. Tunde, what happened between you and her is shared success, not love. Love can't be mimicked."

Tunde's fingers curled into tight fists. "Wait a damn minute, Min Lee. You're being this confident because you had something almost two years ago? You are the one who left her. You are the one who hurt her. I was the one who saved her. So, what if she hasn't said yes, yet?! It's only a matter of time. She *will* be my wife, and I will not look on or behave kindly toward you if you do something to interrupt this. I am hoping you'll be a gracious host." This time Tunde felt the ventricles of his heart collapsing.

"That's the nature of love, Tunde. It has its up and downs. If love can't take a little chaos, what kind of love is that? I'm hoping you, too, understand that you can't force someone to love you. If Min Jade doesn't have a shred of feeling for me, you'll have nothing to worry about my friend because she won't accept my proposal." Min Lee clasped a hand on Tunde's shoulder. "Money can't buy love, and even the adrenaline of shared success can't sustain pure love. Love—true love—is its own love potion No. 9. Ask Min Jade."

Tunde's fists remained balled up at his sides. It took every ounce of self-restraint not to sock the sodding kimchi-eating pianist into tomorrow. Ha Yun was coming their way, and Min Lee took the opportunity to leave a fuming Tunde. "Excuse me," Min Lee bowed, leaving the Lion to stew. "Ha Yun," he greeted the woman approaching. "I need your help. I need fifteen minutes with Min Jade—can you tie up the Lion?"

Ha Yun nodded and proceeded to engage Tunde, whose eyes glared as they followed Min Lee.

More in The Garden

Hy Soo and Min Jade were engaged in conversation when Min Lee came into the garden. "What are you two talking about?"

"You," his father hugged him, patting his back in comfort.

Min Jade could only stare at the two men. They seem to have gotten close even with all their years of separation. Min Lee had done the right thing in coming home.

Hy Soo leaned into his son and whispered, "She's beautiful and brilliant, but you'll have a fight on your hands from the man with her, my boy. That man won't give up easily, so you'd best decide tonight." Hy Soo walked toward the door, his son following him. "She looks like your mother when she smiles." He patted his son again. "I'll go tend to the guests. You go tend to your love."

Min Lee grabbed his dad's wrist. "*Abeoji*, is she the one?"

"For you, yes."

"Thank you, *Aboeji*."

Hy Soo felt satisfaction as he headed back to the party. He'd fulfilled Yu-Sun Ha's final wish. If Min Jade loved Min Lee, he didn't have to worry at all. Back in the great hall, he hurriedly sought out Tunde, so he could tie him up in conversation and give the Mins a chance to talk. Ha Yun, who was smiling and chatting away, seemed to have been doing a good job, but he'd lend a hand and prolong the separation time.

Min Lee walked over to where Min Jade stood. They were alone for the first time, and he pulled her into the garden cove. "Alone at last." He embraced her.

"Someone could walk in."

"Who cares. I can't believe I am seeing you."

"Me either," she waited for the chatter to cease so he could kiss her.

Instead, Min Lee said, "Why would you encourage a man like Tunde into thinking he has a chance with you? You don't think I would ever believe all that, do you, even if it were to make me jealous?"

"You should. I've spent a lot more time with Tunde than with you. I'm going to…."

"No, you are not. *Jeoldae.* I'll never let you make such a decision!"

"You don't even know what I was about to say."

"It doesn't matter. *You* will only be with me."

"Why?"

"Because I am the man who popped your cherry," Min Lee put a finger in his cheek and made a popping sound.

"Min Lee!"

"Come with me," he began pulling her by the hand. "If you have doubt, I will make you cry out only my name…not the man you are sporting as cover. I have a bedroom upstairs."

"I didn't mean to mislead Tunde. I just wanted to sort out my feelings. Is that a crime?"

"A crime against love? Yes, it is. Why would you want to do that?"

"Well, for starters, your mother doesn't like me! Maybe I need a backup plan."

"She's not my mother. My mother *would* love you. Look, Min Jade, I did all this so my father could rest in peace. I hate parties, but my father is dying, and he promised my mother he would not leave me alone in the world. I wanted him to see I was not alone."

"Min Lee…."

The duck beak came up. "Marry me, Min Jade."

"What? You are being crazy right now!"

"You knew that from the beginning. We both are." In a swift move, he pulled her into him. "Do you love me? Tell me, Min Jade, that you don't know the answer to my question, and I'll walk away."

"Let go of me," she tried to pull away, pretending her heart hadn't already left her body.

"*Saranghae,* Min Jade."

Min Jade was melting. His warm breath on her face started so loud a hum it was deafening.

"*Saranghae,*" he repeated softly, kissing her forehead, then the tip of her nose before bringing his lips to cover hers in searing passion. When their lips locked in passion, Min Jade knew what her answer had to be.

Min Lee pulled back and tilted her face to him. "Will you marry me, Min Jade?"

"Min Lee…."

"Don't say another word," he clamped her lips with his fingers. "Yes, or no?"

"What about Tunde?" She said, her voice hardly above a whisper.

"All is fair in love and war…isn't it? Yes, or no?" he demanded.

"Yes."

"You are absolutely sure you wanted to spend the rest of your life with me," he pulled her closer. "I'm not sure what we will face or how our life will be; all I know is, I want to go there with you."

"Yes, I'm sure," Min Jade closed her eyes, "And yes, I do."

"Let's go tell everyone."

"Right now? Min Lee, please…let's spare Tunde the embarrassment."

"Only if…." he trailed off as his passion got the better of him. "I'm going to kiss you again, right now."

When his lips met hers again, she felt the familiar heat his touch always elicited rising from her body. She nestled into him, inhaling the smell of orange she loved so much. "Let's at least go and show them," Min Lee said as they stepped out of the cove. "Tonight, I'll come to you."

"Min Jade," a familiar voice was approaching. Min Lee and Min Jade stepped back from each other. "There you are," Tunde said. "Min Lee, I think you are on stage about now."

"Ah, yes." Min Lee moved toward the door, his eyes holding that of the woman he loved. Min Jade smiled ever so slightly before lowering her head. That's how it had started for him; this thing called love—with her smile. "Please come in, Min Jade. Sit up front," he said.

Min Jade walked toward Tunde. Glaring at her as she approached him, he pulled her back into the garden. "I hope you were telling him what needs to be said." His voice was terse, and he searched her eyes for any emotion she was feeling. Did he mistake the look in her eyes? She'd never looked at him the way she was looking at Min Lee. Tunde slapped a shrub as he followed her into the great room. He was quickly losing his patience.

"I was." She hurried toward the door.

Ha Yun sat to the left of Min Jade, Hy Soo to her right. Tunde was next to Hy Soo, who was next to In-Tak Hyun, her so back erect, it seemed it would snap. In-Tak Hyun stole peeks at the woman next to her husband and wondered how all this was possible. There were about fifteen people in the room. Conspicuously missing was Seung-Le, which gave In-Tak Hyun smug satisfaction. Min Lee sat at the piano and asked his father to join him. "Dad and I have been collaborating on a Korean album. Today, we'd like to play a special rendition of *Serenade*." The men looked at each other in understanding. In-Tak Hyun was furious. Well aware of the meaning of the stupid tribute to Min Lee's dead mother, she clenched her jaws, her flared nostrils blowing invisible smoke. When the chilling song finally came to an end, it took all her strength to sit still when Min Lee, who spoke first in Korean, then in English for Min Jade's and Tunde's benefit, said, "Min Jade has the voice of an angel. I hope she will consent to sing for you tonight. If she doesn't win a Nobel for her amazing work in Physics, when you hear her, I'm sure you'll agree she should try for a Grammy."

Min Jade flushed with embarrassment. So, this was *how* he would show them their togetherness? How could he? *Outtake?* She realized she had just thought in Korean! Leaning in, Min Lee whispered something to his father, who nodded, and they began playing. He would declare his love publicly, this time through song. In this life, he would never let her go ever again.

"Time, I've been passing time watching trains go by all of my life..." Min Lee began. He had a terrific voice! She had not known that. He nodded at Min Jade to sing with them when he got to the chorus. Min Jade reluctantly joined in with Hy Soo and Min Lee. How could she refuse, even though he had gone too far? *"Maybe it's you...it's you...I've been waiting for all of my life. Something's telling me it might be you. I've been waiting for all of my life."* It seemed father and son had conspired. In-Tak Hyun was frothing at the mouth. Was that bastard child planning to bring this American into her family? Tunde's insides were on fire. This was a declaration of war. How dare Min Lee bring him into his home and make a fool of him? He would not stand for it. As soon as the music stopped, Tunde was on his feet, his body quivering in rage. "That was grand," Tunde

ignored Min Lee walking directly over to Min Jade's side and pulled her close to him. "As always, your voice is amazing," he said, gazing at her. He grabbed her by the wrist. "We are out of here. Now."

Min Jade delicately removed her hand from his. *Who did he think he was talking to?*

Tunde's steely black eyes met Min Lee's almond browns. *I will never lose,* Tunde thought as he straightened his shoulders. This was indeed a declaration of war. Everyone was soon distracted from the live drama playing out before them by a commotion in the hallway.

"*Hyung….*" Seung-Le staggered into the room. "Sorry, I'm late. Am I too late for the celebration?" Everyone, wanting to know what the hullabaloo was about, crowded around.

In-Tak Hyun, embarrassed by Seung-Le's drunkenness, instantly went over to her son. "What are you doing?" she said through clenched teeth.

"I'm drowning my sorrow, Ma. *Oma,* look who I brought with me. My ex! She wanted to celebrate too, no longer having to be your daughter-in-law."

"Seung-Le, stop this immediately," In-Tak Hyun tried to usher him up the stairs.

"No, *Eomeoni,*" he shrugged off her hands. "I brought a guest; I can't be rude."

Choi Shin walked in behind Seung-Le. In-Tak Hyun, who had been holding her cool, was seething. "Why would you bring this woman here?" she demanded.

"She wanted to see Min Lee, *Eomeoni,*" Seung-Le slurred. "She has something to tell him." Seung-Le went to the bar and poured a drink. "*Oma.* I am my brother's keeper."

In-Tak Hyun signaled the help to remove Seung-Le to his room.

"Hello, *Eomeoni*." Choi smiled wickedly, hugging In-Tak. She herself was quite sloshed.

"Get out," In-Tak Hyun hissed, her pursed lips close to Choi's ear, pushing the woman off her.

"I can't do that, *Eomeoni*."

Ji-Joon immediately went over to Choi. He hoped she wouldn't do anything stupid. "Why are you doing this?" He spoke quietly. "Leave now. For everyone's sake, leave now."

"*Oppa*," Choi Shin's voice became loud and grating. She stumbled over to where Min Lee stood. "Why? Why? Why is everyone telling me to leave? It's because of *you that I'm here*," she said, pointing an accusatory finger at Ji-Joon. "You are always keeping me away from Min Lee. He doesn't answer his phone, he doesn't answer his door, he cancels all my appointments, and now he won't let me play with him. How else can I see him?"

"Doesn't it dawn on you that he doesn't want to see you again?" Ji-Joon whispered to her.

"I don't care if he wants to see me again. I don't, but *Oppa*, you have to see our child. I'm pregnant."

"I am my brother's keeper," Seung-Le, who was being ushered from the room, lifted his glass, and emptied its contents in one swig.

A hush came over the room. In-Tak Hyun fainted. Tunde grabbed Min Jade's arm, "Let's go now," he ordered. Before she could collect herself, Tunde was dragging her across the room. Hy Soo instructed that In-Tak Hyun be taken upstairs and that the doctor be called. Ha Yun was staring at Choi Shin, her eyes glistening with shock, while Ji-Joon ushered Min Lee out of the room. Choi Shin smiled triumphantly, staggering after Min Lee. "*Oppa, Oppa*," Choi shouted. "Come back and talk to me. Come back to your child and me."

"Are you satisfied?" Tunde spat as he pushed Min Jade toward the door. "Is this what you expected? Just what did you think, Min Jade? I guess you have your answer now. Let this end here. We leave tomorrow right after your lecture."

"Let go of me," Min Jade shrugged free of his grip.

Tunde pushed her into the car and got in beside her.

Min Jade put as much distance between them as she could, moving to the far side of the car. "Are you crazy?" She was furious. "Who do you think you are? Better yet, who do you think I am to speak to me this way?"

"How rude can you be?" Tunde bellowed. "Never in my life have I ever been so insulted and humiliated. Didn't you know why he asked you to sing that song? Didn't you?" Tunde demanded.

"It's just a song. So what?"

Tunde raised his hand. It took all his strength to bring it back to his side. "So, you want to be his concubine?"

"Oh, stop." Min Jade

"Don't you think it's strange that he had a woman there who thinks he's hers and a baby-mother at that…whom he's spurned? What does that make you? Damn it, Min Jade. Is this who you want to become? Some Korean concubine?"

"Tunde! We're done here."

But he was right. What could she say? How could she have allowed herself to get caught up in this nonsense? *Stupid, stupid girl.* How could she have been so bamboozled?

"You will leave with me tomorrow," Tunde insisted. "Even if I have to lift you over my shoulder and take you to the airport. That's final!"

She would leave tomorrow, alright, but not with Tunde. This was the end of the drama. It had all played out. She would go back to the life she knew. Min Jade felt hot tears well in her eyes, but she refused to let them fall. How could he? Hadn't he just told her how much he loved her? Hadn't he just asked her to marry him? Hadn't she told him repeatedly how much she loved him and how much she wanted to marry him? Their love, which had hummed so loudly, had once again betrayed her head.

Min Jade rushed from the car into the hotel. Her heart felt as though it had been dissected without anesthesia. She had gone crazy with all this attention, and it served her right for straying from her promise to herself. Her work was her happiness. How dare she dream for more? With shaky hands, Min Jade opened the door to her room. Sinking to the floor, her back braced against the door, she wailed like a wounded animal. How could she have been so foolish? She was the stupidest woman on earth, a colossal idiot. Min Jade ignored the unceasing knocks and Tunde's commands for her to open the door. When she'd finally pulled herself together, she called the front desk. "This is Min Jade in suite 1506. I am checking out in the morning. I'll need a car to take me to the KAIST, and then to the airport. Will you arrange it?"

"With pleasure, Madam. What time?"

Min Jade made reservations for the first flight out of Korea after her lecture. This was some helluva melodrama. Korean Style. Her phone pinged.

Crazy Korean: *Min Jade, this is not what you are thinking. Please answer the phone. Please let me explain. Please let me up. I'm in the lobby. I can explain. It's all a huge misunderstanding. I would never hurt you this way. You know me better than that! Will you please let me up so I can tell you everything? Min Jade. Please. Sa rang-hae.*"

She ignored the texts and phone calls and finally shut off the phone.

Min Jade quickly made her way to the lecture hall's pre-arranged spot behind curtains. After her lecture, a car was waiting for her when she exited the private entrance. "Incheon Airport," she said, handing her luggage to the driver, "and please hurry."

Tunde, who'd been in the audience, went to her green room. To his surprise, Min Jade had already left, the attendant informed him. "I'll be a monkey's uncle," Tunde said, rushing to his car. "Incheon Airport," he instructed.

Min Lee's driver pulled up to the auditorium. He did not see Min Jade's car glide by him.

Min Jade made it to the gate just in time to board the plane. There would be no more tears or drama for her. Taking her seat in first-class, she could feel herself slipping into that place she had always feared, into that abyss, the frightening darkness she knew would one day call her name again. This was too much for her, entirely too much. Min Jade ordered two Vodkas and tonic. With no piano to soothe her burdened soul, she plugged in her iPhone only to hear Min Lee's rendition of *Serenade* on the selection. Putting on the eye mask provided, she cried.

CHAPTER TWENTY-FIVE

MIN JADE, ANN ARBOR
GOOD NEWS

MIN JADE BLEW HER NOSE INTO A PILE OF TISSUES. She felt miserable. Her body was worn out, her mind in turmoil, and she hated herself for being weak. She stuck a thermometer in her ear. Her fever was 102. She should go to the hospital. This kind of temperature was too high for an adult. Maybe she should get an ice pack to cool her body down. That was too much of a chore. Instead, she took two Tylenol, climbed into bed, and pulled the covers over her head. She felt as though a part of her had died, and the rest was about to follow. How could Min Lee have done this to her? A loud, ringing sound ripped through the silence. It stopped, then started again.

Drenched in sweat, searing pain in her head, Min Jade felt around the night table for her cell. 5:00 a.m. Apart from her mother once calling when her father had an acute attack of appendicitis, no one except Tunde had ever called at this hour. Unconscionable and infuriating. He, her guardian angel to whom she should be eternally grateful, the man who had moved heaven and earth for her, the man whose words matched his actions, the man who put her above himself, and whose love was shown daily in deeds and action, deserved her devotion, much more than the cad Min Lee. Still, he too was just a man ready to spread his peacock feathers to catch his mate Min Jade clicked off the phone and powered it down. Never again would she trust a man.

When Min Jade roused again, it was midday. Her fever had subsided somewhat. "Shit," she turned on her phone to call her secretary. She just could not go into the labs today, and her office hours needed to be canceled. As she was about to dial, she noticed a missed call. She punched up her voicemail. "Dr. Jade. This is the Royal Academy of Sciences. We are so pleased to inform you that you have been nominated for the Nobel Prize in Physics. Please return our call so we can be sure you got this message."

Maybe she was dreaming. Delirious. Min Jade pinched her cheek. It seemed so real. Was she wide awake, or was this a damn dream? Min Jade swung her legs out of bed and went to the bathroom. She was awake. This can't be. It just couldn't be. Did they say she was nominated for the Nobel Prize? The moment felt surreal, and Min Jade couldn't think of what to do. What should she do? If this was not a dream, shouldn't she be jumping for joy? She pinched her arm again to make sure she indeed was not in a dream. The mind could play such tricks on someone who was grasping at straws. This surely would have been her life raft…in an otherwise-sinking world. What does one do in situations like this? She should call her mother. Winful? Tunde? Were it not for his help, she may never have been able to publish her definitive research on time. Though her mind was in overdrive, her body felt catatonic, so she just sat on the mirror stool, staring into space. She felt something hot on her cheeks and touched her face, only to realize she was crying. Her moment, the moment she waited for her entire life, felt so anticlimactic. Min Jade did what anyone too frightened to face reality did. She took an anti-anxiety pill and climbed back into bed.

A strident knock had Min Jade padding to the door. She pulled it open and collapsed in Winful's arms. "Min Jade…" he grabbed her before she hit the floor. He'd never known her to miss a day of work, much less on the biggest day of her life. "Min Jade, I've been calling. Are you okay?" She was burning up.

"What did I do now?" Her voice was so soft, Winful stopped in his tracks.

"We're going to the hospital."

"No. Please, I am fine. I was nominated, you know."

"I do. You did it, Min Jade. You really did. But right now, we need to go to the hospital."

The following day, when Min Jade opened her eyes, she was feeling much better. Did she dream all this? She was in her bed, an IV in her arm, and Professor Winful was napping in a chair nearby.

"Professor?"

A groggy Winful stirred. "Are you feeling better?"

"Yes. But…."

"I had your doctor come. You were adamant about not going to the hospital, so I called him. He gave you a heavy dose of antibiotics. The news hasn't yet been announced to the world, so I needed to protect you. You don't mind, do you?"

Her dear, dear Winful. "Thank you," Min Jade said.

"Shall we call your parents now?"

"May I just have another day? I feel better, but I'd like a little more time. So, what will we do now?"

"We'll celebrate, darling. You'll celebrate. We'll tell your parents together tomorrow and then call Professor Tunde. I think he must be the next to know."

Yes. Tunde. The lifesaving Lion.

Chair Winful and Min Jade shared the news with Jessica Jade the following day. All composure had gone out the window for everyone when Jessica Jade held onto the banister, sunk to the ground, and sobbed. Min Jade had never seen her mother cry. Never understood the weight she must have carried. Only then did Min Jade truly appreciate her mother's sacrifice and the weight she had lifted on her behalf. Her father had already left for work, but Jessica, through tears and more tears, called to let him know. They had to compose themselves again to meet the President of the University and the Dean of the College. Min Jade felt like a rag doll, all the emotion draining her of any force. Next, they called Tunde.

"Tunde. Professor Winful here." The phone was on speaker. "Min Jade is right here beside me. She got the nomination! We couldn't have done this without you."

Tunde was happy to hear from Professor Winful, but he was annoyed that it was not Min Jade who had made the call. They had not spoken since she left Korea. He was glad this had happened now. Surely it would be a distraction.

"Hold on a moment, Min Jade wants to speak to you." Winful handed her the handset.

"Wow, Min Jade, that's a wow."

"Wow, back to you. I have added your name to my paper."

"Don't be daft. I did nothing. Just supported you so you could do what you do so brilliantly."

"I beg to differ. How can I ever thank you?" There was no way to get around this courtesy though she never wanted to see him again. Adding his name to her paper was gratitude enough.

"Shall we celebrate?"

"I think you know the answer to that." Min Jade was only too grateful the emotional letdown she'd experienced in Korea had not sent her spiraling.

Chair Winful's stride was decidedly more assured than Min Jade's as he led her across campus. Peacock feathers might have well been sticking out of his rear end. Winful buzzed around. He preened and oiled his feathers.

"It's only a nomination," Min Jade said.

After the official nomination was announced, the next few days felt like they were right out of a storybook. Reporters from all over the world were flying to the University to get interviews. Local and international news jammed the phone lines. When did the world care about this kind of thing? Yeah, it was a big deal in the scientific community, of course, but many of the reporters who showed up were from the general media. The reason, of course, she was black. People from all over campus were dropping in to congratulate her, inviting her to lunches, dinners, and conferences. Granted, she was the first-ever black woman and certainly one of the youngest, nominated for the Nobel Prize in Physics, but she hadn't won yet. What would they do if she did win? Min Jade would be the third woman in the history of the Academy to win a Nobel in Physics, joining the ranks of the likes of Marie Curie, who received the prize in 1903 for discovering radioactivity and a second time in 1911 for isolating pure radium. The other Marie, Maria Goeppert-Mayer, like Min Jade, was also from the United States. Since its inception, only one hundred and ninety-eight people had won a Nobel in Physics, and fewer than four percent of them were in their thirties. She'd be making history on all fronts for sure. At that moment, she couldn't begin to fathom how bad the circus would become. Min Jade was eternally grateful for the distraction because she'd been unsure how she'd have handled her splintered heart. With her skyrocketing popularity, she began to understand the importance of anonymity. What took the cake and sent her mother into a catalectic state was the White House call inviting Min Jade to sit on the President's Council for the Sciences. She had even received two marriage proposals. It was only then that Min Jade thought of Min Lee. She'd ignored his calls and texts and would continue to do so. But just tonight, just for a moment, she thought of how much she missed him. She pressed the button to read his texts.

Crazy Korean: *Min Jade, I will be coming to Ann Arbor if you don't pick up the phone or text me!*

Crazy Korean: *Min Jade, I am so sorry. Nothing is as it seems. Please let me explain. I will come to Ann Arbor right now.*

Crazy Korean: *Listen to me. I need you to listen to me.*

Crazy Korean: *Min Jade. Please. Please.*

Crazy Korean: *First, congratulations. I just heard the news.*

Min Jade started to sob. At a knock on her door, she flew into the bathroom and locked herself in. Whoever it was needed to go away.

When the circus got too crazy, she and her dad had their hands full, keeping her mother in check. Her mom started spending entire days calling everyone in the universe and organizing parties to celebrate Min Jade's accomplishment. Min Jade decided that to remain sane, she would jet off for a five-day sequestered vacation, and she would tell no one where she was going, not even her mother.

CHAPTER TWENTY-SIX

SOUTH KOREA, MIN LEE WOO
THE TRUTH

JI-JOON SAT WITH HIS HEAD IN HIS HAND. This was bad. He had tried to keep the news under wraps, but someone in the room, close friends, and family at that, got greedy. He was watching the news. Min Lee had destroyed their lives in one moment of irrational behavior! There was only one solution. Choi Shin had to get rid of that child, and then they could claim the accusations were false. Ji-Joon worried that Min Lee might have second thoughts if Choi were pregnant, knowing his own birth circumstances. There was no way he'd marry Choi, so what now? Ji-Joon was all the more eager to get him to focus on a plan, but Min Lee was obsessing so much about going to Ann Arbor that he could not focus. The debacle was too much.

"*Appa*, I will marry Min Jade. That I promise you."

"I know it will be hard, and I know Korean society can be harsh and provincial, but don't you care about that. You don't have to live here. You can manage Soo Industries from wherever you are."

"Yes, *Appa*. I won't let you down." The conversation was one that made Min Lee think he was asking permission to leave this world behind. He was in pain, and Min Lee wanted it to stop.

On his next visit to his father, Min Lee desperately wanted to tell his father he'd found Min Jade and that all would be well. He wanted to keep his promise to his mother, but Min Jade had just vanished into thin air. How could he and his father both have faced the same fate in love? Min Lee now understood how frantic his father must have been when he couldn't find his mother. He had to find Min Jade. With his father's health slipping daily, he had to.

Min Lee was at his computer the following day, checking flights to Michigan when his doorbell rang. Padding to the door, he pressed the video pad only to see In-Tak Hyun at his door – at eight o'clock in the morning! He hurriedly pushed the buzzer. Something must have happened to his father. "*Eomeoni*, has something happened to *Appa*?"

In-Tak Hyun entered with a flourish. "I want you to leave Korea this instant. Pack up, leave and never come back. You have disgraced this family beyond repair in the few months you've been here. Your father is spending his last days worrying, having to hear on the news all the debauchery of a son who does not deserve him. You have disgraced his good reputation and dragged our family name through the mud. *Ca*. I want you to leave now. Go carry on your shenanigans elsewhere. This is Korea, and you no longer belong here."

"*Eomeoni*."

"Don't you dare call me, Mother! I could never be the mother of someone like you!"

Min Lee got dangerously close to the ill-mannered woman. "You're right. You could never be my mother. You could never hold a candle, even to a little finger of my mother. Father knew that didn't he? Why else would you spend your entire life scheming and hating a dead woman? You are heartless and vile. No wonder father has never loved you."

In-Tak Hyun's face contorted, her eyes widened. There was nothing short of murder in them as her hand connected with Min Lee's face. "How dare you?"

"Get out." Min Lee's voice was low. "Now, before I kill you."

"If you don't leave Korea, it will be me who will kill you. Do you hear me? I will make you wish you were never born to your trollop of a mother." In-Tak Hyun turned on her heels to leave.

Min Jade grabbed the revolting woman by the arm and spun her to face him. This time it was his hand that connected with her face. "Get out of my sight, or I will kill you, right here, right now," he chucked her out the door, and she fell to the floor. "If you ever speak my mother's name ever again, I will, without hesitation, kill you." He slammed the door so hard it reverberated on its hinges. Min Lee stood at the door shaking, blood purpling his face. He has never been this mad or felt such hatred in his entire life.

Hearing the commotion outside, Ji-Joon opened his door to see what was going on. In-Tak Hyun was sprawled on the hallway floor, her face flushed with anger. She jumped to her feet when she saw him, smoothed her hair and clothes, and approached him. The scorn on her face was pure she devil-evil. "Get that bastard out of here, or not only will I kill him, I'll kill you also."

Ji-Joon watched the crazy loon march down the hallway, her steps so angry that her shoe heels buckled. He let himself into Min Lee's apartment and found Min Lee shaking with anger. "What the hell happened just now?"

"Something that should have happened years ago. That woman is beyond evil."

Ji-Joon took on a calming demeanor. "It was about Choi, wasn't it? We really should talk about Choi!"

"Don't ever bring that woman's name up to me again. I'm telling you this for the last time. I don't care what she said. I can't be the father of Choi's child if I didn't sleep with her, right? I did not sleep with her. Why can't you get that?"

"I was here. I saw...."

"I don't care what you saw," Min Lee shouted. "I don't give a damn. I never slept with that woman. End of story."

"We should at least get a doctor to confirm her pregnancy."

"Do what you want. I don't give a flying fuck. Just keep that woman away from me. Even if I did sleep with her, and I am the father of her child, I don't care."

"What if she is really pregnant?"

"Have her get rid of it. Give her whatever she wants. She is the quintessential gold digger."

"Min Lee...."

"Ji-Joon, fuckin' kill the bitch if you have to. I'm done talking about this. If she is pregnant, get a DNA test. I suspect the child—if she is even pregnant—could belong to anyone in Korea! Call me in Ann Arbor and tell me whose!" Min Lee screamed at the top of his lungs. Thank God the place was soundproof.

Ji-Joon's phone rang. "What?" He barked.

She'd never been lucky in love. Ha Yun was drowning her sorrow at her favorite after-work spot, the Glam lounge. With Min Lee fading into the shadows of love, she was back to her favorite corner table shrouded with foliage. The place was packed as usual, and Ha Yun began looking around for someone she might know or might be interested in getting to know.

Ordering a bottle of rosé, she scrolled through her phone. She stopped at Se Na, her best friend, the world's best listener of sob stories. She'd never told Min Lee how she felt, but she had been hoping. Se Na would reassure her that her turn for love would come one day. She punched up the number but did not press the call button, stopping to listen in on a lost love conversation.

"I can't believe he's ignoring me. Do you know what I had to do to get to this point? *Aigooo.*"

"What did you have to do?"

"All I wanted was to get our album done. I don't care about anything else but that stupid brother of his…."

"You mean your ex-fiancé."

"Seung-Le has been blocking my every turn to get my solo album contract signed. I didn't think Min Lee would go along with such a crazy scheme. He knows how good I am. I thought for sure he'd back me up, but no, he went into a hands-off mode. No matter how I tried to get to him, his watchdog manager was always guarding him."

Ha Yun's ears perked up when she heard Seung-Le's name. Discreetly peering through the foliage, she saw Choi Shin sitting at a table with two people, and they were chatting away as though nothing had transpired weeks before. And Choi was drinking! Ha Yun turned on the recorder on her phone, scooting closer to the trio without revealing herself.

"What will you do?" One of the women said.

"What did I do? I took advantage of the situation. One night, I overheard him talking about some American woman at the bar. He was getting sloppy drunk, so I offered to drink with him. His manager, the gatekeeper, left in frustration, asking the bartender to make sure he got home safely. I saw my chance. I took him home." Choi Shin sat with smug satisfaction. As calm as she pretended to be, she was pissed that neither Min Lee nor Ji-Joon had reached out to her since her Oscar-winning performance. She had destroyed two brothers with one blow, and it felt revengeful, almost satiating, though deep down, it left her empty. That's what In-Tak Hyun got for looking down on her. Seung-Le thought she was some play-mate and didn't give a hoot about her dreams, and Min Lee should've supported her.

"So, what exactly are you saying?" One of her friends asked.

"I'm saying that man is no man at all. Imagine a naked woman in your bed. How can you resist?"

"You were naked?" They asked, incredulous, nervous laughter wafting in the air.

"And so was he. I made it easy. I undressed him. All he had to do was a rollover. But even stone drunk, he didn't touch me. Not even for a second. He kept calling out this other woman's name. Min Jade. Can you believe it? I met her, too. She is a *heug-in yeoseong* from America. *Oppa* has lost his mind, I tell you."

"No. Did you say a black woman?"

Ha Yun, too, had been taken back by Min Jade. In general, Koreans were xenophobic about any foreigner, but maybe a little more if they were black, rarer in South Korea. Ha Yun continued to listen. Choi Shin conveniently left out the story about the scene she had made accusing Min Lee of being the father of her child. Here she was, guzzling alcohol and boldly admitting that Min Lee hadn't touched her. That evil woman. How could she?!

"Yup," Choi said. "She is some kind of brainiac, as I under-stand it. I bet I took care of her undying love, too. Anyway, I have to go. I have a gig. See you later."

The women watched her go. "Can you believe her?" one said.

"Her career is over, anyway. Did you see the news?"

Ha Yun waited until Choi slid through the glass doors. What a despicable, scheming woman. What should she do? She dialed Ji-Joon.

CHAPTER TWENTY-SEVEN

MIN JADE
TRAGEDY

MIN JADE RELUCTANTLY TURNED ON THE PHONE she'd stored in her luggage during her five days on the island. Already her muscles were tense, and her secluded beach property in Belize—where she'd fallen asleep at nights to the sound of waves lapping against the shore— was receding. Unfortunately, her time of introspection did not lead to any new conclusions about her future life but had been good for her psyche. Tried as she did to forget, Min Lee's betrayal had invaded her thoughts. She believed him. She was sure things were not as they seemed, but she didn't think she was brave or mentally strong enough to live a dramatic life. She was a damn good physicist, that much she knew beyond a shadow of a doubt, and that's what she would do with her life—devote herself to her career. Min Jade was still pinching herself to believe she'd been nominated for the Nobel and felt deep gratitude to Tunde, wishing there was a way the head could control her heart. As controlling as he was, everything Tunde had done was for her benefit, including being furious at her. Min Jade scrolled through her fifteen missed calls. Ten were from her dad! Three were from Min Lee, and two from Tunde.

She dialed her father. "Dad?"

"Min Jade, why haven't you answered your phone? I've been trying to reach you since early morning."

"I'm at the airport. I just landed."

"Come to the hospital now. Your mom has been admitted."

"What?"

"Hurry, Min Jade. Cardiac unit. I need to get back to her. Hurry."

"Dad. Dad!" The phone went dead.

Min Jade rushed toward an airport official. She explained her situation and was allowed to clear passport security and customs ahead of the line. She jumped into a cab. "U of M hospital, and please hurry." She could barely sit still, her mind swirling with worry. What could possibly be wrong with her mother? The woman was as healthy as an ox. She had been to the hospital once in her entire life, and it was to have Min Jade. She must have eaten something bad. Indigestion could feel like a heart attack.

The cab was still moving toward the curb when Min Jade opened the door and jumped out. She handed the cabbie a wad of cash and bolted through the double glass doors. "The cardiac unit…my mother," she could barely get the words out at the information desk.

"Calm down, Miss," the receptionist said. "What's your mother's name?"

"Jade. Jessica Jade."

The woman typed the name on the keyboard. "Left bank of elevators, cardiac unit, fifth floor. Room 540." Min Jade was already halfway down the hall. On the fifth floor, she kept her hand on the buzzer until she heard the door click. Frantic, she approached the nurses' station. "I'm Min Jade. How is my mother?"

"Miss Jade. Please follow me. The doctor is waiting for you."

Her father was in the room with the doctor, but her mother wasn't there. He looked grave and drawn. How could he look so fragile in five days? "Dad…." Her father turned. "Where is Mom?"

Tears welled in his eyes. "Min Jade. Oh, Min Jade." Her father was inconsolable.

Min Jade rushed over to hold him up. "Dad. Where is Mom?" she repeated. The look in her father's eyes was one she'd never forget as long as she lived.

"She's gone, Min Jade. She's gone."

"Gone where? What…Dad…what are you talking about?"

"Miss Jade," the doctor said, "it was a massive myocardial infarction. "I am sorry we tried."

Min Jade's brows knitted. *What was he saying? Just what on earth was he talking about?* Min Jade looked over at her father. He was crumbled in a chair, devastated, tears steadily falling down his face.

"What exactly is going on here, Doctor?" Min Jade asked.

"I'm afraid your mother passed away minutes ago. She had a massive heart attack. Random. No reason we can see, but it destroyed her heart."

Min Jade still couldn't piece it all together. Dr. Jones was a family friend. He'd known Min Jade since she was but a tot and was a part of many decisions her mother had made when it came to Min Jade's health—from her asthma treatments to her mental hospitalization.

"Dr. Kingsley did everything he could. I came the minute your dad called. I was privy to all he tried to do. I can't explain it, Min Jade, but it happens. I can't believe Jessica is gone, but she is. I know this is going to be hard, but you have to stay calm. You have to stay…."

Min Jade stared blankly at Dr. Jones. She couldn't hear a word. She put her hand to her ear and jiggled it. His mouth was moving, but no sound came from his lips.

"Min, Jade," Can you hear me?"

Min Jade continued to have a mask like look on her face. He was afraid she was shutting down. "Owen, I think Min Jade is not going to be okay."

Suddenly Min Jade began laughing hysterically. "Mom's such a prankster." Her mother dead? Were they crazy? Her mother couldn't die; the woman had never had as much as a cold. It was a bad practical joke. All because she'd left without telling her. And a little spooky. "I'm sorry I didn't tell Mom I was leaving. Tell her it's okay now. I'm back. I really shouldn't have left without telling you guys, but I just needed a moment. Tell her this is a nasty joke to play for something like this." Her mother would never leave her, not this way.

"Min Jade," her father said, holding on to her, "let's go home and rest now."

"Okay, Dad. Go ahead and get Mom. We'll all go together."

"Min Jade," Doctor Jones kept repeating, "Min Jade, do you understand what I'm saying? This is not a joke. Your mother has passed away."

Min Jade became agitated. Her mother was too organized to be dead. And certainly not while Min Jade was away. That could never happen. Her mother wouldn't die like this. It just would never happen. They were so wrong.

Her father shook her by the shoulders. "Min Jade. Min Jade."

"I think she's in shock." Dr. Jones summoned a nurse. "Please call Dr. Robbins. He's Min Jade's psychiatrist. Ask him to come now."

The nurse ran out of the room. Frightened to death at the immediate change in Min Jade. Owen felt his world crashing down around him. He just lost his wife, and now his daughter was falling apart. "Help her, John." He said.

"Dr. Robbins might want to give her a sedative. He might even want to keep her overnight. I think she's having a dissociative episode," Dr. Jones explained.

"Mom," Min Jade kept repeating loudly, "I was only gone a week. Isn't being dead a little drastic, Mom?" Min Jade was laughing. Her mother was such a prankster. Then she felt it. The snap and then darkness descending, like thunderous clouds rolling in.

When Min Jade woke, she was in an unfamiliar bed. She sat up to get her bearings. Why was she here? It looked like a hospital. She rang the buzzer, and a nurse came in. "Why am I here?"

"Just a moment," the nurse said. A few minutes later, she returned with Dr. Robbins in tow.

"Min Jade, are you alright?" His eyes showed grave concern.

"I'm fine. But I'm not sure why I am here. I had such a bad dream. Did I…Oh, Dr. Robbins," reality seeped in. "Is Mom really gone?"

He nodded his head. "I'm afraid so, Min Jade. I am afraid so. Your father is here. I'll bring him in."

There was such relief on Owen Jade's face when he saw his daughter. "Are you all right, darling?"

"Yes, Dad. I think I'm fine."

The breath her father let out was a deep sigh of relief.

Min Jade asked to see her mother. Doctor Robbins advised against it, worried by her brief psychotic break.

"Min, Jade, let's go home," her father said.

"Doctor Robbins, I need to say goodbye to my mother. I cannot leave this hospital without saying goodbye to my mother," she insisted. "I know you are worried. I understand I had a bit of a setback, but I am fine now. Please arrange for me to see my mom."

Though highly unusual, Dr. Robbins arranged with Dr. Francis, the doctor in charge of the morgue, to move Jessica to a private space so her daughter could say goodbye.

Min Jade took her father's hand, and, together with Dr. Robbins, they walked to the room where her mother lay. Her mother's lifeless body was indeed there. Her mother was dead. Her father's body rocked back and forth, emotions unsettling him, but Min Jade's were as still as the morning after the storm. She felt nothing, not her heart beating, her eyes blinking, her limbs moving, or even the breath coming out of her mouth. She was as dead inside as her mother was, where she lay on the cold, hard gurney. Nothing mattered anymore—none of it.

Min Jade and Owen could barely function. Betsy Spaulding, her mother's best and oldest friend of over forty-five years, stepped in and made all the arrangements for Jessica Jade's home-going ceremony. On the day of the funeral, Min Jade looked like a shadow of her former self. In the three days it took to organize all the arrangements, she had lost enough pounds that her clothes drooped. The light, completely gone from her eyes, left her stare vacant, her and voice silent. Though she seemed confused, Min Jade was very much present.

Betsy worried she'd have another break, had offered her one of the pills Dr. Robbins had prescribed, and Min Jade had gladly taken it. She threaded her fingers through her father's as they walked to the front pew. Jessica Jade's picture, adorned with flowers, smiled at them from an easel. She remembered the picture well. It was her mother's last publicity shot before giving up her career when Min Jade was sixteen. *She'd devoted her life to me, and I wasn't even here when she took her last breath.* The tears came fast, making a large wet spot on the white collar of her black dress. For the first time in her life, Min Jade had worn black. Aunt Betsy had followed her mother's instructions to a T. Apparently, Jessica Jade had written her funeral wishes over twenty years before. Her mother's absolute control and organization extended even to her last day on earth. One of Jessica's friends from her music school days was singing *Requiem Pie Jesu,* her mother's favorite, as they made their way to their seats. *Sleep eternal...*Min Jade's knees buckled. "Dear God," she whispered. "How will I ever go on?" Just as she was about to step into the pew, Chair Winful held her close. "Min Jade, I am sorry. I am so sorry," he said, kissing her cheek then shaking her father's hand. "Owen, I have no words."

Her father nodded his gratitude, pushing back the leveling emotions. He had to be strong for his daughter.

"Take all the time you need to grieve." Winful patted his friend on the shoulder. I am here for you. Whatever you need. I'll handle everything."

The entire physics department, including her students, were all at the church. That was when Min Jade completely lost it. She remembered little after that.

CHAPTER TWENTY-EIGHT

MIN LEE WOO
SOUTH KOREA
HOME AGAIN

JI-JOON WAS USED TO WRAPPING THINGS UP. He still couldn't believe it was over. The doctors had informed them Hy Soo's cancer had infiltrated his entire system and had caused an aneurysm in his brain stem. He had been dead by the time In-Tak Hyun found him, collapsed in his bedroom. "Hy Soo is dead," she had barked into the phone at Ji-Joon. "Now, there is no reason for you and Min Lee to be in Korea anymore. So, get out." The witch didn't even have the courtesy to call Min Lee herself, refusing to acknowledge him as more than a nuisance. Min Lee had to postpone his trip to Ann Arbor. Ji-Joon was glad Min Lee was able to take his father's death in stride. Ji-Joon knew Min Lee loved his father, but their years of separation made this just another sad event in his life. It was hard to tell what he was feeling. He was glad they'd spent the last four months together and that at the end, Min Lee had spent every waking hour with his father. It was a wonderful thing, too, that their relationship was immortalized through their collaboration on *My Mother's Sonata*, Min Lee's new

Korean album. With Hy Soo's death, things were back where they started: In-Tak Hyun blaming Min Lee for her husband's death, Seung-Le blaming Min Lee for taking everything away from him, and Min Lee erecting a wall as long and as deep as the wall of China. He would clean all this up for sure, including Choi Shin. Ji-Joon, who'd received Ha Yun's call, had decided against telling Min Lee what she'd overheard. Choi Shin, he would handle personally. "Have you signed the papers I left on your desk?" Ji-Joon asked, handing him a cup of coffee.

"No, not yet."

"Do it. It's important. It's the power of attorney for the business stuff you need to handle. Your father's Will is quite clear on this, Min Lee."

"We'll get it done today. After your haircut," Min Lee attempted a smile. "You can't go back to England looking like a K-Pop idol."

Ji-Joon touched his spiky hair and laughed. "I have to take care of that, and I have other things to do, so I'll be gone for about two or three hours. Let's make sure we have this wrapped up by then."

"All right," Min Lee said, fishing his ringing cell from his pant pocket. "*Annyeonhaseyo.*"

"Min Lee, it's Ha Yun."

"*Noona.* Forgive me for not being the first to call."

"No need. I know it's been a hectic time, with your leaving and all." *That was what he considered her: a sister.*

"Thank you for everything you did for Dad. If it's okay with you, I'd like to have you and your dad over to dinner before I leave."

"We'll come by for sure." Min Lee did not broach the subject of Choi, so she suspected Ji-Joon had not revealed Choi's confession to him. With his father's rapid decline, she could understand why. "Are you doing, okay?"

"I am, but I just wished I…."

"Min Lee, you should have no regrets when it comes to your father. For years all your dad ever talked about was you back in Korea. You gave him that. I think it was enough for him. All he wants now is for you to go get your girl. He told me to make sure, or he'd pull my toes at night."

Min Lee chuckled. "Sounds like Dad. Thanks, Ha Yun. I'm going to do that. You are a very special person, and…."

"Don't say it."

Choi Shin looked at her watch. Crossing and uncrossing her long legs, she tapped her polished nails on the table. It seemed the fools had finally come to their senses. But what was taking Min Lee so long? He was annoying her just about now. Since she had the upper hand, shouldn't he be the one waiting? Ten minutes later, Ji-Joon walked in.

"It's about time. Where the hell is Min Lee?"

"He won't be here."

"What does that mean?"

"He has no reason to be here. He sent me to see what you wanted."

Choi Shin felt like a blood vessel popped in her head. "He sent you? Does that mean he doesn't care that his reputation will be further ruined or about his child?"

"Yes, I suppose that's what it means. What else can you do? You've already leaked information to the press, but you may be the one suffering most."

"You'd better get him over here right now before this gets ugly."

"Afraid I can't do that. Min Lee has gone back to London." Ji-Joon lied.

"What!" Choi jumped up from her chair. "Gone back to London?"

"Yes," Ji-Joon pushed her back into the chair and brought his face close to hers. "If you don't want this to get very, very ugly, you should stop with this charade now. You know Min Lee never slept with you."

"How can you prove that?"

"Well, I can drag you by the hair to the doctor to see if you're pregnant. See those guys over there? They are ready to do that at my command. Who will be ruined then? But this should suffice." Ji-Joon shoved headphones into her ear. "Do you remember this conversation?"

The color in Choi's face drained. Her eyes widened as she listened to the conversation she'd had with her friends at Glam Lounge. Which one of those bastards had betrayed her? She'd kill them. To save face, she jerked the earplugs out and threw them on the table. "How do you know that's me?" she barked.

"Do you want us to find out? Choi, this jig is up."

"That's what you think!" she huffed.

"A word to the wise." Ji-Joon got even closer to her face. "If you continue, you don't want to find out what will happen. Lots of ambitious, scheming, vile people like you commit suicide every day, right? Think of the shame and the fact that you would never work again, much less be a top violinist, or worse, ever get a record contract. All that talent of yours will be washed right down the drain. The gossip you leaked to the press will work against you. They will find out the woman in the story is you! Choose."

Choi felt cornered. She should at least get some money out of this. "What deal are you offering?"

"Your life to go on as though this never happened. We'll keep the entire thing quiet as far as you're concerned and resolve the nuisance news story. A 'woman scorned' story will suffice, but that woman does not have to be you."

"I'll do it if he signs the papers for my record deal for ten million *won*."

"You'll do it, period," Ji-Joon grabbed her purse and removed her cell phone just in case. "Don't try anything stupid. Those men," he said, nodding to the four men in black, "are only too happy to help you get to heaven." Ji-Joon turned on his heels and left the restaurant. Checkmate, he thought, as he moved steadily toward the door, winking at his pretend goons. Thank you, Ha Yun. On to the next problem. Min Jade wouldn't be easy to fix.

CHAPTER TWENTY-NINE

ANN ARBOR, MICHIGAN
MIN JADE
DESPERATE

TUNDE DISEMBARKED AT DETROIT METROPOLI-TAN Airport at 12:30 p.m. Despite his faith, he'd downed a couple of brandies in the car and, to keep him from over-reacting, would have another two before he saw Min Jade. Tunde checked into the godforsaken Campus Inn Hotel and made a few calls. After working closely with her, he pretty much knew her routine. He set his iPhone alarm for 5:30 p.m. and took a nap.

At 7:00 p.m., Tunde summoned his driver, directing him to Min Jade's house. He would be stern and to the point and would not leave without a firm answer of yes or no. He didn't care to play games anymore, and Min Jade tested his reserve. Korea was a debacle, and he was still fuming that Min Lee had pulled such stunts on him. Now she'd taken to not answering her phone? Did she really think that would stop him from claiming her heart? She needed to belong to him, and that was all that mattered. "Enough!" he said out loud.

"Sir?"

"Nothing."

The house was dark, except for the porch light. Tunde walked up the driveway and knocked on the door. No answer. He looked through the window. Stillness. He knocked louder. After ten minutes, he strode back to his waiting car. Where in the world was Min Jade? He tried her cell again from inside the car. The same message, the caller is unavailable. Maybe she was at her mother's. He drove to her parent's home. That, too, was shrouded in darkness. The lab. That had to be it. He instructed his driver to go to her lab. Sealed tight. He thought of calling Professor Winful, but that was a bit too desperate. He'd come back in the morning.

On Sunday morning, try as she did, Min Jade could not get out of bed. Darkness enveloped her. She could hear knocking at the door, but her body would not move. Registering she should check in on her father, who was staying with Aunt Betsy, Min Jade reached for her cell. It was dead. Scanning her room, she found her charger and plugged in her phone. The knocking continued, and she finally found the strength to make it to the door.

"What do you think you're doing right now?" Tunde loomed large.

"What?" Min Jade left the door open and walked back into the house.

"Do you know what I've been going through? I've been running around Ann Arbor trying to find you. How can you disappear for weeks without a word? Isn't that overkill? And why is your phone not working?"

No answer.

"Min Jade," his tone softened. "What's going on?"

"Why are you here? Why are you here?" Min Jade screamed. "What do you want?"

Tunde grabbed her shoulders. "Tell me," he said, "what's going on? Min Jade. I'm here..."

"I don't want you here. I don't want you here. I don't want anyone here," Min Jade broke free from his embrace.

Suddenly, they heard a voice. "What's that?" Tunde asked.

"I think it's my phone. I just plugged it in. Tunde followed the voice to Min Jade's bedroom. Her cell was announcing *Crazy Korean calling. Crazy Korean calling.*

"Hello, Min Lee."

Taken aback, Min Lee was silent for a moment. "Who is this?"

"Tunde."

"Why are you answering Min Jade's phone?"

"Because she is unavailable to answer it."

"Where is she?" Min Lee demanded.

"In her living room."

"*Aishheee.*" Complete exasperation. "You are at her house?"

"Yes. I am at her house, and I'm afraid she can't take your call right now."

"Put Min Jade on the phone, now," Min Lee shouted.

"Why? You may be responsible for her state right now. I came over because I hadn't been able to reach her for four weeks. She's in quite a state. I don't think, after what happened, you should call again."

"Why was her number off?"

"You'll have to ask her, but you won't be able to right now."

"Who the hell...." Min Lee heard the phone click off. "*Aish-hhhhheeee!*" He banged his desk. She would want to know his father had passed away. His father had liked Min Jade a lot. He regretted all that had happened and that it was dampening her greatest moment of being nominated. He needed to be with her, but how. Min Lee poured whiskey over clinking ice and raised the glass to his lips. He couldn't cancel his performances. He sat at his piano, feeling defeated and trapped. That Tunde was relentless. What did he have to do? He lifted the lid of his piano and stared at the keys. For the first time in his life, his music failed him. "*Eomeoni*," he whispered. "I am so lost."

"Why are you here—and why are you answering my phone? I told you to get it for me, not answer it. Who was it?" She asked as he returned to the living room.

"A wrong number," Tunde said without hesitation. "Min Jade, I'm here because I care about you. I've been calling you for weeks. What the hell is going on?"

Min Jade stared at him. "I'd like you to leave."

"I don't know what's going on, but you don't need to be strong with me." Tunde was not giving up. He pulled her down next to him on her couch. "I have strength enough for both of us. Let me help you, Min Jade. This can't be about the Korean, can it? It looks to me right now that you need a friend to lean on."

This time Min Jade blinked. "Thank you. I am sorry."

What on earth was she saying? It didn't even make sense. Something was wrong. But what? Tunde tried to look through Min Jade's phone to find her mother's number, but the phone had immediately gone to auto-lock. "What is your code?"

Min Jade looked at him. Lost. "My code?" What code?

"Min Jade. I want the unlock screen code for your phone. I need to call your mother."

"My mother is dead."

"Min Jade, you are not making any sense. Please tell me what's going on."

"My mother is dead! DEAD. DEAD. What don't you understand? DEAD. DEAD," she screamed. "My mother is dead. She's dead," sobs racked her body. Tunde could not believe his ears. "What did you say?"

"I said my mother is freakin' dead. Call her. I don't have her number in heaven but call her."

"What is your code?" Tunde insisted.

"0321."

Tunde keyed in the code and scrolled through the address book. He found the number for her mother and dialed it. It went to voicemail. He then tried her father's number. It rang five times, and then he answered.

"Hello, Min Jade."

"Hello. Is this Mr. Jade?"

"Yes, it is. Who is this?"

"I am Tunde, you remember, a friend of Min Jade's. I am with her at her home right now, and I'm afraid she's not doing very well."

"I know. She was very close to her mother. She's in shock right now. We all are. It is good of you to come. I'm glad she called you."

"Sir, may I please stay with Min Jade? I am so very sorry for your loss. I am so sorry."

"Thank you, young man. I'll have Betsy bring me over a little later."

So, indeed, her mother had died. It was unbelievable. How could such a vibrant woman die so suddenly? It was sad, but Tunde, Allah would have to forgive him, realized it was the perfect storm to have her lean on him. Tunde took a weeping Min Jade by the hand and led her back to bed. Going to her kitchen, he made a toddy of lemon, rum, and honey. He held her as she drank the cure-all medicine, never letting go of her until she'd fallen asleep in his arms. Tunde called his office to let them know he'd be away for at least another week. Maybe he should take her back with him. She'd never agree to that. He wanted her to depend on him now. What would he do? *Allah help me.*

By the time Tunde's meeting with Mr. Jade had ended, he knew just what to do. He'd found the door. Now all he had to do was walk through it. Would he? Could he?

On Monday morning, Tunde insisted Min Jade see someone. He called Dr. Winful.

"I'm glad you're here. Yes. I think Dr. Robbins should see her. She'd held up well, considering. The faster she can manage this thing, the better because we need her at the University." Dr. Winful was saying. "Work will get her back to normal, plus we can't jeopardize her chances if this gets out."

"Will you call Dr. Robbins?" Tunde asked.

"Yes. I'm glad you are here." Winful said again. "You're an impressive young man. It'd be good for Min Jade to have you around all the time. She's a genius, you know. We all teeter on the edge from time to time. Her mother was everything to her. She could use a good friend like you by her side at a time like this."

"I will be here. Thank you, Dr. Winful."

Dr. Robbins staged an intervention. It took a couple of days afterward for Min Jade to surface fully. Thursday morning, Min Jade woke bright and early and hurried to the kitchen. Her appetite had returned, and she was ravenous. Suddenly she stopped. There was a man in her kitchen! She was about to pick up a vase to smash his head when Tunde turned around and smiled.

"Finally," he said. "I was worried about you."

"Tunde? What are you doing in my house?"

"What?"

"I said, what are you doing in my house?" Flashes of memory started coming into her head. When Min Jade grasped the entire scenario, she was furious. Maybe she should have been grateful, but she was stronger than they all thought. Her

mother, the greatest of all mothers, hadn't spent her life grooming her daughter for nothing. Min Jade's strength would now
have to be her own. "Get out," she screamed. "Get out NOW!"

Tunde advanced. He thought she was getting better. "It's
alright, Min Jade."

"It's not alright," she screamed louder. "How dare you?
What did you think, Tunde, that you could save me? I can save
my damn self. How did you even get in here?" Min Jade spun
on her heels and returned to her bedroom. When she returned,
she was dressed. Min Jade grabbed her keys from the key hook
and went to stand before Tunde. "When I get back," she said,
"you had better be gone. I don't need you. I don't need anyone.
I now have my mother's strength."

Tunde stood mouth agape. She was quite ill. People often
got maddest with the people they loved the most. He'd be
patient. "I know you can take care of yourself. I just want to be
close. What are friends for?"

Min Jade's eyes narrowed. "Friends are mere distractions.
Get out of my house. I mean it, Tunde."

Tunde stood in the kitchen, shaking with anger. He got
it! She was angry, but never in his life had anyone spoken to
him that way. In his culture, that deserved a thrashing, crazy
or no crazy! His pride was severely injured. What else would
she do to his battered ego? Maybe it was best not to be here.
Tunde summoned his driver, feeling like a complete failure.
He started to pack the few things he'd brought over: shaving
cream, a few slacks, shirts, and sundries, then decided to leave
them. They would remind her of the sacrifice he'd made for her.
Plus, if his clothes remained there, it would mean things were
not over between them. Tunde took a last look at the average
but comfortable home where he had found purpose. He pulled
the door behind him. He would no longer call Min Jade. She

had to call him. From the car, he called his pilot. "We're heading home. I'm on my way to the airport." He didn't go back to the hotel to fetch his things. He left everything behind in Ann Arbor. He wanted no reminders of his failure.

Two weeks had now passed since Min Jade returned to her lab. Resuming her daily visits with Winful gave her something to look forward to, and she relied heavily on his strength to help her get through each day. At the thought of never seeing her mother again, Min Jade still often broke down in tears, but her headspace had survived the pressure of the psychological onslaught. Min Jade exhaled loudly as she made her way up the steps to Winful's office. Flopping down in her usual chair, she looked at the bustling professor and appreciated how great a friend he was. Winful didn't say anything when she walked in; instead, he went to the makeshift kitchen ledge to brew tea. Waddling over a few minutes later, he set a steaming cup of tea on the table next to Min Jade. "Drink it. It's good for your nerves. It's my Saint John's Wort."

"Your calming tea."

"Yup. Now that marijuana is legal, I thought about using that, but…."

Min Jade laughed, surprising herself. "This is good enough. It's Valium, you know."

"Don't tell anyone." Chair Winful sat behind his desk. He touched the tips of his fingers together and rested his elbows on the desk. "How is your sanity?"

"I was close to the edge, wasn't I? So very close. It's good. Good, though I'm still deeply sad. But you know what, I have come to appreciate how strong I am, thanks to my amazing mother. You know another funny thing, Dr. Winful, I think I now have everything my mother ever wanted to give me. I don't just feel mentally strong; I am mentally strong. Mom did a great job with my life." Her voice faltered.

"That's true. Her wingspan was large and sheltering. I think she knew all along you'd be fine and that once nominated, you'd find your way. She knew it all."

"Maybe." Min Jade sipped her tea contemplatively. "You're probably right," Min Jade rested the cup back onto the saucer. She leaned back in the chair and closed her eyes. "So, what happens if I don't win the Nobel?" She asked.

"That is highly unlikely. I believe you already have the Nobel, dear. The only thing you can do now, is not show up to accept it."

Min Jade was getting better every day. She resumed her daily walks by the music school and weekly trips to the farmer's market. The one thing that surprised her more than anything was her loneliness from not talking to Min Lee every night. Her mind, no matter how much she tried to implement her thought-stopping technique, kept straying to him. On one of those occasions, she came very close to calling him. She should at least hear him out. At Zingermans, Min Jade ordered a double espresso and took it out to the patio where she and her mom would often sit. She watched a mixed-couple family go by and wondered if she would ever have one of her own. If only Choi Shin had not pierced her bubble, she might have been planning a wedding. Back to her full senses, she also felt awful about her behavior toward Tunde. He'd been her rock when Julian left, and he was there when she opened her eyes from her near breakdown. She made a promise to call him and ask for forgiveness. Life was unpredictable; she sighed, draining her cup.

Bright and early Monday morning, Dr. Winful's secretary summoned her. "Chair Winful would like to see you right away, Dr. Jade."

What now? Min Jade, who'd done everything in her power to show him that she was all right, wondered what her watchful mentor wanted this time. She hadn't planned on dropping by his office, as he was supposed to be away anyway. Winful had taken to summoning her twice or thrice a week extra and insisted they had lunch once a week.

"Thank you, Jeannie. Isn't he supposed to be out of town?"

"His plans changed," Jeannie said.

"Okay, I'll be right there." Once and for all, she'd put his worries to rest today.

"Blah, blah, blah." Min Jade flapped her lips as she walked into his office. She rolled her eyes back in her head and feigned a tic. Her head jerked, and her body twitched. Crazy Eyes in *Orange Is the New Black* had nothing on her.

"What is wrong with you?" Winful rushed to her side.

"You, Professor. You are driving me batty. I'm okay. I told you. Really, I am. So, can you now go back to your duties instead of babysitting me? I'm good. I'm really good!"

"You got jokes." Winful laughed. "Funny girl. Are you saying you don't need my Saint John's Wort tea anymore? Fine. How about this?" he handed her a letter, and it was he this time who needed consoling. "A special letter. Have you opened your mail?" he said softly, tears glistening in his eyes. "This is just a copy. See, I'm copied as your Chair."

"Not in a few weeks. Did we get another big grant?" Min Jade rubbed her palms together.

"You, Min Jade, are the Nobel Laureate in Physics." Winful was in tears, and in one great stride, he swooped her up so tightly in his arms, she could hardly breathe.

"Is it for real?" Min Jade's voice was but a whisper.

"Yes," he said, stroking her hair. "You are my little genius."

Tears welled in Min Jade's eyes. The moment was anticlimactic. The moment was meaningless without her mother. Min Jade unfolded the letter. She struggled to see through the tears. She read the letter a few times before grasping it all.

The Royal Academy of the Sciences

Lilla Frescativägen 4A
SE-114 18 Stockholm

Dear Professor Jade,

It is with great honor and extreme pleasure that we welcome you as a Nobel Laureate in Physics. The Award Ceremony will take place on December 10th. We request the honor of your presence at a special gathering we will host at the Palace. We have reserved ten tickets for your guests. Please forward your guest list to us as soon as possible.

Again, Dr. Jade, it's an honor and congratulations. Please also accept our condolences on your mother's passing. May she rest in peace.

His Majesty Carl XVI Gustaf and Queen Silvia

"Dr. Winful," a teary Min Jade said into his shoulder, her tears drenched his jacket. "I don't think I can accept this. I just don't think I can."

"Don't be silly, dear. You can't give back a Nobel prize. You must go. Make your mother proud. You have no choice. But, since I knew you'd say something crazy like this, I've come up with a plan. I have this sneaky suspicion it could help. Let's shift our focus a bit to your love life. What do you think if

I offered that nice man of yours, Tunde, a position here? He could be closer, and it could be good for you."

Min Jade backed up fast, knocking over the side table, spilling her tea. "You cannot," she said. "Absolutely not."

"Why not? He seems to like you very much. He's been supportive of you in many ways. I think he is God-sent. Isn't it time to think about sharing your life with someone who loves you? He seems like a perfect match, and he is a physics man!"

"First of all, he is a Muslim, so he can't be God-sent, and Dr. Winful, you just can't."

"I thought you liked this guy. He is good to you."

Min Jade thought of the last time she had seen Tunde. She had been vile. With Winful singing his praises, she chided herself for not following through on the call she'd promised herself to make. He had indeed been good to her, and he was partly responsible for her nomination, but he was not the man she loved. With her mom's sudden death, she realized how fragile life itself was, and she would rather spend her life as a physicist than as the wife of a man she would never love. "I do but not that way." Min Jade finally said. "Tunde is a dear and valued friend, and I'm afraid I've been awful to him after all he's done, but I do not love him as a man. I'd like to set the record straight with him too."

"I see. Is there someone you like as a man?"

Min Jade hesitated. She began cleaning up the mess she'd made, grabbing a handful of paper towels from Winful's make-shift kitchen. She got down on the floor to avoid looking at him. He knew her too well.

"That sounds like a yes to me," Winful pressed.

"Why is it important?" Min Jade stopped cleaning and looked at Winful.

"Tell me about him," Winful said.

And Min Jade did.

If there was anyone Min Jade loved, it was Min Lee Woo. But love was folly. Even if she were foolish enough to acknowledge it, why would she want to be with someone who wasn't hers to love? For sure, they were star-crossed lovers, and the night in Korea would always be a painful reminder of her stupidity. It was best to leave things as they were. After all, he too had stopped calling, which meant he had moved on and probably married to Choi Shin. Soon he'd have a bouncing baby to pour out all his love. When Min Jade finally rested the letter on Winful's desk, she knelt in prayer. "Dear God, I know you don't do this usually, but just this once, please let my mother see her daughter accept the Nobel Prize in Physics. Please give her a front-row seat from heaven."

Winful helped her to her feet, and, together, they sat in reverend silence. On his window ledge, on the other side of his beloved orchid, a bird landed, and as it did, the light in his office flickered. They looked at each other, and, even as scientists, they were sure of the all-knowing. Finally, Min Jade said, "I should go and tell Daddy."

Back at her office, Min Jade's secretary had taken another call. For the tenth time that day, Joan wrote the name Min Lee on a memo slip and stuck it in a folder of mounting messages that Min Jade had yet to review.

CHAPTER THIRTY

LONDON
MIN LEE
STILL WAITING

MIN LEE WOO WAS PREPARING TO GO ON TOUR. It was the last thing in the world he wanted to do. Every day he toyed with the idea of just getting on a plane to Ann Arbor before his tour started, but Ji-Joon had convinced him to give Min Jade some time and some space. But just how much?

"She is very much like you, Min Lee. Think about how you would've handled the situation. Very much the same. Don't push too hard if you want a future with Min Jade. She loves you. She agreed to marry you. She is disappointed, but you can share Ha Yun's recording with her when she calms down. It will surely clear things up. We've been absent from the stage for five months. Let's refocus on that and give her some time," he'd said.

Ji-Joon was right, of course. Min Lee doubled down on his practice; so exhausted was he at night, he could only fall into bed. And when he went back to the stage, no one but Ji-Joon could tell he was not at his best. Mechanically he continued to play, each recital becoming harder and harder. Music no longer offered solace, and for the first time since he was twelve, Min Lee felt rudderless. Min Lee rarely left his house now, nor did he visit his old haunts. Every morning he'd crumple the yellow sticky note Ji-Joon stuck on the refrigerator and throw it in the trash. GONE TO THE BANK. GONE TO APOLOGIZE FOR YOUR RUDENESS. GONE FISHIN,' DAMN IT! Ji-Joon was none too pleased with him, but he could do little. Nothing was left of his logic. Nothing magical left in his music. His heart had completely trampled on his life, leaving him listless, anxious, and downright sad. He was, after all, a maladaptive.

Min Lee tried to distract himself from the rising feeling of hopelessness with cooking. He was an excellent cook, after all. He diced tomatoes and chopped scallions, peeled carrots, and beat eggs. He ate ramen, a testament to how sad he had become. Today, he would try his hand at beef soup. Min Lee switched on the television, poured more whiskey, and removed a cut of beef from the refrigerator. He had gotten hooked on Korean dramas, too. They kept him hopeful with their soppy lines and predictable happy endings.

"The winner for the Nobel Prize in Physics has just been announced. American-born Min Jade, an African American professor at the University of Michigan, is the first black woman to win a Nobel Prize in the sciences. For the third time in the history of this prize, a woman has won the Nobel in Physics and the second American. Marie Curie, Maria Goeppert-Mayer, and now Min Jade. It's curious that all their names begin with the letter; M, so you might consider that when naming your future newborn scientist. Professor Jade is only thirty-two years old. She became the youngest tenured professor at the University at twenty-five. She attended the prestigious RAIN Academy high school, graduating two years early. She studied at Oxford for her undergraduate work and then at the University of Michigan for her master's and Ph.D. Her win has been dampened by the loss of her mother just a few months before this announcement was made public. She says it's a bittersweet moment and that she is happy she was able to share her nomination with her mother before she died." Pictures of Min Jade flashed on the screen. "Due to her hectic schedule, we only have a voice clip. Here is what she has to say."

> *"The question I have been asked most is how does it feel to be a first? I am not a first. Two women have won before me. By first, they mean, of course, the color of my skin, but I am far more interested in the color of light. I don't put much stock in anything but my brain. I am, of course, glad that I am a black woman and a Nobel Prize winner. Whatever gets people up in the morning to strive every day for excellence is what I am about, and if a little black girl takes inspiration from me, I am happy. But I am equally happy when a little Asian, Indian, African, Arab, or Caucasian girl does the same. The world is not easy for women in any shade. For me, skin color leads to subjective conversations. I deal in facts and objectivity, and proof. Anything else is useless noise."*

Min Lee Woo dropped his whiskey glass. This could not be. The warm, loving, and beautiful woman he had met in New York had died? Jessica Jade? Dead! This just could not be. Min Lee quickly scrolled through his phone until he reached Min Jade's number. What could he say to her? He had to say something. He looked at his watch. 6:00 p.m. Midnight her time. Dare he call? He selected the number, then decided to text her, but lost his courage before pressing 'send.' They were both mourning the death of a parent. They could have buried their pain in each other's hearts. He wanted to share so much with Min Jade, and he yearned to see her once more to set the record straight. He'd call her office in the morning. He could only imagine how distraught she had to be. He'd keep his promise and be there for her always.

He called the next day and left a message. Then he called nine more times and left more messages. It was now three days later, and Min Jade had not returned his condolence call. He tried to rationalize how busy she had to be with the announcement of her win, but he was sinking into a sadness that felt apocalyptic. With each passing day, Min Lee drowned his broken heart in more and more spirits.

Ji-Joon was getting tired of lifting a drunken Min Lee into bed. What the hell? Was he becoming an alcoholic? On more than one occasion, Ji-Joon had been tempted to throw in the towel. Just up and quit! At thirty-five, he'd had a great life living inside Min Lee's life, and that was okay as long as they still had fun. Lately, he'd become the whipping boy. He was tired of Min Lee Woo's pity party. If he didn't get his ass in gear, Ji-Joon would have to do something drastic. He missed the surety of his old, cocky pal, and he was not going to be screamed at anymore. That Min Jade was a lot tougher than he had thought. Ji-Joon dropped Min Lee on the bed and threw a cover over him. *What a wuss*, Ji-Joon thought. *Just a lonely kid in grown-up clothing.*

"Let's take a walk." Ji-Joon pushed open Min Lee's bedroom door the following morning. It was 11 a.m., and he was still in bed.

"Go away," Min Lee pulled the cover over his head.

"I am not going anywhere. Get your ass up, and let's get on with life. You are such a fake, and now you are headed to being a loser!"

That got Min Lee's head to come out from under the cover. "What did you say?"

"A fake. A loser. Yes, I said it. You are a fake and a loser. You pretend to be strong and mighty, but you are nothing but a wuss. A girl if you ask me. And don't let me add coward."

Min Lee's entire body now emerged. Hair stuck up on ends; he looked like the mad musician. "You're fired. How is that?"

Ji-Joon rolled his eyes. "Fine with me. I'll go work for Lang Lang." Something from the bedside table came flying toward him. Ji-Joon ducked. "Look, Min Lee, get up and be ready to go in thirty minutes, or I will quit. I mean it." He left the bedroom, slamming the door loudly.

Thirty minutes later, Min Lee was waiting inside Ji-Joon's flat. Ji-Joon was not there.

Min Lee's phone trilled.

"Hey, wimpy, are you ready?"

"Ji-Joon..."

"Guess who I just got off the phone with?"

Min Lee perked up. Maybe Min Jade had finally reached out, even if it was to Ji-Joon instead of him. He waited with bated breath.

"Well?"

"Well, what? I said, guess who. That means you're supposed to guess."

"Ji-Joon, why are you taunting me?"

"Taunting you! Who is taunting who here? Do you know what a right stick in the mud you've been these past few months? Man, you're killing me with this moping around. This will make you snap out of it."

"If you were in front of me, I'd wring your neck. Where are you anyway? I'm here in your flat. You said, thirty minutes."

"*Ashlee.* You are truly no fun anymore. I'll be up in a bit, just at the mailbox."

"Thirty minutes is thirty minutes," Min Lee shouted. "*Aishhheeee.*"

Ji-Joon could hear Min Lee still screaming at him as he hung up the phone. The only person who could put an end to this nonsense was Min Jade.

"The mail." Ji-Joon bounced out of the elevator. "Let's take a few minutes before heading out." He walked back into Min Lee's living room and flopped down on the chair. He held one letter behind his back.

"Who called you?" Min Lee said, annoyed.

"Well, it was someone from Sweden," Ji-Joon said.

"Why did you make it sound like it was important? I need to fire you. Really, I do."

"And when will that be?" Ji-Joon walked over to the counter and put the letter on the table. "It was a guy called Dr. Winful," he said, tapping the letter, "he wanted to make sure we'd received this." Ji-Joon handed the letter to Min Lee. "That's why I went to the mailbox."

The return address read, "The Academy of the Nobel Sciences." Min Lee ripped it open. Did Min Jade get him an invite? He was beyond ecstatic.

Dear Maestro Woo,

This year's Nobel Laureate Gala will take place on December 10 at the Royal Swedish Academy and City Hall in Stockholm, Sweden. We are extending an invitation for you to perform a concert as part of our festivities. We hope you will consider this invitation with the utmost regard, and we look forward to an answer post-haste, as our planning committee is anxious for your response. Of course, a speedy response will allow us the opportunity for the best planning possible to receive you as our distinguished guest."

With deep gratitude,

Lars Bergström (Secretary), Chair of the Nobel Foundation Gala Committee.

The following day Ji-Joon walked in to find a new and improved jovial, Min Lee Woo, standing in front of a mirror.

"What on earth are you wearing?"

"My tux for the gala."

"Are you crazy?" Ji-Joon looked at the contraption Min Lee had on. Yellow jacket with purple sleeves and purple pants. "Any reason?"

"It's what Min Jade was wearing when I first met her. A yellow dress with a bold purple slash. I want her to know I remembered our meeting."

"I don't think so. Take it off right now. Here," Ji-Joon handed him a suit bag. "This is what you will wear." It was a classic tailor-made black tux.

"*Aishhheee.*" Min Lee threw the yellow jacket over the chair.

"Here, this was in the mail. Do you know who this Winful person is?"

"No. Must be someone from the Academy. He was the one who called, right?"

"Yeah, but this is from the University of Michigan. Isn't that where Min Jade is?

It's an invitation for you to meet him for lunch in Switzerland."

Min Lee grabbed the letter. It simply said, "Please be my guest. I hope you're curious."

Curious? Min Lee was intrigued. How would Chair Winful know of him or where to find him unless Min Jade had told him? Did she even know where to find him? Min Lee's mood surged. If she had forgiven him, he would never let her go ever again, not ever in this life. A bouncy Min Lee took the envelope to his room and tucked it in his special drawer where he kept his mother's photograph. "*Eomeoni*," he whispered. "Help me find the woman I love."

I'm going to the practice hall," Min Lee announced. He was still wearing purple pants.

Normalcy, at last. This was good, Ji-Joon thought, very good. He called the driver.

Two days later, Ji -Joon found himself operating on a tight schedule. His flight was in five hours. He had to stop by the practice hall on his way to the airport to get Min Lee to sign the Korean estate documents left by his father, which In-Tak Hyun was now contesting. The woman gave him a bitch of a headache. Min Lee had refused to even look at them, instructing him to have the attorneys handle it. Even so, he still needed his signature and had little time to squabble.

As he approached the door to the practice room, Ji-Joon halted. Was that Min Lee playing? My God, he had never heard music as beautiful in all his years. Min Lee had reached a whole new level. Not only was the music technically brilliant— his strong suit—but it was filled with an emotional maturity he'd never heard before. Ji-Joon's heart swelled with pride. He almost felt like crying. Is this what love does? Ever since he'd received the invitation and the letter from Chair Winful, Min Lee was a different person. A completely new man. He was convinced Min Jade still cared about him and was now fully living inside his music rather than just playing it with emotion. What he heard today was music resonating from a soul in flight. Ji-Joon shivered, watching the hairs on his handstand on end. He hated to interrupt this moment, but he had to make his flight.

"Ji-Joon," Min Lee smiled. "Are you leaving now?" Dear God, even his face glowed, Ji-Joon thought. Ji-Joon looked closely at his friend. "Min Lee, the music is heavenly. You have outdone yourself."

"Ah, it's not me. It's *Eomeoni*. She has to be here with me. She always said to feel the music inside you. Close your eyes and let the music be you. I've become the music, Ji-Joon."

CHAPTER THIRTY-ONE

MIN JADE
INVITATION

"**D**AMN IT." Tunde was throwing couch pillows onto the floor. He could hear his phone ringing down in the bowels of the couch.

"Hello," he said, hoping the caller hadn't hung up. "Hello."

"Hello, old chap. What took you so long to answer?"

"My phone fell into the couch. What's up, Albert?"

"Did you by any chance get the news?"

"What news?"

"Min Jade has won the Nobel Prize."

"What. My God, that's great." Tunde said. "She deserves it."

"Yes. She does…so, old chap, do you think we'll get invitations to the crowning of the incomparable Queen Min Jade, our new Physics Laureate? After all, you were listed on the paper."

"I was? I certainly hope so," Tunde said. "She's quite the girl, isn't she? If only she'd come to her senses about my love."

"From the sound of things, I take it she's not quite your girl anymore."

"Bloke, do you have to be so blunt?"

"That's the British in me. Sorry, old chap."

"And stop that, too," Tunde shouted at him. "How old can a thirty-three-year-old be? I am not one to give up easily, my boy. This story has no ending yet."

"I see."

"If we get invitations, we're going, right?" Tunde said.

"Wouldn't miss it for the world. I hope we all got invitations. Maybe Chin can hook us up with a gig in Viking country. It will be almost the time of our yearly PH get-together. Why not kill two...he paused...is that too crass?"

"As are you."

"We should travel together," Albert said. Let's coordinate our flights."

"Coordinate? You can fly with me."

"Ah, there is that—the King. I forgot. Happy to."

"Bye."

Chair Winful had not been exaggerating about the media circus. For two weeks non-stop, Min Jade felt like a hamster. Calls poured in for television and radio interviews, to visit schools, for keynote speeches, to join boards, for jobs and, again, even romantic suitors. Min Jade no longer went to her office and could no longer leave home without planning an escape route. Did all Laureates get this kind of attention? Shuffling from one station to another, Min Jade refused to go anywhere else after two weeks from one city to the next. If they wanted to interview her, they'd have to do it by satellite or come to her office. Finally, back in her office, Min Jade sat at her office desk and picked up the folders stuffed with yellow sticky messages. Not now, she thought, filing the folder into her desk drawer. A rap on her door sent shivers through her body. Did some reporter find her? It turned out to be Sigmund, her dear colleague who'd taught her sabbatical semester. She didn't mind Sigmund interrupting her first moment of quiet in two weeks.

"Hey, Star. Can you spare a moment for an old friend?" He pushed his head further around the door.

"Oh, shut up!" Min Jade waved him in. "Shut the door quickly and put the 'not in' sign on it."

"It's only the beginning, you know. Congrats, kiddo. You deserve this. I won't have to resort to 'I knew her when,' will I?"

"Sigmund. Sit down and shut up."

"And bossy, too, now. I like that. Congrats, Min Jade. Really. We are proud of you. How are things going personally?"

"Up and down. I really miss my mom. I wished she…." Her voice trailed off.

"You think Jessica Jade doesn't know all this? She has been and will always be your guardian angel. Can you imagine how she is bragging up there right this minute?" He pointed to the heavens.

"Aren't you a physicist?"

"Yep. But don't you feel it? We can't explain everything."

"You know, I do. I really do…I hope you're right, Sigmund."

That evening at home, Min Jade sat down to make a list of the people to invite. She was given invitations for ten people. When she was done, she looked over the list and began crossing out and adding names. She started the list at ten because number one belonged to her mother, and each time she was about to get there, she'd started crying. She crossed out another name. She couldn't possibly invite the other Perfect Harmonies and not Tunde, who probably should be on stage with her. She added him at number seven. The one person her heart wanted on the list was Min Lee, but how could she, after all these months? She added his name anyway. Immediately she scratched it out. He was the reason her heart had overruled her head, and, clean sweep, he'd shot a poison arrow through it. No more pain for me—never. Min Jade scratched out his name until it was no longer visible on the page. So much for love... Min Jade felt sad, a sadness she couldn't deny.

The List

1. Mom ∞
2. Dad
3. Chair Winful
4. Aunt Betsy
5. Min Lee Woo, Ansel Schmitt Han Wis, University of Innsbruck
6. Sigmund Fletcher
7. Tunde
8. Anastase
9. Chin
10. Alfred

Min Jade would be off to Sweden to attend the formal prize ceremony in two days. Min Jade wished she didn't have to go. She didn't want to make a fool of herself, sobbing all over the place, and couldn't bear to think of such an event without her mother. Could she accept by satellite? Winful would never allow it. She would have her father by her side, which made her very happy. He had been amazing through this entire ordeal. When she'd asked him how he managed, he'd simply replied. "I love with my heart. I have forty-two years of memories tucked away in this heart. Those never go away. All I need to do is remember them, and your mom's right here beside me. I am grateful for the life we had and look who she left me." He'd kissed her cheek. Would she ever have a love like that? Min Jade began pulling items from her closet. A pocketbook bopped her on the head. She loved that pocketbook. It's the one she'd sported in Innsbruck, and she'd take it to Sweden. Min Jade unclipped the lock and began cleaning it out. Inside were a bunch of old notes and messages she'd received from students. She sat on the bed and started reading. "Oh my God," she exclaimed as she read a crazy note she'd received from Tunde. "So, Miss Lady in the yellow dress, want to have a spot of tea with me?" Min Jade found herself laughing. It was from when they first met. She needed to right her wrong with Tunde.

Min Jade pulled out her phone and scrolled to Cocky Nigerian. He answered on the first ring.

"Hello, Tunde. It's Min Jade."

"I know. I'm glad you called," Tunde said.

"First, I'd like you to know how much I appreciate you and how much I need to ask for your forgiveness."

"Better late than never."

She could tell he was not going to make it easy for her. "I'm truly, truly sorry." Min Jade said.

"I get that. How are you? And congratulations."

"Better, thanks. Did you get my invitation?"

"Yes. I did, and I accepted."

"I hope you will not mind my mentioning you in Sweden. "

"There is no need to mention me. You would have had the same results with Julian, eventually. But if you permit me, I'd like to say I'm sorry, too, Min Jade, I am. I overstepped our friendship and boundaries. I was not playing fair." Since leaving Ann Arbor, Tunde had been doing a bit of soul searching. Although he'd been genuinely sad for her loss, he realized he had manipulated the situation to his advantage, just as he had in Austria. He felt ashamed.

"I know you were only trying to help. I was out of my mind. Literally."

"Yes. I realized. I adored your mother, and I'm truly sorry for your loss."

Tunde misjudged Min Jade. She was intense, brilliant, and a winner to the bitter end. He was deeply attracted to her, but he was also a very practical man. For the long haul, he would need a woman far less powerful than Min Jade. Indeed, the sun and the moon cannot occupy the sky at the same time. Still, he was thrilled she was on the line, and frankly, it wasn't over until it was! "I have more to be sorry for, too."

"You do?"

"Yes. In Austria, I accidentally took the mail from your mailbox instead of mine. There was a message from Min Lee. I was obsessed with you back then, so I put all of your mail back except his message. For weeks I'd beat you to the mailbox to purge all his messages, which came every day for a month. I know that was a caddish thing to do, but I was hoping…I am truly sorry. I understand now that the heart cannot be manipulated, and I am very sorry I interfered with your and Min Lee's relationship. If I hadn't done that, things would have been different. I can never forgive myself for the pain I caused you, but I'm asking for your forgiveness."

"I see." Min Jade said. "But why are you confessing now?"

"Because I don't want to carry this guilt anymore, and although I realized I might love you until eternity, we are not meant to be together. I knew when your mother passed away that it was time to let go, but I will always be here for you, Min Jade."

Min Jade inhaled and held her breath for as long as she could.

"Min Jade, are you still there?"

"Yes, Tunde, I am. I'll see you in Stockholm. We no longer need to say sorry to each other...." Min Jade said.

"Yes, you will. And again, Min Jade, congratulations."

"Thank you."

Min Jade sat on the bed, her mind in chaos. Min Lee Woo had indeed called. He'd been calling for an entire month. She sighed, dropping her shoulders in an exaggerated movement. What's done is done, she thought...there are no accidents. It's the way it was supposed to be.

Min Jade was in her office, putting the final touches on her acceptance speech. She had been to Sweden many times, but Winful still gave her a Fodor's guide. Opening the junk drawer to stuff it in, she noticed the folder she'd stuffed in it a few weeks back. She pulled out the folder and methodically began to review the messages. Most of them didn't matter anymore, just calls about her becoming the new Laureate. Min Jade crumpled them up and threw them in the wastebasket.

The next memo she picked up was from Min Lee Woo! Min Jade checked the date. It was the day after her win was announced. As she continued, there were ten more calls from Min Lee Woo. He had called, after all. How had she misjudged him so?! She would make everything right with everyone and then leave well enough alone. Losing her mother reminded her how fragile life is and how she should appreciate the people she cared about while they were here with her. She would forgive them both, but she would never trust her heart again.

CHAPTER THIRTY-TWO

STOCKHOLM, SWEDEN, ROCKIN' DA HOUSE

"WHY CAN'T WE PLAY OUR GIG?" Chin was at a loss.

"Because it's corny," Tunde said.

"I think it would be swell," Albert said, earning him a glare from Tunde. Hadn't they had this conversation?

"I think so, too." Anastase piped in. "It would be news. Imagine the Nobel Laureate rocking the stage at the Award Ceremony. I think it would be great."

"We're still not doing it." Tunde banged the table.

"But that's why we came early," Anastase said

They were at a watering hole having their usual cocktails.

"Watch it!" Chin bellowed at Tunde. "You are outnumbered anyway, so shut your kingly mouth up. Let's see what Min Jade says."

"Do you think we're going to get near her before the awards? She'll have a non-stop schedule. You'll be lucky if she even greets us personally," Tunde scoffed.

"I don't know who you're talking about, but Min Jade will contact us," Chin said. "Who's betting? Put your money on the table now. Tunde, you put five times as much as the rest of us."

"Why?"

"Because I want you to lose big!"

"All right. Let's do this." Tunde dropped a wad on the table. Everyone placed their bets that she would call, except Tunde.

City Hall

Min Lee's driver waited until his luggage was unloaded at his hotel and then drove him to the hall where he'd play. Ji-Joon was already there, and so were his hosts.

"Maestro Woo. What an honor to meet you. Thank you for coming in early. I can't tell you how excited the community is to have you with us. We are most pleased."

"Thank you. This is such an honor. I am delighted to be here. I do, however, have a favor to ask," Min Lee said, whisking the head guy away from the pack. In the far end of the room, they talked for several minutes, the host's head bobbing up and down. "Funny, you should ask. I am aware of the Perfect Harmonies. Dr. Chin has approached me about it. I think it's a marvelous idea. It will show our sometimes-too-serious scientists that we can have fun and win prizes just the same. And it will be great for news items."

"That is terrific. Do you mind sharing Dr. Chin's details with me?"

"Absolutely. Let me see here…." He scrolled through his phone. "Ah, here it is. Can we bump phones?"

"Yes, we can," Min laughed. "I wouldn't have guessed you to be up on the latest technologies." Min Lee smiled again.

"Trying to get out of the dark ages." The man chuckled. The room is yours as long as you need." Gunnar Ingelman, deputy to Lars, clasped Min Lee's hand. "We are very honored. Everyone here is at your disposal."

The Bar

"Who's buying the next round?" Albert said.

"I'll buy," Anastase said, "Tunde will have no money after he loses."

At that moment, Chin's phone rang. He moved away from the noise in the room into the hallway to take the call.

"Hello."

"This is Min Lee Woo."

"Mr. Woo. This is quite unexpected. To what do I owe this honor?"

"I understand that you spoke with Gunnar Ingelman. If it's okay with you guys, I'd like to play a tribute song with the Perfect Harmonies to Min Jade."

"*Yahoo!* That's totally rad."

"Of course, you can't let Min Jade know."

"I'll keep it a secret from Min Jade. You'll play piano on the song, I'm guessing."

"Yes. If that's okay."

"We're all here already. I'll round up the guys for rehearsals and get back to you."

"That'd be great. Let's chat later, then."

Chin walked back to the table with a self-satisfied look on his face. All that needed to happen now was for Min Jade to call.

Arlanda Airport, Sweden

Min Jade, her father, Dr. Winful, Aunt Betsy, and Sigmund deplaned at 4:00 p.m., Stockholm time. A limo was waiting to whisk them away to the Grand Hotel. There were still a few days before the Award Ceremony. Min Jade and her family were whisked away to a gathering where she met the other nominees and found out how busy her schedule would be for the next few days. The Committee had set up her dad and

Aunt Betsy with a personal tour guide. Sigmund would entertain himself, and no doubt Chair Winful would be anywhere Min Jade was going to be. Her shadow, as always. To her surprise, he begged off, saying he had something to take care of but would join her at the ceremony.

Min Jade settled her father and Aunt Betsy and then went to her room. Many delectable treats and gifts awaited her, some sent by colleagues and others from the Nobel Committee. Min Jade ditched her high heels, indulged in a few of the delectable treats, and felt relieved that her schedule was pretty free for the rest of the day. She decided to meet up with the Perfect Harmonies. Albert had said they would be coming in early.

"Why are you grinning like a Cheshire cat?" Tunde grunted at Chin.

"Oops, hold that thought," Albert said, reaching for his phone. His grin was even bigger. "Jackpot!" He put the phone on the table and turned on the speaker.

"Hey, Albert."

"Hey, Min Jade. You're on speakerphone. We are all here."

"*Hello!*...to the brightest stars in Stockholm. Where are you guys?"

Chin was pointing to the phone, Tunde was sulking, and Anastase grabbed all the money.

"Hey," everyone but Tunde echoed. "We're at...hold on...." Chin picked up the menu. "The Icebar."

Tunde sulked even more. Why had she called Albert and not him?

"Any gigs in town for us, Chin? I'm staying a few extra days so that we can jam."

"Yes! You know I never disappoint. Where are you? Come on over. We're getting drunk."

"Well, I can come over, but I can't get drunk. I'm sure my driver knows where the Icebar is. See you soon."

Tunde pretended to pick feathers from his mouth. How cool and unpretentious. Maybe he was going to fall in love with Min Jade all over again…not that he had fallen out of love.

She showed up an hour later. Tunde was proud of how well he played it off, seeing her again. No one would ever know how much he hurt on the inside.

Albert pulled up a chair for Min Jade. "Sit," he said, pulling his chair close to her. I have big news I am not supposed to repeat. It's a major hush-hush at the University."

"Out with it then," Tunde scoffed. "Why are you being obscure?"

"Because it's top secret. Heads are rolling in the Physics Department…bloody heads line the hallways every day."

"Oh, for Pete's sake!" Tunde chugged his drink.

Min Jade smiled. The Lion never changes. "Go on, Albert."

"Remember the article that came out saying our university thought they had solved the matter-from-nothing problem."

"Yes. But I won." Min Jade gloated.

"Well, it turned out that Dr. Kessler and your Julian were involved. Julian's breakdown was nothing more than a ploy to join her in England. The sly fox Kessler used age-old seduction to get information from Julian about your research."

"No way?"

"Yes. I'm afraid so. Julian followed Kessler back to England. The truth was that Kessler's boyfriend was the lead physicist on the Fusion Project at the Imperial College. Poor, stupid Julian, brilliant but socially stunted, really thought she loved him. The poor sod. When she began to spurn him, Julian spilled the beans. I guess he's not as stupid as he seemed. Now heads are lining the hall…

"We get the idea." Tunde cut him off.

"My God," Anastase said, "how stupid."

"Yeah. How do you throw away your career like that?" Chin was shaking his head.

"Let's invite him to join our band," Vadim said. "It's probably the closest he'll come to sound dissonance ever again."

Min Jade wanted to be mad at Julian, but she couldn't. Yes, he was an unexpected Uriah Heep, but she, too, had gone tipping through the tulips with the crazy man. Love potion number 9 was no joke. Thank God she'd woken up before it was too late. She hoped Julian would take a page from her book and chuck love out the window.

Morning came too soon, and before Min Jade knew it, she was being whisked off to media junkets and official functions, part of the week's festivities. She'd always appreciated the gravity of receiving the Nobel Prize, but this was overwhelming. In the car, she smoothed her muted skirt, her usual wardrobe significantly toned down, and looked over the program. She gasped loudly when she got to the program page detailing the Award Ceremony. Min Lee Woo? She did a double take, her eyes as big as saucers. Min Lee Woo would be giving the Gala Concert? *Oh, my God.* Min Jade almost spilled the coffee she'd asked for on the way out the door. How did this happen? She remembered the time in London when he'd said that if she won, he'd lobby to play, but that wasn't probable. Had the Academy actually invited him? That was plausible. If memory served her right, Lang had played at the Nobel Peace Prize in Oslo last year. The Royal Academy of Science, however, was quite a bit more conservative.

The Preparation Mashup

It was a day to be pampered before the big night. Min Jade booked the works. Mani-pedi, body scrub, massage, and facial. She skipped the hair salon treatment. She was paranoid about what a hair salon visit might yield in a place full of blonde, blue-eyed people. There were a fair number of Africans in Sweden, but Min Jade hadn't found a salon that could do her hair. Her natural hair was not a real issue, anyway. A wash, *Miss Jessie's Sweetback Treatment* for her curls, and she was good to go.

Min Jade ordered a heavy lunch. Swedish meatballs, fruits, a cheese platter, and coffee. That should keep her full as she'd be too nervous to eat at the gala. After lunch, Min Jade checked in on her father and Aunt Betsy, who were just returning from their tour. She'd hardly seen them!

"I have to go to the venue early, so someone will come to escort you as usual. Thank you so much for being my strength. You guys are the best."

"I wouldn't want to hear Jessica's mouth when we get there, would you, Owen?" Aunty Betsy said.

"You got that right. See you later, scallywag." Her father kissed her cheek. "We are proud of you."

Band Rehearsal

It was their third practice. Tunde had not cheered up one bit. When he learned Min Lee Woo was the Gala's revered guest of honor, he was downright pissed. And when he learned Min Lee would horn in on their band, the one thing he still shared with Min Jade, he became hostile.

"Why are we doing a classical song with K-pop beats? Shouldn't those beats be African?"

"There you go again. This is the Perfect Harmonies, bro. Any beat works, remember?" Chin said.

"Don't call me, bro."

"Mate, you're a pain in the ass," Albert said. "It's a special song he composed for Min Jade. She does have a Korean name."

Tunde slapped the drum and crossed his eyes. "Every beat comes from Africa."

"We know."

Min Lee walked in. Tunde, as usual, ignored him. He'd even ordered his shoes to be lifted so the difference in their height would disappear. They leveled each other's gazes. "Are you going to play the music as written today, or do we get more African flourish?" Min Lee asked Tunde. "It's great, but it throws off the song. Can I count on you to stick with the music?"

Tunde didn't answer. He tapped out an African rhythm on the drums.

"Why don't we have a talk?" Min Lee said. The men stepped over to a corner of the room.

"Look," Min Lee said, "I can't say I'm happy to see you. But I'll respect Min Jade's choice. You win, but will you let me do this one last thing for her? I owe Min Jade an apology. She's refused to answer any of my calls. I want her to know I am deeply sorry, and I'll wish you both the best. Just this one song, that's all I ask."

Tunde was ecstatic. Does this mean Min Jade had not been in contact with Kimchi Man? The field was still wide open, but it was not fertile. "No need to ask me for permission, man. She's made her choice. We've *both* lost."

"Okay, everyone. Two hours. That's all we have. Are we feeling confident?" Albert said.

"Yeah. We're good."

After a rehearsal with the Perfect Harmonies, Min Lee dropped by to see Chair Winful before putting in more rehearsal hours for his performance. Winful confided in Min Lee about Min Jade's feelings for him and confessed he'd ask the committee to consider him as the musical guest so they could reunite.

"How did you get them to agree?" Min Lee asked.

"Well, it wasn't that hard. You are a world-renowned pianist. But I did tell a little white lie. I told them Min Jade was going to be your fiancée and that I wanted this to be a surprise for her. They gave me your address and number. I know it's against protocol."

"You didn't say I was Min Jade's fiancé!"

"I did. I also told them it would ease her pain of not having her mother with her to have you by her side."

"Professor Winful, how sneaky."

"Look, I'll do anything for Min Jade. I'd tell a thousand lies, but I'm not lying about you, right?"

"Not if I have anything to do with it."

"We've got this, right?"

"Yes, sir. I think so."

"That's great. Make it good. She is my pride and joy."

"I will, sir. And thank you for everything."

"Make her happy, son. She deserves it."

"You can be sure of that, sir."

"Good. Now, I'm just about as close to Min Jade as anyone can be. Consider me a great uncle and stop calling me sir."

"Yes, Chair Winful."

"Not that either. Call me…What do you call an uncle in Korean?"

"*Samchon.*"

"Call me that."

Min Lee bowed deeply and took his leave. He felt like he had wings.

Everything was laid out when Min Lee got back to his room. He'd succeeded in getting Ji-Joon to let him jazz up his look. Still a classic black tux, its lapels thinly piped with light grey, but he would wear a grey vest instead of a cummerbund to compliment the white shirt, its grey buttons peeking out below a grey bowtie. Min Lee put a barely visible yellow and purple handkerchief in his pocket. He then stretched out on the couch. *Maybe it's you, I've been waiting for all of my life,* he hummed. Min Lee set his watch to alarm in two hours, having no trouble at all dozing off. As his mind lulled, his last thought was, *Min Jade, I'll never let you go again.*

Grand Hotel

Min Jade woke from her nap. She felt relaxed and rejuvenated. She glanced over her speech once more. She had pretty much memorized it. It was just a guideline anyway. She'd rather speak extemporaneously than read from a piece of paper. She lifted the beautiful gown from the bed and hung it inside the bathroom door. The steam from her shower would smooth any leftover wrinkles. She'd never worn anything like this in her life. A tribute to the University of Michigan, Go Blue, the maize-colored dress trimmed with a blue hem that could only be seen when she walked. The bodice of the V-neck dress was banded with blue Swarovski crystals spaced every two inches. At the waist, in an opposite V formation, more crystals hugged her long torso before the dress flared dramatically from the knees, dropping elegantly into a gathered train. Modest and appealing, the V-neck extended down her back, ending in a single blue crystal mid-back. Matching crystal shoes would adorn her feet, the exact blue of the dress hem. Cinderella couldn't have been more beautiful, Min Jade thought.

"*I feel pretty*," Min Jade sang, donning a shower cap to cover her curls. As she buffed her body with bath gel, she couldn't believe this was all happening. Usually cautious of scents that could provoke her asthma, she decided to dab her body anyway in *Datura Noir*. A bold scent for a strong woman. *Look at me, Mom.*

Coiffed and pampered, Min Jade was ready for the maddening crowd. Her escort was right on time. Tucking the last curl in place, Min Jade spun around and around in front of the mirror. Her face saddened. Her mother would have been pleased. Grabbing her glasses from the nightstand, Min Jade put on her maize-framed specs.

Grand Hotel, Min Lee's Room

Min Lee straightened his grey bow tie. He was glad he hadn't worn the yellow jacket with purple sleeves after all. He'd pull it out one day when Min Jade wore her dress again. He'd be around for that; of that, he was sure.

Grand Hotel, Tunde's Room

Tunde slid his feet into the softest leather shoes known to man. His tailor-made tux fit to perfection. He would make peace tonight, one way or the other. Albert was right. It was time to let go fully. Tonight, he felt his heart would break into a thousand pieces.

CHAPTER THIRTY-THREE

THE AWARD CEREMONY AND GALA, MIN JADE DEDICATION

MIN JADE GATHERED HER SKIRT A quarter inch as she ascended the steps of the Roman-columned, ochre-brick building that housed the Royal Academy of Sciences. There was a pre-ceremony reception where past and present Laureates would meet the Royal Family, Heads of State, major patrons of the Nobel Foundation, and other distinguished guests. Other than those on her list, guests would join them at the official Award Ceremony and the Gala.

Compared to the 1,300 guests who would fill the hall in the next hour, about 150 people were milling around. The first person she laid eyes on was Min Lee Woo. She mentally slapped herself for not realizing he would be there under the distinguished guest category. He looked absolutely stunning. Standing inches above most, he was hard to miss. Tunde and the Perfect Harmonies were coming toward her. Min Jade's throat went dry at the possibility of the two of them meeting. She was glad when her escort led her and her father to the receiving line of the Royals.

When she was introduced, Min Jade curtsied and introduced her father. Carl XVI Gustaf was the seventh King in the Bernadotte dynasty who'd ruled Sweden for more than a thousand years. He was a handsome man with receding white hair, and his wife, Queen Silvia, was equally attractive. The other Royals and their spouses were also present.

"Congratulations to you both. I am so sorry to hear of your loss. Please accept our condolences." His Majesty clasped Min Jade's hand in his.

"Thank you, Your Majesty," Min Jade said.

Min Jade moved down the line of dignitaries. By the time she had completed the rounds of shaking hands, bowing, and curtseying, Min Lee was no longer in the room. The entire evening was surreal, and she could convince herself she hadn't seen him at all. They were led into the concert hall.

It was magnificent. Umber stained wooden walls, proudly displayed past Laureates. She would be on that wall, Min Jade thought, as she climbed the steps to the stage. The chairs on the stage were set in half circles with an aisle between them. A small name tag for each Laureate was discreetly put on the back of each seat, and they were lined up in that order. The Royals had already been seated in the front row. Past Laureates were also seated on stage. Min Jade searched for her father, beaming right behind the Royals. Dr. Winful and Aunt Betsy were next to him with Cheshire smiles plastered on their faces.

Svante Lindqvist, President of the Academy, took the microphone. "Let's welcome the Nobel Laureates in Sciences to sit." The eleven recipients crossed the stage and took their seats to thunderous applause.

"*The Nobel Prize,*" Lindqvist continued when the clapping died down, "*is the most prestigious prize in the world, reserved for those whose works and efforts have given us solutions to some of the earth's most complex problems. Let's take a look back on the history of the Nobel Prize, which also commemorates the life of its founder, Alfred Nobel, who died on this day in 1896."*

A most impressive video was shown after that, with countless speeches extolling the brilliant scientists and their works. His Majesty then took the stage to hand out diplomas and medals. Each Laureate was allowed to speak.

The Perfect Harmonies were in awe. They couldn't wait to touch the gold medal, hoping it would bring them closer to the prize. Even Tunde was impressed as they watched the evergraceful Min Jade rise to receive her prize and medal. She was the most beautiful woman in the room, Tunde thought, fighting the feeling of possession that threatened his resolve to let go. As a Laureate's guests, they were seated near the stage and in full view. No matter how hard he tried, he still very much loved the woman on stage. Aware of Min Lee Woo's presence two rows in front of them, Tunde, annoyed, watched every twitch on his face. He, too, was definitely in love with his Min Jade. May the best man win, he thought, as his resolve to let go dissolved into thin air.

Min Lee watched Min Jade. She was exquisite beyond words. Her golden dress moved in fluid motion as she walked up to accept her medal from the King. Before walking to the microphone, she did the triad bow to give her acceptance speech as the new Laureate in Physics. If his heart didn't stop pounding, he might just die on the spot. He mopped his brows and pressed his hands together.

Min Jade stood at the podium. She scanned the audience, resting her eyes on her father, the woman next to him, Professor Winful, and on Min Lee. She then found the Perfect Harmonies and began, *"Your Highnesses, Excellencies,*

Heads of State, distinguished guests, the Royal Academy, Patrons of the Nobel Foundation, family, and friends. Thank you. Thank you for this most prestigious award and for this magical moment.

"*No one does anything meaningful by themselves. I want to say a special thanks to my father, Owen Jade, and to the man who's been my academic father and wings, Dr. George Winful, Chair of the Physics Department at the University of Michigan, of which I am proud to be a graduate and professor. To my colleagues, the Perfect Harmonies, a long story from my sabbatical in Austria, I'll be happy to share with anyone who wants to know later. A very special thanks to one person, in particular, Dr. Tunde Oghenekohwo, who was next to me when our discovery was finally confirmed.*"

Tunde beamed and wished he was sitting in front of Min Lee!

"*To my Aunt Betsy, a rock, thank you. To our special guest tonight, pianist Min Lee Woo, whose music my mother loved. Thank you.*"

Tunde could not help himself. Why was this man always in the same sentence as him?

"*Tonight, means more to me than you can ever imagine. Tonight, is about realizing a dream. I want this dream to come true for every little girl who loves the sciences. Yet, many little girls will succumb to the hardships, ridicule, and loneliness they often face being different or for being a girl in a field most often occupied by men. I was one of those little girls. My mother gave up her career to ensure her fragile, yet gifted daughter did not succumb to those pressures or veer off onto the wrong path.*

"*I know you can't believe it now, but I was once a nerdy, knobby-kneed, bespectacled, and bullied little girl, who, as you can only imagine, had to endure a lot to stand before you today.*

They say kids like me, born with special God-given gifts and talents, often walk the fine line between genius and madness. Many times, the only difference between the two outcomes is in the love that holds your space. For me, that love came in the form of my father...."

Min Jade paused, swallowing hard; she could not cry.

"And my incredible, devoted, unselfish and loving mother, who always told me I'd bring home this prize because, as she said, 'There is nothing that you can't do.'

"I'm sure by now you've noticed that I am black." The room chuckled. *"It has been a conversation throughout this life of mine. I am black, and I am enormously proud to represent my race of people. Nothing and no one can define who you are or who you will become. In a country that struggles with diversity, for a nerdy, black, fashion-challenged child, I dressed up for you tonight...."* A laugh waved through the room. *"Life was not always easy. I stand before you today largely because of my mother's love and sacrifices. The lonely road on which I could have lost my way without my parents' love has led to a triumphant destination. My mother lived for this day, but unfortunately did not live to see this day, as she passed away just months ago."* Min Jade could hear sniffles throughout the room. *"She lived long enough, thank God, to know that I was nominated for this most prestigious prize.*

"My mother's love was large and extended way beyond me to the vulnerable but gifted students supported by her foundation. Her moral compass was always pointing in the direction of equality. I will continue her work, so if any of you need someone to hold your space, regardless of your race, creed, or other choices, you can count on me.

"Even as a physicist, though you may think this a little hocus-pocus, I somehow feel my mother is right here beside me

tonight, cheering me on, saying 'Welcome to the finish line my, dear daughter. You did it.'"

Min Jade paused, and someone handed her a handkerchief.

"I share this award with my mother, my father, and with all of you who need someone to hold your space when the light dims. I thank you for this great honor. I look forward to continuing to grow as a scientist and hope that one day, many students in this very audience will be standing where I am right now, simply because you know you can and because you will."

At the Gala, Min Jade was mobbed. She felt like the 1,300 people in the room surrounded her. Soon the lights dimmed, and the festivities were to begin. The evening would start with a concert by Min Lee Woo. Min Lee walked on stage and bowed to the audience. Then he did something he rarely did. He spoke. "Tonight, is a special night for very special people. Congratulations to our new Laureates. I am especially pleased to have been invited this year because I know one of those Laureates personally. I met Min Jade in Austria, and her mother, Jessica Jade, in New York. I promised her mother then that I would play a benefit concert for her foundation, which, as you heard tonight, holds the space for gifted young men and women. I dedicate my concert to her tonight, and I'd like to thank the Academy, which has allowed me to ask for your help in allowing her work to continue. There is more information in your program. And to Min Jade," he said, sitting at the piano, "This is a special request from Dr. George Winful for his star." The Michigan fight song, *Pomp, and Circumstance,* rose through the hall in all its effervescence.

Min Jade was crying now, and she didn't want to do anything about it. Her father squeezed one hand and Winful the other. For one hour and fifteen minutes, Min Lee held sway. The music had reached a new high.

It was time for dinner to be served. The emcee came back on stage. "Our dinner entertainment tonight will be by a group called the Perfect Harmonies."

Min Jade gasped.

"Professor Jade mentioned them in her speech. They met on sabbatical in Innsbruck, and they are all physicists. They represent the world's nationalities, hence the name the Perfect Harmonies. Dr. Min Jade, the pianist, is replaced tonight by none other than our esteemed guest, Min Lee Woo. Please help me welcome the Perfect Harmonies: Vadim Abarnikov, Bauman Moscow State Technical University; Tunde Oghenekohwo, Cambridge University via Nigeria; Albert Brimble, Cambridge University, England; Chin Zhang, University of Science and Technology of China, and Anastase Durot, Sorbonne, France, with a guest appearance by Min Lee Woo. Yes, physicists can rock, too!" the emcee said.

Min Jade was beside herself. Winful looked at her, as did Aunt Betsy and her dad. She raised her shoulders in a shrug. The room was abuzz.

Tunde, unable to help himself, tapped an African beat as the band assembled. When Anastase hit the stage in black tuxedo tights, the room was uncontrollable. The band played background music throughout dinner and picked up the tempo as the night advanced toward the end of dinner. People were on the dance floor. Min Lee Woo and the band dedicated a K-pop classical song to the ever-cool Min Jade, who broke barriers and shattered boxes. Again, the crowd loved it. Tunde played the right notes, even though he was fuming that Min Lee had met Min Jade's mother.

Finally, Chin asked if the crowd wanted to hear Min Jade rock the mic before leaving the stage. "Min Jade, Min Jade, Min Jade," chanted the conservative scientific community in a conga line. Min Jade reluctantly climbed up to the stage, laughing so hard she could barely breathe. "What on earth?" She wanted to kick Chin in his shin.

The piano played trills and led into the song *All of My Life*. Min Jade quickly looked at Min Lee Woo, who discreetly nodded at her.

"Time, I've been passing time watching trains go by...all of my life." By the time they reached the chorus, *"something's telling me it might be you...Baby, it's you, it's you, I've been waiting for all of my life,"* the entire room was singing and swaying. Tunde was beside himself. That sneaky kimchi eater. But he conceded.

Min Lee Woo was never surer Min Jade was the woman he'd been waiting for all of his life.

Ji-Joon, moved by the moment, was ready to find the woman he'd been waiting for all of his life.

In Stockholm, the Royal Academy of Sciences had never seen a gala like this, nor did Min Jade suspect they would ever see one like it again. The evening was in Perfect Harmony, as the press would later report. *"The cool, brilliant, zany, and multi-talented Nobel Laureate Min Jade 'lasered' away the stuffiness of the Nobel Prize Gala with her band of physicists and the incomparable classical pianist Min Lee Woo. Patrons danced into the night, the young Royals letting loose."*

CHAPTER THIRTY-FOUR

MIN JADE AND MIN LEE WOO
THE MAKE-UP

THEY MADE UP WITHOUT SAYING A WORD. As the night drew to a close, Min Jade sent her father, Aunt Betsy and Winful ahead and then went to find Min Lee Woo. She found him in his luxuriously appointed green room that boasted paneled walls like the great hall. He was lying on the sofa, his feet propped up on the arm. His eyes turned toward the door as she walked in.

"You must be famished," she said, handing him a candy bar from her purse.

"I am famished." He rose from the chair and walked over to Min, Jade, "For you." In one quick movement, he pulled her into his arms and brought his lips down on hers. "Oh, Min Jade," he murmured against her ears, "I have missed you so much." He kissed her again, deeply, searingly, passionately.

As always, he smelled like orange, spicy, tangy orange. Min Jade closed her eyes and listened to his breathing, hers rising to match his. He was holding her tightly, pulling her closer and closer. She never wanted him to let her go. She'd waited for him all her life, her heart knew it, her soul knew it, and her body knew it.

Finally, he stepped back and looked at her. She was glowing, beautifully at peace. What had taken him so long? "I've been going mad waiting for you."

"You knew I'd come?"

"I was hoping, but if you didn't, I'd come. I had Ji-Joon on the case to tell me the moment you were free."

"Spying on me?"

"Just making sure you'd never get away again."

Min Jade moved out of his embrace. *God, was he handsome!* She stared at him for a long time, holding his gaze, wanting those lips of his to leave honey as they traveled over her body.

Suddenly all the bad memories came flooding back.

"Shall we go home?" he said, pulling her back into his arms, his hand cupping her head into his broad shoulders.

She inhaled deeply—Orange...spicy orange.

"Come," he said, pulling her behind him. "I want to go home." Min Jade hesitated.

"Meaning home, as in where the heart is?"

"Wherever you want it to be. As long as you're by my side."

"Isn't your side taken?" Min Jade shattered the mood. "I don't think so, Min Lee. I am not...."

"Please listen to me."

"*Shireoyo.*"

"But you have to. If I am unforgivable, I'll let you walk out the door. But...."

"But. Min Lee, how can love be but...."

"Aren't you the one changing your tune?"

"Well, I never said.... Well, the science of love is all brain chemicals. That's what I said, a false illusion...or a delusion. I never...."

The duck beak came up. "Let's go home, Min Jade. I'll tell you everything." Min Lee dialed for his driver. They fetched their coats and walked into the night, his hand firmly clasping hers.

"Darling."

"Huh," Min Jade answered quite naturally.

"You look wonderful tonight."

She rested her head against his shoulders. Could she trust him? Maybe she could. He tilted her face to his. In her eyes, he saw her entire world.

"I'm so sorry about your mom," he pulled her head to his shoulder when they got into the car. "I know she heard you. She once said that my mother heard my music, so I know she heard you tonight. Congratulations, Min Jade. I'll say it for her since she entrusted you to me."

"She would be pleased," Min Jade said.

Min Lee opened the door to his suite. It was as magnificent as hers. Appointed in hunter green, very manly, she thought, hers was a pale yellow, but the layout was identical - the king bed with the cushioned headboard, a sitting area, working area, and a small dining area. The bathroom was enormous, with a rainforest showerhead. Min Jade loved it.

"Let's toast to the most brilliant woman on the planet and the woman I'd like to be my wife." Min Lee pulled a box from his pant pocket.

"Huh? What? What?"

"Well, it's a long story. I said if you forgave me, I'd never let you go ever again. So, I bought an engagement ring. I had Ji-Joon leave it in the car just in case you decided to kill me instead. But I think I know the answer. We've wasted enough time. Marry me, Min Jade. My sun no longer shines without your moon."

"You have a lot of explaining to do."

"I know." He kissed her again. His eyes glistened.

"You big baby." Min Jade caressed his hair. "All the time, you act brave and untouchable."

"I'm only weak with you." He gave her another long, satisfying kiss before popping the cork on the champagne. "Ji-Joon's doing, just in case."

Min Jade laughed.

"May I do something I've wanted to do since we met?"

Her eyebrows went up as his index fingers disappeared into her dimples. "I used to love doing that to my mother."

"Is that why you love me because I have dimples like your mother?"

"One of the reasons." He poured some bubbly and handed her a glass. They interlaced arms and drank from each other's glasses. "But mostly because I can no longer imagine my life without you."

"Yum…this is good. Tell me more about the moon and the sun. Is that a Korean metaphor?" She emptied her glass and held it up for more.

Min Lee moved the bucket over to the sofa. He sat and pulled her down beside him.

"Not only Korean, but we use it a lot. There are two schools of thought. First, the sun and the moon are opposites but complementary. They can't occupy the sky simultaneously, yet there is no moon without the sun because the moon only reflects the sun's light. If they are not in harmony, an eclipse happens when the moon dominates the sun, and the sky goes black."

"That's all true, the interdependence of things theory. And your sky went dark?" She poured more champagne.

"A total eclipse."

Min Lee raised her to her feet and unzipped her maize dress. Woozy, Min Jade didn't flinch as the dress fell in a heap at her feet. She tried to undress Min Lee, but she was tipsy, so he helped her. "Let's shower," he said, leading her to the rainforest.

"Don't you just love this shower?" Min Jade flopped around. "Min Lee," she said softly, her body limp, *"saranghaeyo."*

"Saranghaeyo. Saranghaeyo, my Min Jade."

They sat up the entire night talking, clearing up the misunderstandings and coincidences that had kept them apart sharing the loss of their parents only two weeks apart. The wee hours of satisfying love making made them exhausted when the sun rose through the blinds. They showered and went to breakfast. Min Lee was flying out at 3:00 p.m. He had no desire to leave her. As he sat across from her, his body kept jerking in rapid succession. Min Lee Woo ached to hold his woman in his arms. He ached to feel himself inside of her again. He ached to touch her over and over and over again.

"When do you fly home?" he asked.

"Day after tomorrow. We're playing a gig tomorrow night."

"Wish I could be here with you."

"Wish I could go with you."

"I'll come to you just as soon as I've finished this stretch. Two weeks. Can you do without me for two weeks?" He fed her a slice of cheese, slipping his finger into her mouth. She gently nibbled its tip.

"Let's go right now," he said, pulling her from the chair.

"Where are we going? I am hungry."

"Where do you think? I will fill you up."

They were half-dressed by the time they were inside the door. "I don't think I can stand your leaving me," Min Jade said.

"I'll hurry back to you. I won't ever leave you again."

CHAPTER THIRTY-FIVE

MIN JADE

THE PERFECT HARMONIES ROCKED AS USUAL. With the news about them from their gala gig, it seemed the entire population of Stockholm had come out to see them. People thought it was so cool that these brainiacs were so rad, whatever that meant.

"One million buckaroos," Albert said. "That's a reason in itself to win the prize."

"Sure enough," Chin said.

Anastase and Vadim were nodding their heads. Tunde was looking at Min Jade's hand.

"This was one cool place for a reunion. How do we top this next year?"

"Maybe we won't," Tunde said. "Min Jade, will we?"

"What do you mean?"

"Maybe we'll be jamming at a baby shower," he said, staring at the ring.

"Mmmm. I was about to tell you guys. I got engaged last night."

"Is that why you're glowing radiantly? Congrats. A baby shower is fine with me," Albert said, glancing over at Tunde.

"Yeah. This is rad," Chin said.

Anastase and Vadim nodded their heads.

"Tunde…." Min Jade touched his hand.

He moved her hand and got up; he wasn't exactly recovered.

Min Jade followed him. "Tunde," she said, "I can't control my heart. You know, deep down, we are too alike. We don't fit. We're the story of two hearts, but ours don't beat as one. You need someone different, and you know it, too. Please be my friend. It would mean so much to me."

"In love, we all lose our hearts. I can't control mine any more than you can control yours. But what can I say? We weren't meant to be. A life without regrets, without pain, is no life at all, I suppose. I'll be your friend, Min Jade. And if the wind changes, remember I'm here for you." She was right. He needed his perfect fit.

"Thank you, Tunde. I know you'll find the happiness you deserve. Next time, don't try to fit a square peg…."

"What do you mean by that?"

"This." She handed him back the envelope with her name on it.

The Decision

"Crazy Korean Calling," the phone announced. Min Jade dashed from the shower and grabbed her phone.

"Are you getting ready to leave?" This was Min Lee's tenth call since he'd departed yesterday.

"Yes. You got me out of the shower."

"Oh…the shower," he said dreamily. "I love showering with you."

She ignored him. "Min Lee, you wouldn't believe how much they collected to support mother's charity. Almost one million dollars! I'll donate part of my prize money, and they'll have a good endowment. Thank you."

"That's great, *Yeobo.*"

"Huh?"

"Honey. It means honey. My wife, honey."

Min Jade blushed. "Honey. Thank you, *Yeobo.*"

"Have a safe flight. Call me when you get in and see you in two weeks."

"Can't wait."

"Hey, if you were in the shower, you're naked, right?"

"Yah."

"Say hi to that body for me. I miss it."

"And me?"

"I'll die for you."

Ann Arbor

Winful and Min Jade's assistant Joan personally managed the media circus. Winful only allowed Min Jade to take essential calls, jettisoning the never-ending requests with great kindness. That's what the AP Newswire was for, to disseminate information.

Though he tried to shield her from some of the threats and negative comments they'd received, Min Jade read them all. *A disgrace! Those party animals, those black folks, desecrated the Nobel with their jungle music. Can't take them anywhere!* Others decried the dumbing down of the educational system that had allowed this to happen. *Of all the people in America, they could have chosen! Was the Nobel lowering their standards?* Yet, others praised the Academy and Min Jade.

Chair Winful was especially harsh when the job offers came in. He instructed Joan to discard them immediately.

"That's not necessary," Min Jade reassured. "I won't ever leave you."

"You'd better not. How about that gentleman friend of yours? He's fantastic, isn't he? Are you going to leave me for him?"

Min Jade kissed him. "I wouldn't leave you for the world. And as I understand it, you were a bit of a meddler."

A sheepish grin crossed his face. "Good." He ignored her last comment. "Now, let's see what other firsts and barriers we can shatter."

Min Jade handed him an envelope and a rare orchid.

"What is this?" Chair Winful tore open the envelope. There was a check for $250,000. "For our 'break the mold fund,' and for you to take a vacation."

Winful turned away, tears welling in his eyes. He couldn't remember the last time he felt so many emotions at once. Jessica Jade had done one helluva job with her daughter. "Are you sure you'll never leave me?"

"I'm sure. Now get back to work watering those orchids. Oh, just one thing. Can I take a few weeks off? I'll tell you why very soon."

Two Weeks Later

Min Jade cleaned every crevice of the house. She didn't even trust her housekeeper, so there they were, cleaning side-by-side. Rugs were shampooed, the refrigerator was cleaned, bathtubs sparkled, linens were sprayed with Seduce Me pheromone spray, curtains were changed, and the furniture gleamed. Jo Malone candles were lit in every room, and fresh flowers were placed throughout the house. On a trip to the farmer's market, Min Jade bought the best cheeses, French bread, *foie gras*, and wild salmon. She'd bought enough food to last all winter!

Tonight, they'd be alone, but tomorrow was their big day when they would tell her dad, Aunt Betsy, and Winful that they were engaged. Min Lee was due to arrive in an hour. She showered, dressed, and was on her way to the airport when her phone rang.

"Where are you?" She looked at her watch. She couldn't be late!

"On the tarmac. We landed early."

Min Jade breathed a sigh of relief. By the time he cleared customs, she'd be there. "I can't believe you're finally here."

"I will always be wherever you are."

"In little old Ann Arbor?"

"Are you planning on leaving your job? I'm the nomadic one. I can live anywhere, although I'm not sure about Ji-Joon. He'll join us next week to check out the place. And Winful made me promise."

Things were moving so fast Min Jade's head was spinning. In the almost three years they'd known each other, they were about to spend more time together than they ever had. Twelve days in Austria was the longest time they had ever been together, but Min Jade felt no fear or doubt. She was home, and she knew it. Finally, she could breathe.

"Dr. Winful will kiss you," she said, "but know that I'll go wherever you will go, and then he'd kill me. So, I think we'd best stay here."

"Ann Arbor it is. I don't want you to meet with a tragic end from Winful. After all, he's partly responsible for my happiness."

The butterflies fluttered, and Min Jade wanted him then and there. And then he was there: standing at the baggage claim exit in Ann Arbor. Min Jade jumped from the car and ran into his arms.

"Hey, someone missed me."

"I did, I did," she said, kissing him.

"Lady, the officer was saying you can't leave your car here."

"Okay. I couldn't wait for him to get here."

The officer winked at her. "I know the feeling."

The drive home was only half an hour. Min Jade would now know what day-to-day life felt like with him. He'd be in Ann Arbor for a month. He hadn't been in any one place for a month except for Korea. Min Jade pressed the garage door opener, and the door rose. How civilized. London and Ann Arbor were a far cry from each other. When Min Jade let him into the house, he was beyond impressed. Not just with her piano, but with the house's eclecticism, the spirit of a true creative being. He'd be happy here, but they'd have to move. He needed a soundproof studio.

"Welcome home, *Yeobo.*"

"Mmmm," he pulled her into an embrace. "It's good to be home. You smell delicious."

"And you smell like spiced orange."

"I do," he said and yanked open the front of her dress, buttons flying.

"I know how to sew." She was breathless with desire, and she let him take her there, right there on the living room divan.

They woke coiled into each other, the fireplace spitting yellow flames. "I'll make Korean food for our dinner party tomorrow. Shall we go shopping later?" He eased from her snake tangle. She watched him cross the room. Min Jade marveled at his fit body and that he was the only man she'd ever seen naked in her life. He was a sight to behold. Min Jade rolled over in utter satisfaction. When he came out of the bathroom, she quickly showered, but before he could dress, she pulled him back into her web. It was noon before they finally left to shop.

Dinner was superb. Her father was delighted to meet Min Lee again, and Aunt Betsy was just downright happy. "Jessica would love him," she whispered to Min Jade.

"She did. They met in New York."

"Ah, yes. She said that."

Min Lee popped a bottle of champagne. "Min Jade and I have some news," he began.

"Oh," Aunt Betsy squealed. The Mins are going to give us good news, Owen."

"Yes. We'd like your permission to marry."

Min Jade held out her finger. "Dad?"

"With all my blessings, scallywag. With my blessings."

"But she cannot leave Ann Arbor," Winful piped up.

"No, sir…I mean, Uncle. We will live here in Ann Arbor."

"Then you have my blessings, too."

Aunt Betsy was turning around like a top. "Where did she put it?" she kept saying.

"What are you looking for, Aunt Betsy?"

"I remember now. When your mother came back from your New York trip, she showed me a package. She said that she thought you'd met your future husband. She was going to give it to you on the day you announced your engagement. Oh, where did she put it?"

"In her dresser drawer," Owen Jade said.

"I'll just run up and get it." Aunt Betsy sprinted off, returning moments later with a beautifully wrapped package. In it was a box with a double strand of pearls and matching earrings. *Something old*, it was labeled. *Your grandma's*. A copy of her Nobel Laureate nomination letter. *Something new*. And a pair of ruby earrings... *Something borrowed…from your grandmother, too. I don't think she knew I borrowed these.* A pair of blue frames. *Something blue.* There were, of course, a few inhalers, Tiger Balm, and Vicks. *Excitement can cause shortness of breath.* A smiley face with a wink was drawn at the bottom of the note.

Min Lee held her close as Min Jade wept.

A month went by fast. Ji-Joon, who'd been with them now for three weeks, was so comfortable playing house that Min Lee didn't think he would ever leave again. But they were packed and ready to go.

Chair Winful had given her four weeks off, but no more.

"You know I only have four weeks, right?" Min Jade said to Min Lee.

"We'll be back in three weeks. We're going to Korea. I'd like you to meet my *Eomeoni.*"

Ji-Joon's head twisted like the exorcist. Did he say Korea?

"No surprises, right?"

"No surprises."

CHAPTER THIRTY-SIX

THE MINS
AT LAST

MIN JADE PLEADED WITH MIN LEE TO TRY and repair his relationship with Seung-Le. He was his only living blood relative, and she reminded him he'd promised his *Abeoji* to take care of him.

Min Lee waited until Friday night to have dinner with Seung-Le. Their relationship had once again soured because of Choi Shin. "I am doing this because you asked. I can't imagine what I can do to make him a real brother. He's been so poisoned by In-Tak Hyun's hatred of me and now by the Choi Shin fiasco. What did I do?"

"Min Lee, it's not about who did what. I bet Seung-Le was as lonely as you were as a child. I bet he, too, had to find a way to cope with his own challenges. A busy, busy father who loved another woman, a mother who waited for a father who loved another woman. Where was there room for him? There have been many misunderstandings and misgivings. Where would we be if I wasn't willing to listen—really listen to you and try to understand?"

"But Min Jade."

"You can always walk away if you try, and it's all in vain. I won't ask more of you."

"Okay." He tucked a lock of curl behind her ear and kissed the tip of her nose. "I'll try. You are very good for me."

"You hold my space, too, you know, darling. How do you say that in Korean?"

"*Neon nae gong-gan-eul jab-a.*"

"Yeah. What you said. *Ahn-yoh hah-say-yoh. Yeobo.*"

Min Lee laughed and tucked her head into his shoulders. "What'd you say we get married the moment we get back? Do you want a big wedding?"

"With whom there? Remember, we are the maladaptives who fit perfectly together. How many friends do you have?"

"One. Ji-Joon. You?"

"I have more than you. Let me see…two-plus Winful, Dad and Aunt Betsy. That'd be seven. So, eight people at our wedding, including us. I think in my parent's garden at home will do. In the spring, it will be perfect. Can you wait that long?"

"That'll be a whole two months away. *Aiiiiishhhh.* Okay. We'll focus on the plans for our new home until then. Something to distract me."

"I can distract you, alright…but I'm going to miss my beautiful home."

"Then keep it. You can turn it into an office."

Min Jade looked at the Crazy Korean. She loved him so much.

"Wanna hear something funny?" She noodled.

"Uh, huh."

"Call me from your cell right now."

"Why. I'm right here."

"Just do it."

Min Lee took his phone from his breast pocket and dialed Min Jade.

"Crazy Korean calling. Crazy Korean Calling," the ring tone announced.

"Hah. That's funny." He knuckled her forehead, his smile warm and comforting. "I'll get one for you. Why didn't I think of that before? Let's see."

"Your perfect fit, the duck beak girl, is calling," Min Jade volunteered.

"Ah, yes. That's perfect."

EPILOGUE

TWO YEARS LATER

MIN LEE STOOD LOOKING OUT OVER THE sprawling home on top of a little hill. He had envisioned a life in full bloom, just like the sculpted garden that enclosed the property. It was now summertime. His solitude was interrupted by a car coming up the driveway.

"Min Lee," it was Ji-Joon.

Ann Arbor had been good to him, as he'd found the love of his life, a lovely Wolverine native. He was a married man now. "Why aren't you practicing?"

"Can't I take a break? I *can* do that, right?"

"*Yes*. I guess. How are you today?"

"Good. Great. What about you?"

"Over the moon. Josie just told me I am going to be a father."

"No!" No one could have convinced Min Lee that their lives today would have been so different from the nomadic life they'd lived for twenty-four years. They were on the road only half a year now.

"Yes. Isn't that some kinda news?"

"Congratulations, Ji-Joon. This is great news. I sure wish I had cigars."

"That'd be great, except we don't smoke. So, I was thinking," Ji-Joon said, how do you feel about us slowing down a bit more this year?"

Another car pulled in behind Ji-Joon's.

"*Abeoji, Abeoji.*" Little feet were sprinting toward Min Lee, grabbing him at the knee.

"Kim Woo. What did Mom tell you about running too fast?"

"She's going to be an athlete." Min Lee hoisted his daughter above his head. "Aren't you?"

"No, *Abeoji.* I am going to be like you and Mummy."

Min Lee held his daughter close to his chest. His little walnut pride and joy, with her cool, slanted eyes. He'd gotten his wish, and his world was complete. And soon, it would be even more complete.

"Hi, honey" He leaned over and kissed his wife. "How was shopping? What's the surprise buy this week?"

"Waiting in the trunk for you to find out." She kissed him back. "Hi, Ji-Joon."

"Guess what, *Yeobo.* Ji-Joon is going to be an *Abeoji!*"

"Oh my…how fantastic. Two more?"

"What do you mean? Just one. I hope."

"No. Two. Min Jade is pregnant," Min Lee said proudly. "Maybe we're both having boys. Imagine, our kids will be like us."

"Or girls." Min Jade swatted him on the behind.

"Either way, we're slowing down our schedule for the year," Min Lee said. "Ji-Joon thinks it's a good idea." He winked at his manager.

"It's about time mothers get help," Min Jade said, starting toward the door. "I'll have tea ready in twenty minutes. I'm pleased."

Min Lee put the book on the side table and pulled the cover-up over his daughter. He never believed there could be this much joy in his life. Min Lee went to the music room. He touched his piano. "*Eomeoni,*" he said. "I am so happy." He lifted the lid and played *Serenade.* "Sorry, *Eomeoni.* You are no longer the only woman in my life, so I have to go now... Tonight I really want to be next to the woman I dearly love. Thank you, *Eomeoni,* for watching over me."

"You're up early tonight." Min Jade looked up from her papers as he came into the bedroom. "Finished practicing already?"

"Uh-huh. What are you reading?"

"A paper from one of my students."

"Are they going for a Nobel Prize?"

"In a few years, I hope."

"Good." He took the papers from her hand. He was looking at her with a curious look on his face.

"*Yeobo,* are you okay?"

"I will be if you kiss me," he said, "because I need you tonight."

"Then bring those lips closer. I want to kiss them, too."

"And what about the other part of the request?"

"You can have me tonight and every night," she said, touching her lips to his. "I belong to you."

"God," Min Lee said, "*saranghaeyo. Saranghaeyo.*"

Min Jade held her husband's face between her hands. "*Sa rang hae,*" she repeated softly. "*Saranghaeyo. Saranghaeyo* forever, Min Lee."

Min Jade's phone trilled. "Cocky Nigerian calling. Cocky Nigerian calling. "

Min Lee grabbed the phone off the side table. That man had still not stopped interrupting his life. "Why are you always calling my wife?"

"Man, not you again. Why are you always answering your wife's phone? How's it going, Min Lee?" Tunde said.

"Great. With you?"

"Great, too. How is your daughter?"

"Looking forward to her new sibling. When you are on this side of the pond, let us know."

"I will. Same for you."

"Here's Min, Jade. Take it easy."

Min Jade took the phone. "Hey, Tunde?"

"Hey, kiddo. How's your Russian?"

"Did you say, Russian?"

"Yup. Compliments of Vadim."

"That will be a hoot. Who's going to want to see an old, pregnant physicist prancing on stage?"

"There's that."

"Funny. I'll have you know I'll be rocking until I'm eighty."

"Looking forward to that. I'll send details." Tunde hadn't found the woman of his dreams yet. He was still hoping…and lamenting at times that Min Jade belonged to Min Lee in this life. Next life, she would be his, he thought, as he hung up the phone. "Okay. See you soon. My love to everybody." She hung up the phone.

"What do you think of that?" Min Jade said, turning to her husband. He had fallen asleep. Staring at his handsome face, she knew for sure she had chosen right.

The End!